MARVE… E

MOON GIRL

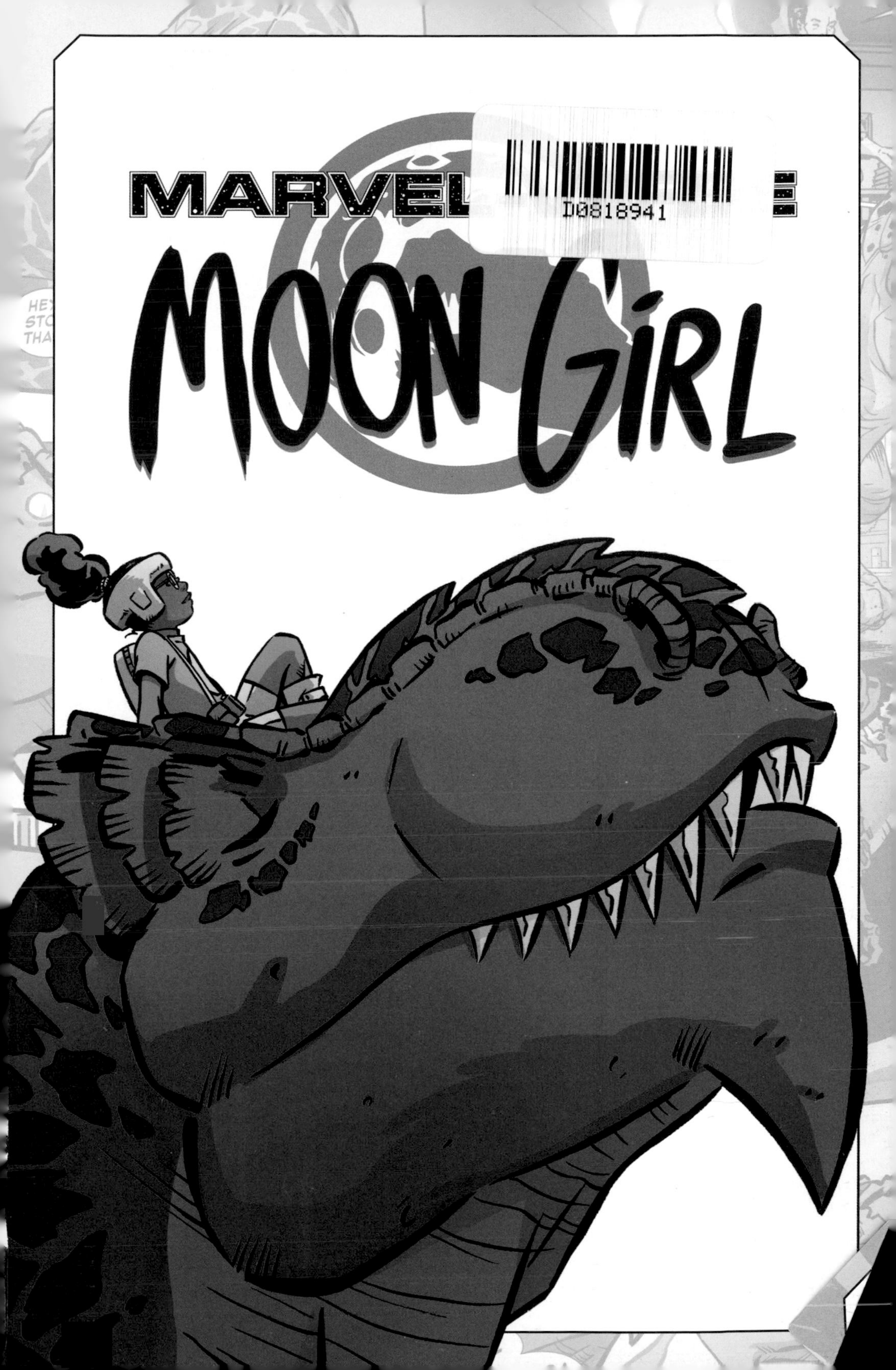

MARVEL-VERSE
MOON GiRL

MOON GIRL AND DEVIL DINOSAUR: MARVEL LEGACY PRIMER

WRITER: **ROBBIE THOMPSON**
ARTIST: **MARCO FAILLA**
COLORIST: **MIKE SPICER**
LETTERER: **VC's TRAVIS LANHAM**
ASSISTANT EDITOR: **KATHLEEN WISNESKI**
EDITOR: **DARREN SHAN**

MOON GIRL AND DEVIL DINOSAUR #1

WRITERS: **BRANDON MONTCLARE & AMY REEDER**
ARTIST: **NATACHA BUSTOS**
COLORIST: **TAMRA BONVILLAIN**
LETTERER: **VC's TRAVIS LANHAM**
COVER ART: **AMY REEDER**
EDITORS: **MARK PANICCIA & EMILY SHAW**

COLLECTION EDITOR: **JENNIFER GRÜNWALD** ASSISTANT EDITOR: **DANIEL KIRCHHOFFER**
ASSISTANT MANAGING EDITOR: **MAIA LOY** ASSISTANT MANAGING EDITOR: **LISA MONTALBANO**
ASSOCIATE MANAGER, DIGITAL ASSETS: **JOE HOCHSTEIN** VP PRODUCTION & SPECIAL PROJECTS: **JEFF YOUNGQUIST**
RESEARCH: **JESS HARROLD** BOOK DESIGNERS: **SARAH SPADACCINI** WITH **JAY BOWEN**
SVP PRINT, SALES & MARKETING: **DAVID GABRIEL** EDITOR IN CHIEF: **C.B. CEBULSKI**

MARVEL-VERSE: MOON GIRL GN-TPB. Contains material originally published in magazine form as MOON GIRL AND DEVIL DINOSAUR (2015) #1, #42-43 and #46-47. First printing 2021. ISBN 978-1-302-93378-4. Published by MARVEL WORLDWIDE, INC., a subsidiary of MARVEL ENTERTAINMENT, LLC. OFFICE OF PUBLICATION: 1290 Avenue of the Americas, New York, NY 10104. © 2021 MARVEL No similarity between any of the names, characters, persons, and/or institutions in this book with those of any living or dead person or institution is intended, and any such similarity which may exist is purely coincidental. **Printed in Canada.** KEVIN FEIGE, Chief Creative Officer; DAN BUCKLEY, President, Marvel Entertainment; JOE QUESADA, EVP & Creative Director; DAVID BOGART, Associate Publisher & SVP of Talent Affairs; TOM BREVOORT, VP, Executive Editor; NICK LOWE, Executive Editor, VP of Content, Digital Publishing; DAVID GABRIEL, VP of Print & Digital Publishing; JEFF YOUNGQUIST, VP of Production & Special Projects; ALEX MORALES, Director of Publishing Operations; DAN EDINGTON, Managing Editor; RICKEY PURDIN, Director of Talent Relations; JENNIFER GRÜNWALD, Senior Editor, Special Projects; SUSAN CRESPI, Production Manager; STAN LEE, Chairman Emeritus. For information regarding advertising in Marvel Comics or on Marvel.com, please contact Vit DeBellis, Custom Solutions & Integrated Advertising Manager, at vdebellis@marvel.com. For Marvel subscription inquiries, please call 888-511-5480. **Manufactured between 11/19/2021 and 12/28/2021 by SOLISCO PRINTERS, SCOTT, QC, CANADA.**

10 9 8 7 6 5 4 3 2 1

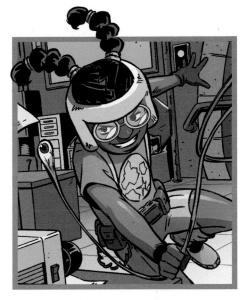

MOON GIRL AND DEVIL DINOSAUR #42

WRITER: **BRANDON MONTCLARE**
PENCILER: **RAY-ANTHONY HEIGHT**
INKERS: **LeBEAU UNDERWOOD,
RAY-ANTHONY HEIGHT & NATE LOVETT**
COLORIST: **TAMRA BONVILLAIN**
LETTERER: **VC's TRAVIS LANHAM**
COVER ART: **NATACHA BUSTOS**
EDITOR: **CHRIS ROBINSON**
CONSULTING EDITOR: **JORDAN D. WHITE**
SPECIAL THANKS TO MARK PANICCIA

MOON GIRL AND DEVIL DINOSAUR #43

WRITER: **BRANDON MONTCLARE**
ARTISTS: **GUSTAVO DUARTE
WITH RAY-ANTHONY HEIGHT**
COLORIST: **TAMRA BONVILLAIN**
LETTERER: **VC's TRAVIS LANHAM**
COVER ART: **NATACHA BUSTOS**
EDITOR: **CHRIS ROBINSON**
CONSULTING EDITOR: **JORDAN D. WHITE**
SPECIAL THANKS TO WIL MOSS & SARAH BRUNSTAD

MOON GIRL AND DEVIL DINOSAUR #46-47

WRITER: **BRANDON MONTCLARE**
ARTIST: **ALITHA E. MARTINEZ**
COLORIST: **TAMRA BONVILLAIN**
LETTERER: **VC's TRAVIS LANHAM**
COVER ART: **RAHZZAH**
EDITOR: **CHRIS ROBINSON**
CONSULTING EDITOR: **JORDAN D. WHITE**
SPECIAL THANKS TO MARK PANICCIA

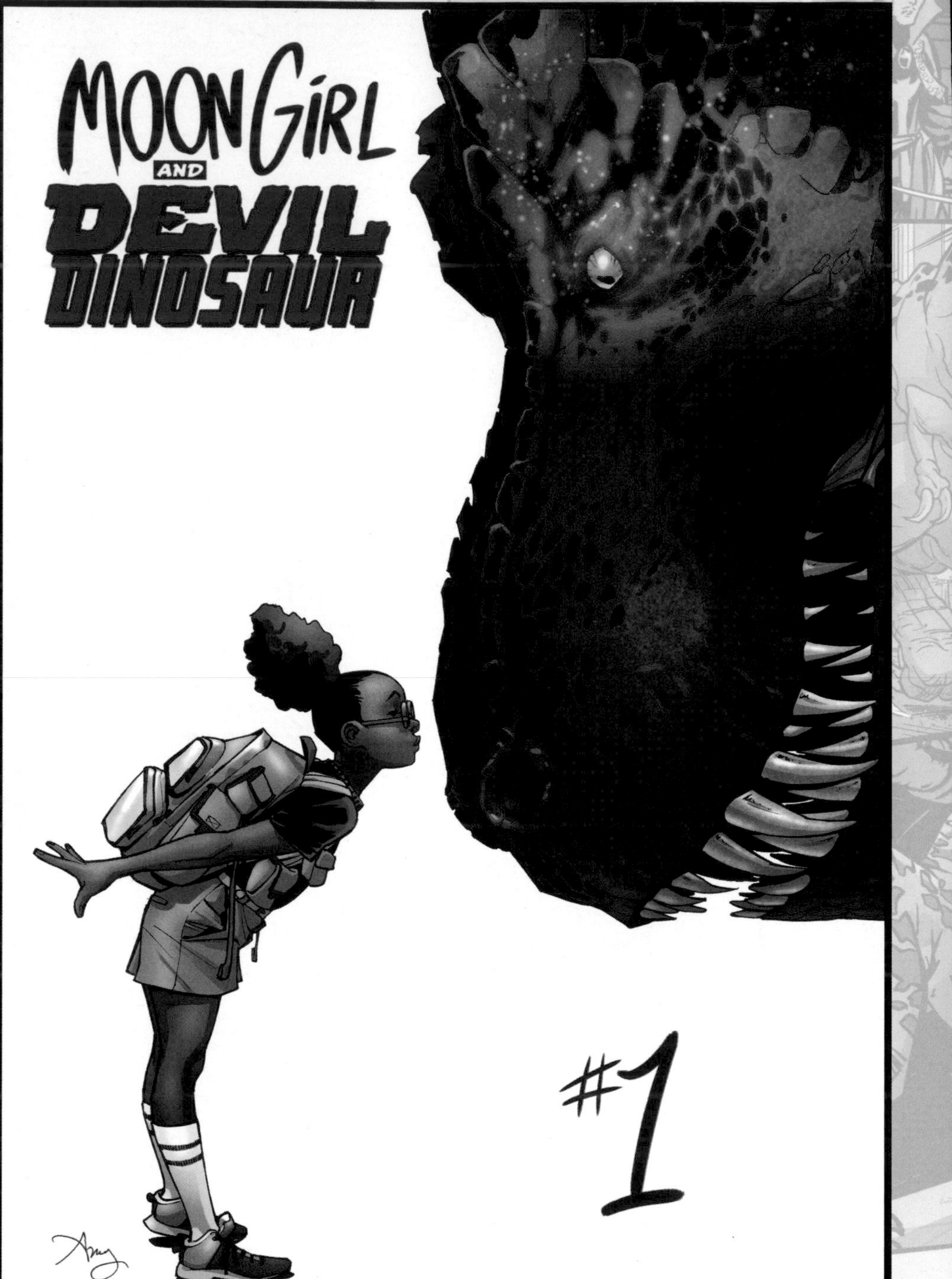
MOON GIRL
AND
DEVIL DINOSAUR
#1

MOON GIRL AND DEVIL DINOSAUR #1

IT'S THE FIRST CHAPTER OF AN AMAZING TEAM-UP! SUPER-GENIUS LUNELLA LAFAYETTE'S WORLD TURNS UPSIDE DOWN WHEN THE PREHISTORIC DEVIL DINOSAUR IS TRANSPORTED TO THE PRESENT!

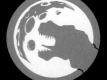

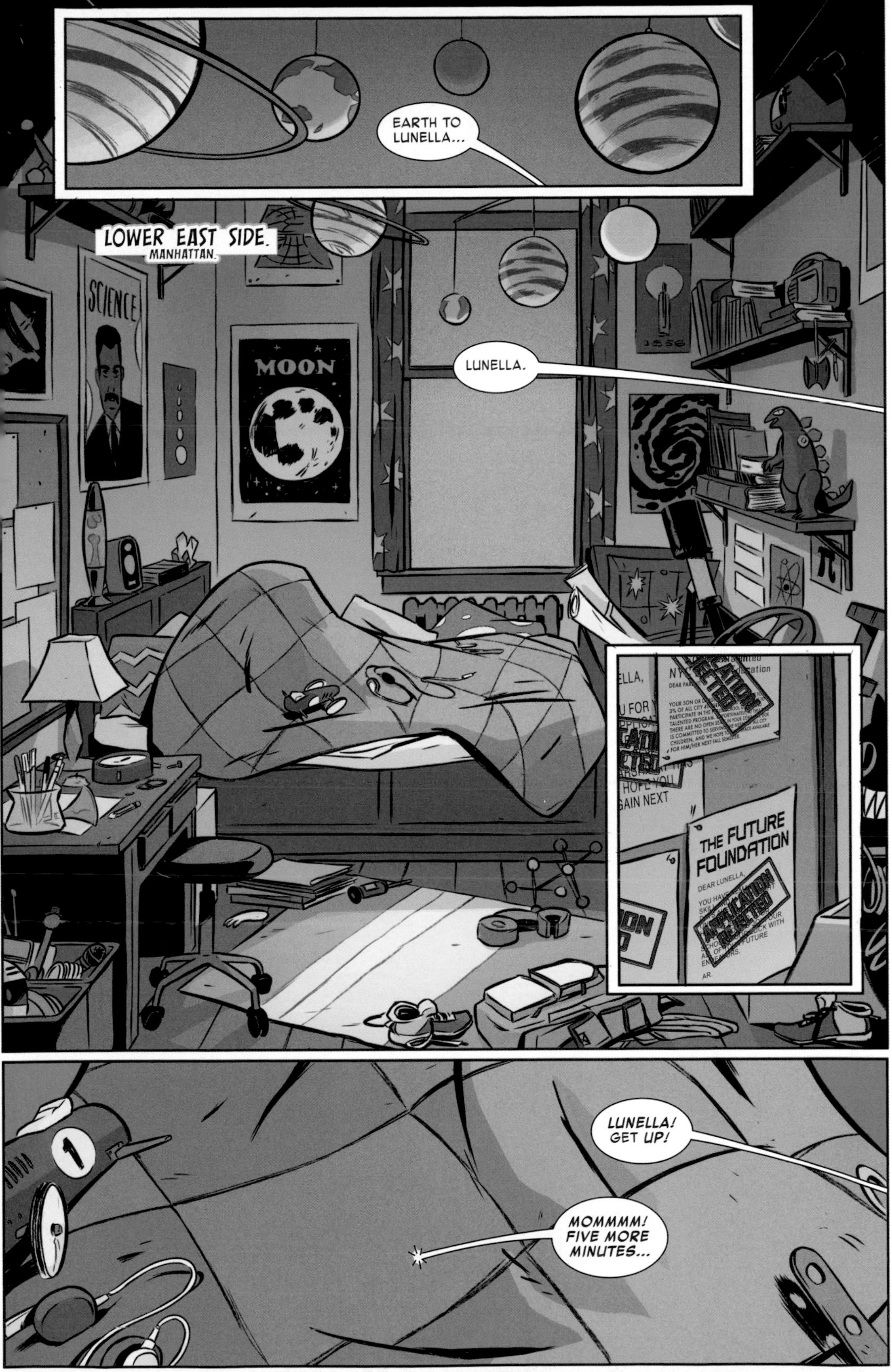
EARTH TO LUNELLA...
LOWER EAST SIDE.
MANHATTAN.
SCIENCE
MOON
LUNELLA.
THE FUTURE FOUNDATION
DEAR LUNELLA,
APPLICATION REJECTED
LUNELLA! GET UP!
MOMMMM! FIVE MORE MINUTES...

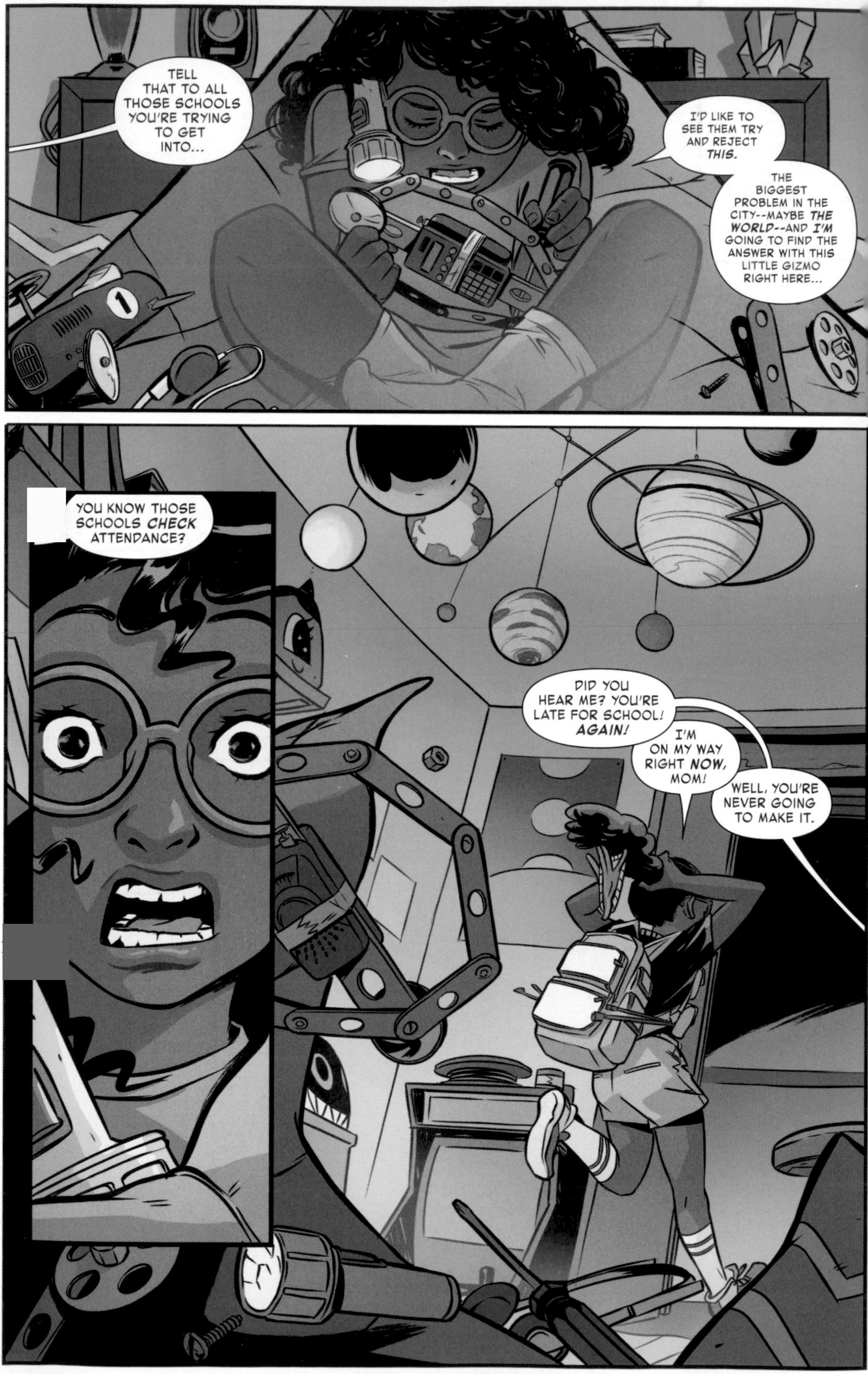
TELL THAT TO ALL THOSE SCHOOLS YOU'RE TRYING TO GET INTO...
I'D LIKE TO SEE THEM TRY AND REJECT *THIS.*
THE BIGGEST PROBLEM IN THE CITY--MAYBE *THE WORLD*--AND *I'M* GOING TO FIND THE ANSWER WITH THIS LITTLE GIZMO RIGHT HERE...
YOU KNOW THOSE SCHOOLS *CHECK* ATTENDANCE?
DID YOU HEAR ME? YOU'RE LATE FOR SCHOOL! *AGAIN!*
I'M ON MY WAY RIGHT *NOW,* MOM!
WELL, YOU'RE NEVER GOING TO MAKE IT.

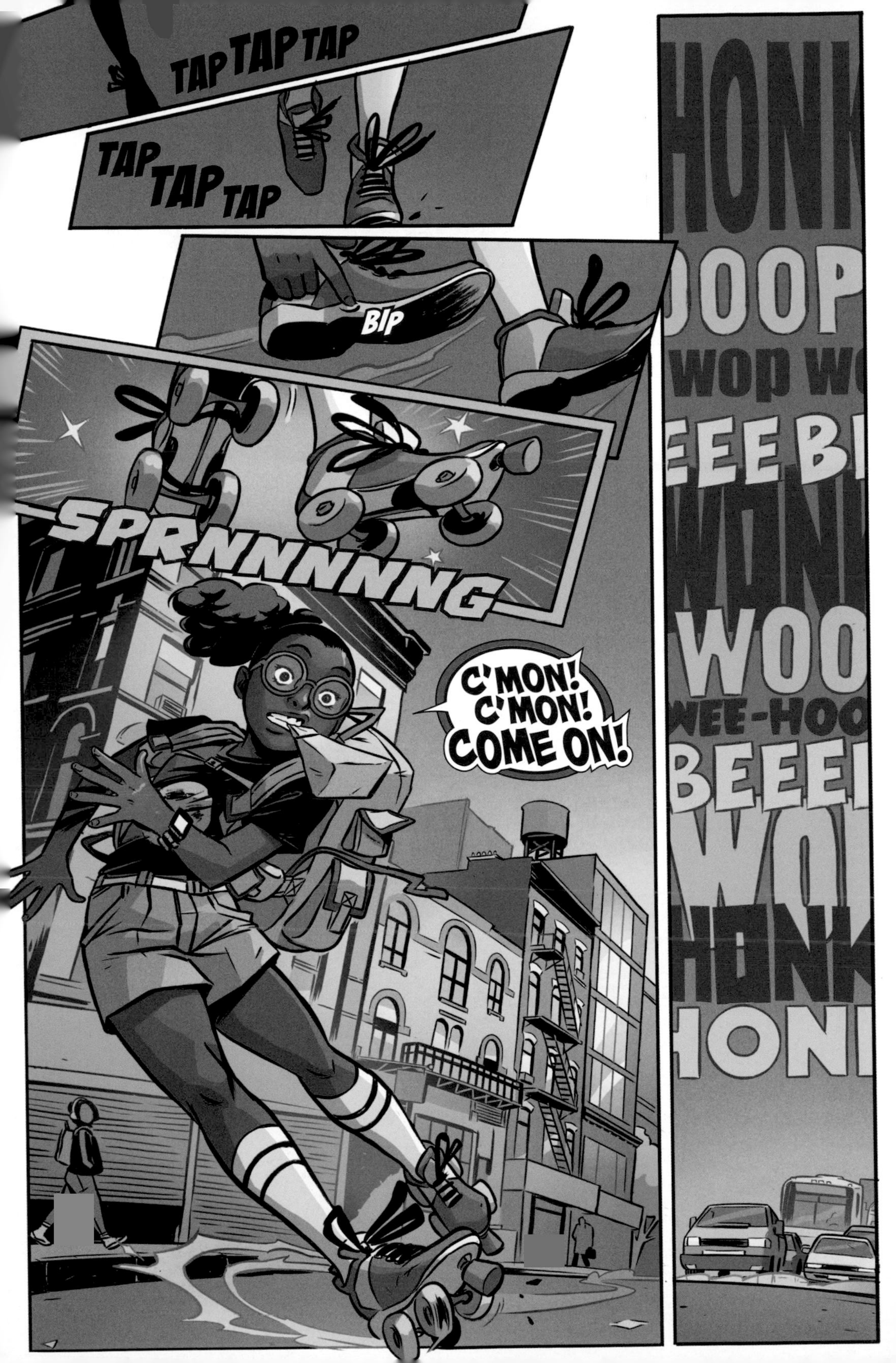

TAP TAP TAP
TAP TAP TAP
BIP
SPRNNNNNNG
C'MON! C'MON! COME ON!
HONK
OOOP
wop
EEEB
WOO
WEE-HOO
BEEE
HONK

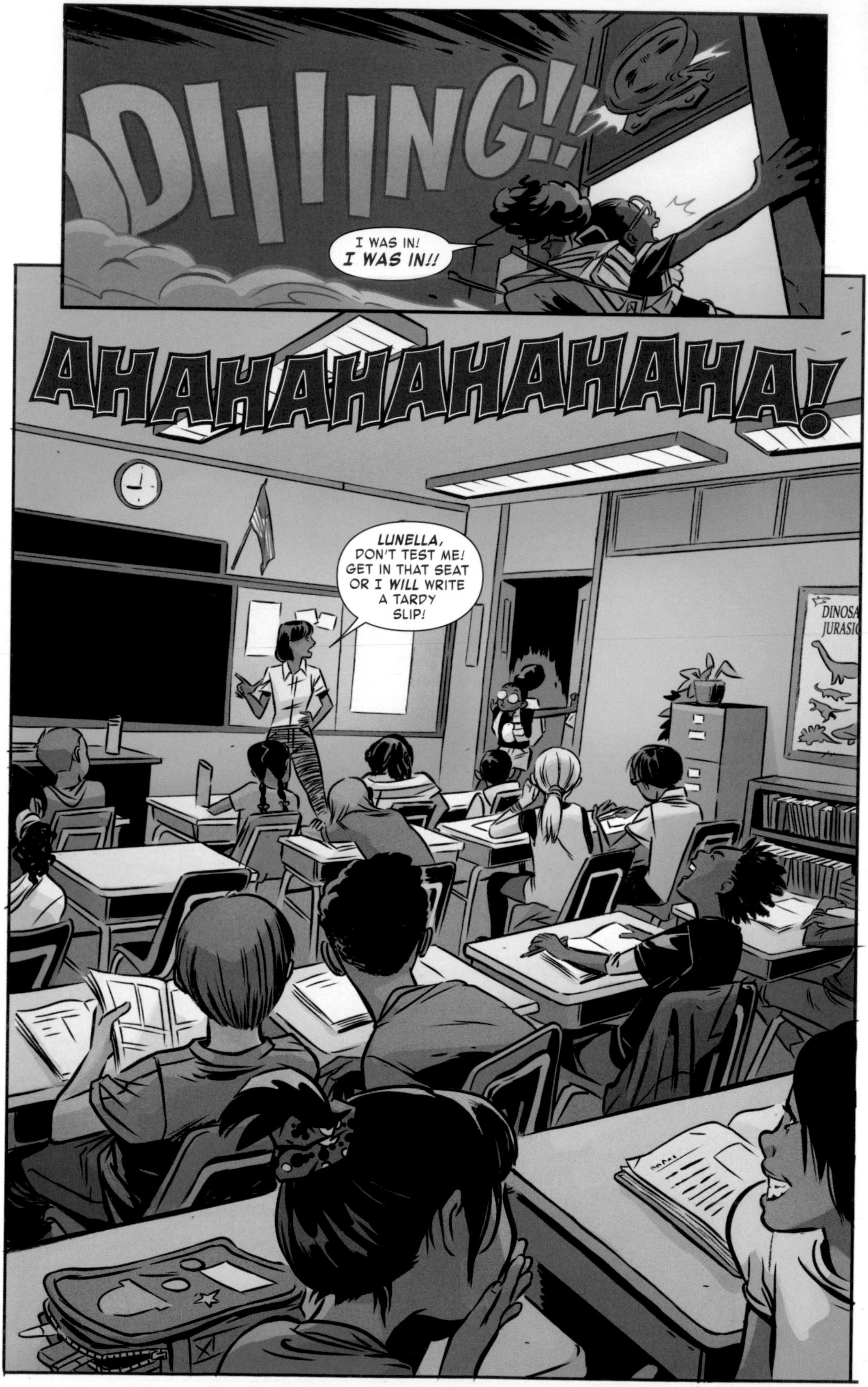
DIIIING!!
I WAS IN! I WAS IN!!
AHAHAHAHAHAHAHA!
LUNELLA, DON'T TEST ME! GET IN THAT SEAT OR I WILL WRITE A TARDY SLIP!

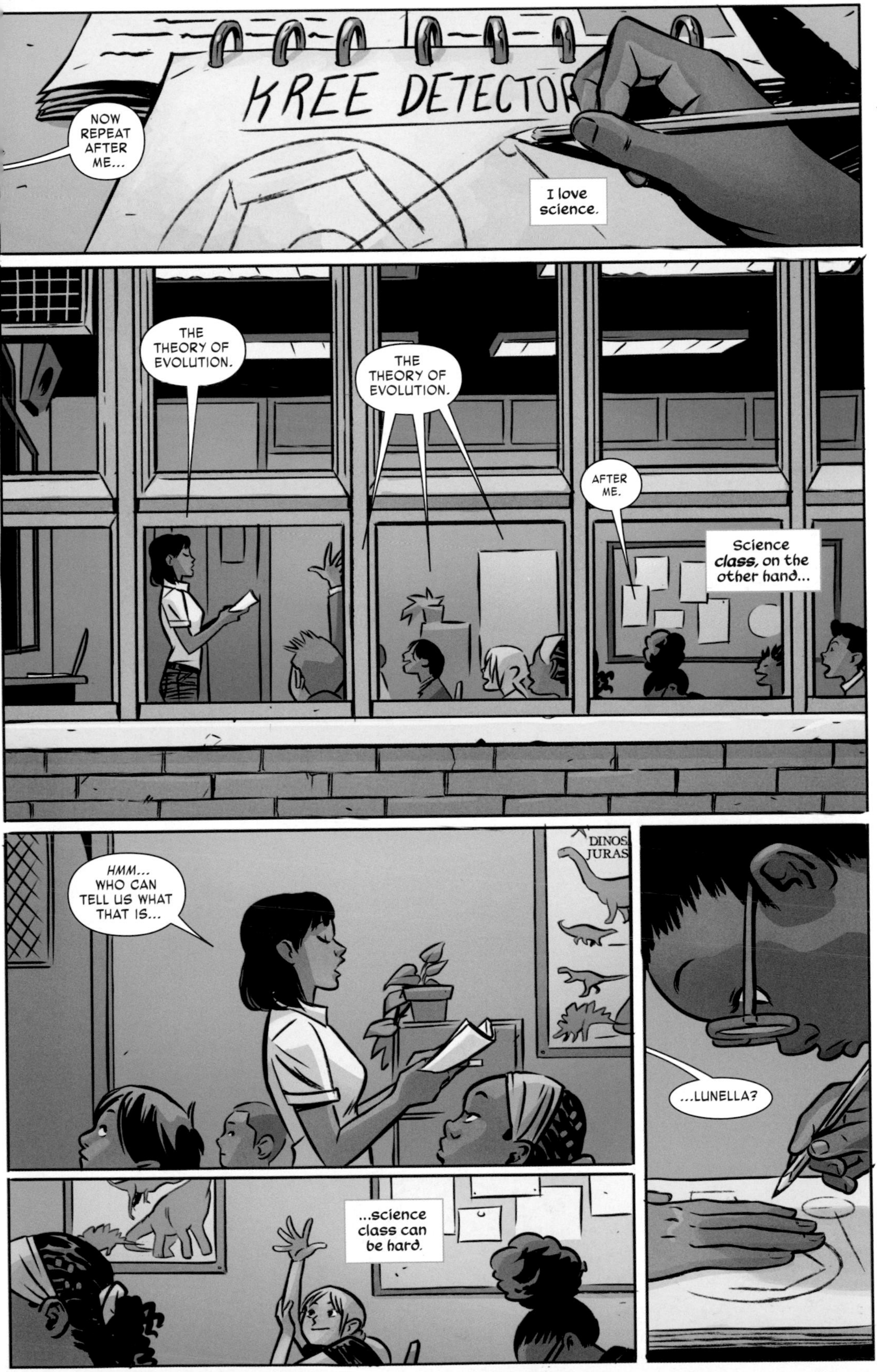
KREE DETECTOR
NOW REPEAT AFTER ME...
I love science.
THE THEORY OF EVOLUTION.
THE THEORY OF EVOLUTION.
AFTER ME.
Science *class*, on the other hand...
HMM... WHO CAN TELL US WHAT THAT IS...
...LUNELLA?
...science class can be hard.

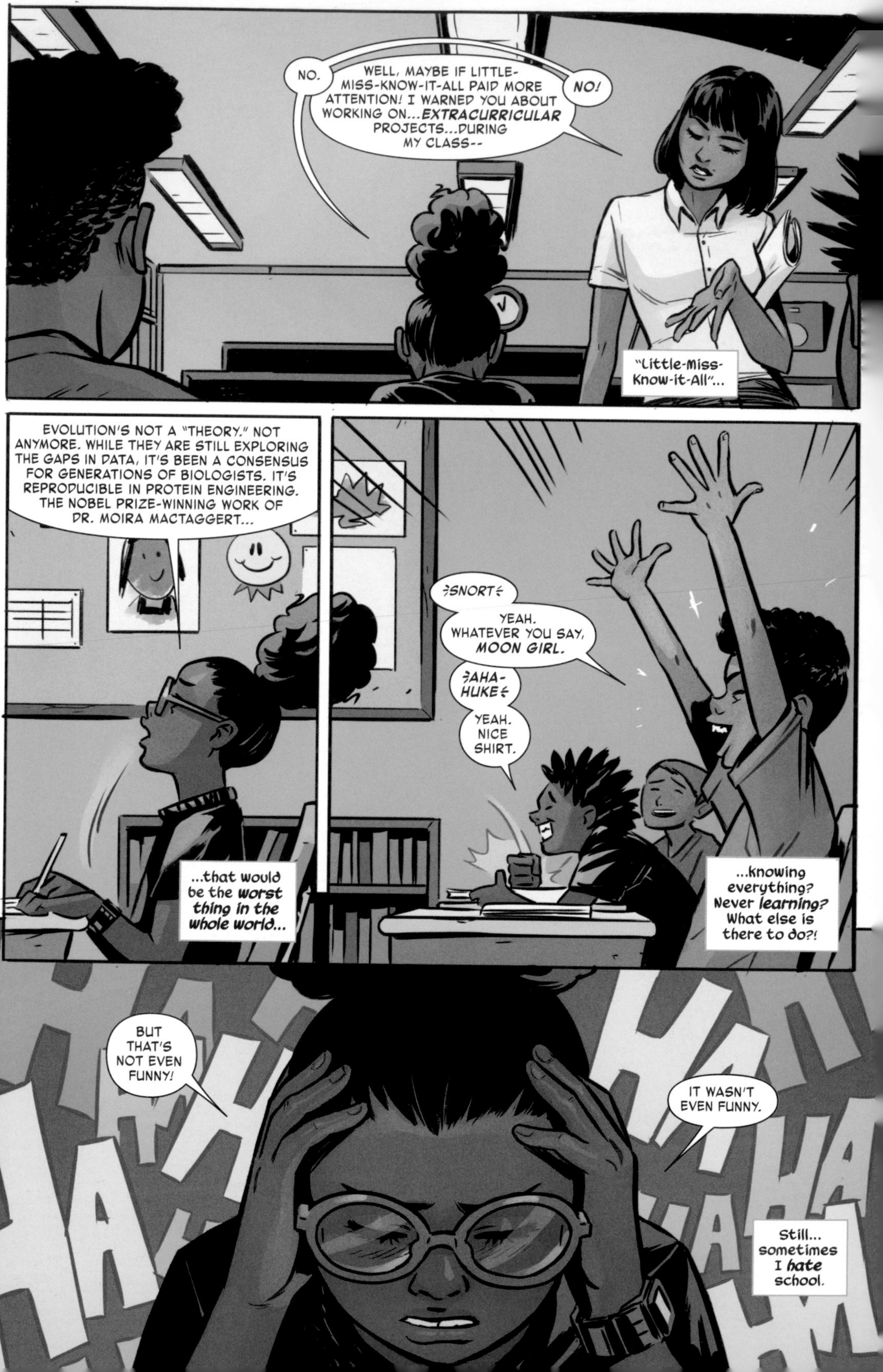
NO.
WELL, MAYBE IF LITTLE-MISS-KNOW-IT-ALL PAID MORE ATTENTION! I WARNED YOU ABOUT WORKING ON...EXTRACURRICULAR PROJECTS...DURING MY CLASS--
NO!
"Little-Miss-Know-it-All"...
EVOLUTION'S NOT A "THEORY." NOT ANYMORE. WHILE THEY ARE STILL EXPLORING THE GAPS IN DATA, IT'S BEEN A CONSENSUS FOR GENERATIONS OF BIOLOGISTS. IT'S REPRODUCIBLE IN PROTEIN ENGINEERING. THE NOBEL PRIZE-WINNING WORK OF DR. MOIRA MACTAGGERT...
...that would be the worst thing in the whole world...
SNORT
YEAH. WHATEVER YOU SAY, MOON GIRL.
AHA-HUKE
YEAH. NICE SHIRT.
...knowing everything? Never learning? What else is there to do?!
BUT THAT'S NOT EVEN FUNNY!
IT WASN'T EVEN FUNNY.
Still... sometimes I hate school.

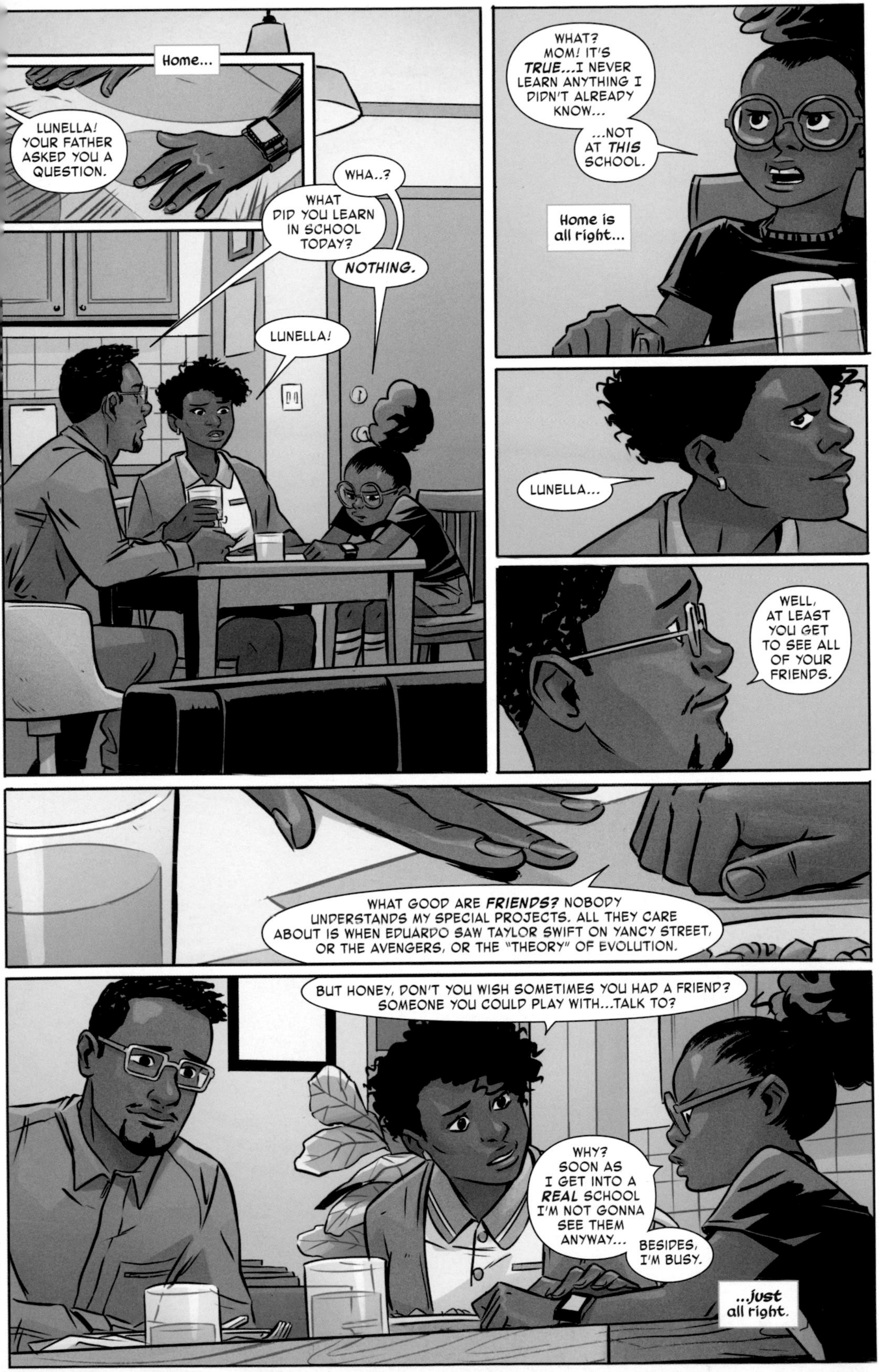
Home...
LUNELLA! YOUR FATHER ASKED YOU A QUESTION.
WHAT DID YOU LEARN IN SCHOOL TODAY?
WHA..?
NOTHING.
LUNELLA!
WHAT? MOM! IT'S TRUE...I NEVER LEARN ANYTHING I DIDN'T ALREADY KNOW...
...NOT AT THIS SCHOOL.
Home is all right...
LUNELLA...
WELL, AT LEAST YOU GET TO SEE ALL OF YOUR FRIENDS.
WHAT GOOD ARE FRIENDS? NOBODY UNDERSTANDS MY SPECIAL PROJECTS. ALL THEY CARE ABOUT IS WHEN EDUARDO SAW TAYLOR SWIFT ON YANCY STREET, OR THE AVENGERS, OR THE "THEORY" OF EVOLUTION.
BUT HONEY, DON'T YOU WISH SOMETIMES YOU HAD A FRIEND? SOMEONE YOU COULD PLAY WITH...TALK TO?
WHY? SOON AS I GET INTO A REAL SCHOOL I'M NOT GONNA SEE THEM ANYWAY...
BESIDES, I'M BUSY.
...just all right.

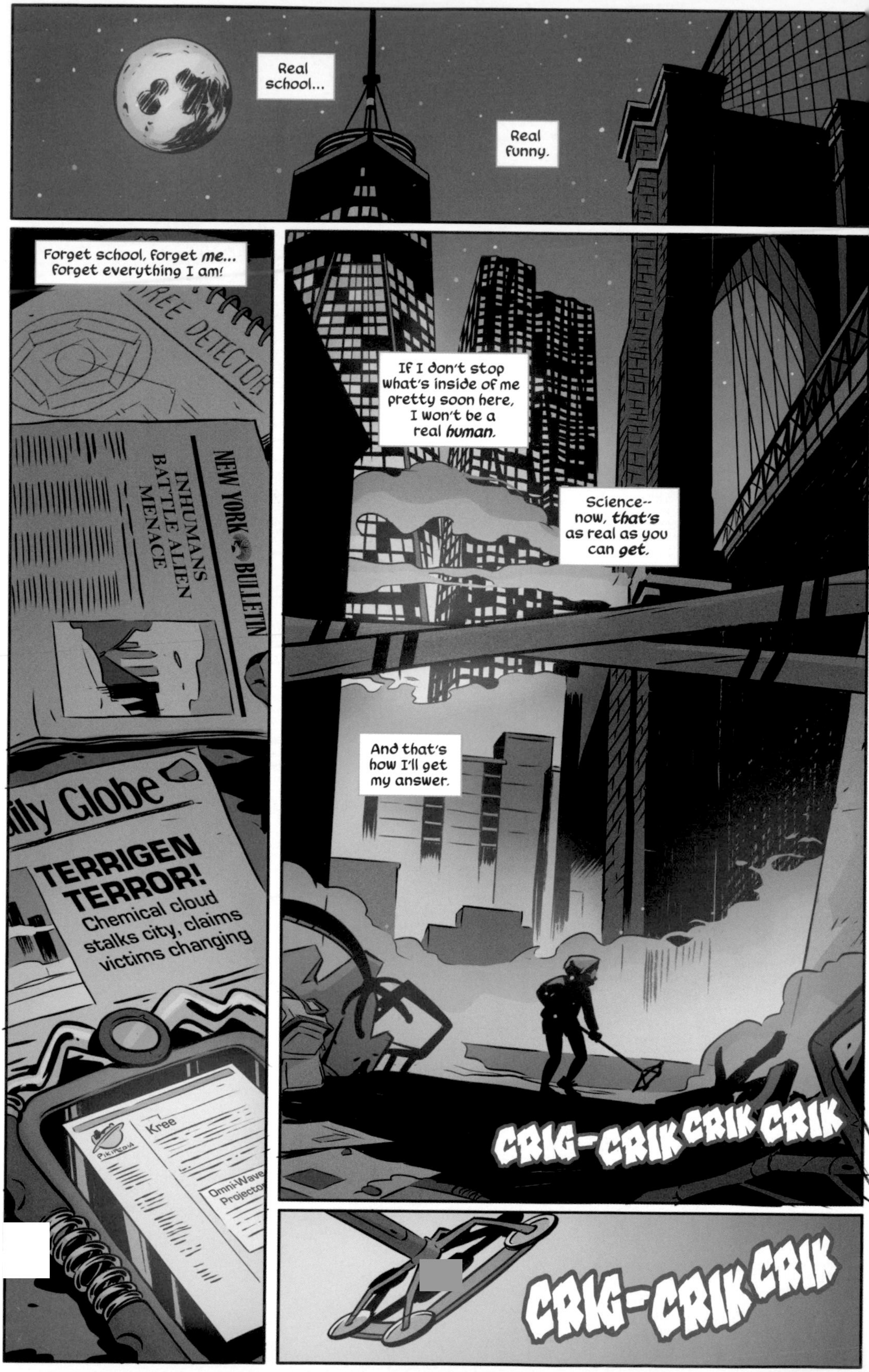
Real school...
Real funny.
Forget school, forget *me*... forget everything I am!
KREE DETECTOR
NEW YORK BULLETIN
INHUMANS BATTLE ALIEN MENACE
Globe
TERRIGEN TERROR!
Chemical cloud stalks city, claims victims changing
Kree
If I don't stop what's inside of me pretty soon here, I won't be a real *human.*
Science-- now, ***that's*** as real as you can ***get.***
And that's how I'll get my answer.
CRIG-CRIK CRIK CRIK
CRIG-CRIK CRIK

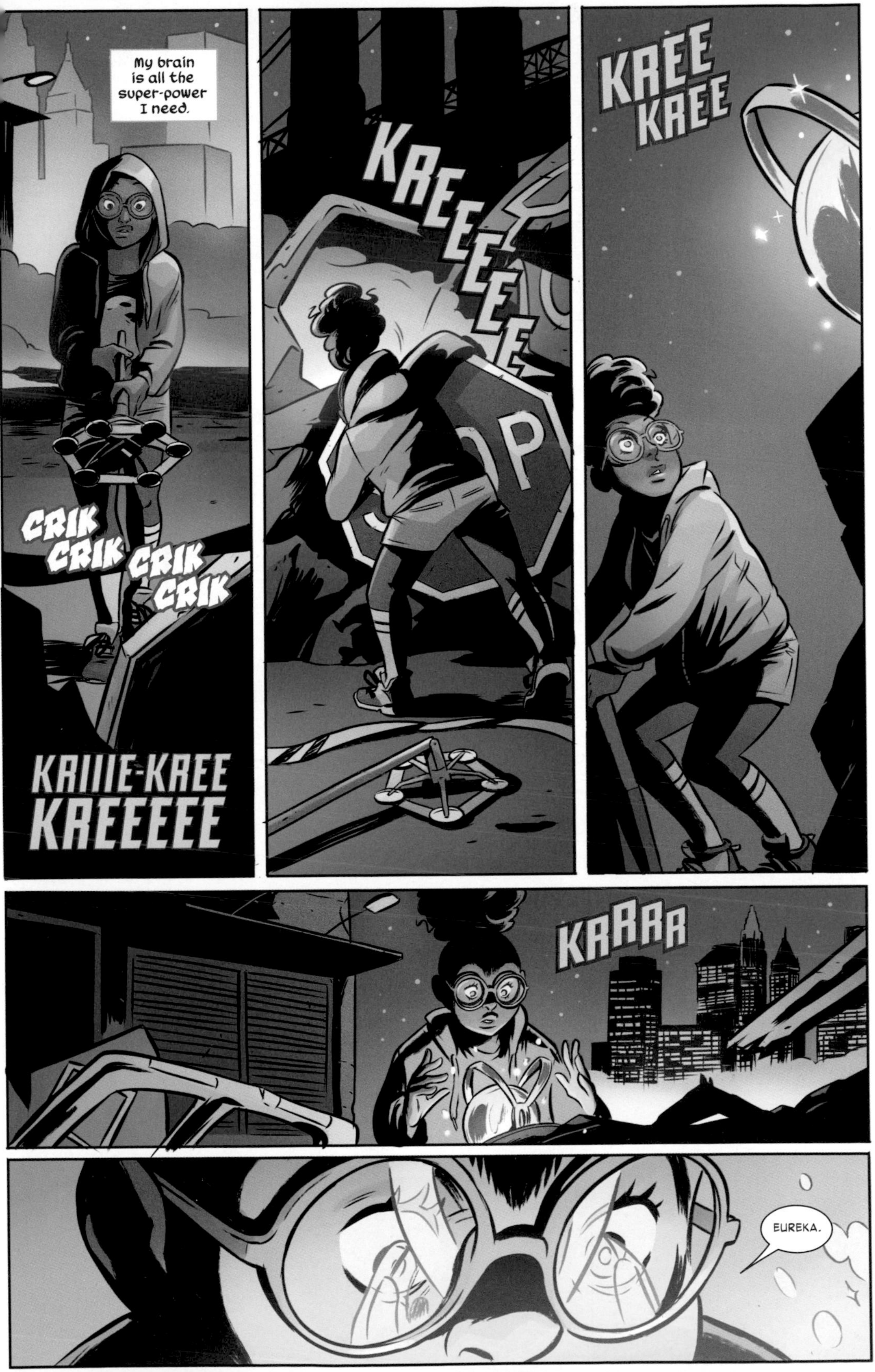
My brain is all the super-power I need.
CRIK CRIK CRIK CRIK
KRIIIIE-KREE KREEEEE
KREEEEEEE
KREE KREE
KRRRR
EUREKA.

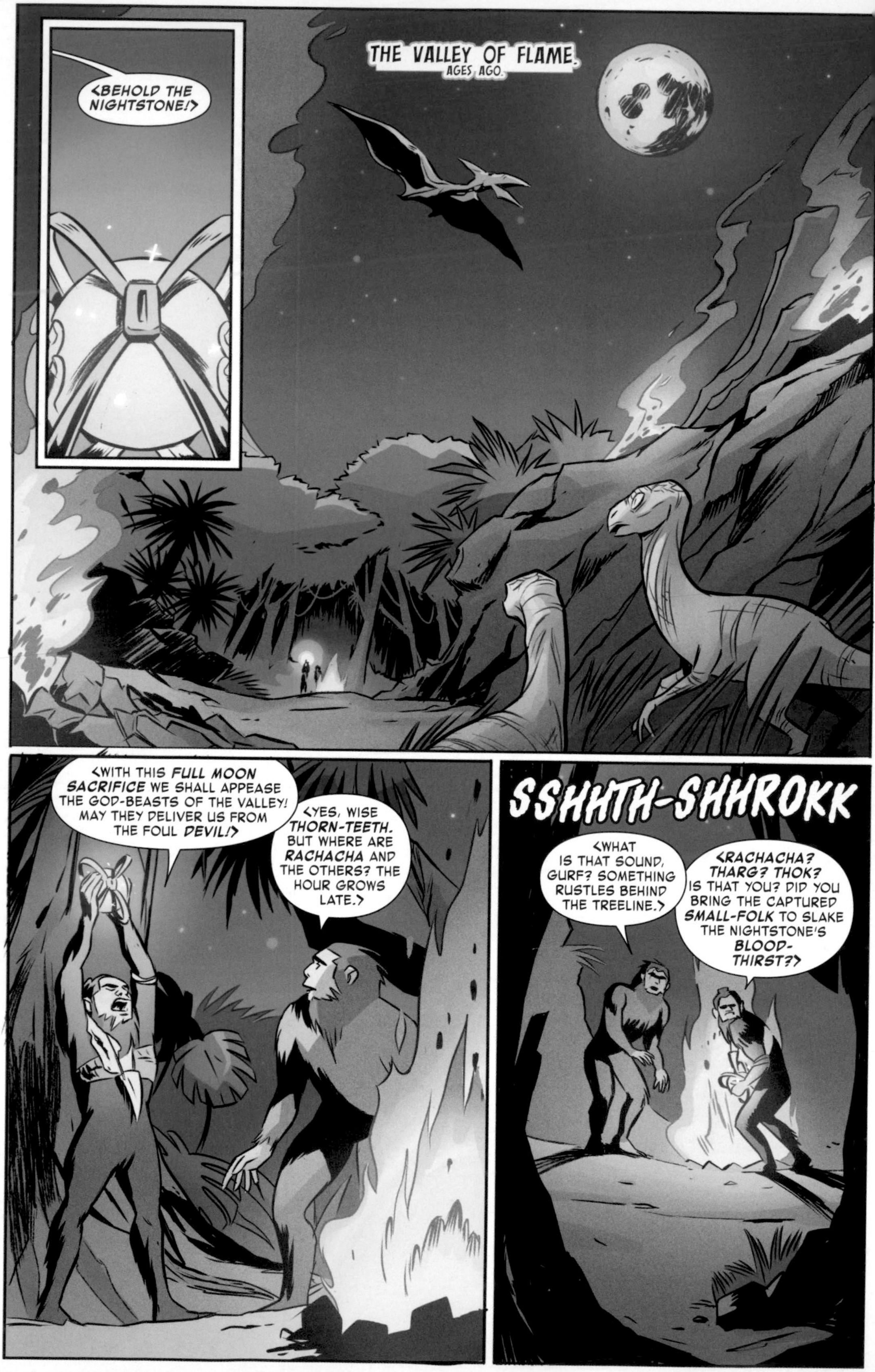
THE VALLEY OF FLAME. AGES AGO.
<BEHOLD THE NIGHTSTONE!>
<WITH THIS FULL MOON SACRIFICE WE SHALL APPEASE THE GOD-BEASTS OF THE VALLEY! MAY THEY DELIVER US FROM THE FOUL DEVIL!>
<YES, WISE THORN-TEETH. BUT WHERE ARE RACHACHA AND THE OTHERS? THE HOUR GROWS LATE.>
SSHHTH-SHHROKK
<WHAT IS THAT SOUND, GURF? SOMETHING RUSTLES BEHIND THE TREELINE.>
<RACHACHA? THARG? THOK? IS THAT YOU? DID YOU BRING THE CAPTURED SMALL-FOLK TO SLAKE THE NIGHTSTONE'S BLOOD-THIRST?>

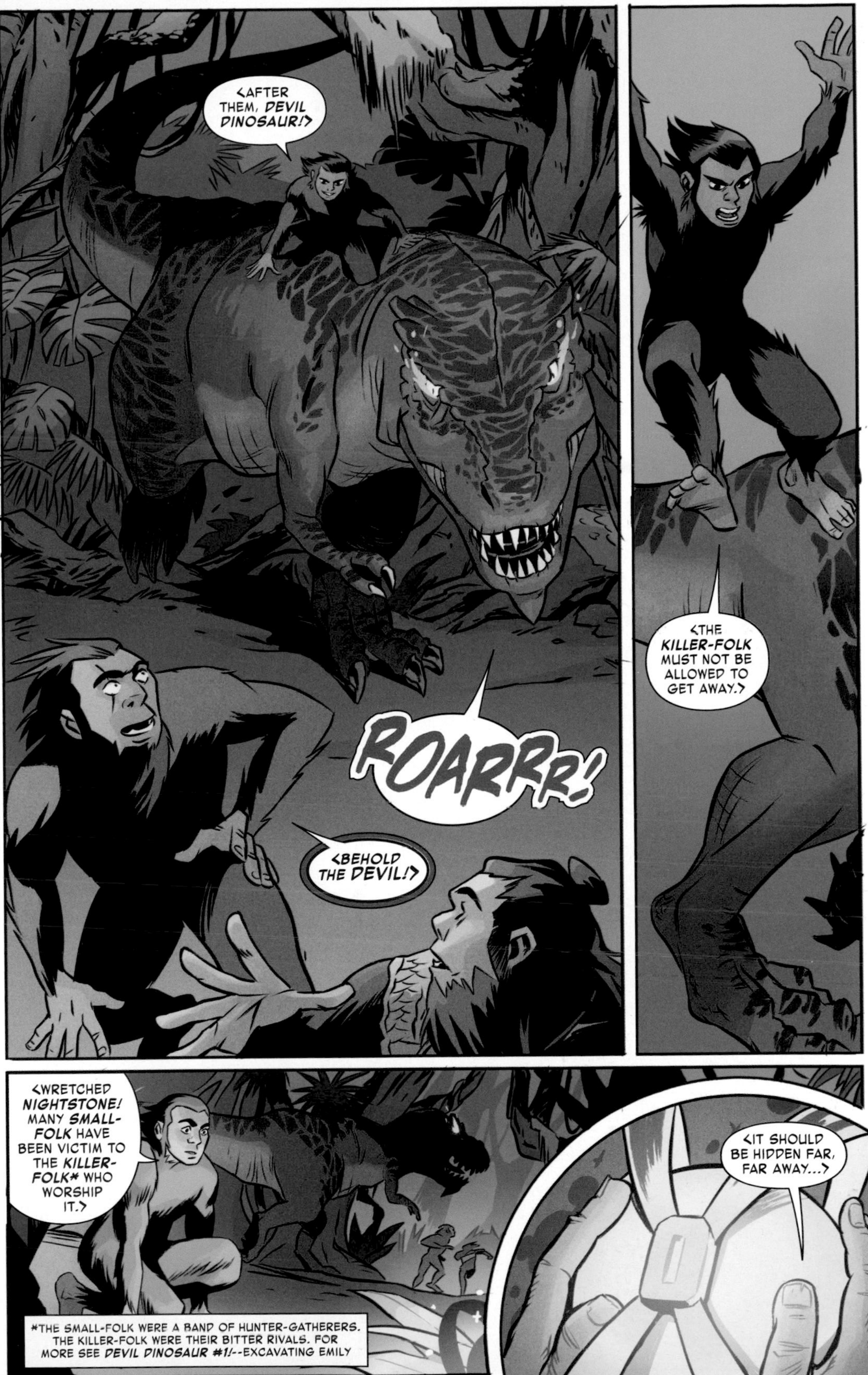
<AFTER THEM, DEVIL DINOSAUR!>
ROARRR!
<BEHOLD THE DEVIL!>
<THE KILLER-FOLK MUST NOT BE ALLOWED TO GET AWAY.>
<WRETCHED NIGHTSTONE! MANY SMALL-FOLK HAVE BEEN VICTIM TO THE KILLER-FOLK* WHO WORSHIP IT.>
*THE SMALL-FOLK WERE A BAND OF HUNTER-GATHERERS. THE KILLER-FOLK WERE THEIR BITTER RIVALS. FOR MORE SEE DEVIL DINOSAUR #1!--EXCAVATING EMILY
<IT SHOULD BE HIDDEN FAR, FAR AWAY...>

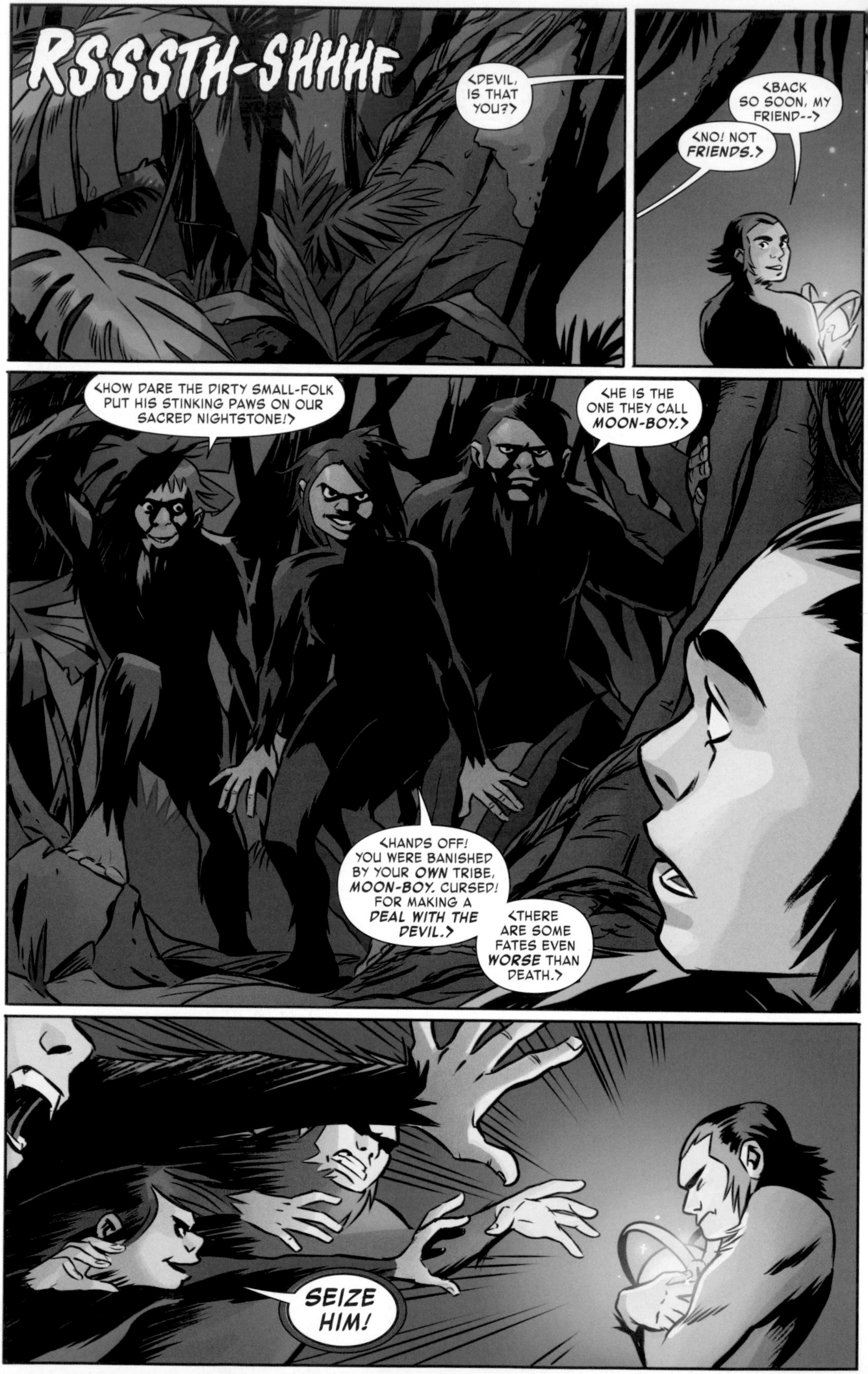
RSSSTH-SHHHF
<DEVIL, IS THAT YOU?>
<BACK SO SOON, MY FRIEND-->
<NO! NOT FRIENDS.>
<HOW DARE THE DIRTY SMALL-FOLK PUT HIS STINKING PAWS ON OUR SACRED NIGHTSTONE!>
<HE IS THE ONE THEY CALL MOON-BOY.>
<HANDS OFF! YOU WERE BANISHED BY YOUR OWN TRIBE, MOON-BOY. CURSED! FOR MAKING A DEAL WITH THE DEVIL.>
<THERE ARE SOME FATES EVEN WORSE THAN DEATH.>
SEIZE HIM!

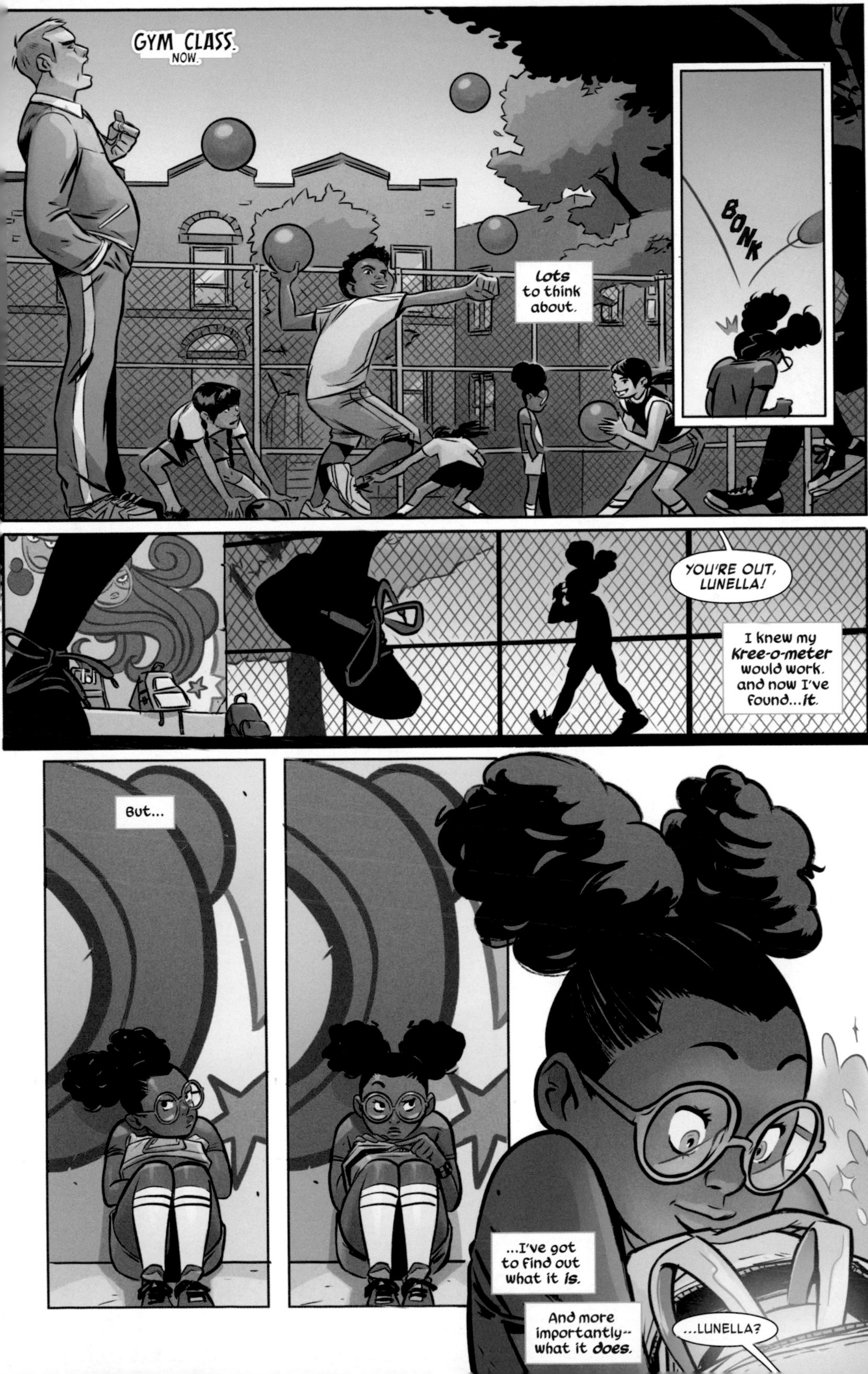
GYM CLASS. NOW.
Lots to think about.
BONK
YOU'RE OUT, LUNELLA!
I knew my Kree-o-meter would work. and now I've found...it.
But...
...I've got to find out what it is.
And more importantly-- what it does.
...LUNELLA?

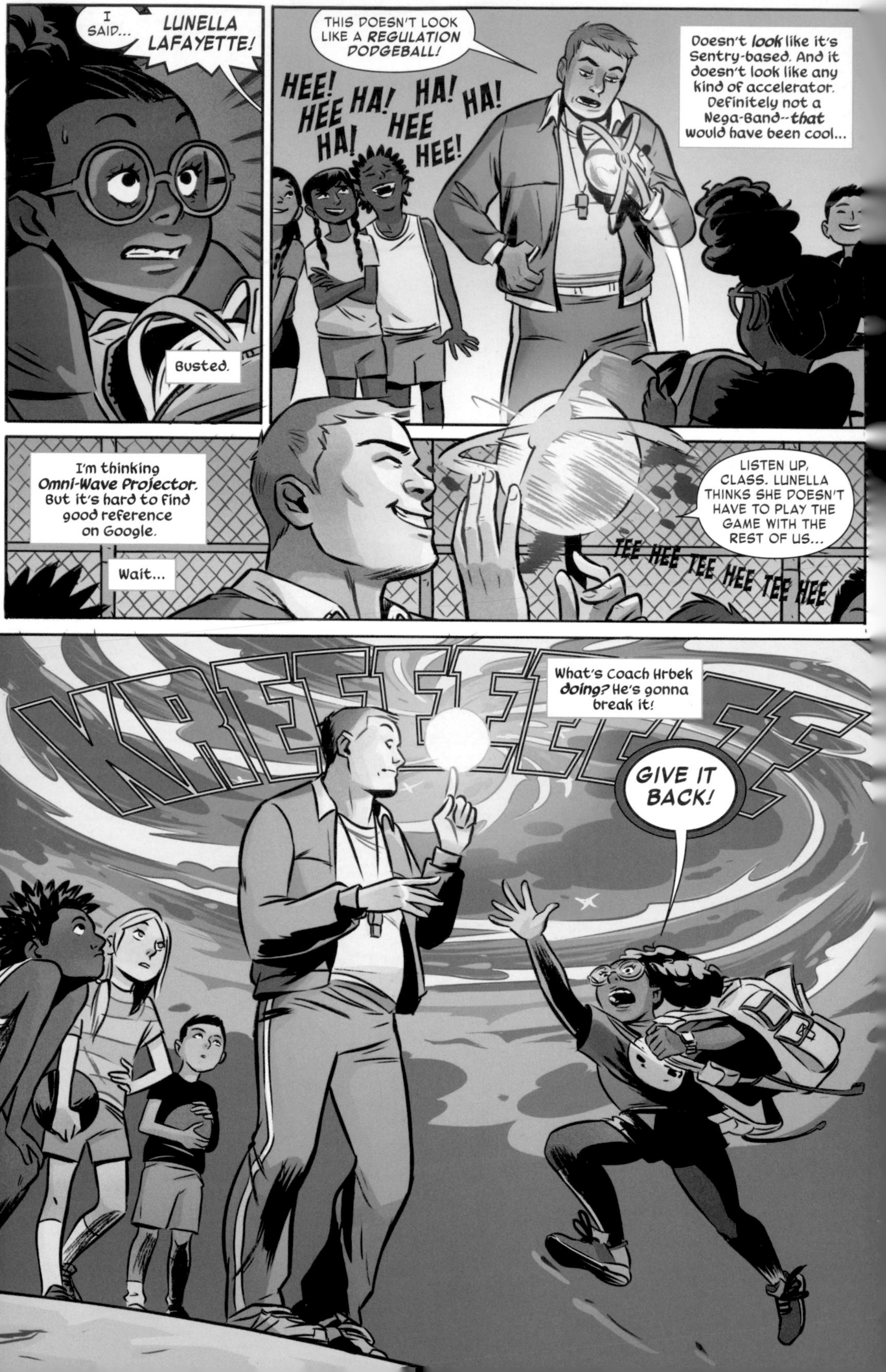
I SAID... LUNELLA LAFAYETTE!
Busted.
THIS DOESN'T LOOK LIKE A *REGULATION DODGEBALL!*
HEE! HEE HA! HA! HEE HA! HEE! HA!
Doesn't *look* like it's Sentry-based. And it doesn't look like any kind of accelerator. Definitely not a Nega-Band--*that* would have been cool...
I'm thinking *Omni-Wave Projector*. But it's hard to find good reference on Google.
Wait...
LISTEN UP, CLASS. LUNELLA THINKS SHE DOESN'T HAVE TO PLAY THE GAME WITH THE REST OF US...
TEE HEE TEE HEE TEE HEE
What's Coach Hrbek *doing?* He's gonna break it!
GIVE IT BACK!

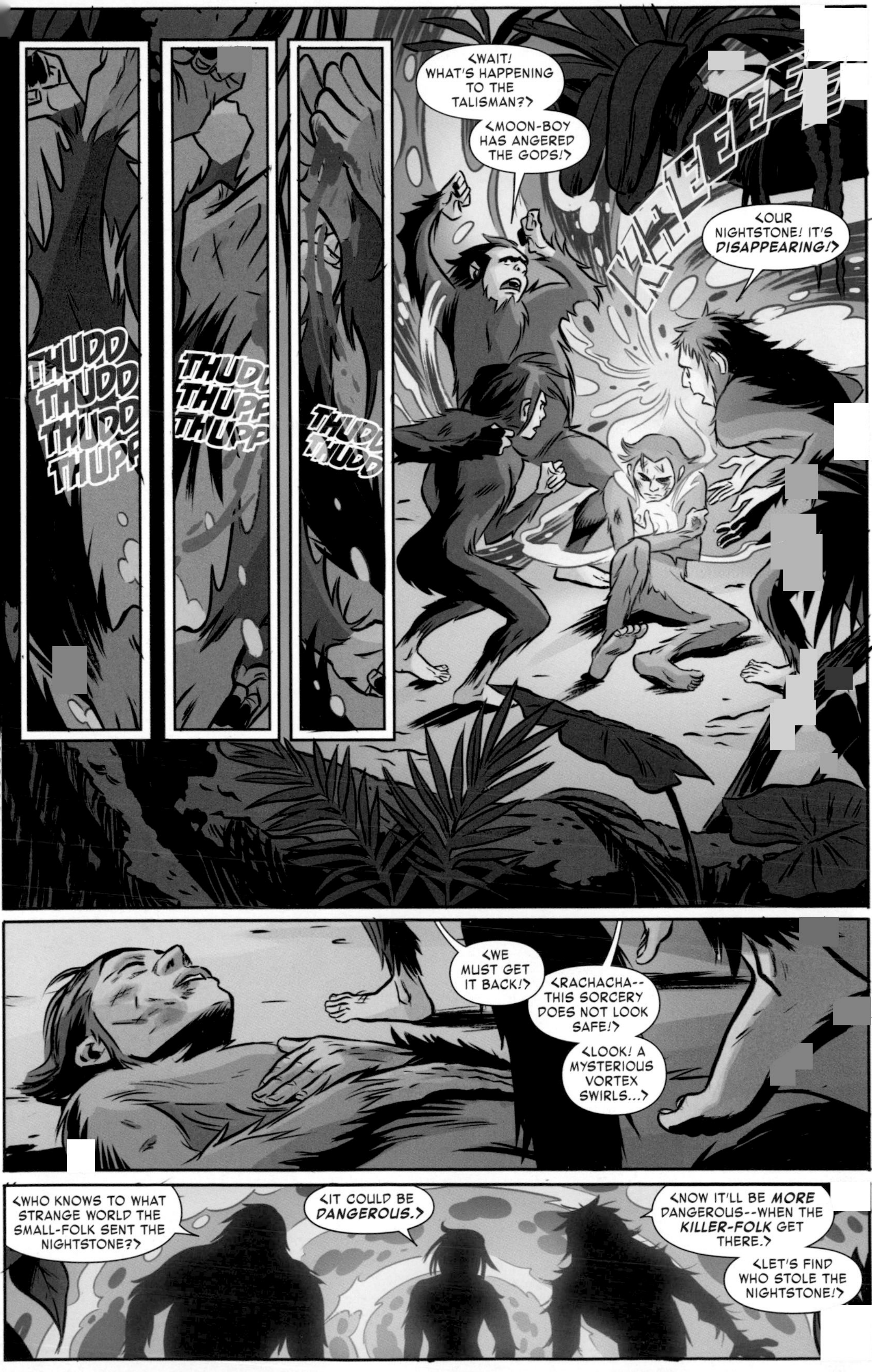

THUDD THUDD THUDD THUPP
THUDD THUPP THUPP
THUDD THUDD
<WAIT! WHAT'S HAPPENING TO THE TALISMAN?>
<MOON-BOY HAS ANGERED THE GODS!>
<OUR NIGHTSTONE! IT'S *DISAPPEARING!*>
<WE MUST GET IT BACK!>
<RACHACHA-- THIS SORCERY DOES NOT LOOK SAFE!>
<LOOK! A MYSTERIOUS VORTEX SWIRLS...>
<WHO KNOWS TO WHAT STRANGE WORLD THE SMALL-FOLK SENT THE NIGHTSTONE?>
<IT COULD BE *DANGEROUS.*>
<NOW IT'LL BE *MORE* DANGEROUS--WHEN THE *KILLER-FOLK* GET THERE.>
<LET'S FIND WHO STOLE THE NIGHTSTONE!>

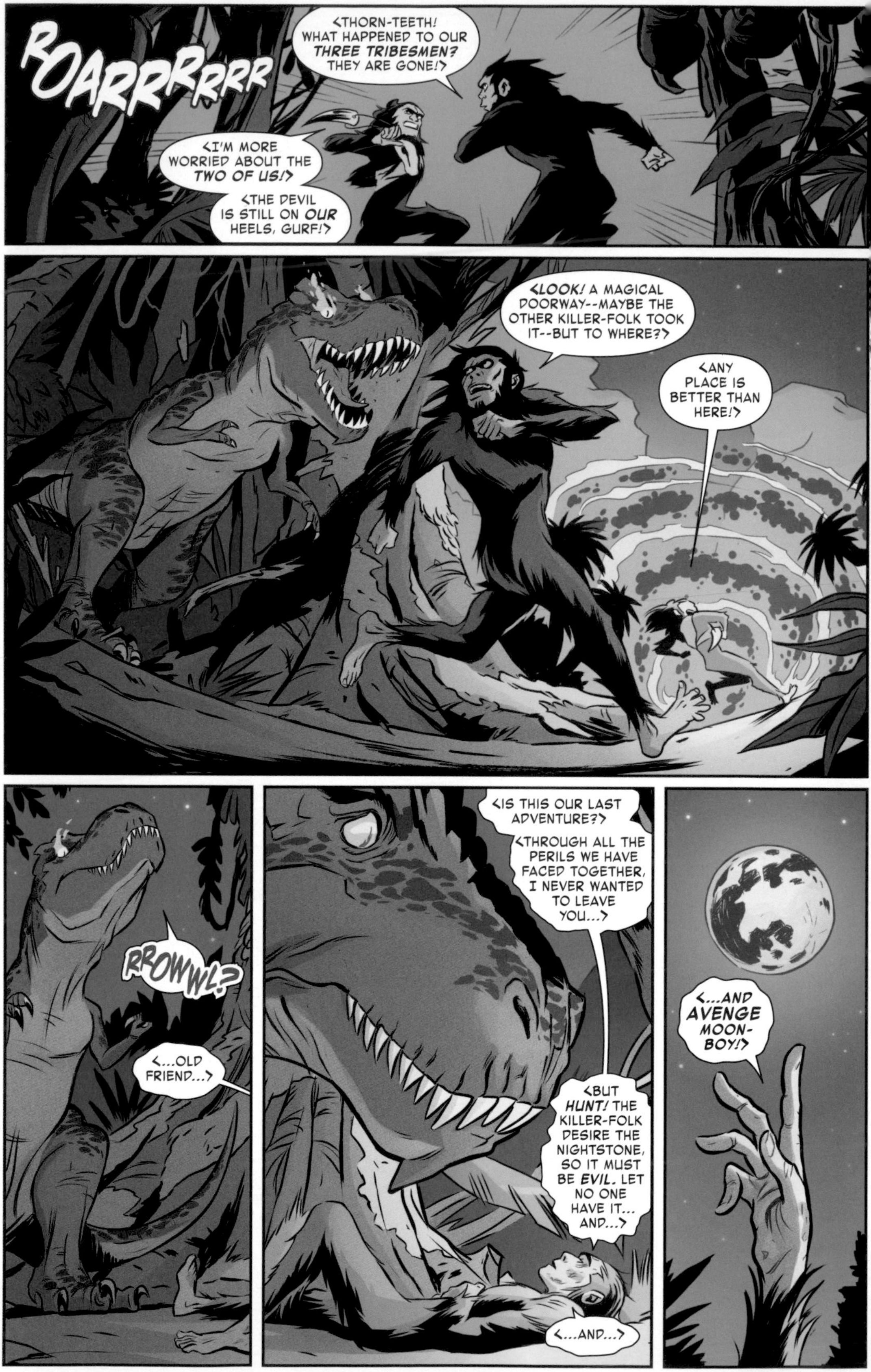
ROARRRRRRR
<THORN-TEETH! WHAT HAPPENED TO OUR THREE TRIBESMEN? THEY ARE GONE!>
<I'M MORE WORRIED ABOUT THE TWO OF US!>
<THE DEVIL IS STILL ON OUR HEELS, GURF!>
<LOOK! A MAGICAL DOORWAY--MAYBE THE OTHER KILLER-FOLK TOOK IT--BUT TO WHERE?>
<ANY PLACE IS BETTER THAN HERE!>
RROWWL?
<...OLD FRIEND...>
<IS THIS OUR LAST ADVENTURE?>
<THROUGH ALL THE PERILS WE HAVE FACED TOGETHER, I NEVER WANTED TO LEAVE YOU...>
<BUT HUNT! THE KILLER-FOLK DESIRE THE NIGHTSTONE, SO IT MUST BE EVIL. LET NO ONE HAVE IT... AND...>
<...AND...>
<...AND AVENGE MOON-BOY!>

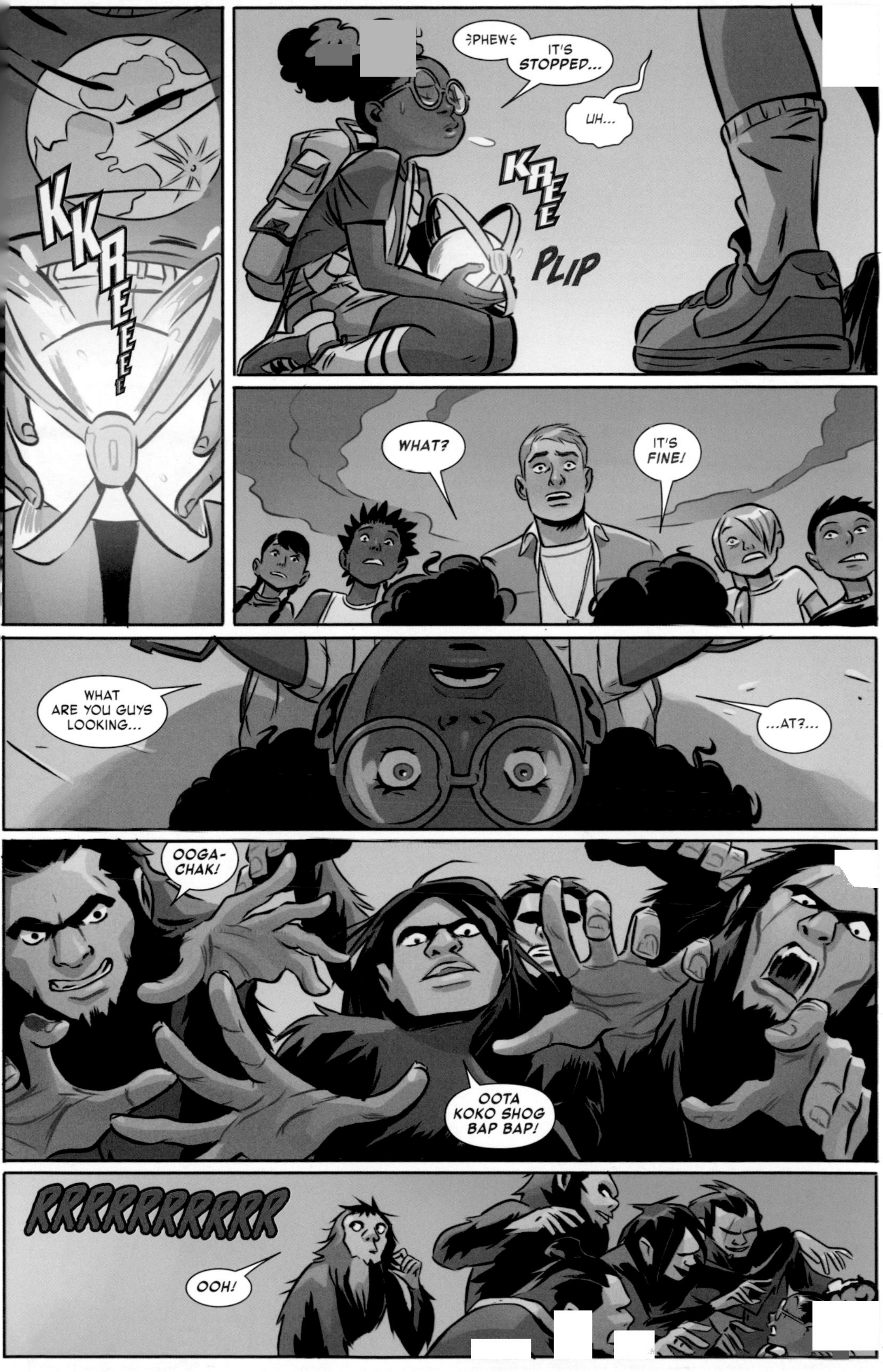
KKREEEEE
PHEW
IT'S STOPPED...
UH...
KREE
PLIP
WHAT?
IT'S FINE!
WHAT ARE YOU GUYS LOOKING...
...AT?...
OOGA-CHAK!
OOTA KOKO SHOG BAP BAP!
RRRRRRRRRRR
OOH!

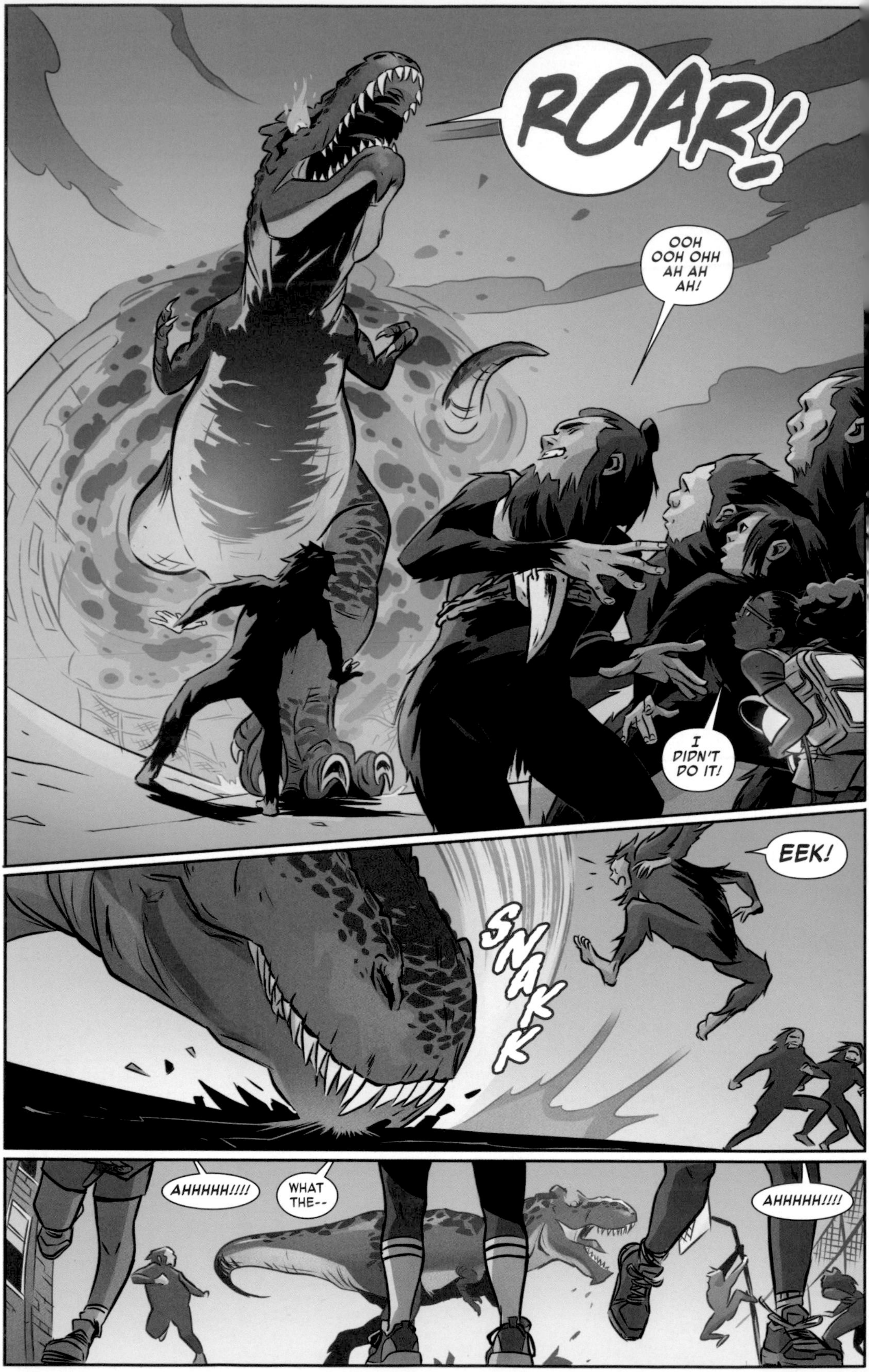
ROAR!
OOH OOH OHH AH AH AH!
I DIDN'T DO IT!
EEK!
SNAKK
AHHHHH!!!!
WHAT THE--
AHHHHH!!!!

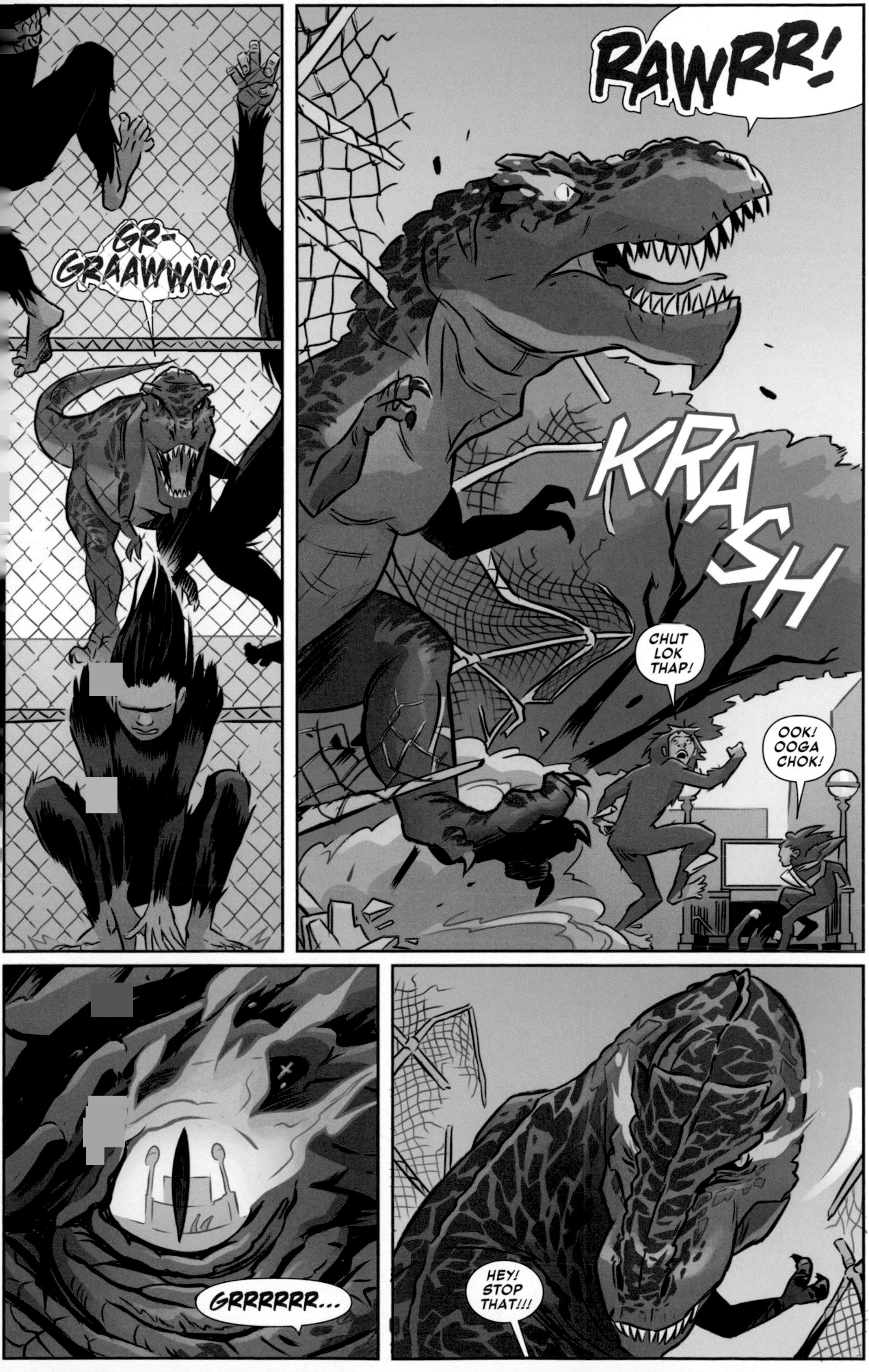
GR-GRAAWWW!
RAWRR!
KRASH
CHUT LOK THAP!
OOK! OOGA CHOK!
GRRRRRR...
HEY! STOP THAT!!!

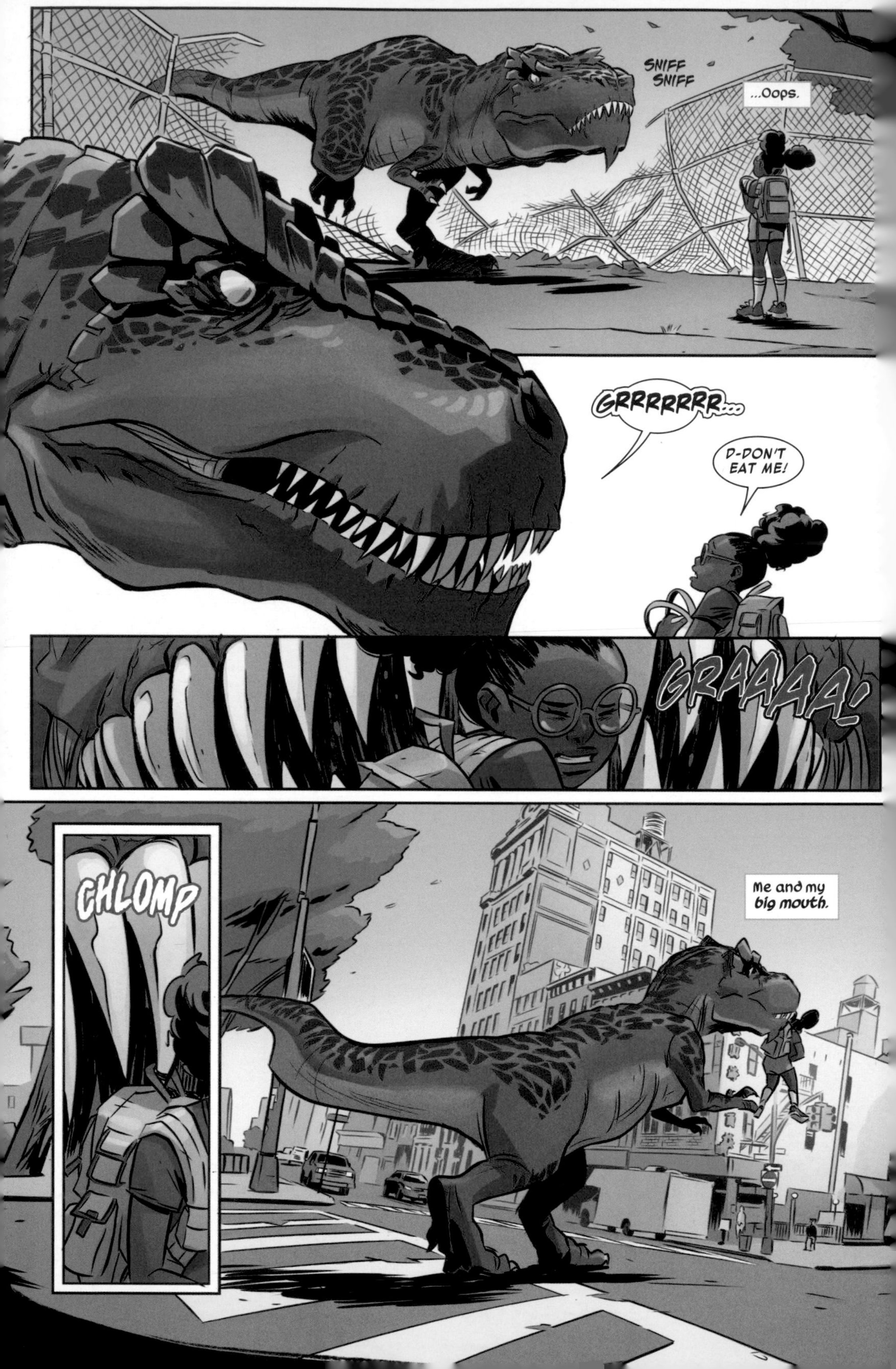
SNIFF SNIFF
...Oops.
GRRRRRRR...
D-DON'T EAT ME!
GRAAAAA!
CHLOMP
Me and my big mouth.

OON GIRL AND DEVIL DINOSAUR: MARVEL LEGACY PRIMER

OU'VE SEEN HOW THEY MET — NOW LEARN THE FULL STORY OF MOON GIRL'S ORIGIN!

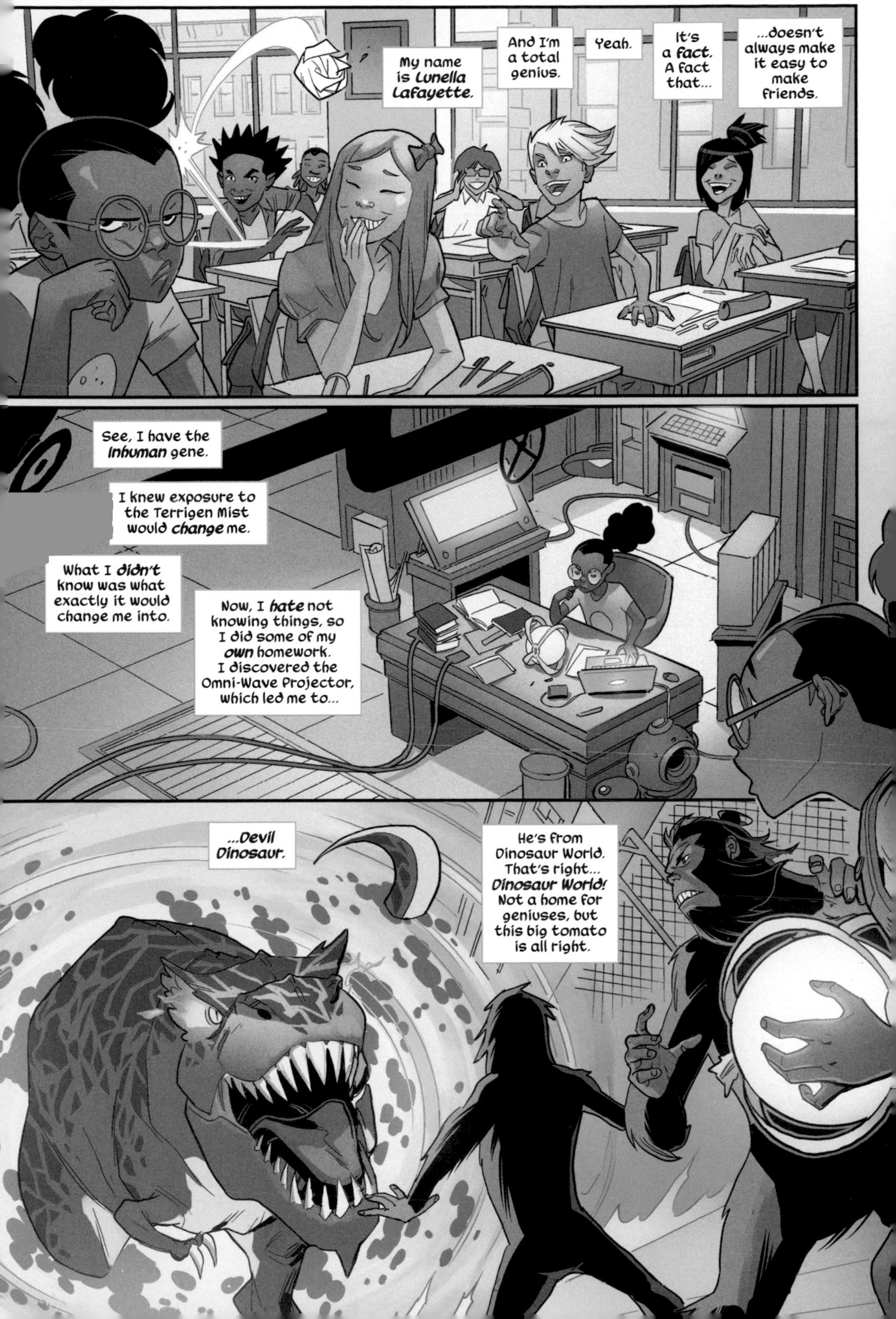

My name is Lunella Lafayette.
And I'm a total genius.
Yeah.
It's a fact. A fact that...
...doesn't always make it easy to make friends.
See, I have the Inhuman gene.
I knew exposure to the Terrigen Mist would change me.
What I didn't know was what exactly it would change me into.
Now, I hate not knowing things, so I did some of my own homework. I discovered the Omni-Wave Projector, which led me to...
...Devil Dinosaur.
He's from Dinosaur World. That's right... Dinosaur World! Not a home for geniuses, but this big tomato is all right.

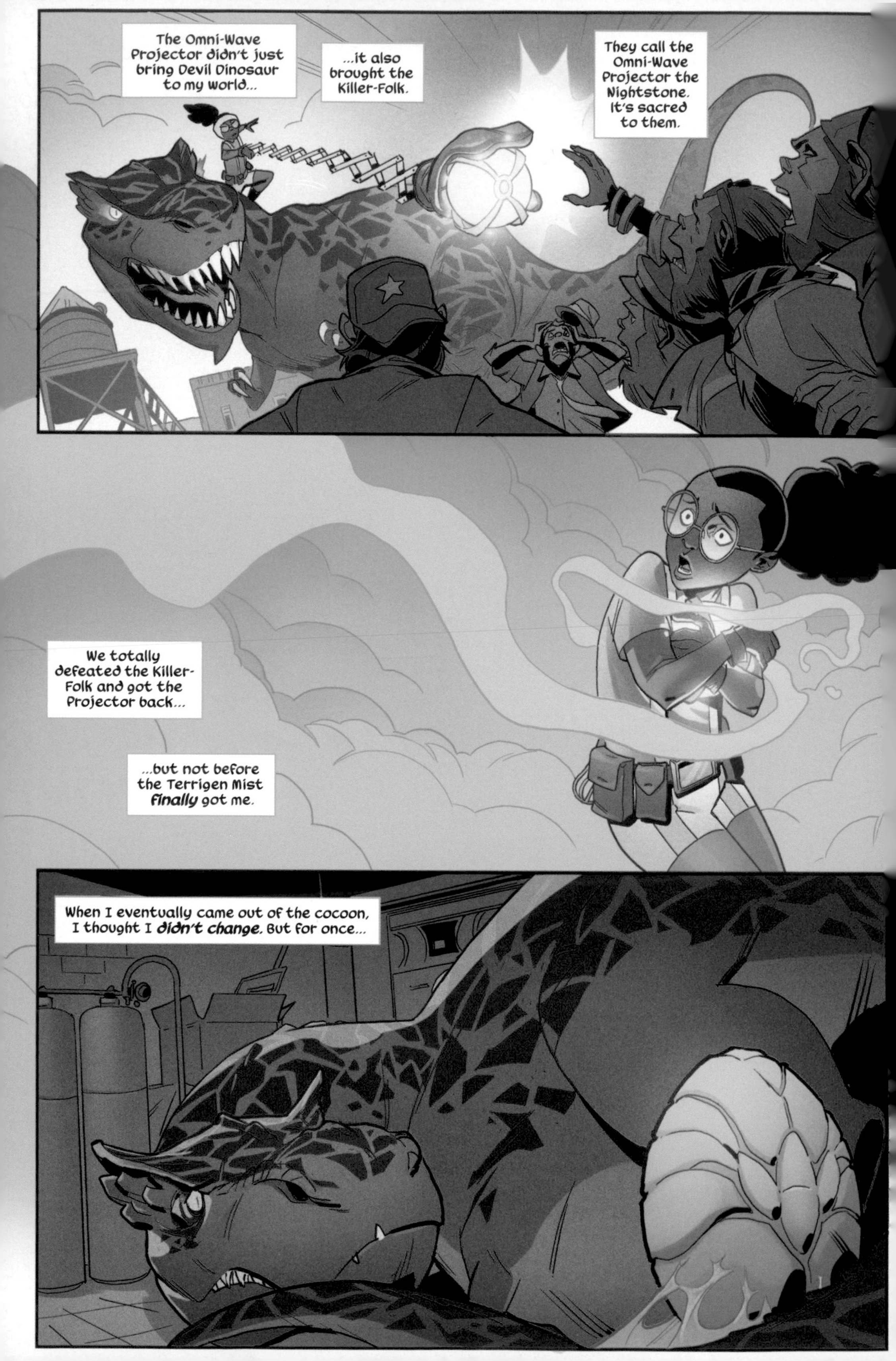
The Omni-Wave Projector didn't just bring Devil Dinosaur to my world...
...it also brought the Killer-Folk.
They call the Omni-Wave Projector the Nightstone. It's sacred to them.
We totally defeated the Killer-Folk and got the Projector back...
...but not before the Terrigen Mist *finally* got me.
When I eventually came out of the cocoon, I thought I *didn't change*. But for once...

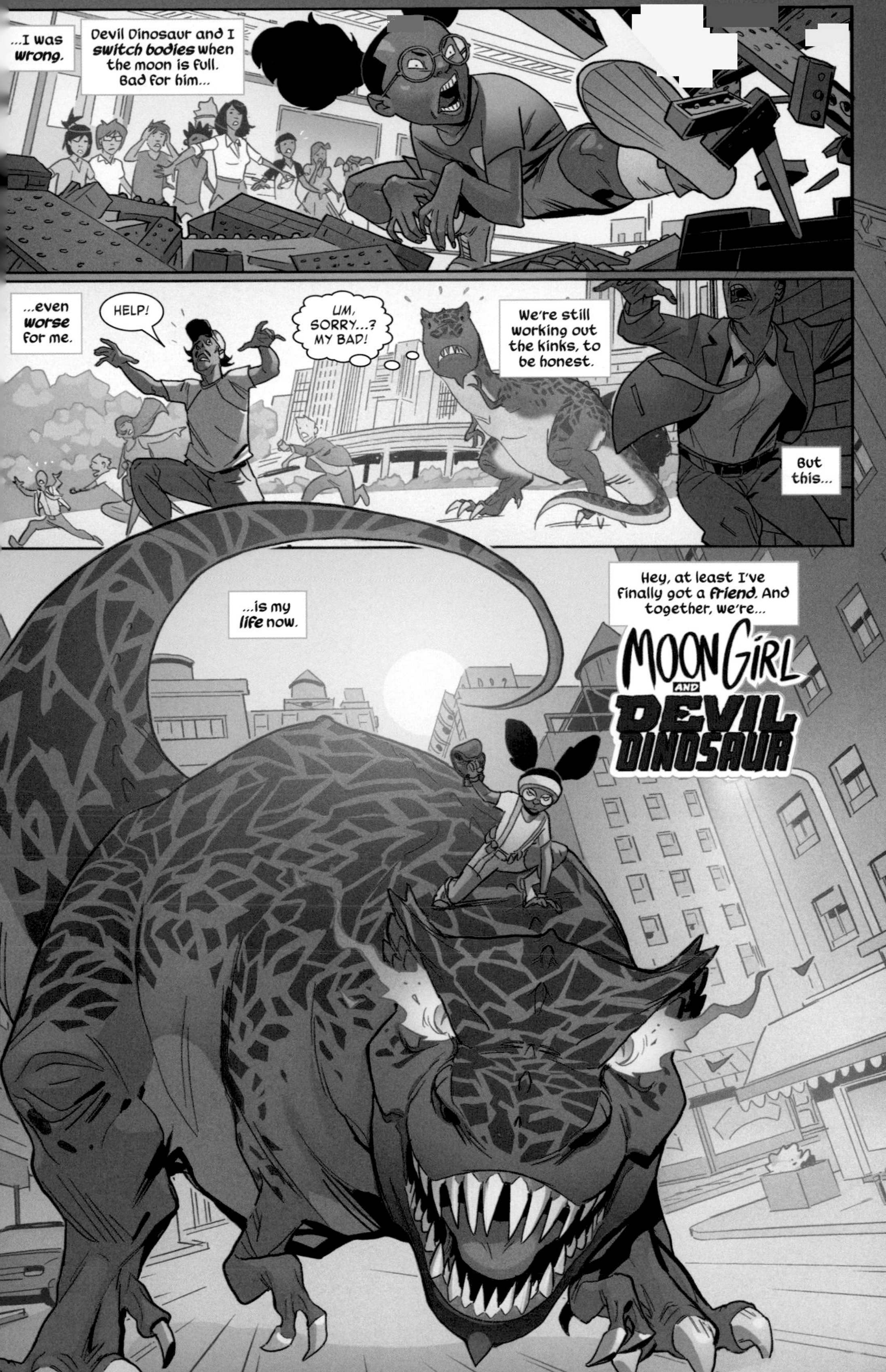
...I was wrong.
Devil Dinosaur and I switch bodies when the moon is full. Bad for him...
...even worse for me.
HELP!
UM, SORRY...? MY BAD!
We're still working out the kinks, to be honest.
But this...
...is my life now.
Hey, at least I've finally got a friend. And together, we're...
MOON GIRL AND DEVIL DINOSAUR

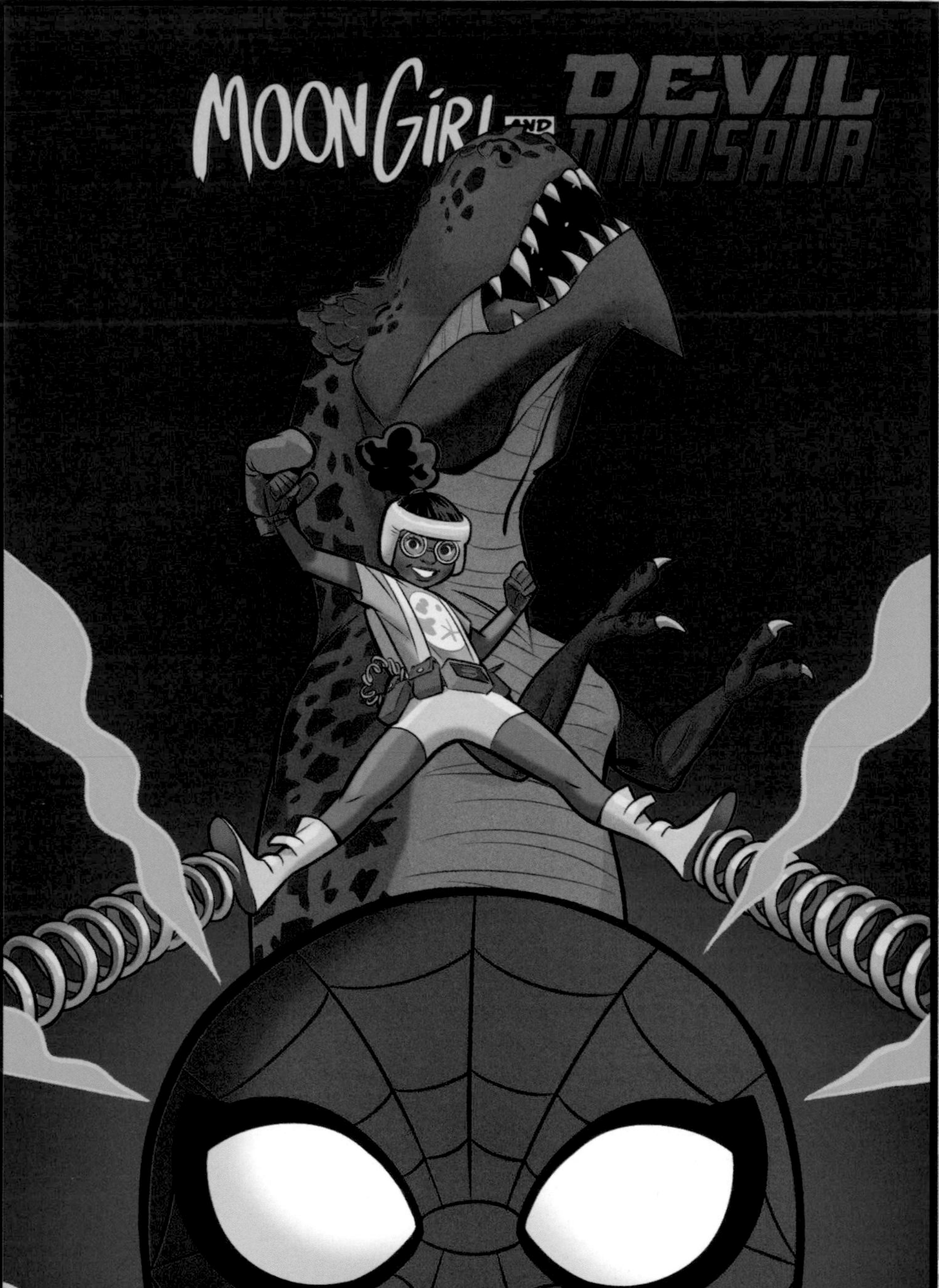
MOON GIRL AND DEVIL DINOSAUR

MOON GIRL AND DEVIL DINOSAUR #42

LUNELLA AND DEVIL MEET THE ORIGINAL
KID HERO HIMSELF, SPIDER-MAN!

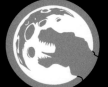

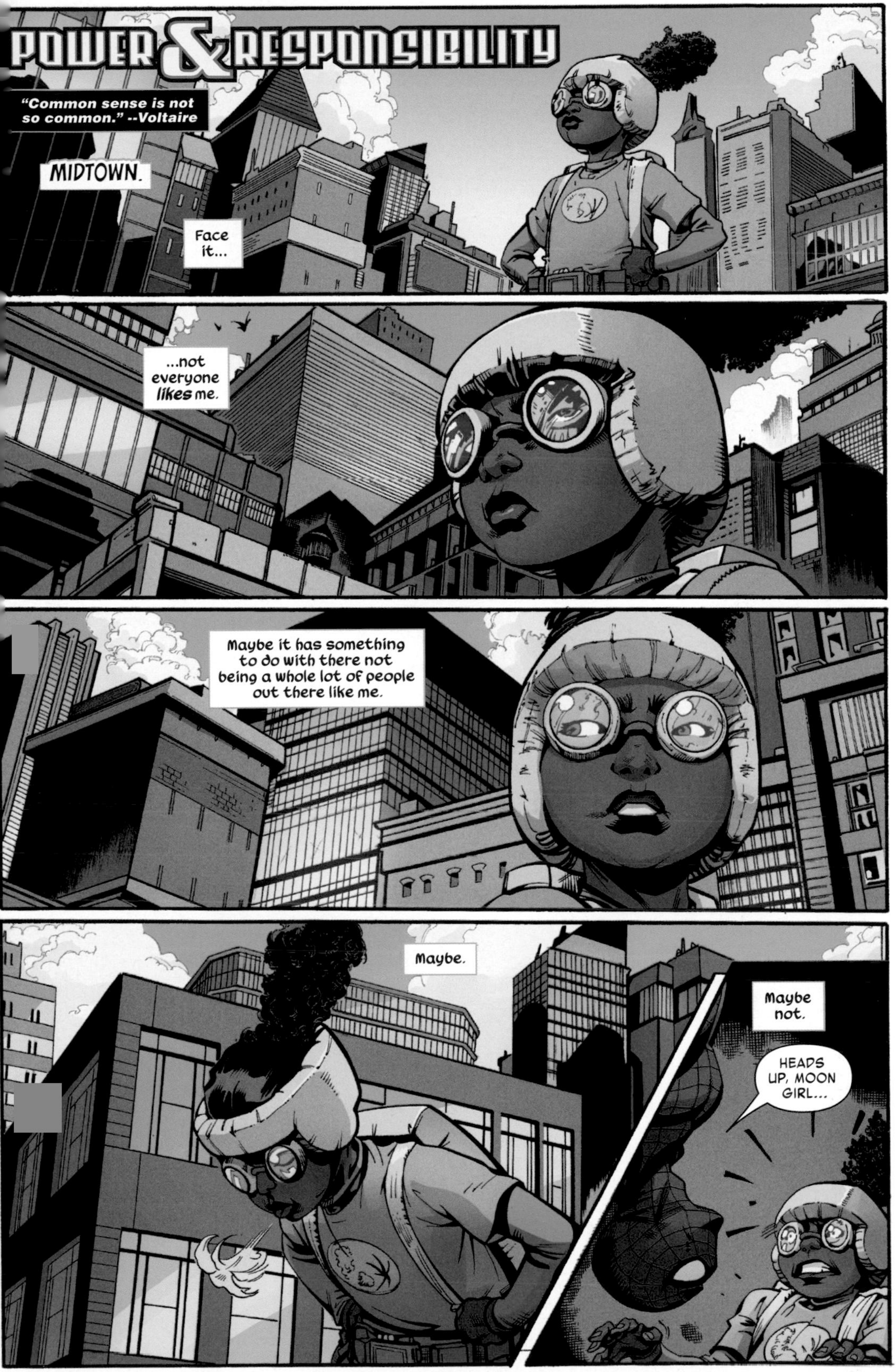
POWER & RESPONSIBILITY
"Common sense is not so common." --Voltaire
MIDTOWN.
Face it...
...not everyone *likes* me.
Maybe it has something to do with there not being a whole lot of people out there like me.
Maybe.
Maybe not.
HEADS UP, MOON GIRL...

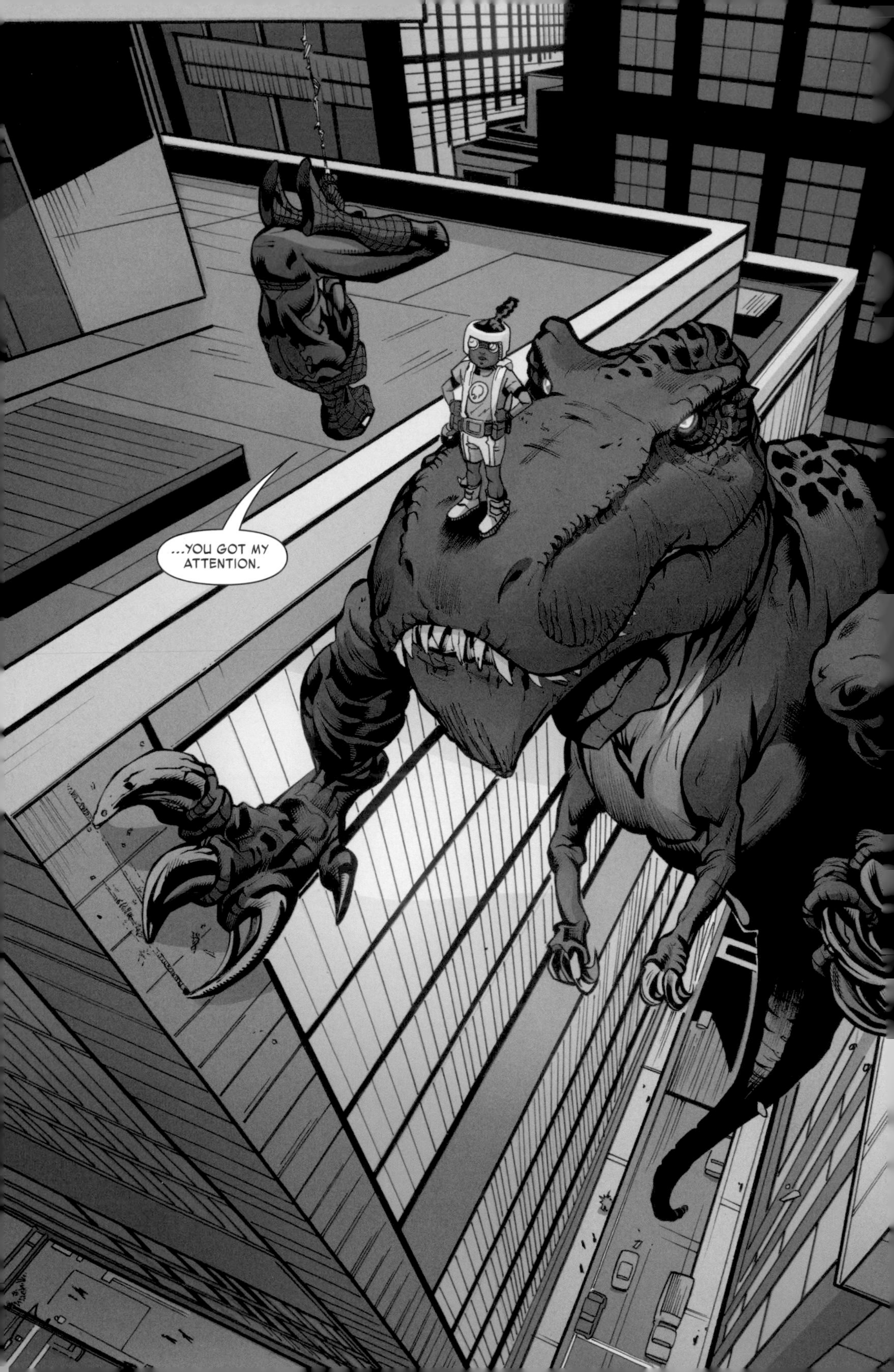
...YOU GOT MY ATTENTION.

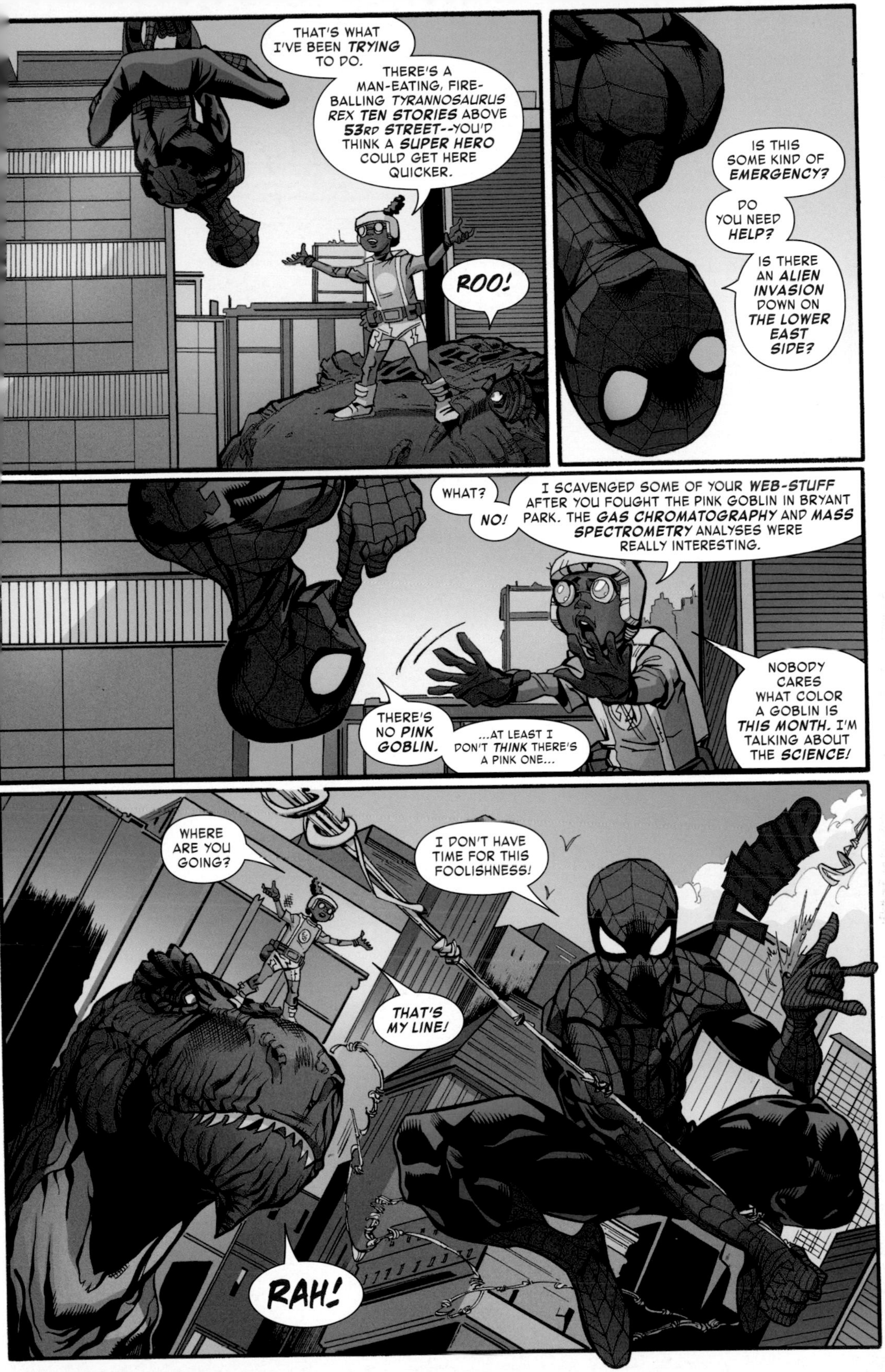
THAT'S WHAT I'VE BEEN TRYING TO DO.
THERE'S A MAN-EATING, FIRE-BALLING TYRANNOSAURUS REX TEN STORIES ABOVE 53RD STREET--YOU'D THINK A SUPER HERO COULD GET HERE QUICKER.
ROO!
IS THIS SOME KIND OF EMERGENCY?
DO YOU NEED HELP?
IS THERE AN ALIEN INVASION DOWN ON THE LOWER EAST SIDE?
WHAT?
NO!
I SCAVENGED SOME OF YOUR WEB-STUFF AFTER YOU FOUGHT THE PINK GOBLIN IN BRYANT PARK. THE GAS CHROMATOGRAPHY AND MASS SPECTROMETRY ANALYSES WERE REALLY INTERESTING.
THERE'S NO PINK GOBLIN.
...AT LEAST I DON'T THINK THERE'S A PINK ONE...
NOBODY CARES WHAT COLOR A GOBLIN IS THIS MONTH. I'M TALKING ABOUT THE SCIENCE!
WHERE ARE YOU GOING?
I DON'T HAVE TIME FOR THIS FOOLISHNESS!
THAT'S MY LINE!
RAH!

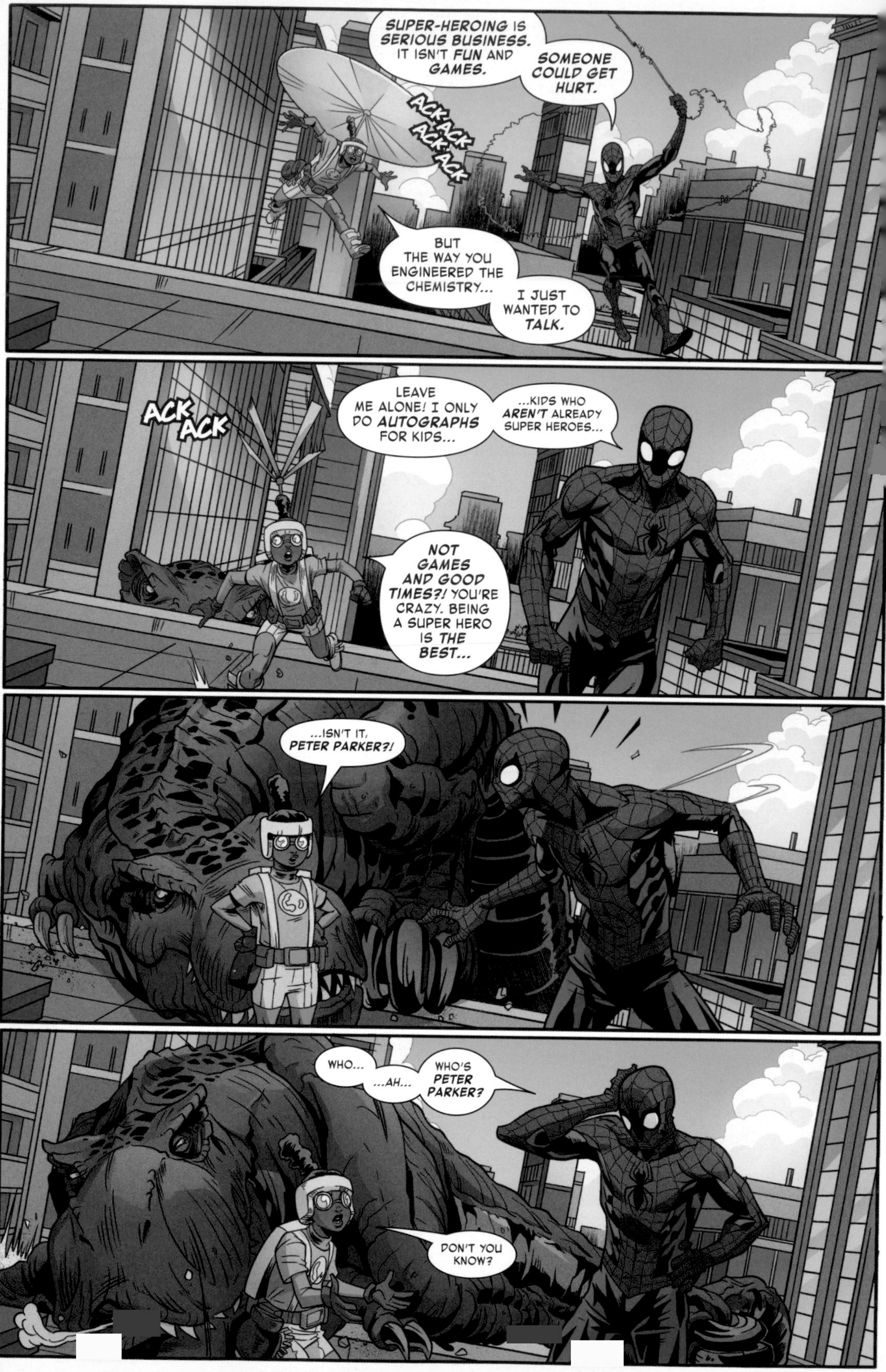
SUPER-HEROING IS SERIOUS BUSINESS. IT ISN'T FUN AND GAMES.
SOMEONE COULD GET HURT.
ACK ACK ACK ACK
BUT THE WAY YOU ENGINEERED THE CHEMISTRY...
I JUST WANTED TO TALK.
ACK ACK
LEAVE ME ALONE! I ONLY DO AUTOGRAPHS FOR KIDS...
...KIDS WHO AREN'T ALREADY SUPER HEROES...
NOT GAMES AND GOOD TIMES?! YOU'RE CRAZY. BEING A SUPER HERO IS THE BEST...
...ISN'T IT, PETER PARKER?!
WHO...
...AH...
WHO'S PETER PARKER?
DON'T YOU KNOW?

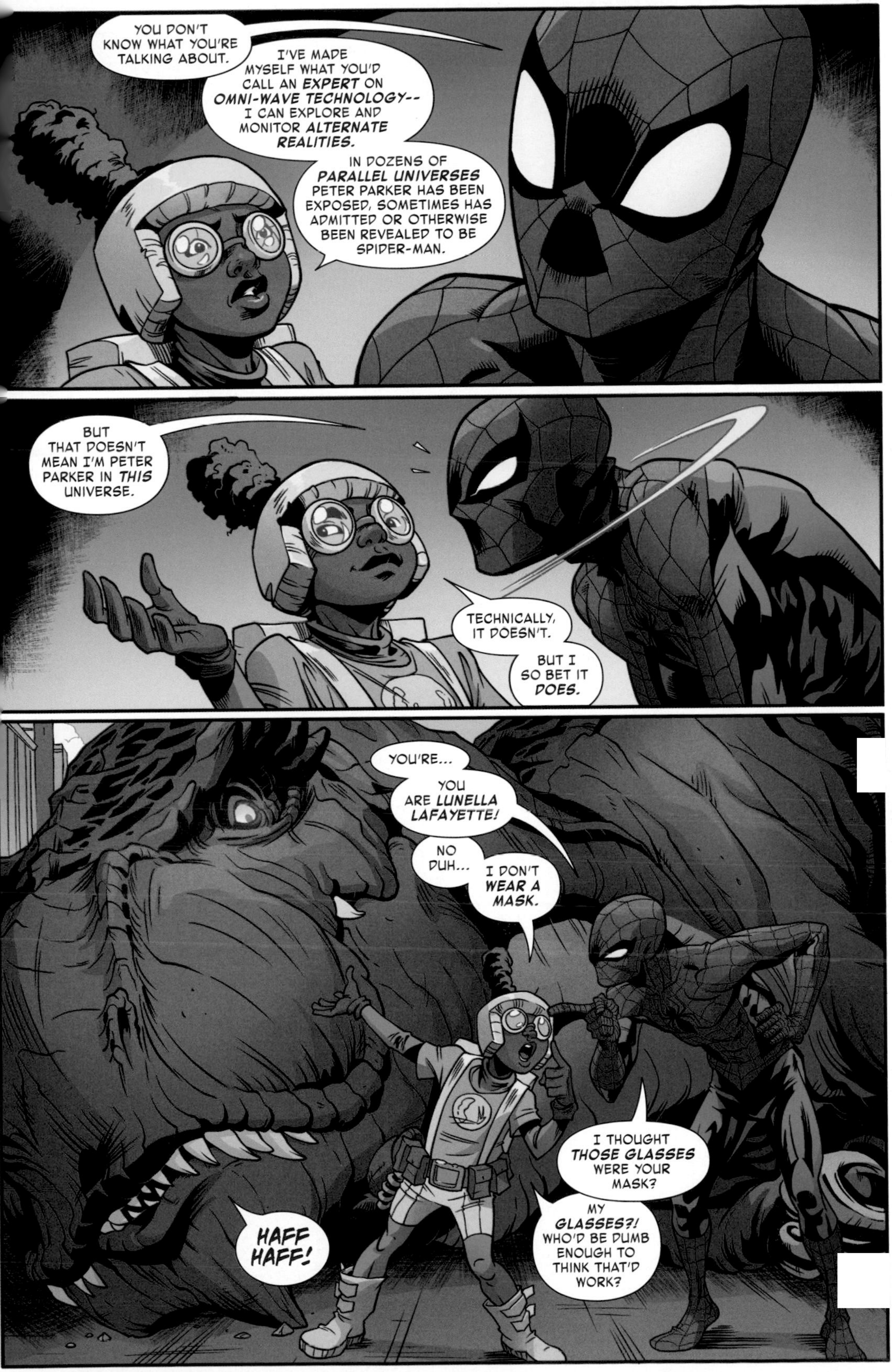

YOU DON'T KNOW WHAT YOU'RE TALKING ABOUT.
I'VE MADE MYSELF WHAT YOU'D CALL AN EXPERT ON OMNI-WAVE TECHNOLOGY-- I CAN EXPLORE AND MONITOR ALTERNATE REALITIES.
IN DOZENS OF PARALLEL UNIVERSES PETER PARKER HAS BEEN EXPOSED, SOMETIMES HAS ADMITTED OR OTHERWISE BEEN REVEALED TO BE SPIDER-MAN.
BUT THAT DOESN'T MEAN I'M PETER PARKER IN THIS UNIVERSE.
TECHNICALLY, IT DOESN'T.
BUT I SO BET IT DOES.
YOU'RE...
YOU ARE LUNELLA LAFAYETTE!
NO DUH...
I DON'T WEAR A MASK.
I THOUGHT THOSE GLASSES WERE YOUR MASK?
MY GLASSES?! WHO'D BE DUMB ENOUGH TO THINK THAT'D WORK?
HAFF HAFF!

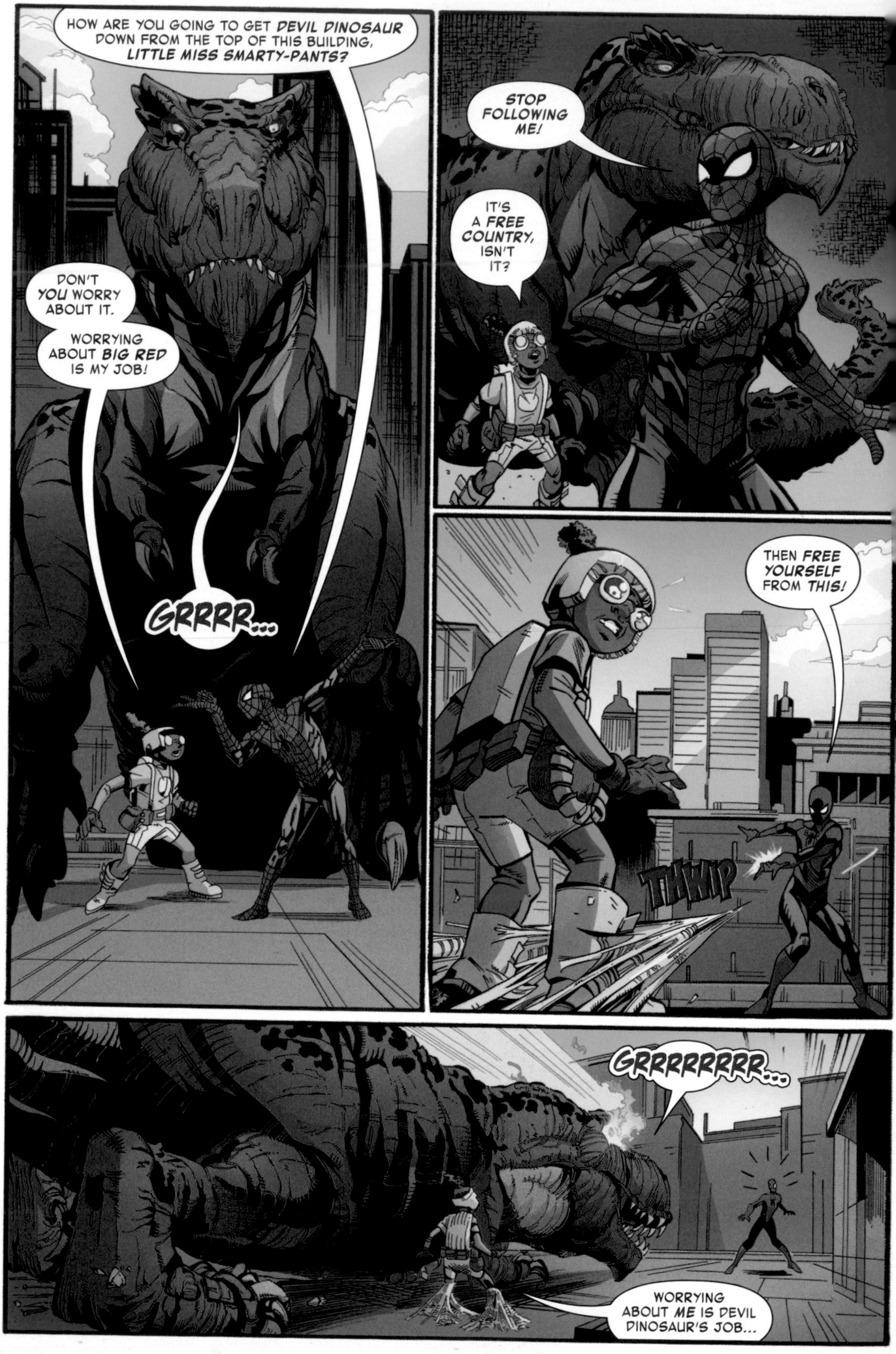
HOW ARE YOU GOING TO GET DEVIL DINOSAUR DOWN FROM THE TOP OF THIS BUILDING, LITTLE MISS SMARTY-PANTS?
DON'T YOU WORRY ABOUT IT.
WORRYING ABOUT BIG RED IS MY JOB!
GRRRR...
STOP FOLLOWING ME!
IT'S A FREE COUNTRY, ISN'T IT?
THEN FREE YOURSELF FROM THIS!
THWIP
GRRRRRRRR...
WORRYING ABOUT ME IS DEVIL DINOSAUR'S JOB...

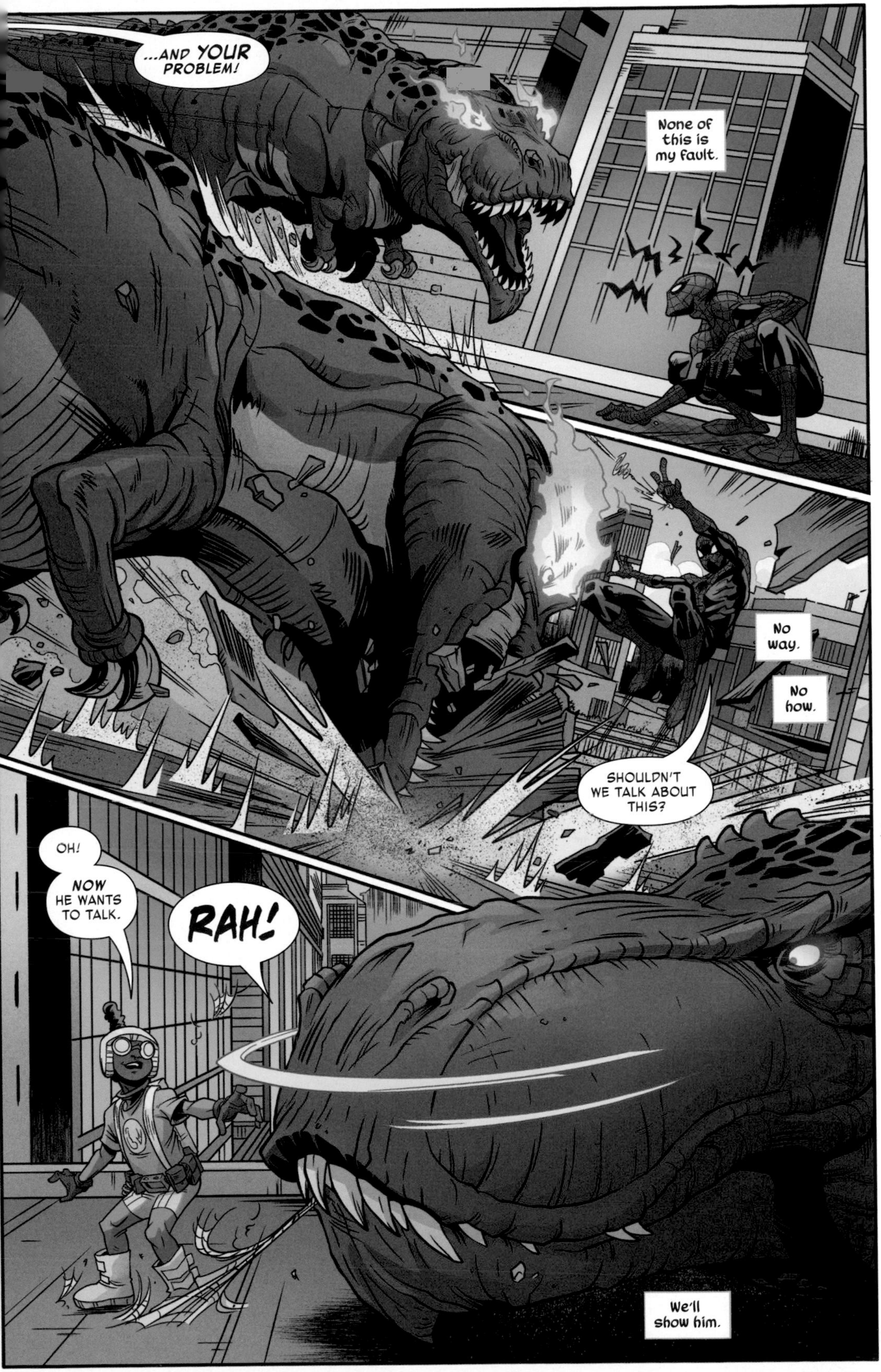
...AND YOUR PROBLEM!
None of this is my fault.
No way.
No how.
SHOULDN'T WE TALK ABOUT THIS?
OH! NOW HE WANTS TO TALK.
RAH!
We'll show him.

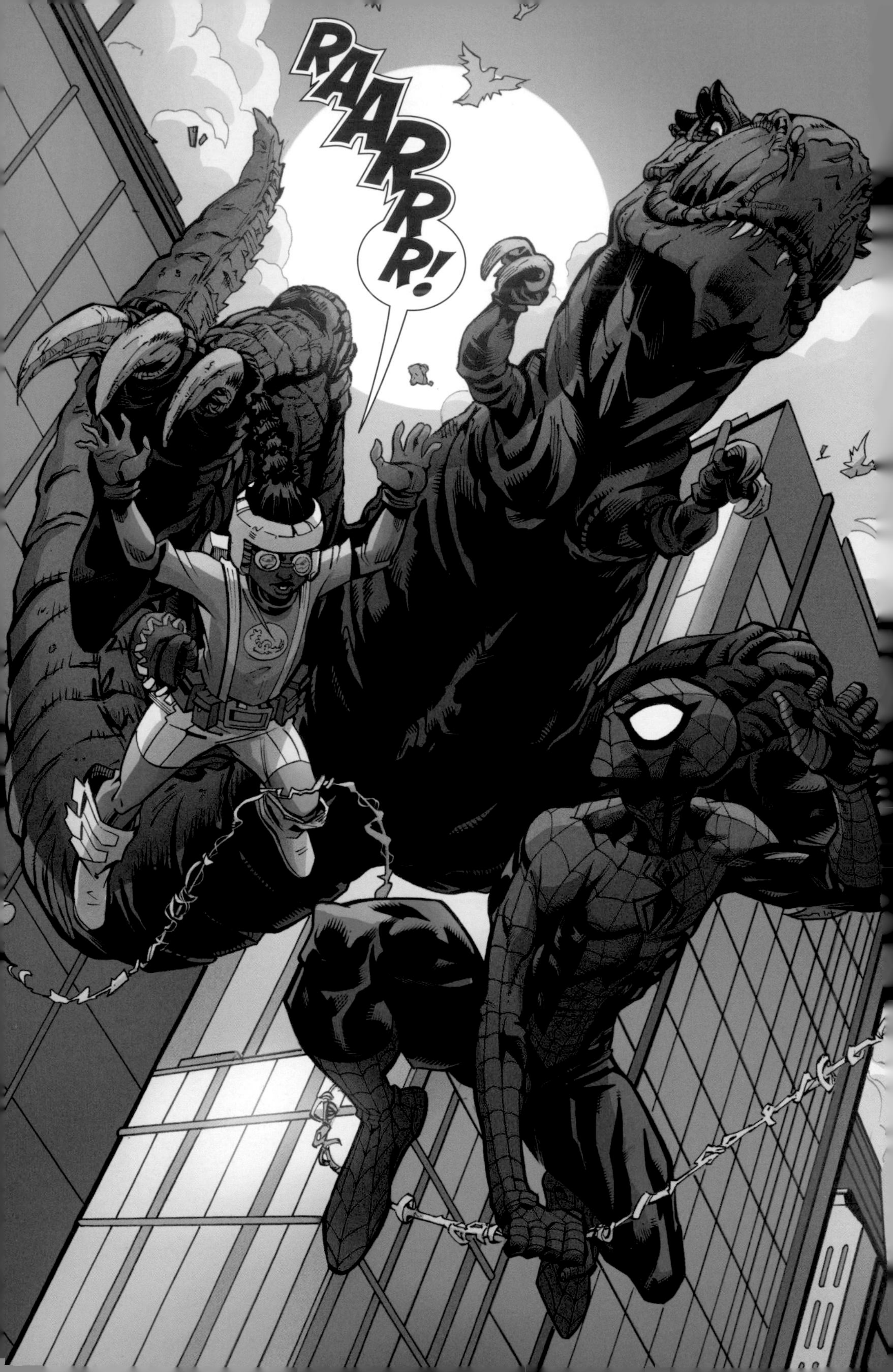
RAARRR!

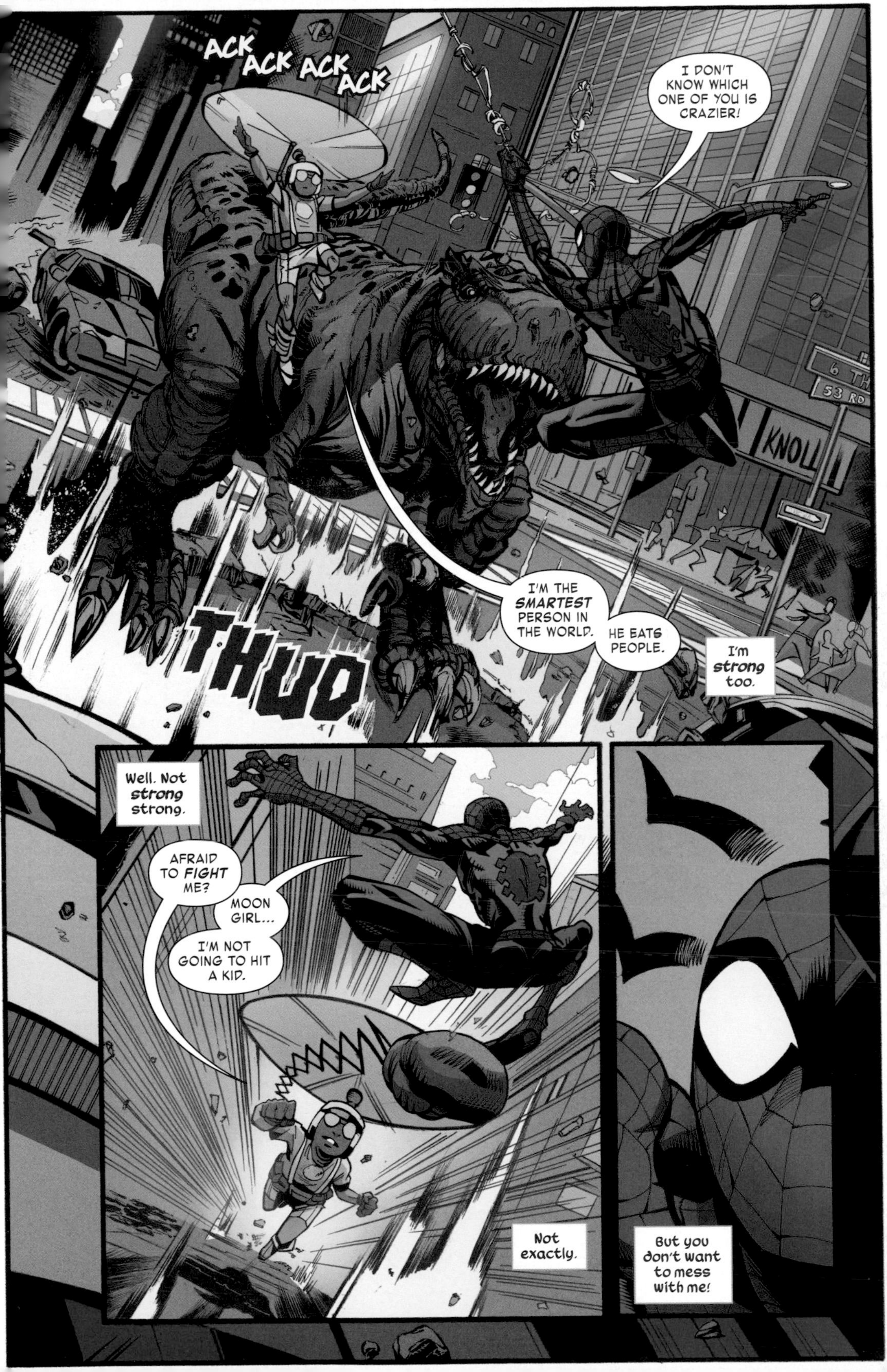
ACK ACK ACK ACK
I DON'T KNOW WHICH ONE OF YOU IS CRAZIER!
KNOLL
53 RD
I'M THE SMARTEST PERSON IN THE WORLD.
HE EATS PEOPLE.
THUD
I'm strong too.
Well. Not strong strong.
AFRAID TO FIGHT ME?
MOON GIRL...
I'M NOT GOING TO HIT A KID.
Not exactly.
But you don't want to mess with me!

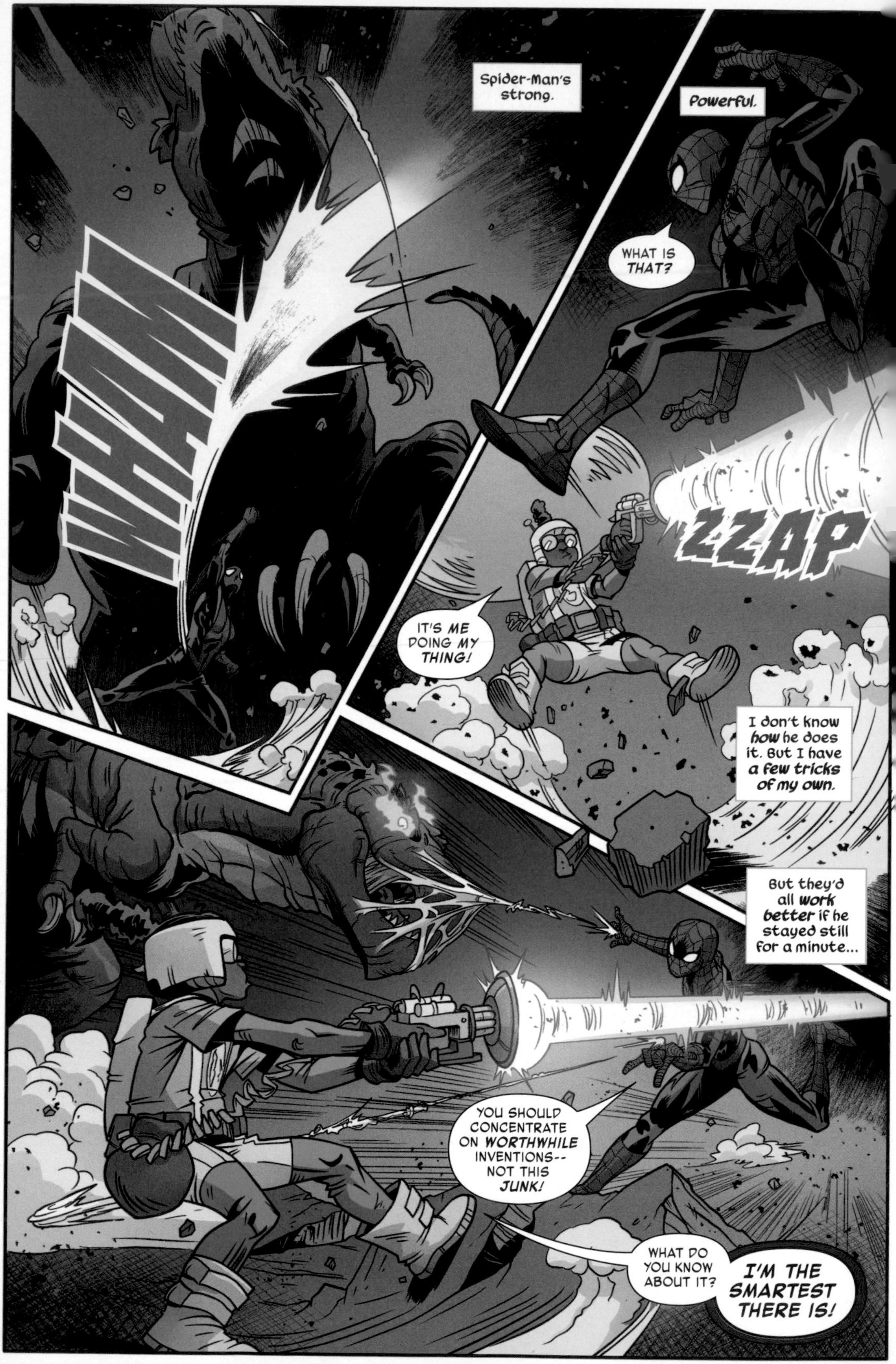

Spider-Man's strong.
Powerful.
WHAT IS THAT?
ZZAP
IT'S ME DOING MY THING!
I don't know how he does it. But I have a few tricks of my own.
But they'd all work better if he stayed still for a minute...
YOU SHOULD CONCENTRATE ON WORTHWHILE INVENTIONS-- NOT THIS JUNK!
WHAT DO YOU KNOW ABOUT IT?
I'M THE SMARTEST THERE IS!

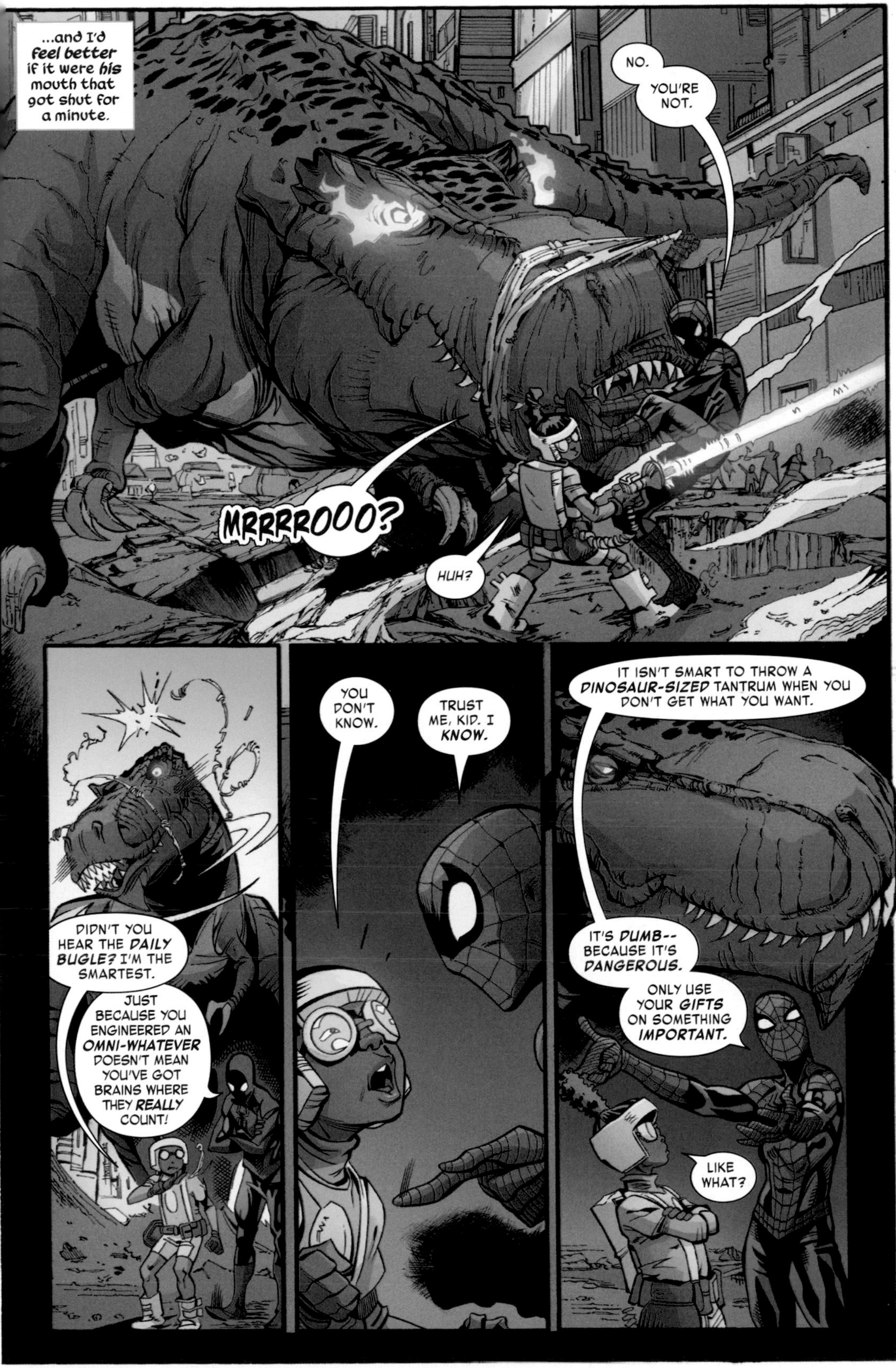
...and I'd feel better if it were his mouth that got shut for a minute.
NO.
YOU'RE NOT.
MRRRROOO?
HUH?
DIDN'T YOU HEAR THE DAILY BUGLE? I'M THE SMARTEST.
JUST BECAUSE YOU ENGINEERED AN OMNI-WHATEVER DOESN'T MEAN YOU'VE GOT BRAINS WHERE THEY REALLY COUNT!
YOU DON'T KNOW.
TRUST ME, KID. I KNOW.
IT ISN'T SMART TO THROW A DINOSAUR-SIZED TANTRUM WHEN YOU DON'T GET WHAT YOU WANT.
IT'S DUMB-- BECAUSE IT'S DANGEROUS.
ONLY USE YOUR GIFTS ON SOMETHING IMPORTANT.
LIKE WHAT?

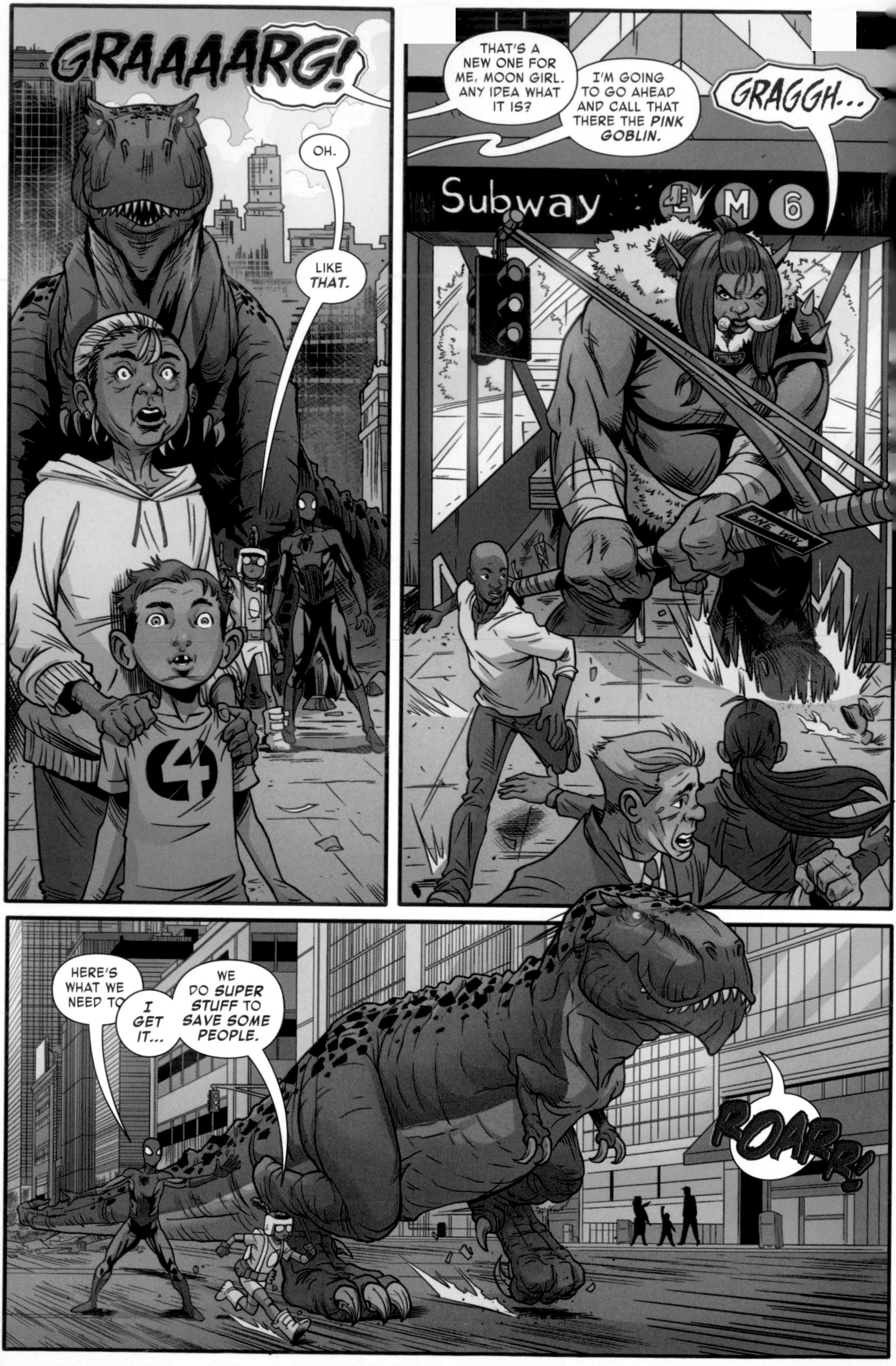
GRAAAARG!
OH.
LIKE THAT.
THAT'S A NEW ONE FOR ME, MOON GIRL. ANY IDEA WHAT IT IS?
I'M GOING TO GO AHEAD AND CALL THAT THERE THE PINK GOBLIN.
GRAGGH...
Subway
M
6
ONE WAY
HERE'S WHAT WE NEED TO
I GET IT...
WE DO SUPER STUFF TO SAVE SOME PEOPLE.
ROARR!

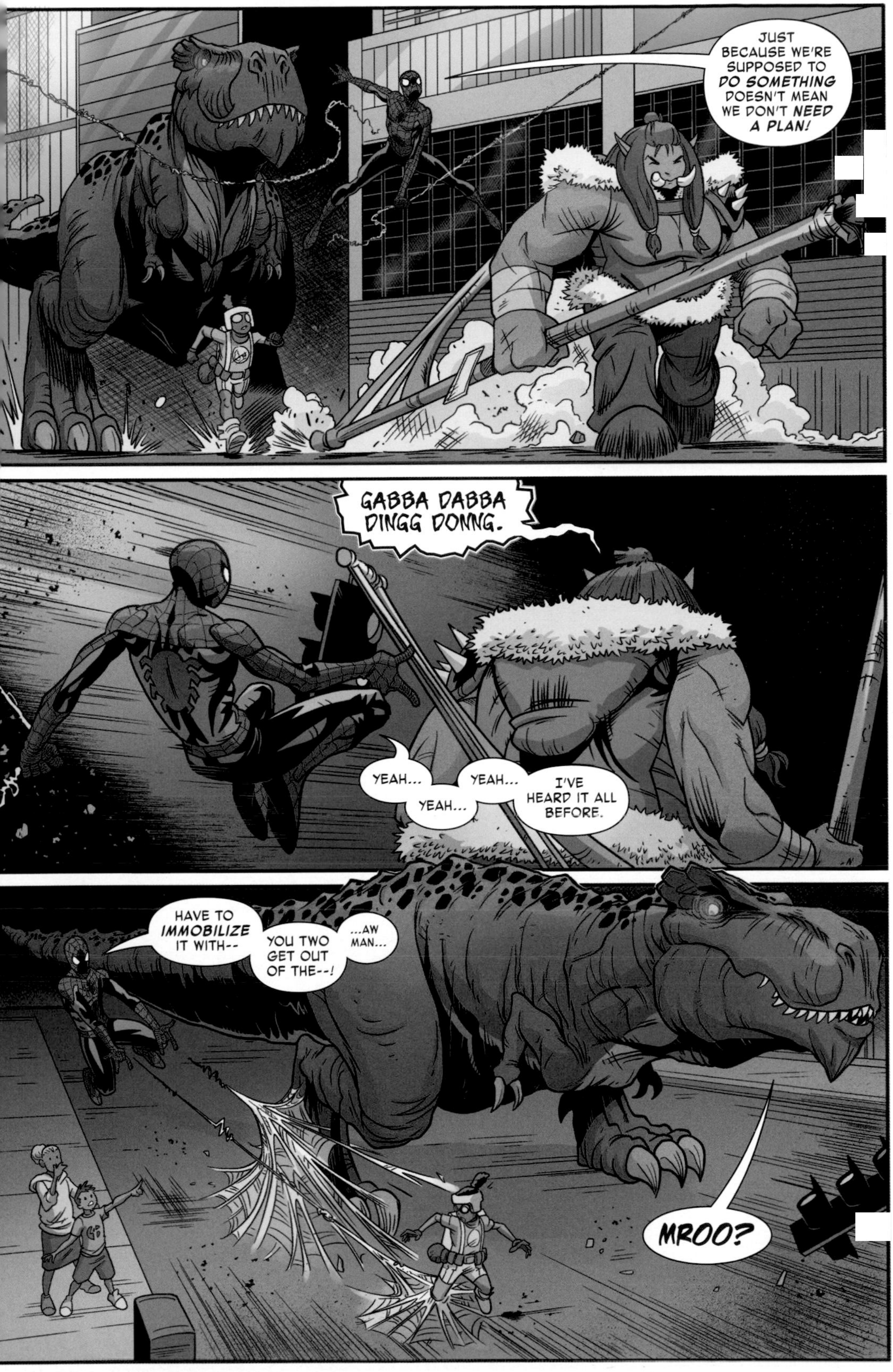
JUST BECAUSE WE'RE SUPPOSED TO DO SOMETHING DOESN'T MEAN WE DON'T NEED A PLAN!
GABBA DABBA DINGG DONNG.
YEAH...
YEAH...
YEAH...
I'VE HEARD IT ALL BEFORE.
HAVE TO IMMOBILIZE IT WITH--
YOU TWO GET OUT OF THE--!
...AW MAN...
MROO?

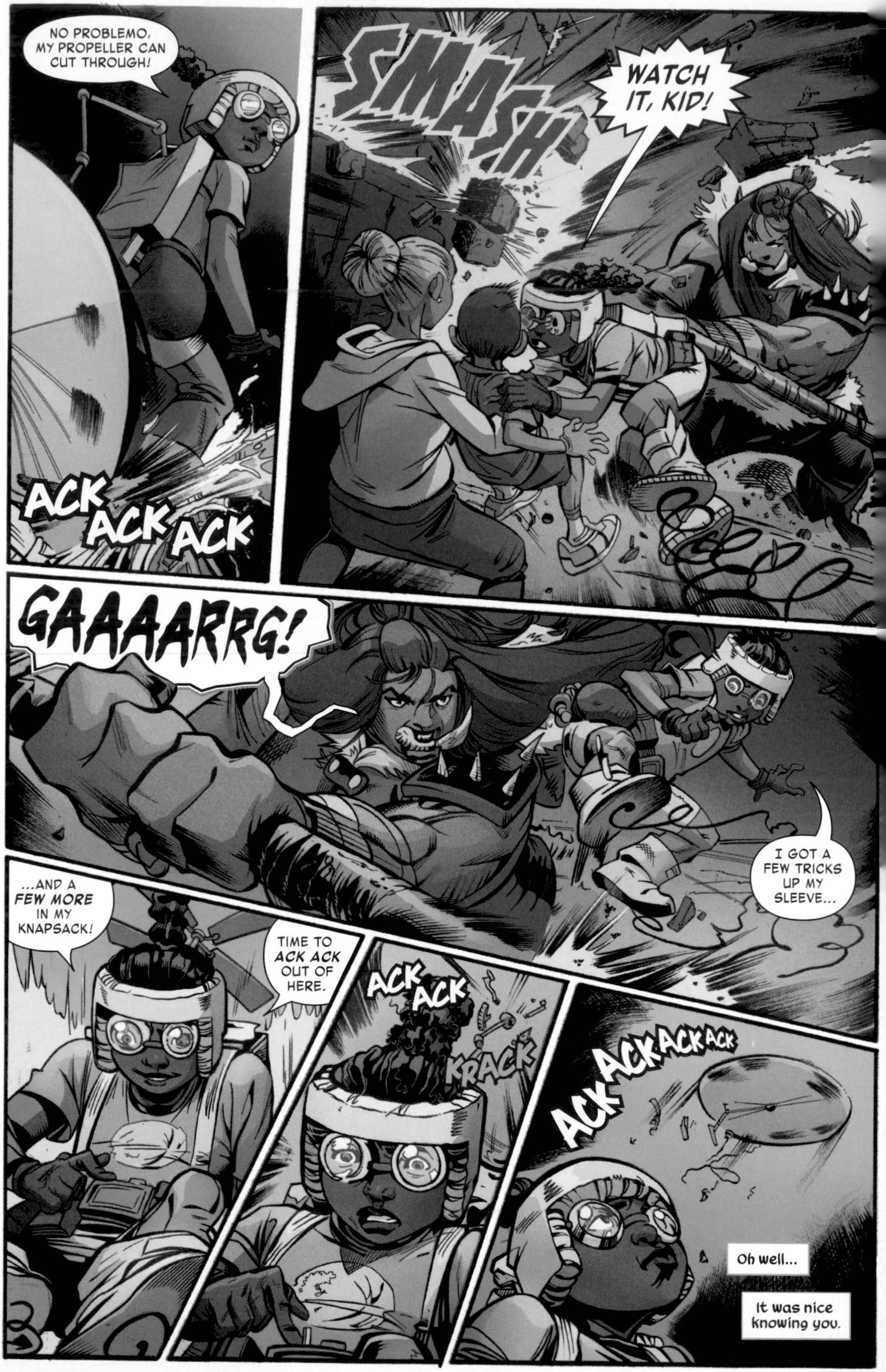
NO PROBLEMO, MY PROPELLER CAN CUT THROUGH!
ACK ACK ACK
SMASH
WATCH IT, KID!
GAAAARRG!
I GOT A FEW TRICKS UP MY SLEEVE...
...AND A *FEW MORE* IN MY KNAPSACK!
TIME TO *ACK ACK* OUT OF HERE.
ACK ACK
KRACK
ACK ACK ACK ACK ACK
Oh well...
It was nice knowing you.

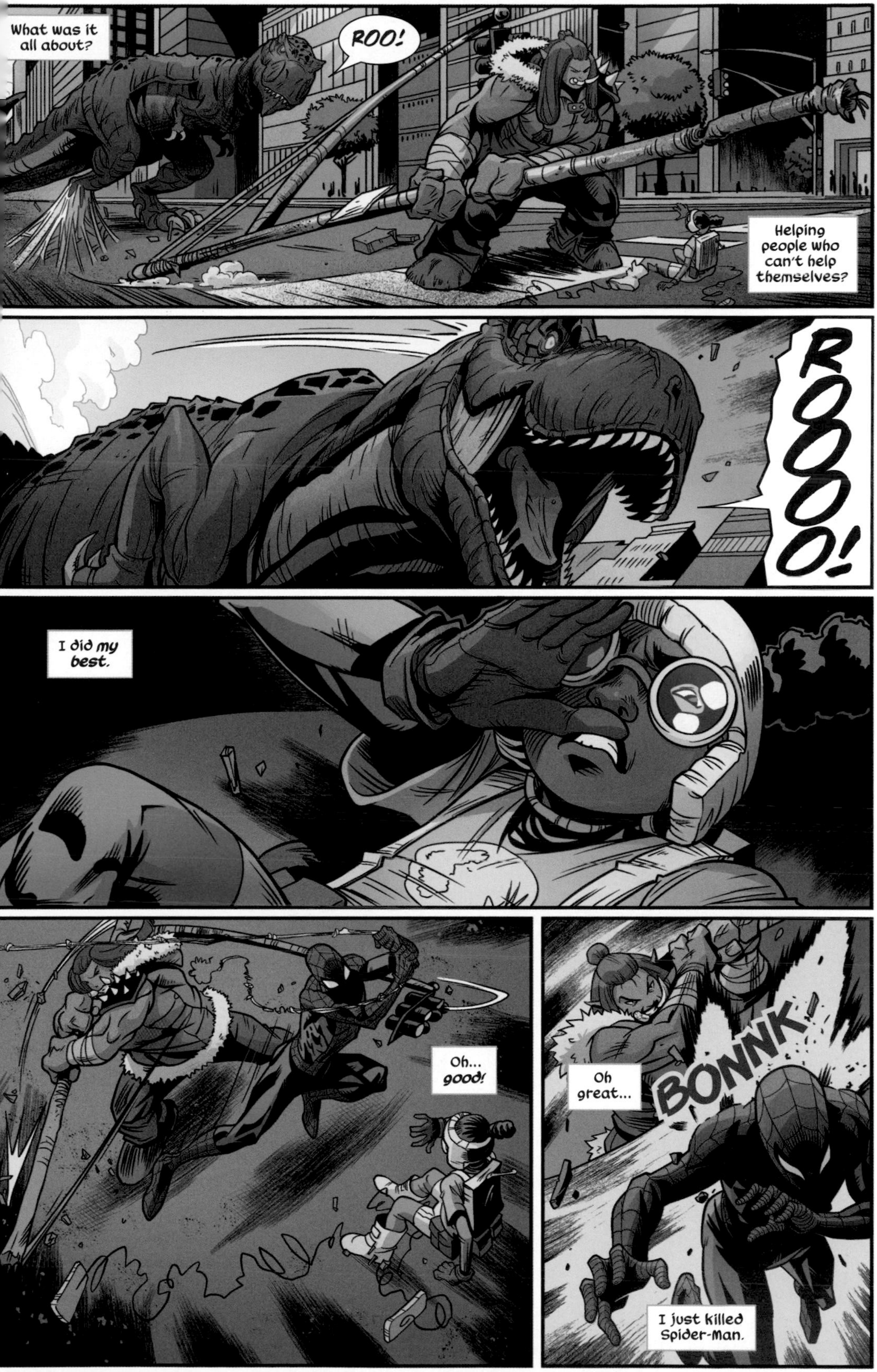
What was it all about?
ROO!
Helping people who can't help themselves?
ROOOOO!
I did *my* *best*.
Oh... *good*!
Oh great...
BONNK
I just killed Spider-Man.

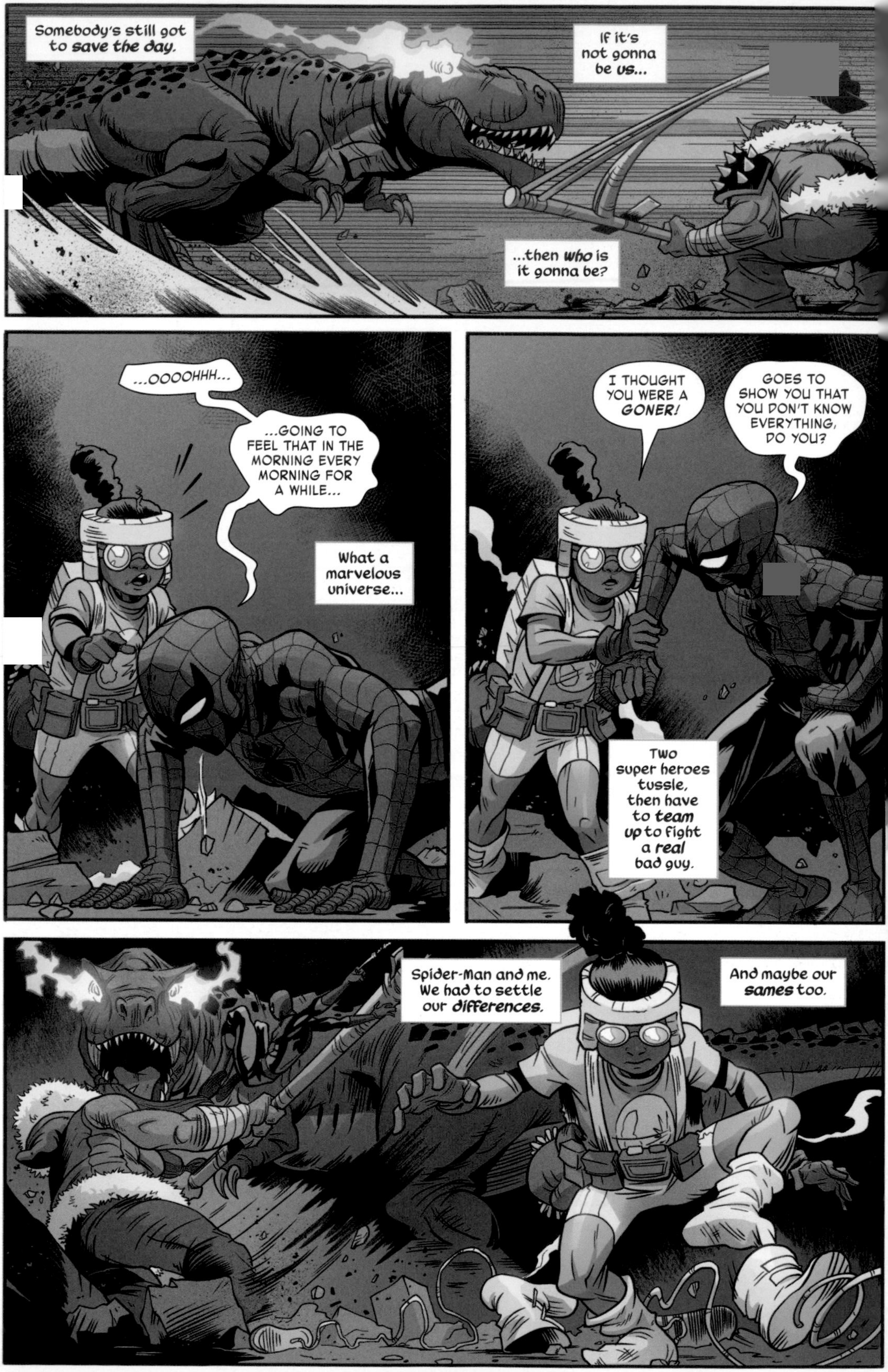

Somebody's still got to save the day.
If it's not gonna be us...
...then who is it gonna be?
...OOOOHHH...
...GOING TO FEEL THAT IN THE MORNING EVERY MORNING FOR A WHILE...
What a marvelous universe...
I THOUGHT YOU WERE A GONER!
GOES TO SHOW YOU THAT YOU DON'T KNOW EVERYTHING, DO YOU?
Two super heroes tussle, then have to team up to fight a real bad guy.
Spider-Man and me. We had to settle our differences.
And maybe our sames too.

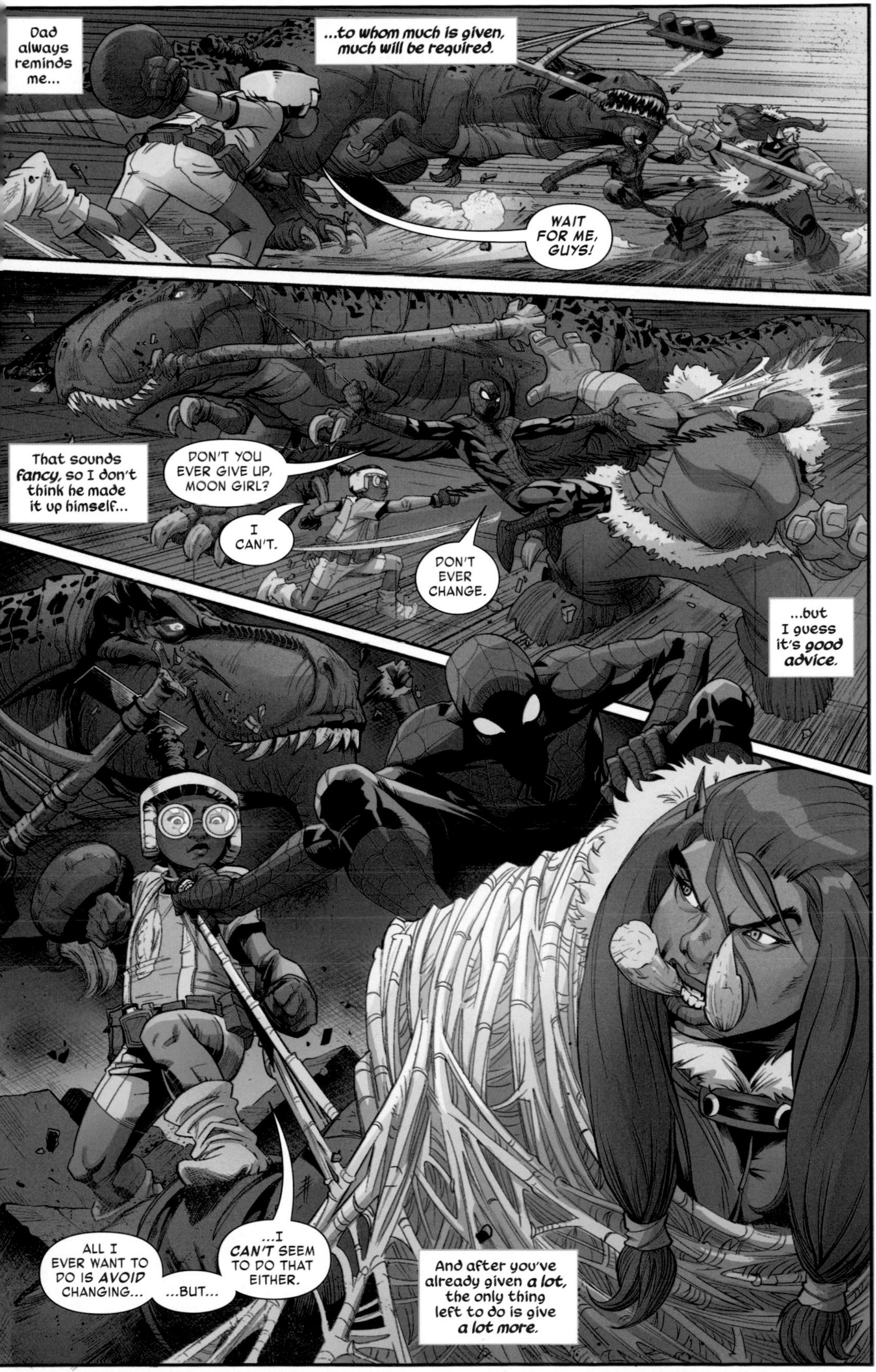
Dad always reminds me...
...to whom much is given, much will be required.
WAIT FOR ME, GUYS!
That sounds fancy, so I don't think he made it up himself...
DON'T YOU EVER GIVE UP, MOON GIRL?
I CAN'T.
DON'T EVER CHANGE.
...but I guess it's good advice.
ALL I EVER WANT TO DO IS AVOID CHANGING...
...BUT...
...I CAN'T SEEM TO DO THAT EITHER.
And after you've already given a lot, the only thing left to do is give a lot more.

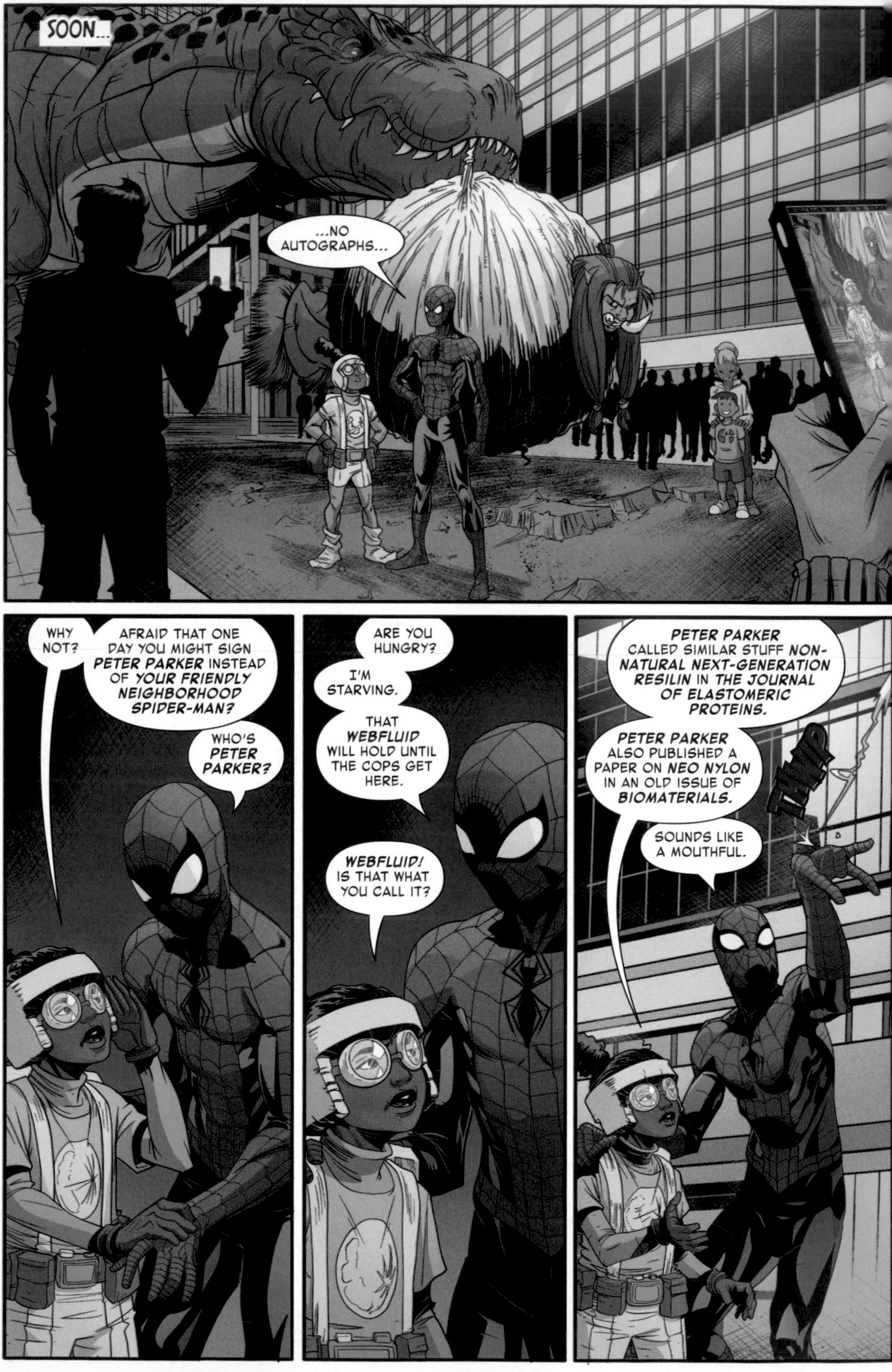
SOON...
...NO AUTOGRAPHS...
WHY NOT?
AFRAID THAT ONE DAY YOU MIGHT SIGN PETER PARKER INSTEAD OF YOUR FRIENDLY NEIGHBORHOOD SPIDER-MAN?
WHO'S PETER PARKER?
ARE YOU HUNGRY?
I'M STARVING.
THAT WEBFLUID WILL HOLD UNTIL THE COPS GET HERE.
WEBFLUID! IS THAT WHAT YOU CALL IT?
PETER PARKER CALLED SIMILAR STUFF NON-NATURAL NEXT-GENERATION RESILIN IN THE JOURNAL OF ELASTOMERIC PROTEINS.
PETER PARKER ALSO PUBLISHED A PAPER ON NEO NYLON IN AN OLD ISSUE OF BIOMATERIALS.
SOUNDS LIKE A MOUTHFUL.

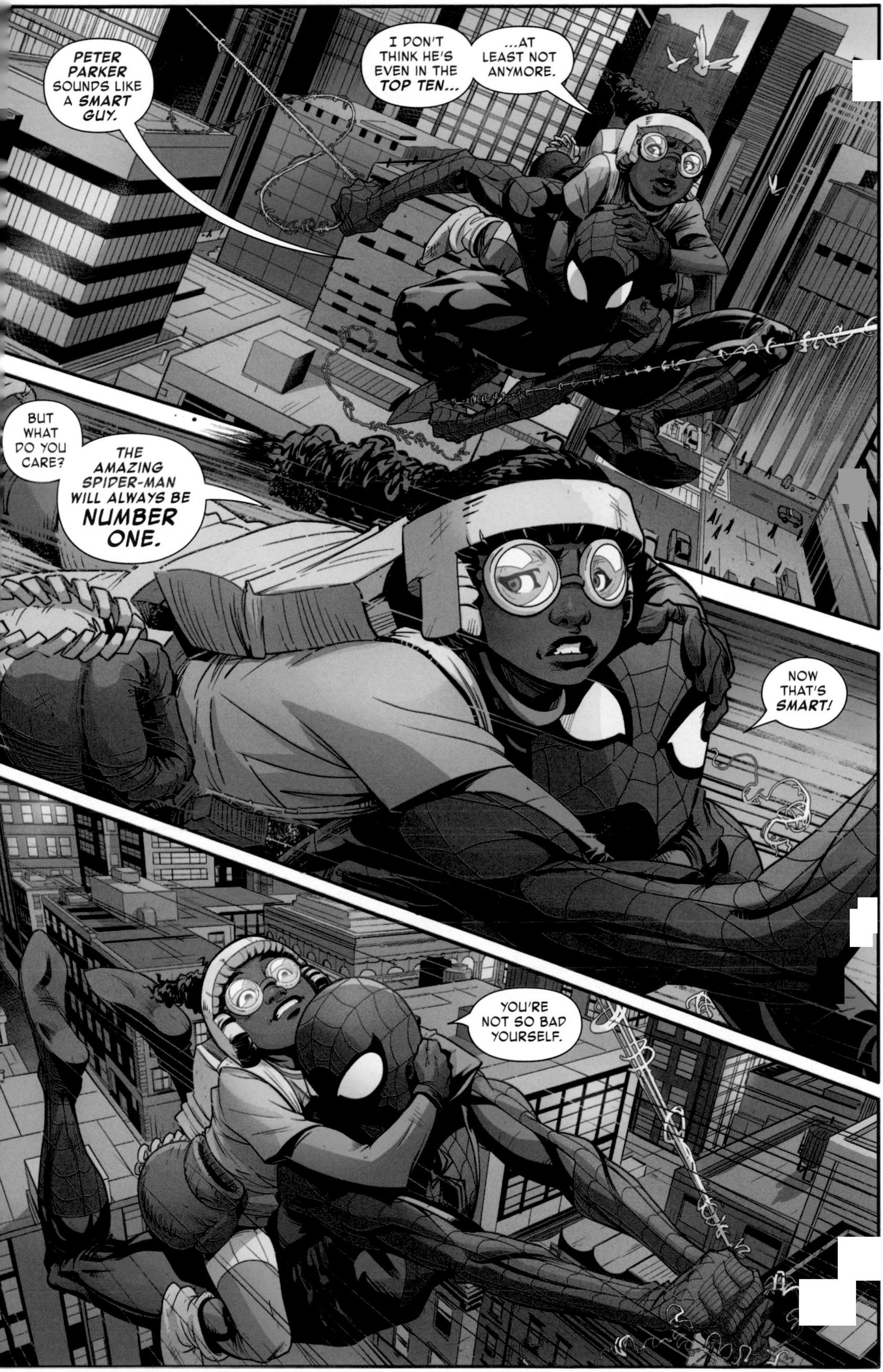
PETER PARKER SOUNDS LIKE A SMART GUY.
I DON'T THINK HE'S EVEN IN THE TOP TEN...
...AT LEAST NOT ANYMORE.
BUT WHAT DO YOU CARE?
THE AMAZING SPIDER-MAN WILL ALWAYS BE NUMBER ONE.
NOW THAT'S SMART!
YOU'RE NOT SO BAD YOURSELF.

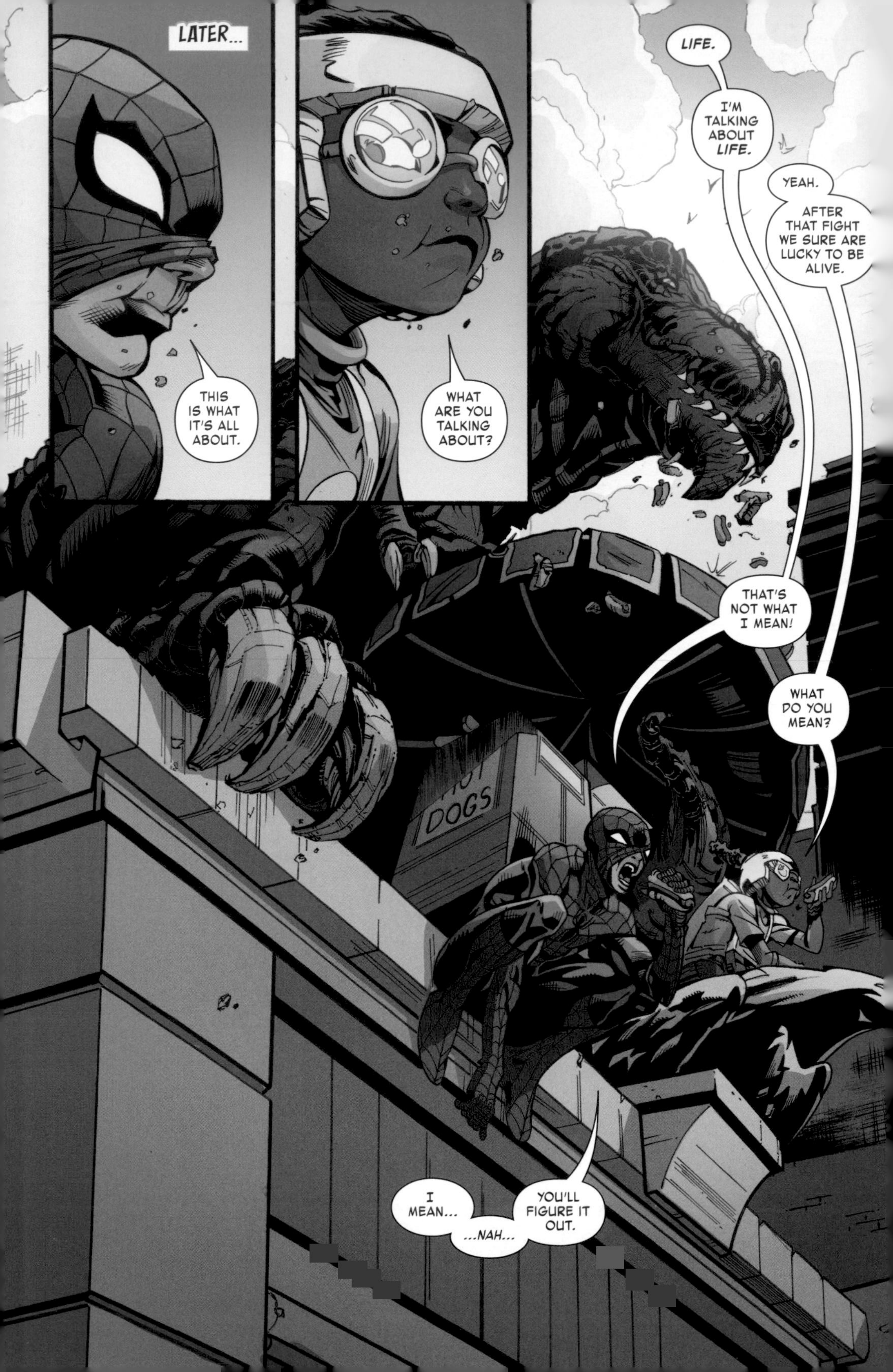
LATER...
THIS IS WHAT IT'S ALL ABOUT.
WHAT ARE YOU TALKING ABOUT?
LIFE.
I'M TALKING ABOUT LIFE.
YEAH.
AFTER THAT FIGHT WE SURE ARE LUCKY TO BE ALIVE.
THAT'S NOT WHAT I MEAN!
WHAT DO YOU MEAN?
DOGS
I MEAN...
...NAH...
YOU'LL FIGURE IT OUT.

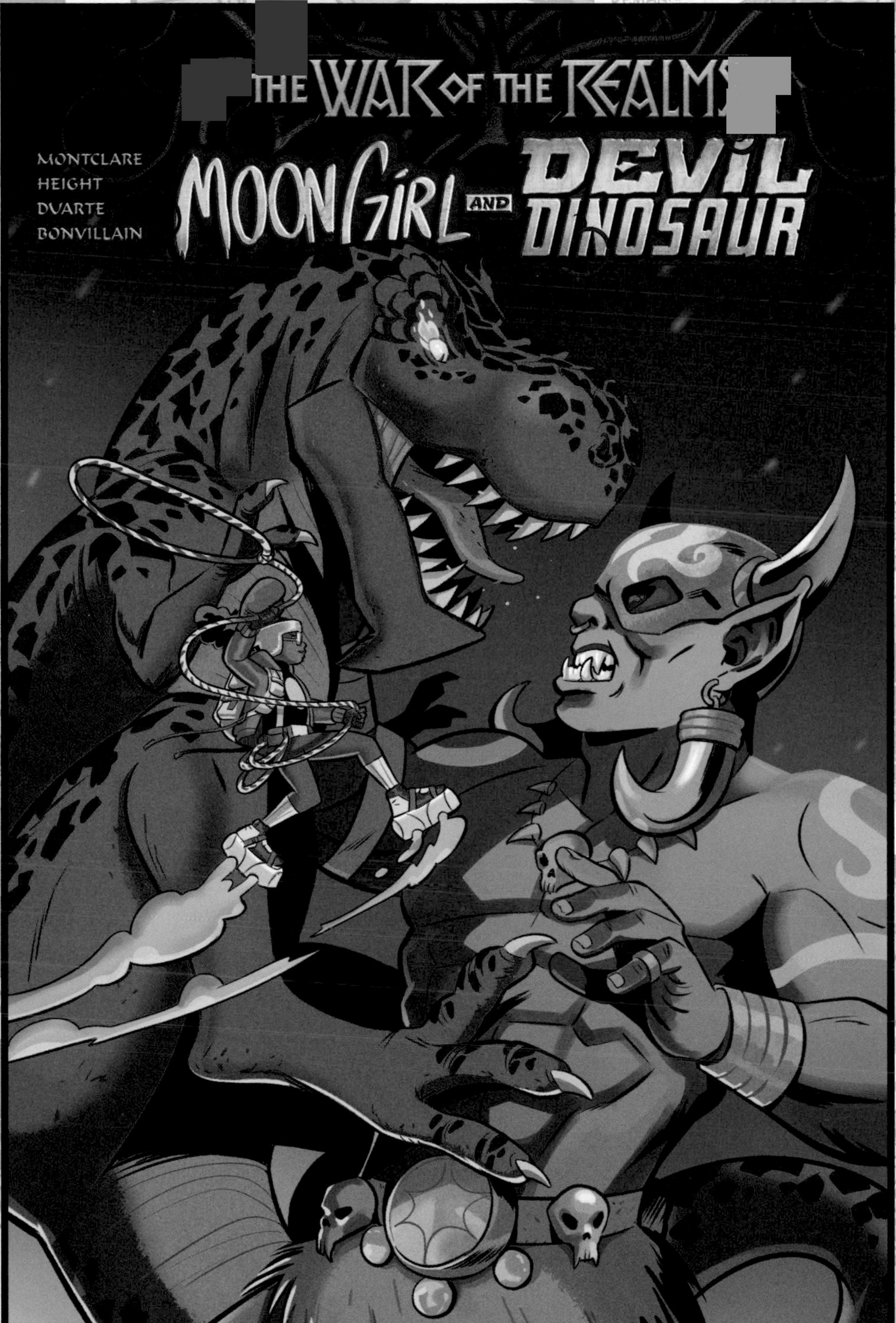
THE WAR OF THE REALMS
MONTCLARE
HEIGHT
DUARTE
BONVILLAIN
MOON GIRL AND DEVIL DINOSAUR

MOON GIRL AND DEVIL DINOSAUR #43

AS FROST GIANTS PROWL THE FROZEN STREETS OF MANHATTAN, MOON GIRL AND DEVIL DINOSAUR RECALL AN ASGARDIAN ADVENTURE ALONGSIDE THOR AND THE WARRIORS THREE!

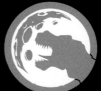

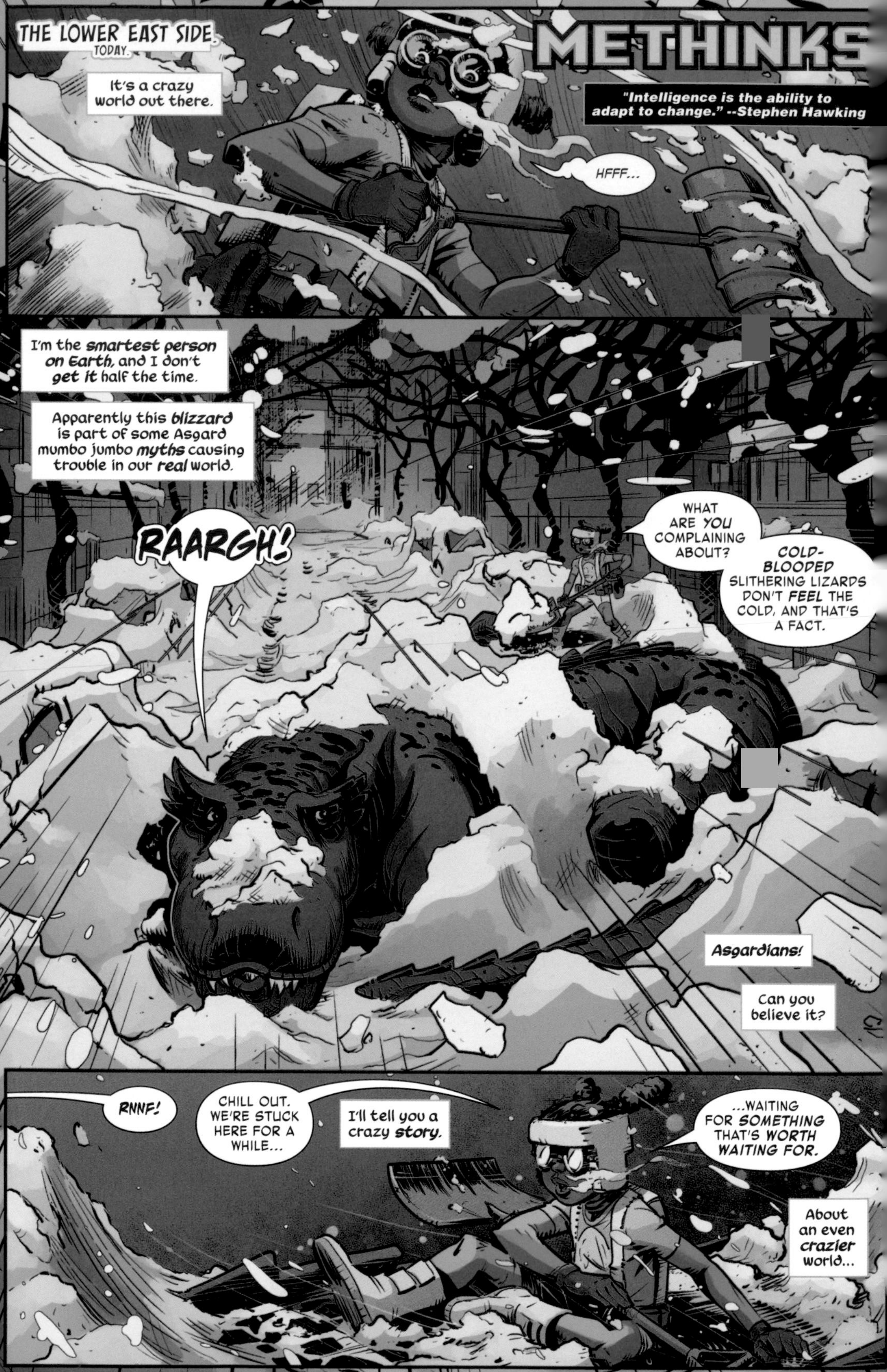
THE LOWER EAST SIDE.
TODAY.
METHINKS
"Intelligence is the ability to adapt to change." --Stephen Hawking
It's a crazy world out there.
HFFF...
I'm the smartest person on Earth, and I don't get it half the time.
Apparently this blizzard is part of some Asgard mumbo jumbo myths causing trouble in our real world.
RAARGH!
WHAT ARE YOU COMPLAINING ABOUT?
COLD-BLOODED SLITHERING LIZARDS DON'T FEEL THE COLD, AND THAT'S A FACT.
Asgardians!
Can you believe it?
RNNF!
CHILL OUT. WE'RE STUCK HERE FOR A WHILE...
I'll tell you a crazy story.
...WAITING FOR SOMETHING THAT'S WORTH WAITING FOR.
About an even crazier world...

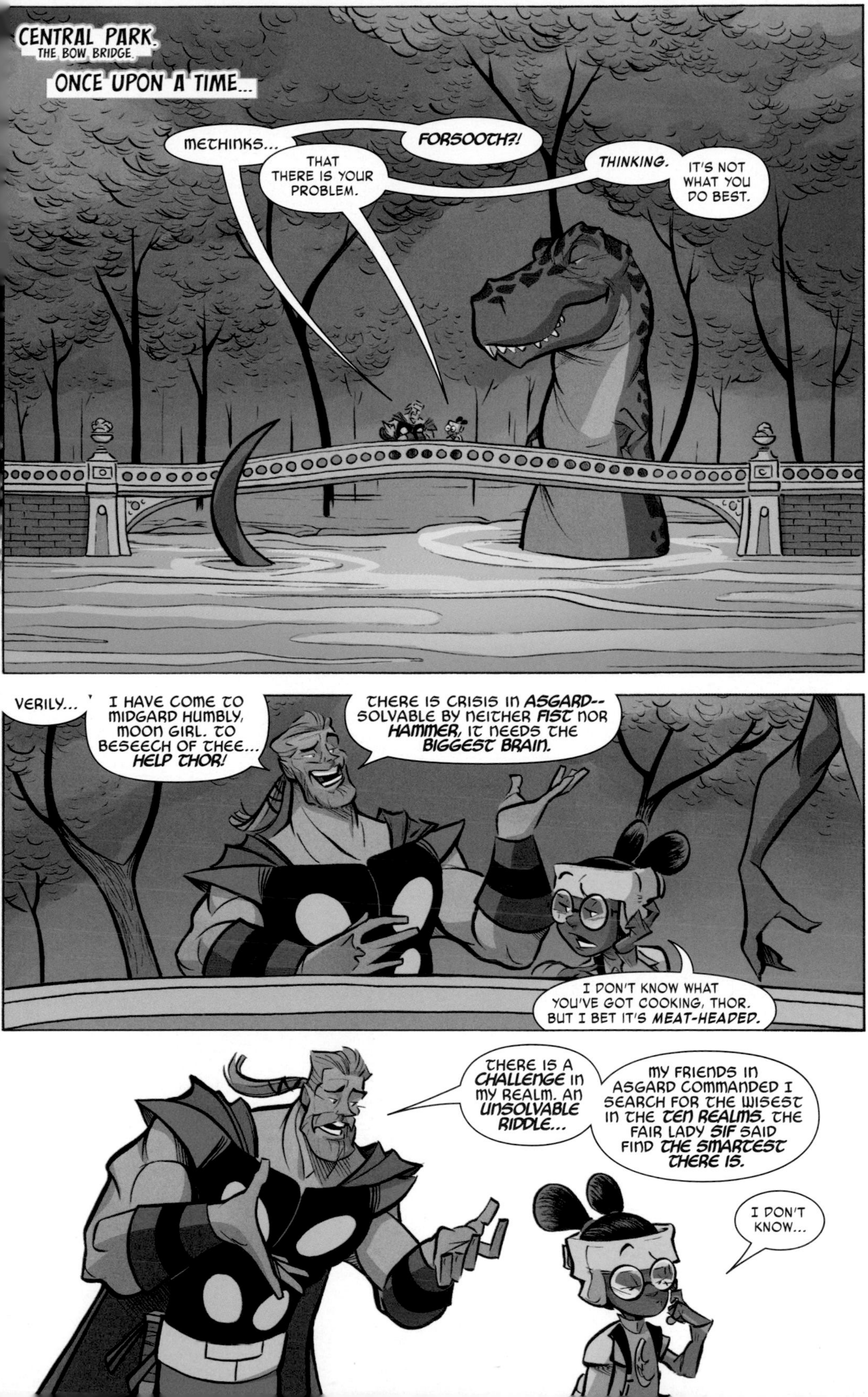
CENTRAL PARK. THE BOW BRIDGE.
ONCE UPON A TIME...
METHINKS...
FORSOOTH?!
THAT THERE IS YOUR PROBLEM.
THINKING.
IT'S NOT WHAT YOU DO BEST.
VERILY...
I HAVE COME TO MIDGARD HUMBLY, MOON GIRL. TO BESEECH OF THEE... HELP THOR!
THERE IS CRISIS IN ASGARD-- SOLVABLE BY NEITHER FIST NOR HAMMER, IT NEEDS THE BIGGEST BRAIN.
I DON'T KNOW WHAT YOU'VE GOT COOKING, THOR. BUT I BET IT'S MEAT-HEADED.
THERE IS A CHALLENGE IN MY REALM. AN UNSOLVABLE RIDDLE...
MY FRIENDS IN ASGARD COMMANDED I SEARCH FOR THE WISEST IN THE TEN REALMS. THE FAIR LADY SIF SAID FIND THE SMARTEST THERE IS.
I DON'T KNOW...

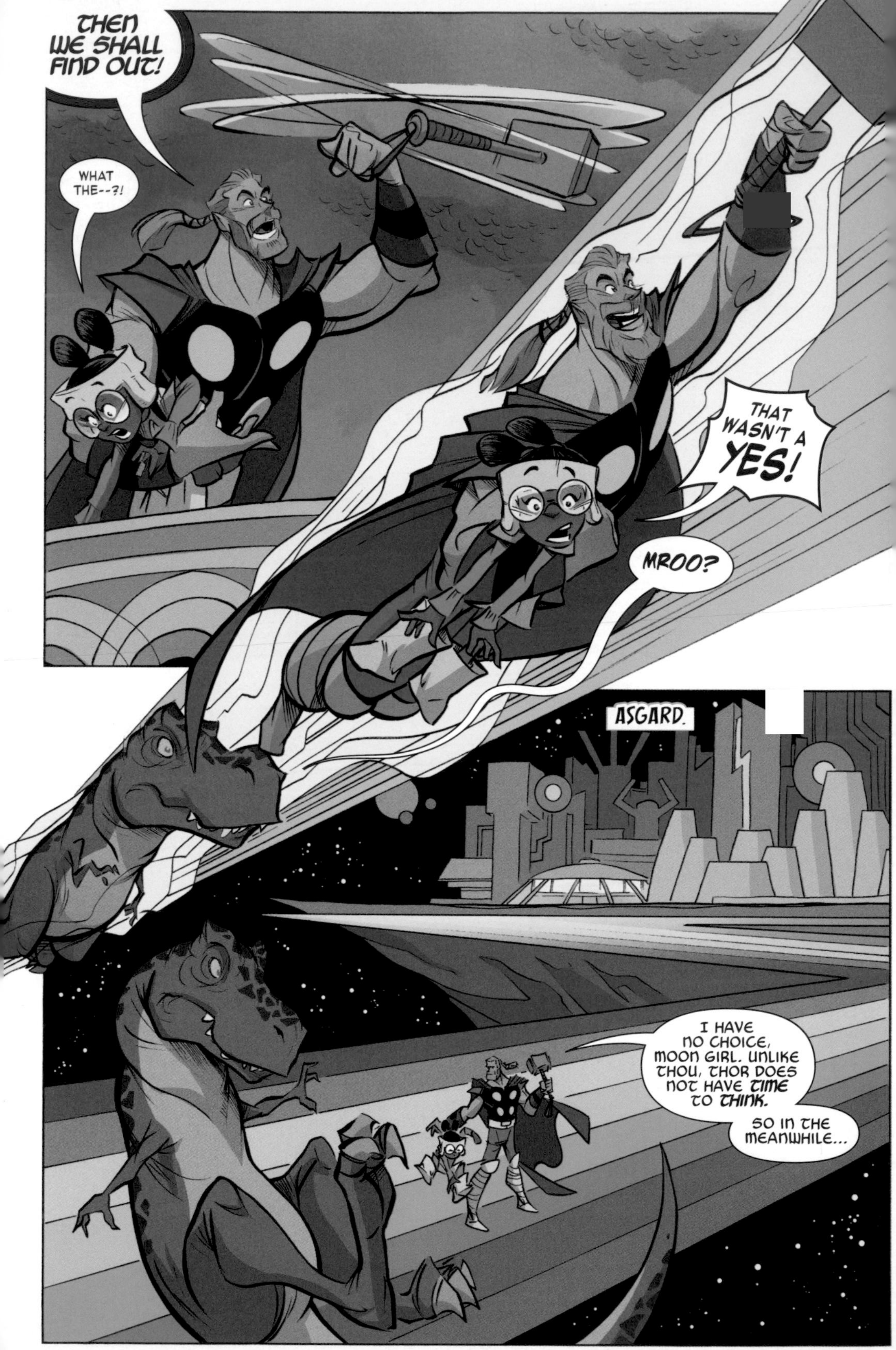
THEN WE SHALL FIND OUT!
WHAT THE--?!
THAT WASN'T A YES!
MROO?
ASGARD.
I HAVE NO CHOICE, MOON GIRL. UNLIKE THOU, THOR DOES NOT HAVE TIME TO THINK.
SO IN THE MEANWHILE...

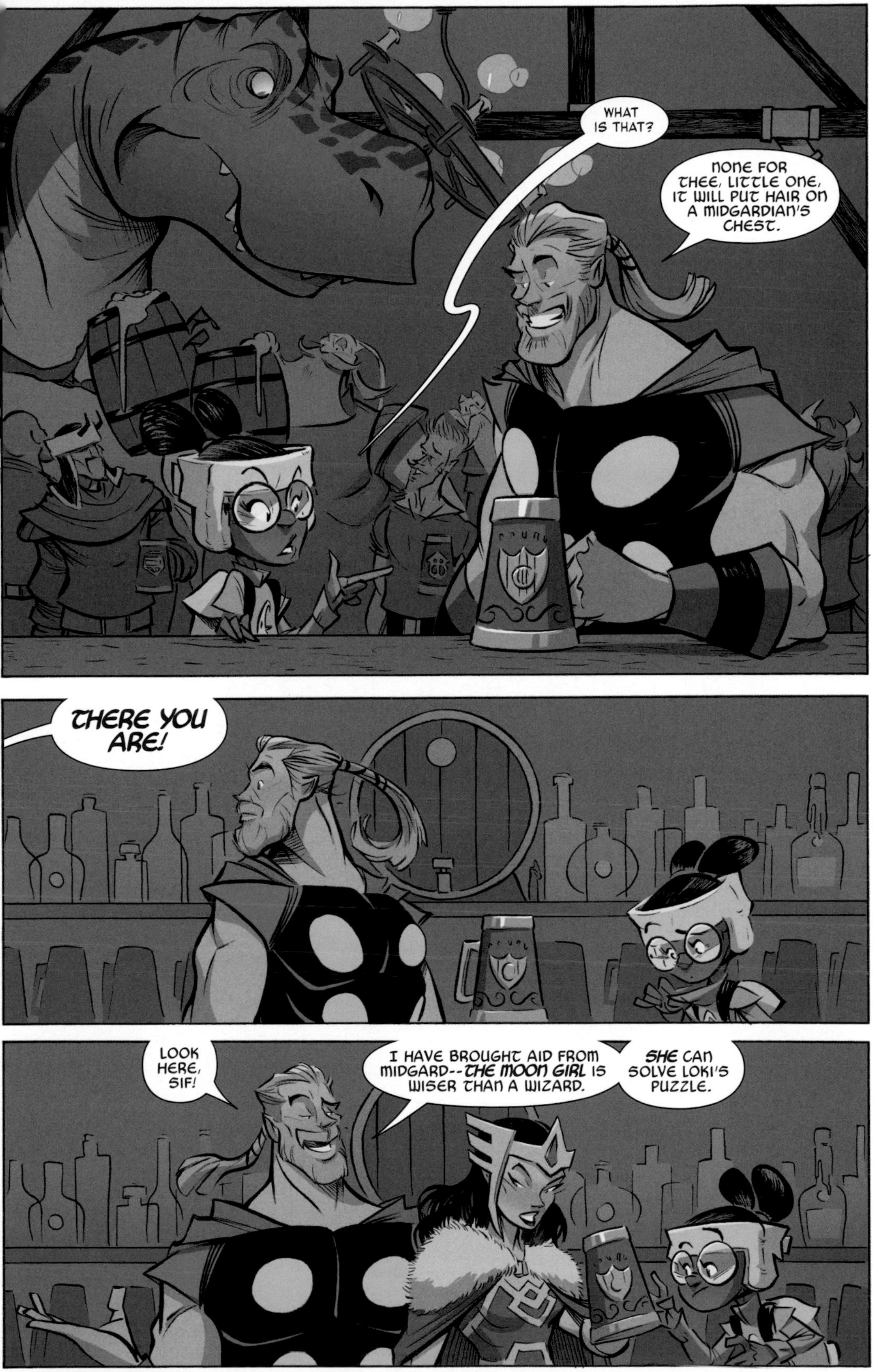
WHAT IS THAT?
NONE FOR THEE, LITTLE ONE, IT WILL PUT HAIR ON A MIDGARDIAN'S CHEST.
THERE YOU ARE!
LOOK HERE, SIF!
I HAVE BROUGHT AID FROM MIDGARD--THE MOON GIRL IS WISER THAN A WIZARD.
SHE CAN SOLVE LOKI'S PUZZLE.

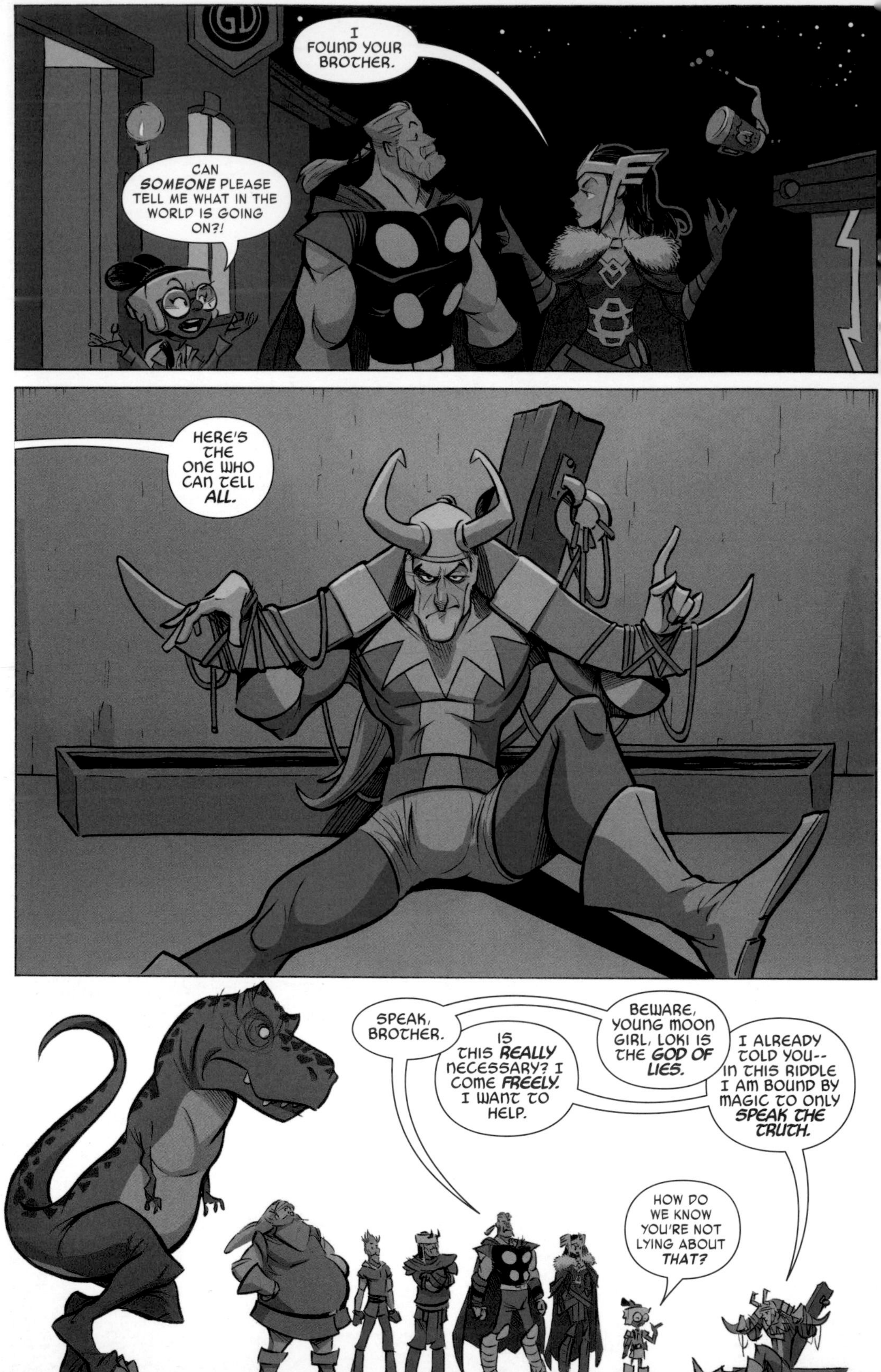

I FOUND YOUR BROTHER.
CAN SOMEONE PLEASE TELL ME WHAT IN THE WORLD IS GOING ON?!
HERE'S THE ONE WHO CAN TELL ALL.
SPEAK, BROTHER.
IS THIS REALLY NECESSARY? I COME FREELY. I WANT TO HELP.
BEWARE, YOUNG MOON GIRL, LOKI IS THE GOD OF LIES.
I ALREADY TOLD YOU-- IN THIS RIDDLE I AM BOUND BY MAGIC TO ONLY SPEAK THE TRUTH.
HOW DO WE KNOW YOU'RE NOT LYING ABOUT THAT?

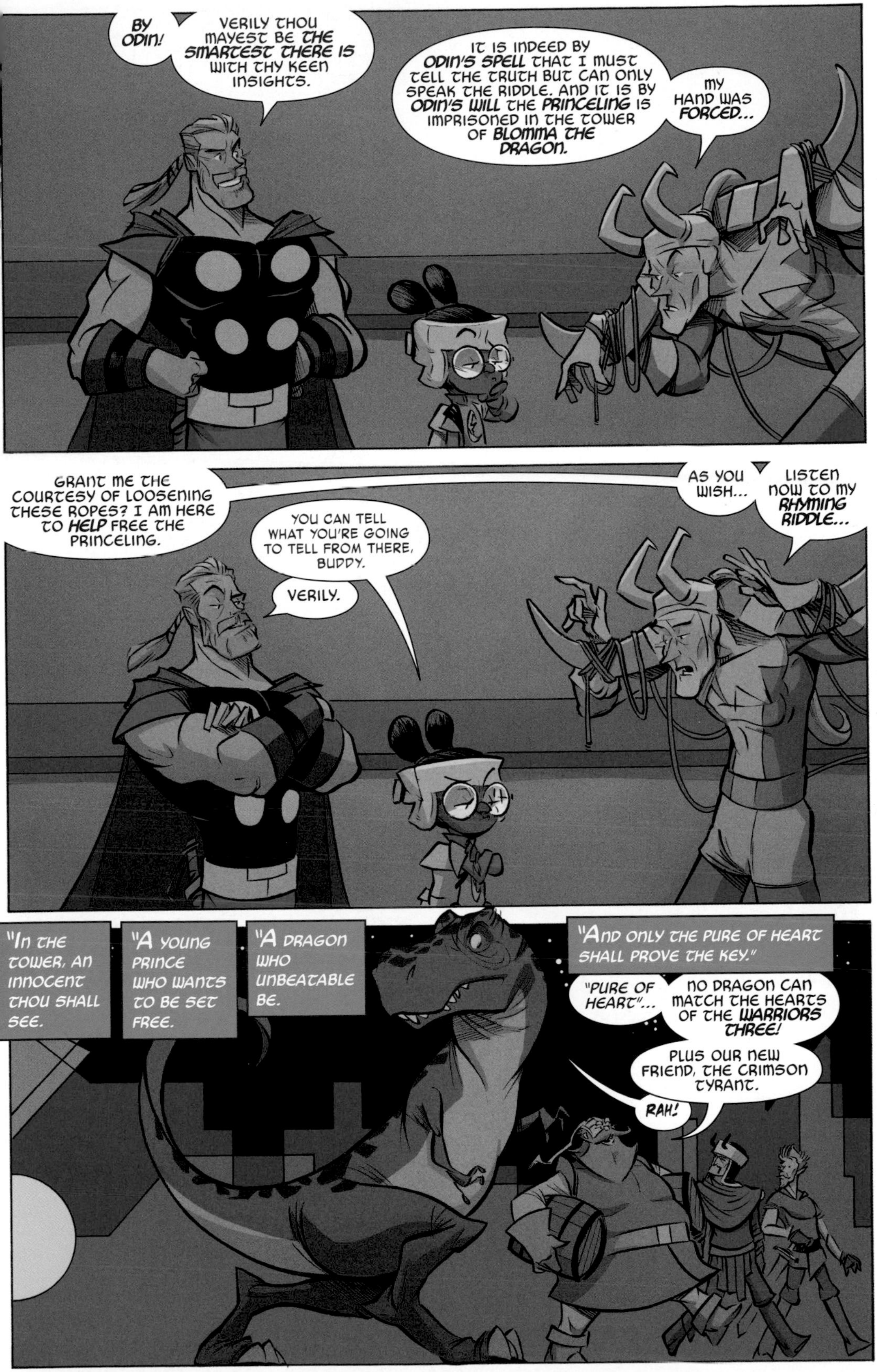
BY ODIN!
VERILY THOU MAYEST BE THE SMARTEST THERE IS WITH THY KEEN INSIGHTS.
IT IS INDEED BY ODIN'S SPELL THAT I MUST TELL THE TRUTH BUT CAN ONLY SPEAK THE RIDDLE. AND IT IS BY ODIN'S WILL THE PRINCELING IS IMPRISONED IN THE TOWER OF BLOMMA THE DRAGON.
MY HAND WAS FORCED...
GRANT ME THE COURTESY OF LOOSENING THESE ROPES? I AM HERE TO HELP FREE THE PRINCELING.
YOU CAN TELL WHAT YOU'RE GOING TO TELL FROM THERE, BUDDY.
VERILY.
AS YOU WISH...
LISTEN NOW TO MY RHYMING RIDDLE...
"IN THE TOWER, AN INNOCENT THOU SHALL SEE.
"A YOUNG PRINCE WHO WANTS TO BE SET FREE.
"A DRAGON WHO UNBEATABLE BE.
"AND ONLY THE PURE OF HEART SHALL PROVE THE KEY."
"PURE OF HEART"...
NO DRAGON CAN MATCH THE HEARTS OF THE WARRIORS THREE!
PLUS OUR NEW FRIEND, THE CRIMSON TYRANT.
RAH!

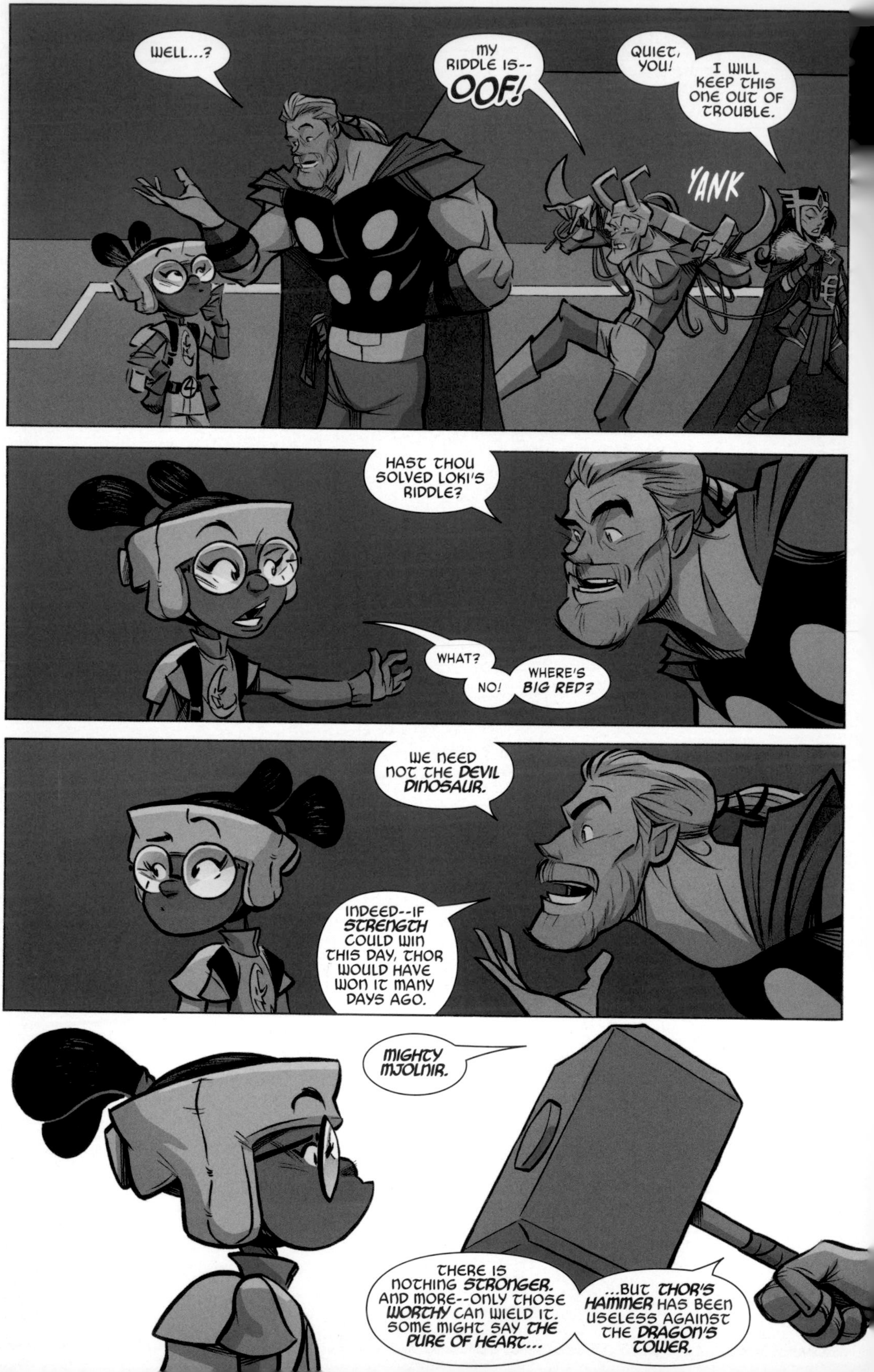
WELL...?
MY RIDDLE IS--
OOF!
QUIET, YOU!
I WILL KEEP THIS ONE OUT OF TROUBLE.
YANK
HAST THOU SOLVED LOKI'S RIDDLE?
WHAT?
NO!
WHERE'S BIG RED?
WE NEED NOT THE DEVIL DINOSAUR.
INDEED--IF STRENGTH COULD WIN THIS DAY, THOR WOULD HAVE WON IT MANY DAYS AGO.
MIGHTY MJOLNIR.
THERE IS NOTHING STRONGER. AND MORE--ONLY THOSE WORTHY CAN WIELD IT. SOME MIGHT SAY THE PURE OF HEART...
...BUT THOR'S HAMMER HAS BEEN USELESS AGAINST THE DRAGON'S TOWER.

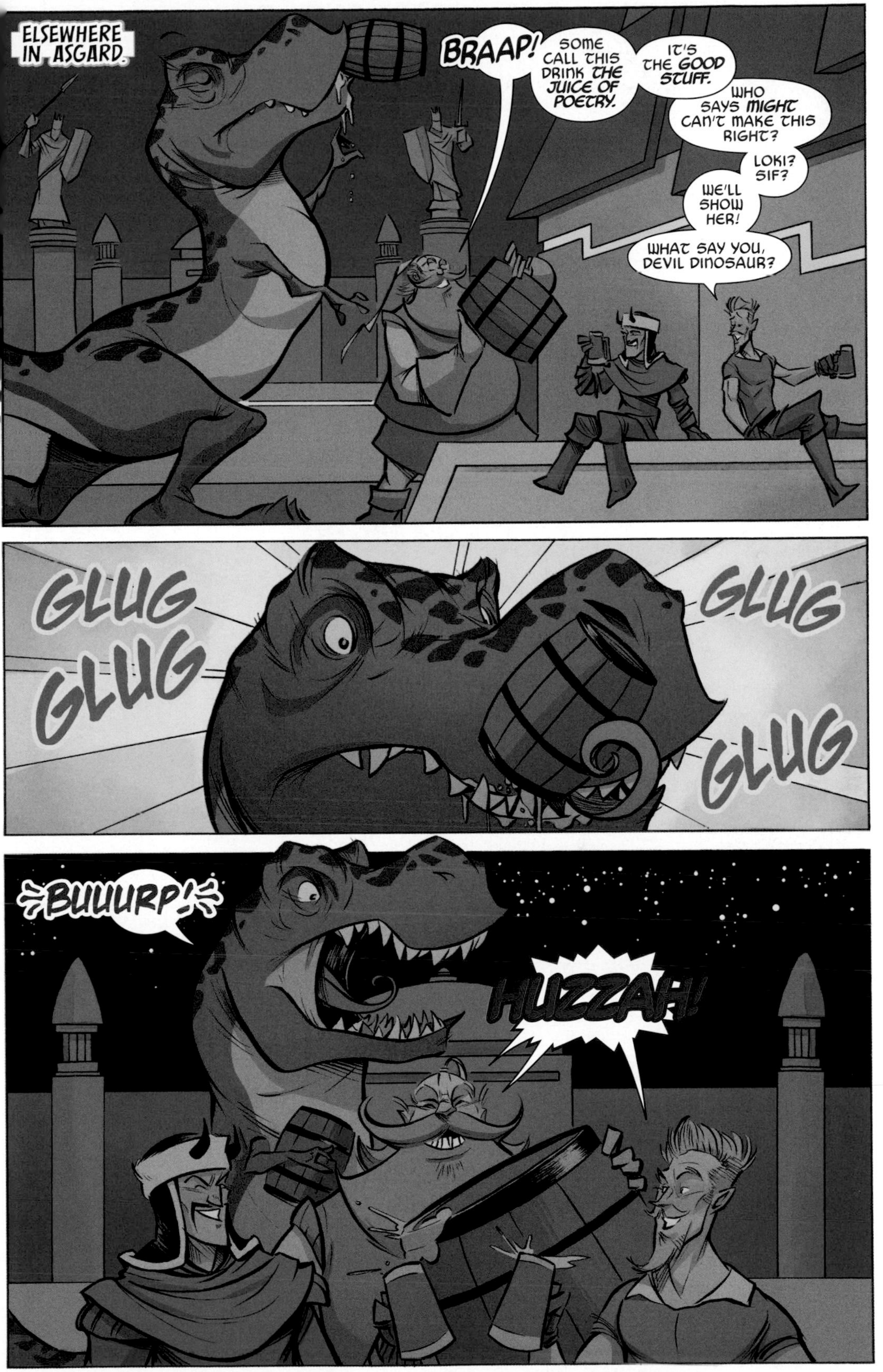
ELSEWHERE IN ASGARD.
BRAAP!
SOME CALL THIS DRINK THE JUICE OF POETRY.
IT'S THE GOOD STUFF.
WHO SAYS MIGHT CAN'T MAKE THIS RIGHT?
LOKI? SIF?
WE'LL SHOW HER!
WHAT SAY YOU, DEVIL DINOSAUR?
GLUG GLUG
GLUG
GLUG
BUUURP!
HUZZAH!

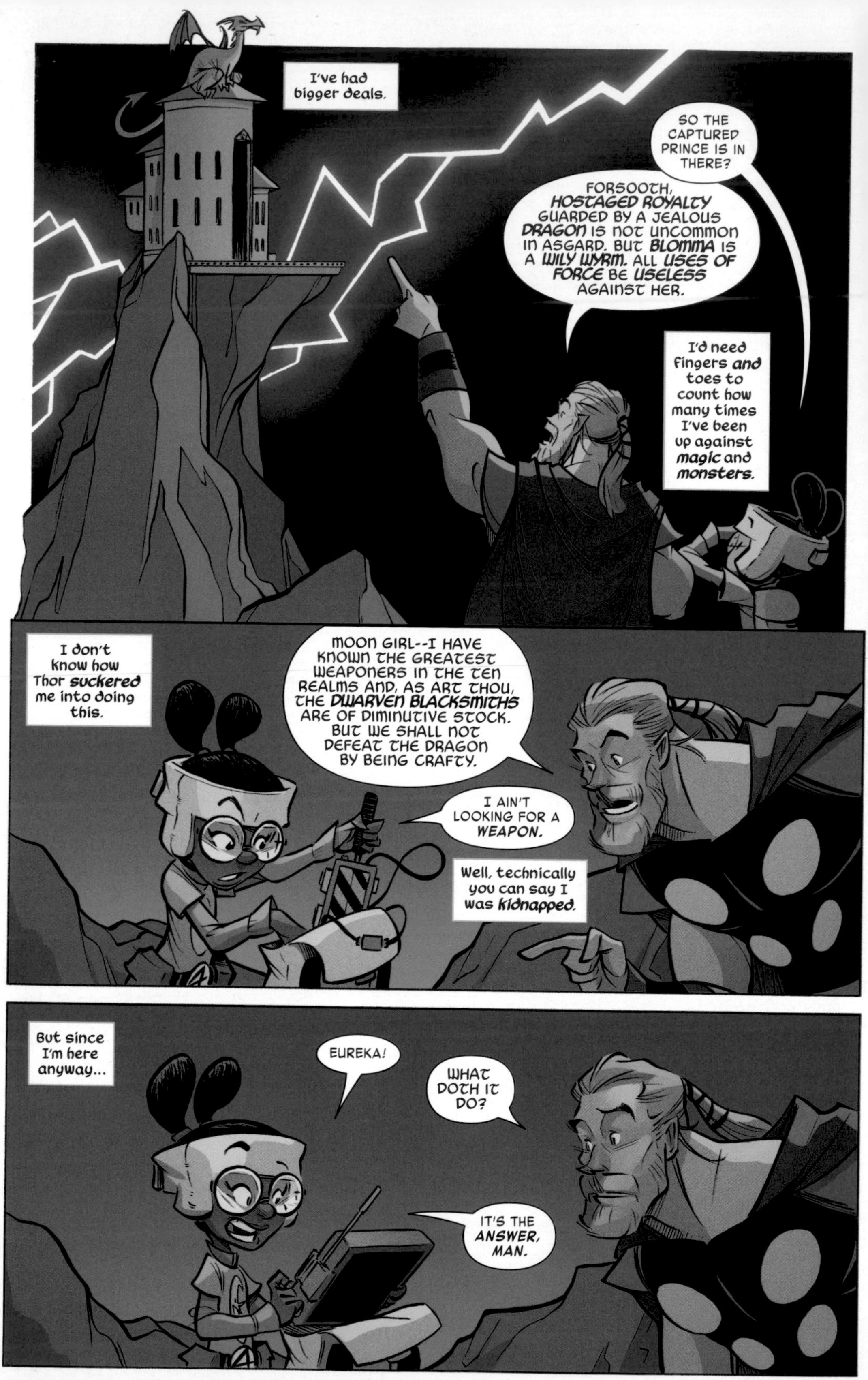
I've had bigger deals.
SO THE CAPTURED PRINCE IS IN THERE?
FORSOOTH, HOSTAGED ROYALTY GUARDED BY A JEALOUS DRAGON IS NOT UNCOMMON IN ASGARD. BUT BLOMMA IS A WILY WYRM. ALL USES OF FORCE BE USELESS AGAINST HER.
I'd need fingers and toes to count how many times I've been up against magic and monsters.
I don't know how Thor suckered me into doing this.
MOON GIRL--I HAVE KNOWN THE GREATEST WEAPONERS IN THE TEN REALMS AND, AS ART THOU, THE DWARVEN BLACKSMITHS ARE OF DIMINUTIVE STOCK. BUT WE SHALL NOT DEFEAT THE DRAGON BY BEING CRAFTY.
I AIN'T LOOKING FOR A WEAPON.
Well, technically you can say I was kidnapped.
But since I'm here anyway...
EUREKA!
WHAT DOTH IT DO?
IT'S THE ANSWER, MAN.

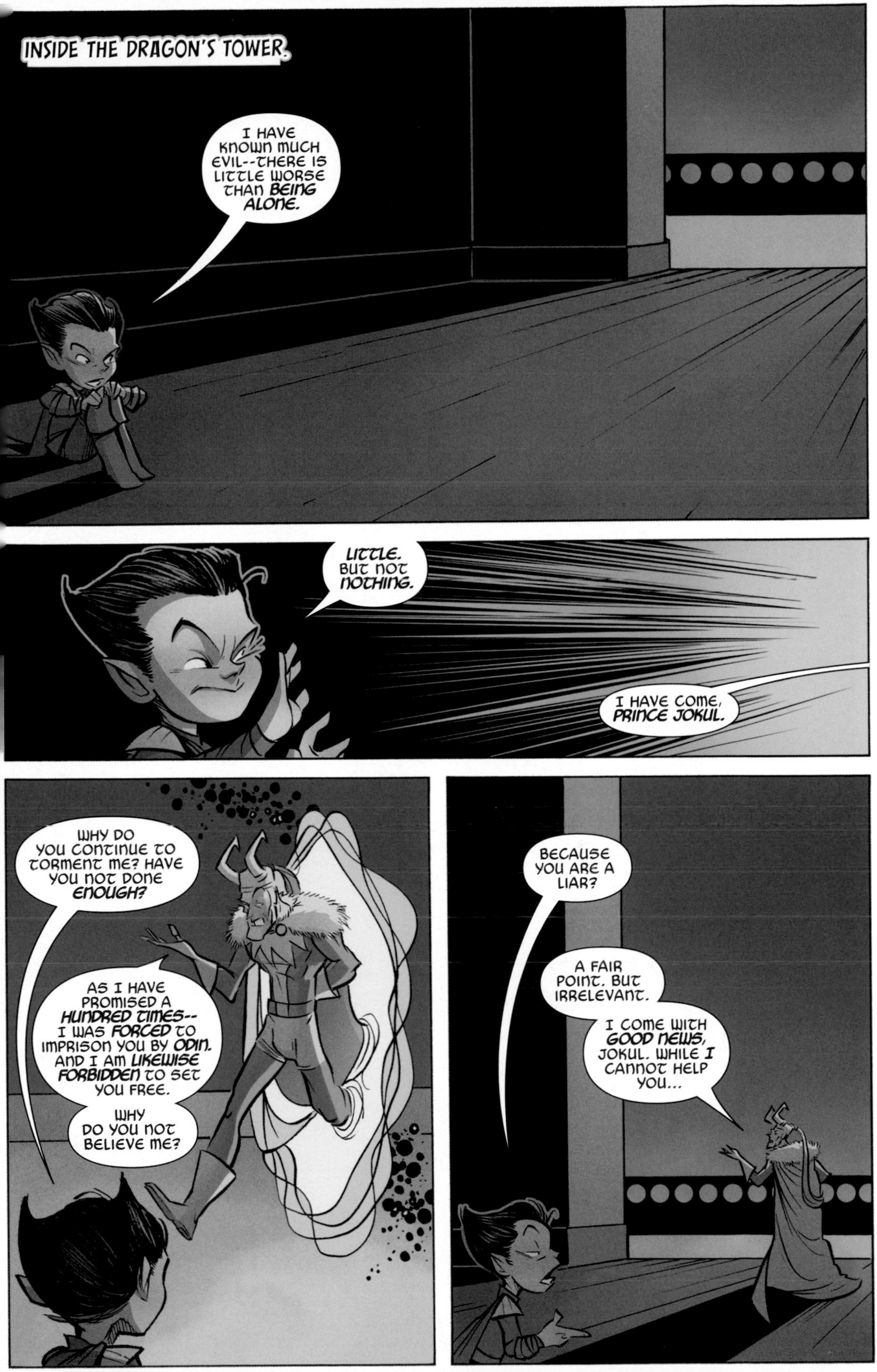
INSIDE THE DRAGON'S TOWER.
I HAVE KNOWN MUCH EVIL--THERE IS LITTLE WORSE THAN BEING ALONE.
LITTLE. BUT NOT NOTHING.
I HAVE COME, PRINCE JOKUL.
WHY DO YOU CONTINUE TO TORMENT ME? HAVE YOU NOT DONE ENOUGH?
AS I HAVE PROMISED A HUNDRED TIMES-- I WAS FORCED TO IMPRISON YOU BY ODIN. AND I AM LIKEWISE FORBIDDEN TO SET YOU FREE.
WHY DO YOU NOT BELIEVE ME?
BECAUSE YOU ARE A LIAR?
A FAIR POINT. BUT IRRELEVANT.
I COME WITH GOOD NEWS, JOKUL. WHILE I CANNOT HELP YOU...

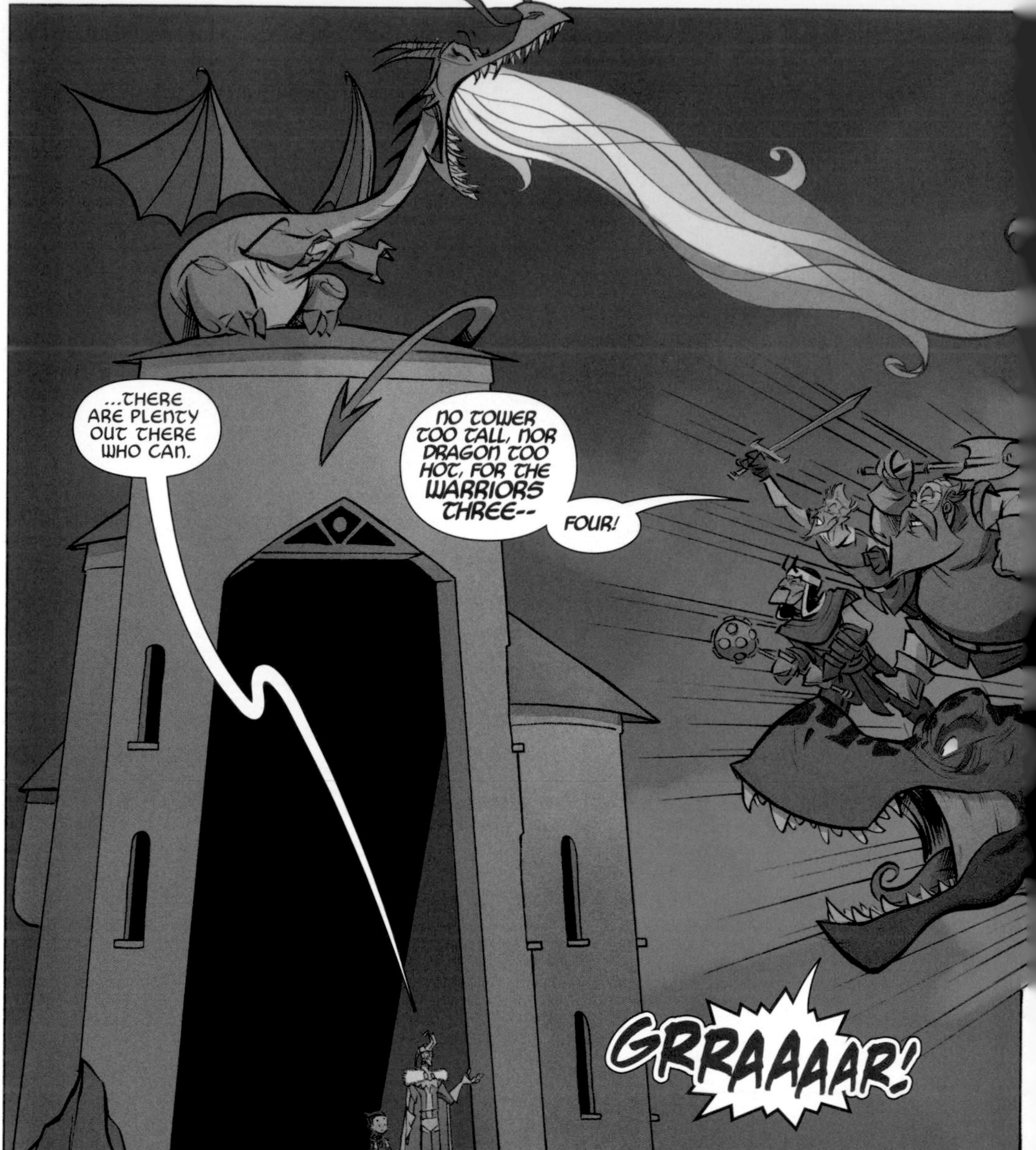
...THERE ARE PLENTY OUT THERE WHO CAN.
NO TOWER TOO TALL, NOR DRAGON TOO HOT, FOR THE WARRIORS THREE--
FOUR!
GRRAAAAR!

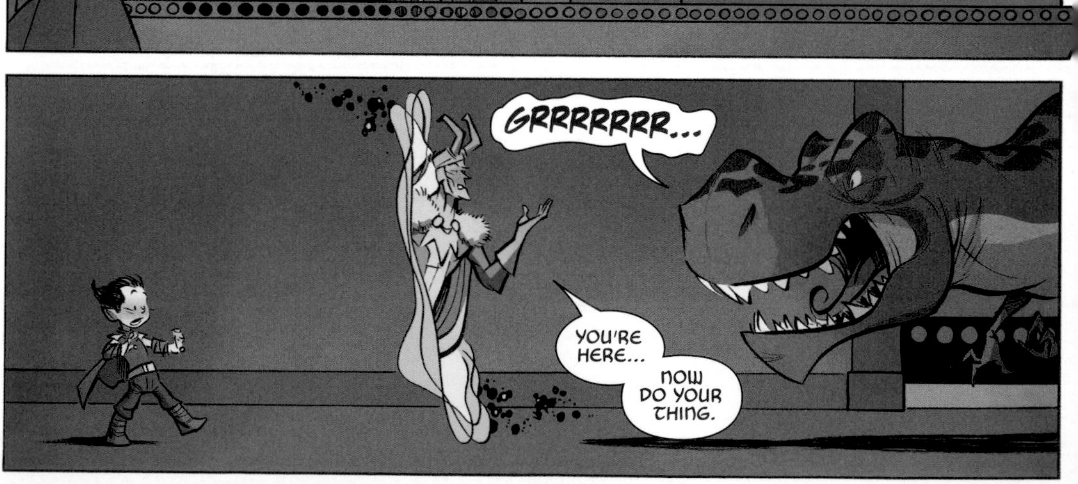
GRRRRRRR...
YOU'RE HERE...
NOW DO YOUR THING.

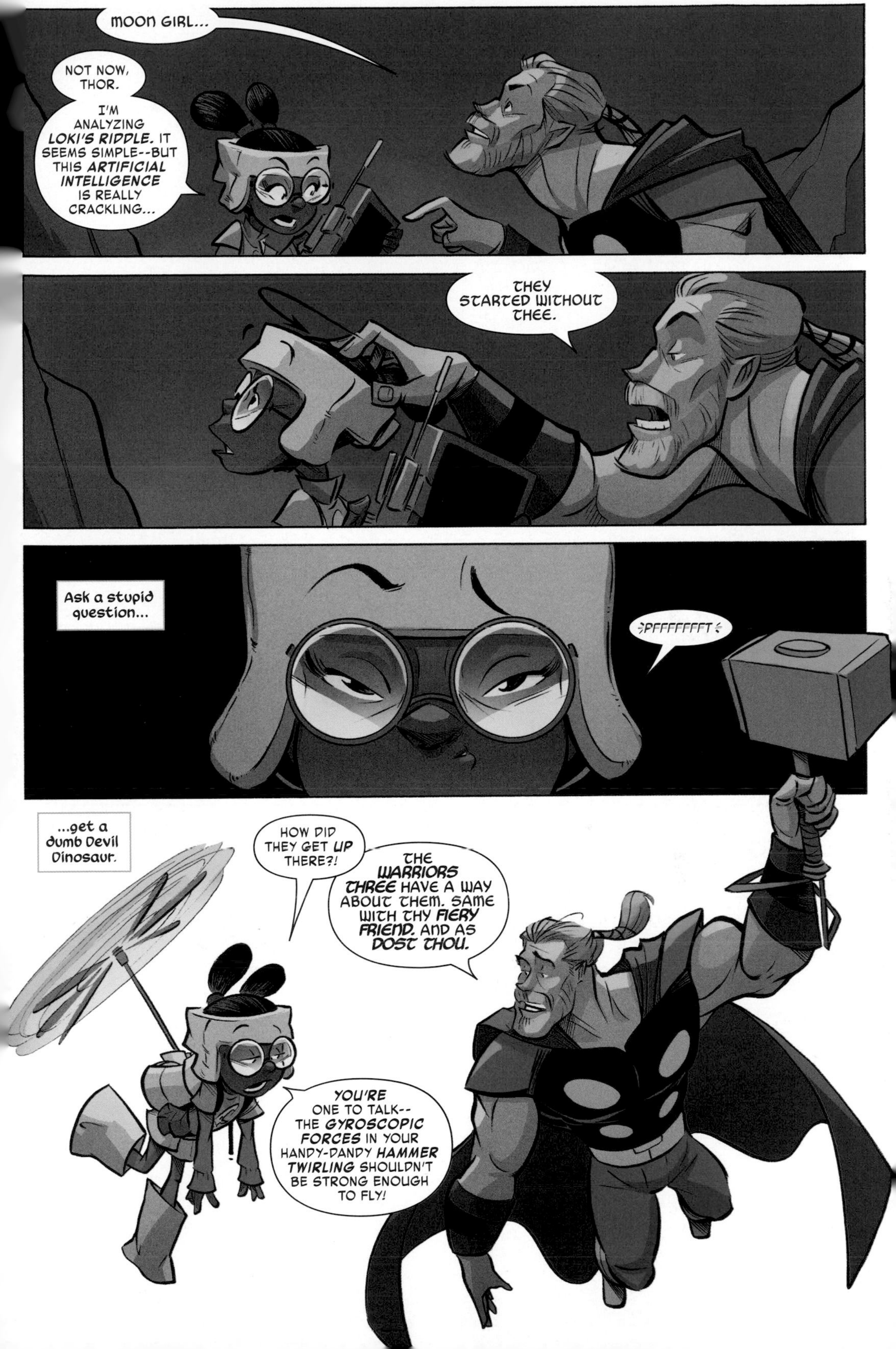
MOON GIRL...
NOT NOW, THOR.
I'M ANALYZING LOKI'S RIDDLE. IT SEEMS SIMPLE--BUT THIS ARTIFICIAL INTELLIGENCE IS REALLY CRACKLING...
THEY STARTED WITHOUT THEE.
Ask a stupid question...
PFFFFFFFFT
...get a dumb Devil Dinosaur.
HOW DID THEY GET UP THERE?!
THE WARRIORS THREE HAVE A WAY ABOUT THEM. SAME WITH THY FIERY FRIEND. AND AS DOST THOU.
YOU'RE ONE TO TALK-- THE GYROSCOPIC FORCES IN YOUR HANDY-DANDY HAMMER TWIRLING SHOULDN'T BE STRONG ENOUGH TO FLY!

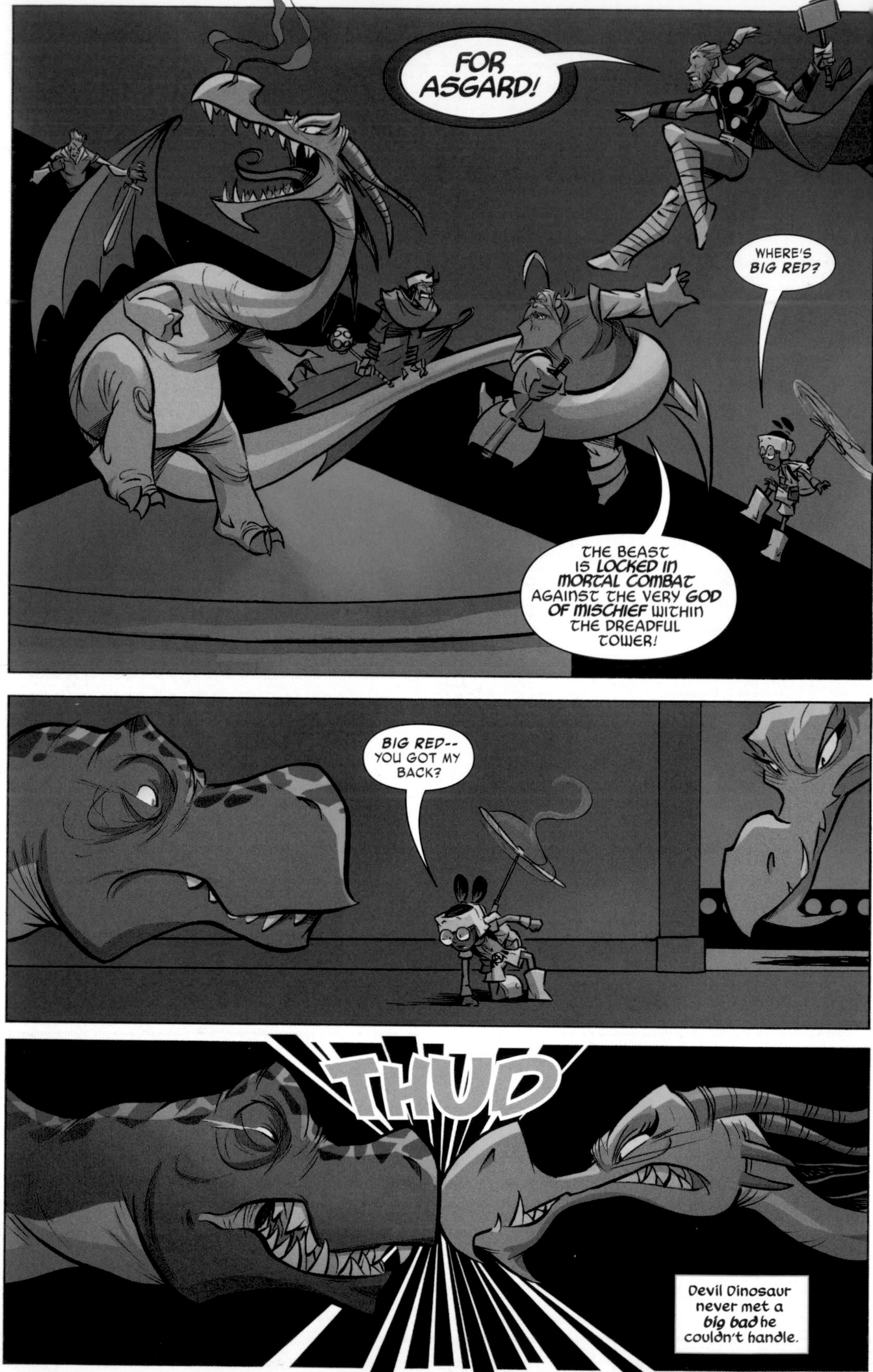

FOR ASGARD!
WHERE'S BIG RED?
THE BEAST IS LOCKED IN MORTAL COMBAT AGAINST THE VERY GOD OF MISCHIEF WITHIN THE DREADFUL TOWER!
BIG RED-- YOU GOT MY BACK?
THUD
Devil Dinosaur never met a big bad he couldn't handle.

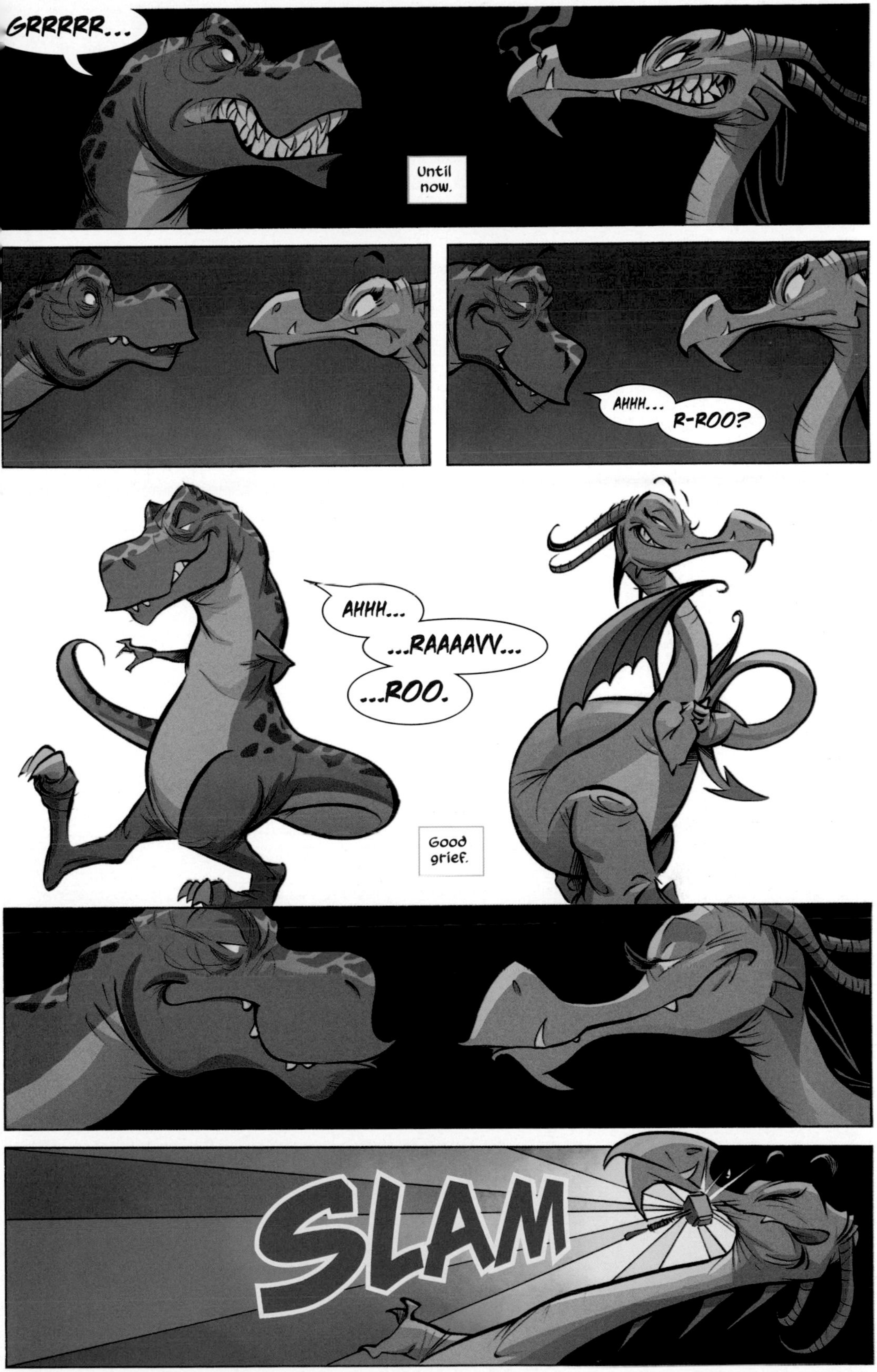
GRRRRR...
Until now.
AHHH...
R-ROO?
AHHH...
...RAAAAVV...
...ROO.
Good grief.
SLAM

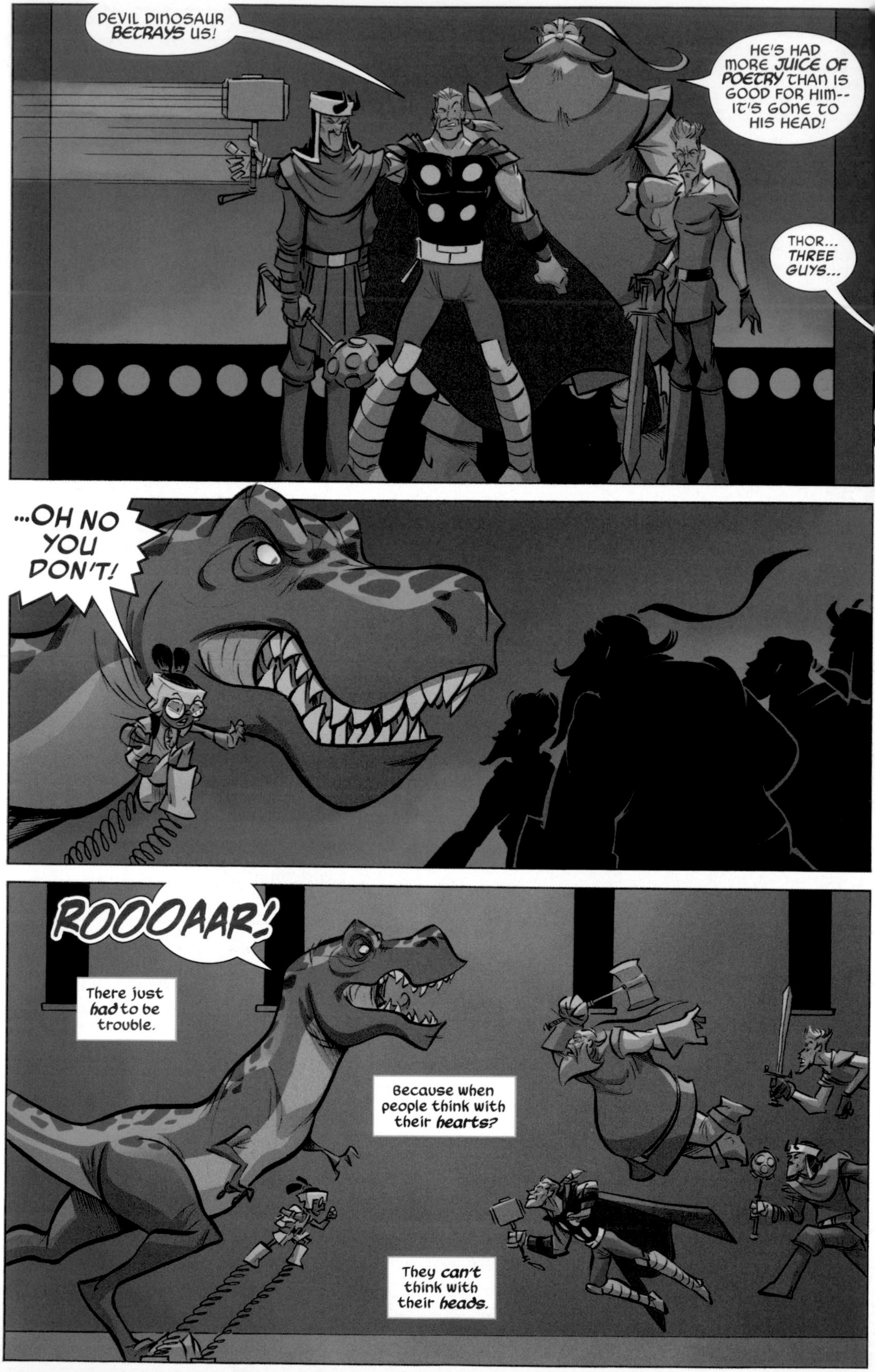
DEVIL DINOSAUR BETRAYS US!
HE'S HAD MORE JUICE OF POETRY THAN IS GOOD FOR HIM-- IT'S GONE TO HIS HEAD!
THOR... THREE GUYS...
...OH NO YOU DON'T!
ROOOAAR!
There just had to be trouble.
Because when people think with their hearts?
They can't think with their heads.

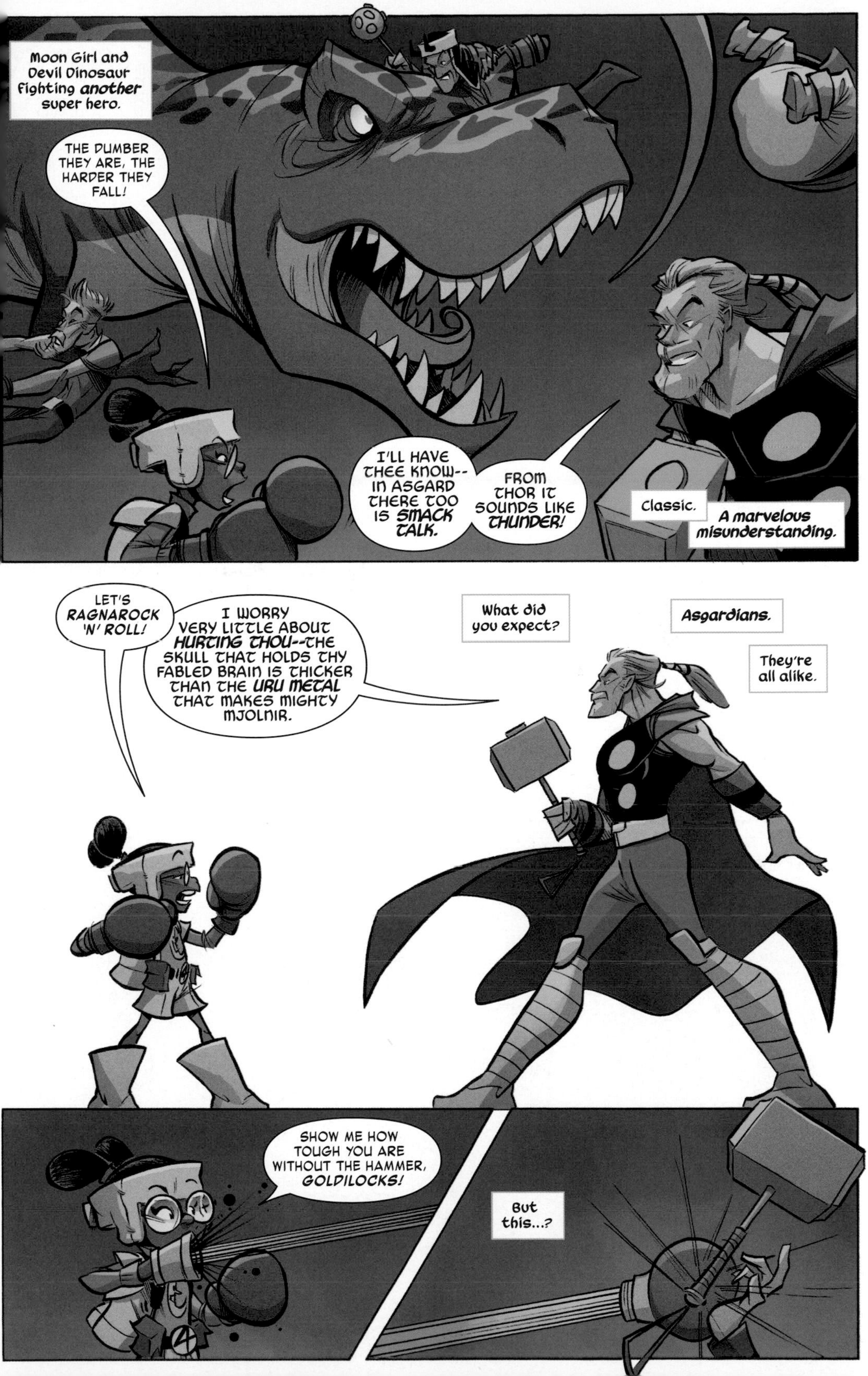

Moon Girl and Devil Dinosaur fighting *another* super hero.
THE DUMBER THEY ARE, THE HARDER THEY FALL!
I'LL HAVE THEE KNOW-- IN ASGARD THERE TOO IS *SMACK TALK.*
FROM THOR IT SOUNDS LIKE *THUNDER!*
Classic.
A marvelous misunderstanding.
LET'S *RAGNAROCK 'N' ROLL!*
I WORRY VERY LITTLE ABOUT *HURTING THOU*--THE SKULL THAT HOLDS THY FABLED BRAIN IS THICKER THAN THE *URU METAL* THAT MAKES MIGHTY MJOLNIR.
What did you expect?
Asgardians.
They're all alike.
SHOW ME HOW TOUGH YOU ARE WITHOUT THE HAMMER, *GOLDILOCKS!*
But this...?

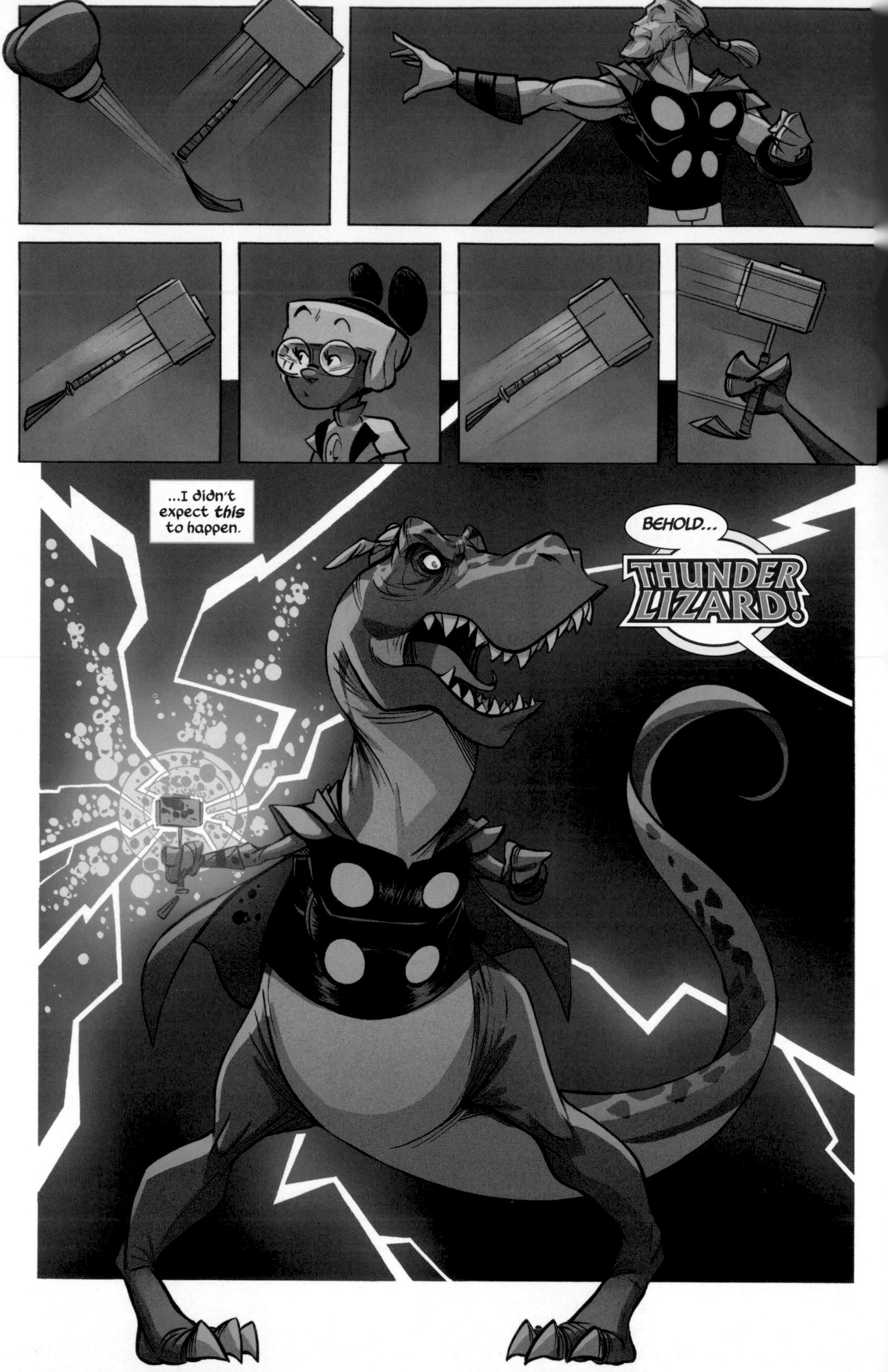

...I didn't expect this to happen.
BEHOLD...
THUNDER LIZARD!

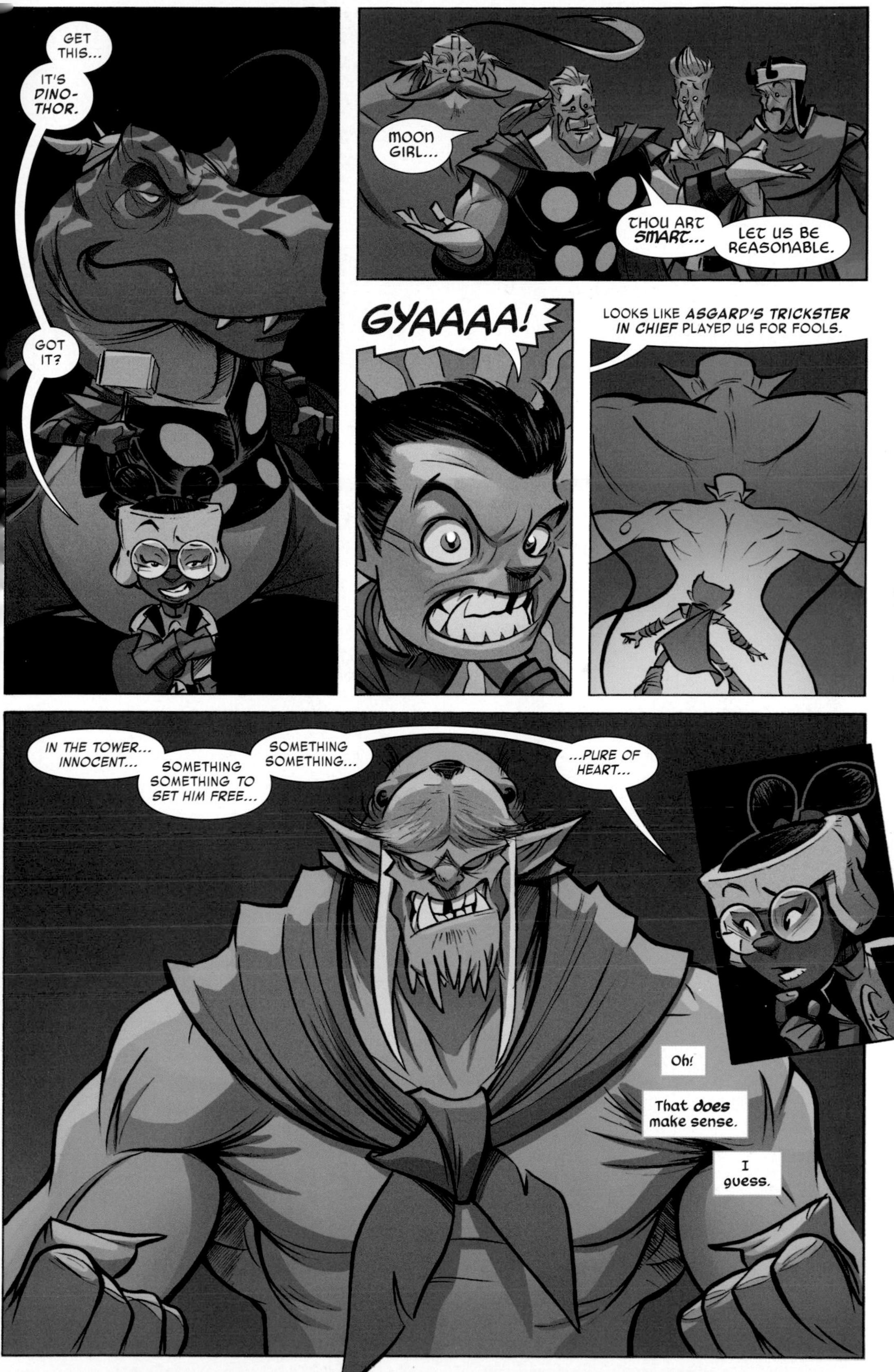

GET THIS...
IT'S DINO-THOR.
GOT IT?
MOON GIRL...
THOU ART SMART...
LET US BE REASONABLE.
GYAAAA!
LOOKS LIKE ASGARD'S TRICKSTER IN CHIEF PLAYED US FOR FOOLS.
IN THE TOWER... INNOCENT...
SOMETHING SOMETHING TO SET HIM FREE...
SOMETHING SOMETHING...
...PURE OF HEART...
Oh!
That does make sense.
I guess.

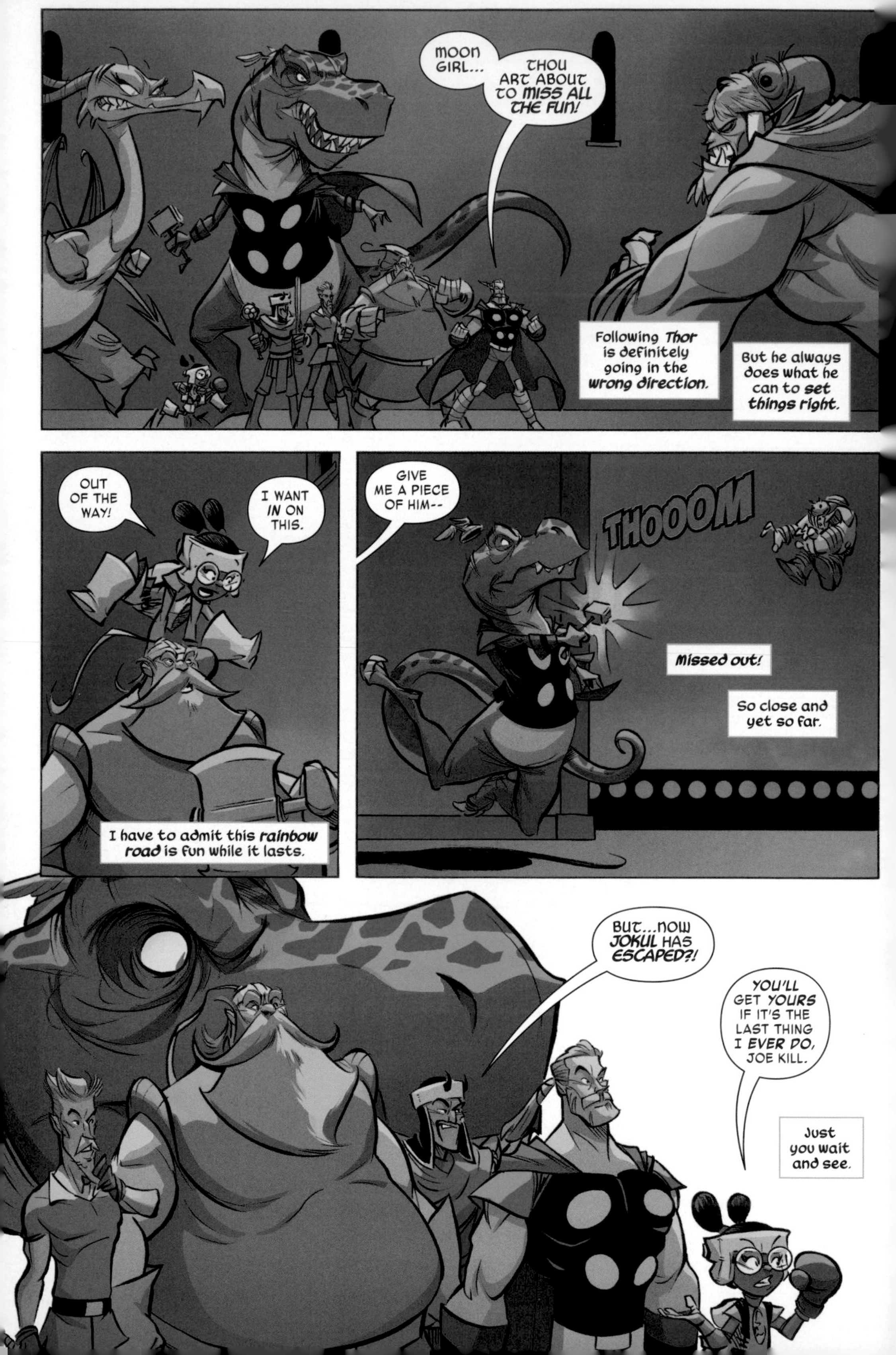

MOON GIRL...
THOU ART ABOUT TO MISS ALL THE FUN!
Following Thor is definitely going in the wrong direction.
But he always does what he can to set things right.
OUT OF THE WAY!
I WANT IN ON THIS.
I have to admit this rainbow road is fun while it lasts.
GIVE ME A PIECE OF HIM--
THOOOM
Missed out!
So close and yet so far.
BUT...NOW JOKUL HAS ESCAPED?!
YOU'LL GET YOURS IF IT'S THE LAST THING I EVER DO, JOE KILL.
Just you wait and see.

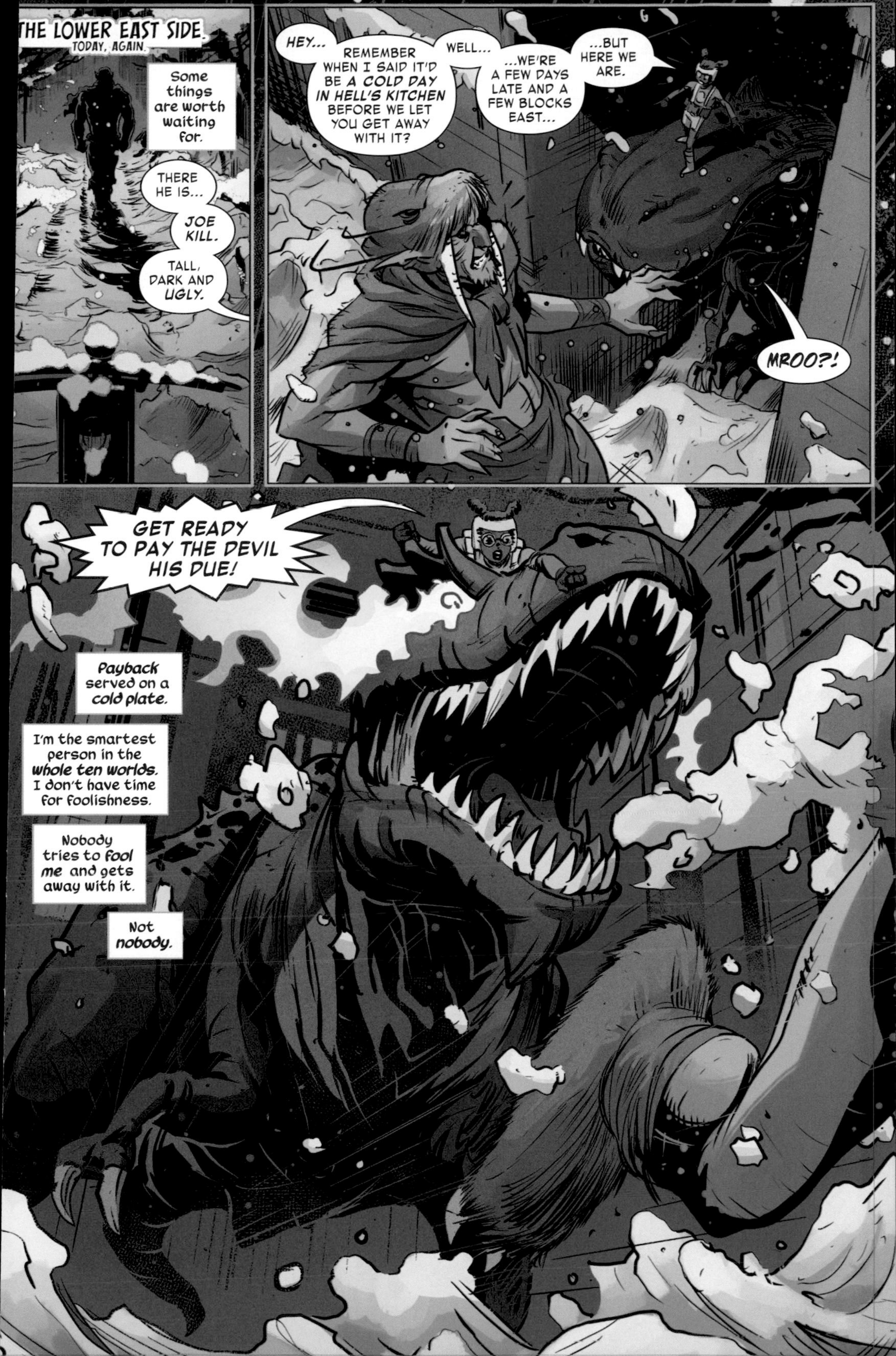

THE LOWER EAST SIDE.
TODAY, AGAIN.
Some things are worth waiting for.
THERE HE IS...
JOE KILL.
TALL, DARK AND UGLY.
HEY...
REMEMBER WHEN I SAID IT'D BE A COLD DAY IN HELL'S KITCHEN BEFORE WE LET YOU GET AWAY WITH IT?
WELL...
...WE'RE A FEW DAYS LATE AND A FEW BLOCKS EAST...
...BUT HERE WE ARE.
MROO?!
GET READY TO PAY THE DEVIL HIS DUE!
Payback served on a cold plate.
I'm the smartest person in the whole ten worlds. I don't have time for foolishness.
Nobody tries to fool me and gets away with it.
Not nobody.

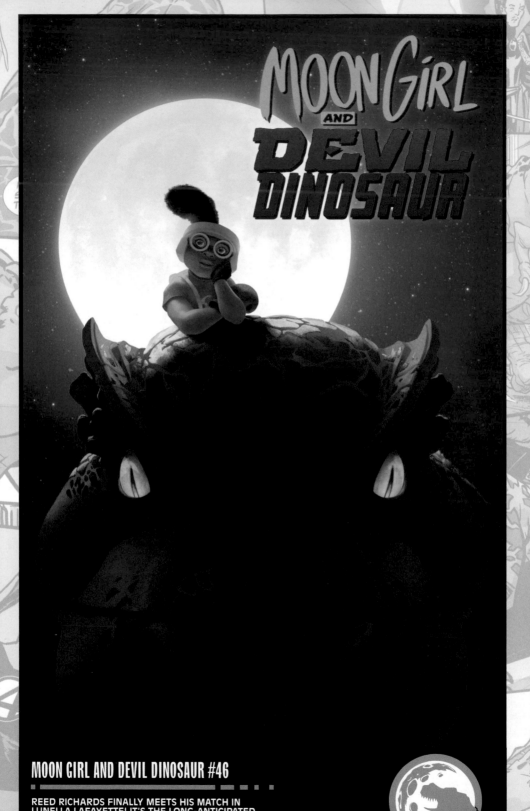

MOON GIRL AND DEVIL DINOSAUR #46

REED RICHARDS FINALLY MEETS HIS MATCH IN
LUNELLA LAFAYETTE! IT'S THE LONG-ANTICIPATED
ULTIMATE BATTLE OF THE BIGGEST BRAINS
IN THE MARVEL UNIVERSE!

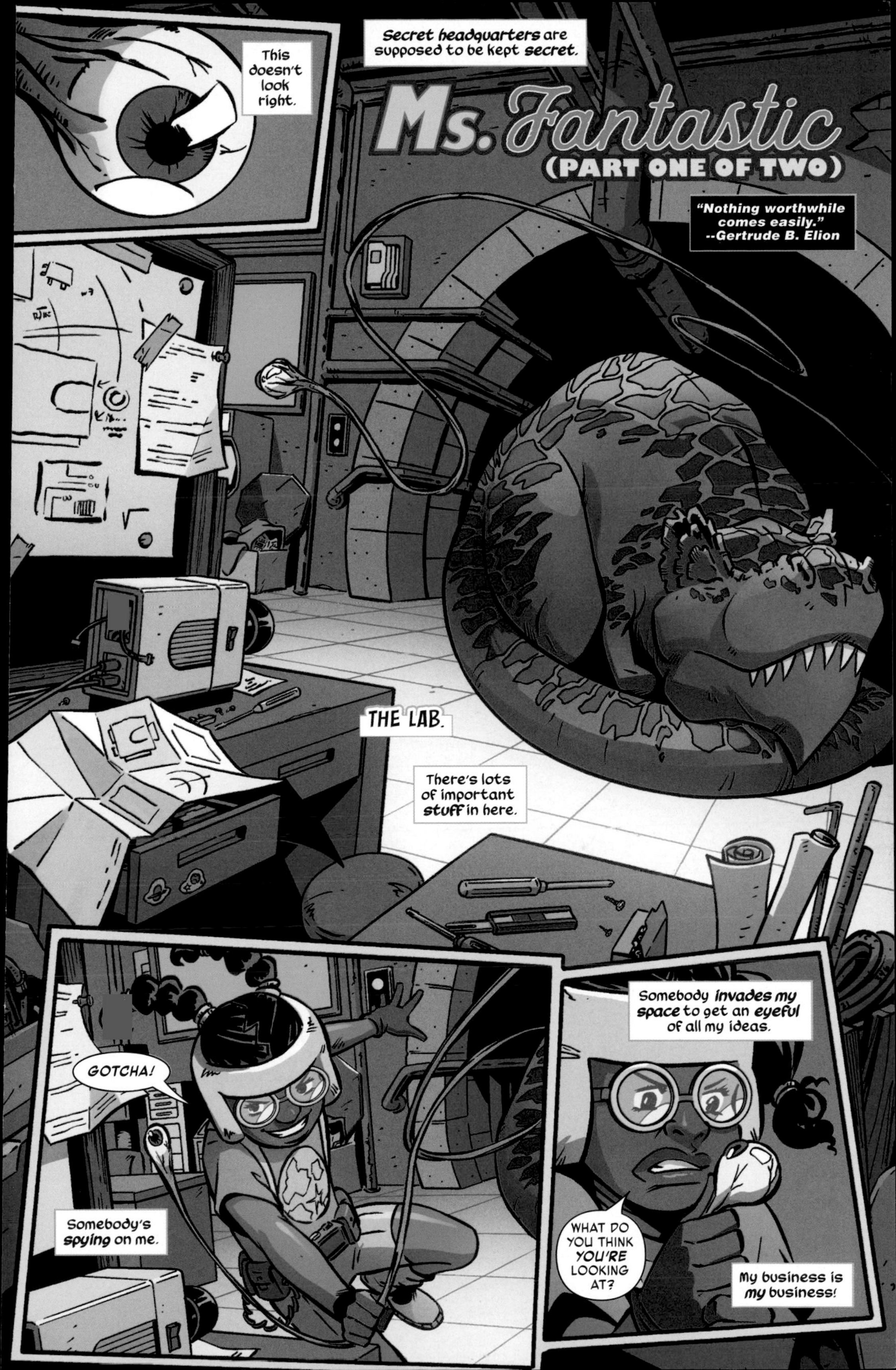

This doesn't look right.
Secret headquarters are supposed to be kept secret.
Ms. Fantastic
(PART ONE OF TWO)
"Nothing worthwhile comes easily." --Gertrude B. Elion
THE LAB.
There's lots of important stuff in here.
GOTCHA!
Somebody's spying on me.
Somebody invades my space to get an eyeful of all my ideas.
WHAT DO YOU THINK YOU'RE LOOKING AT?
My business is my business!

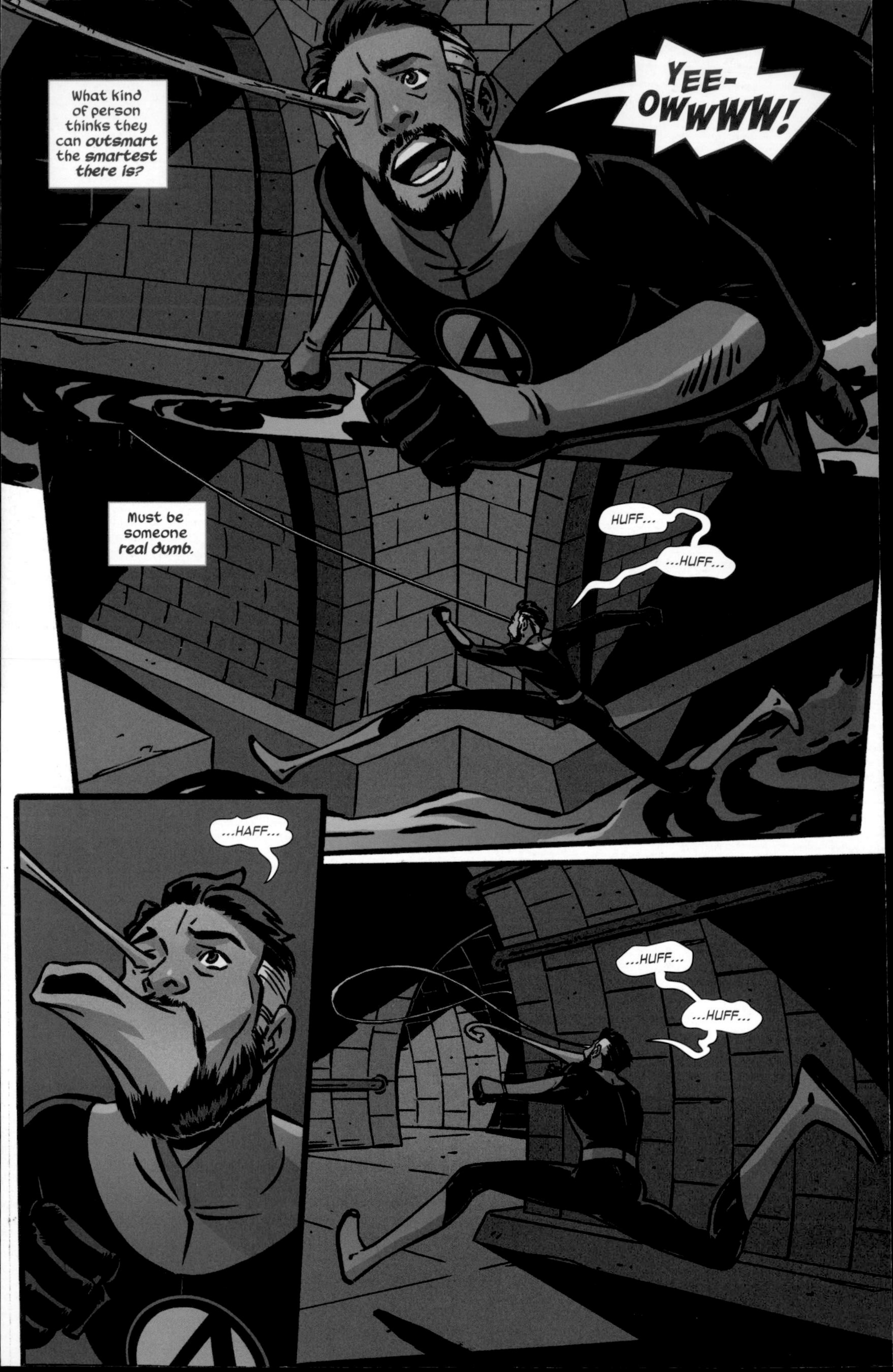
What kind of person thinks they can *outsmart* the *smartest* there is?
YEE-OWWWW!
Must be someone *real dumb.*
HUFF...
...HUFF...
...HAFF...
...HUFF...
...HUFF...

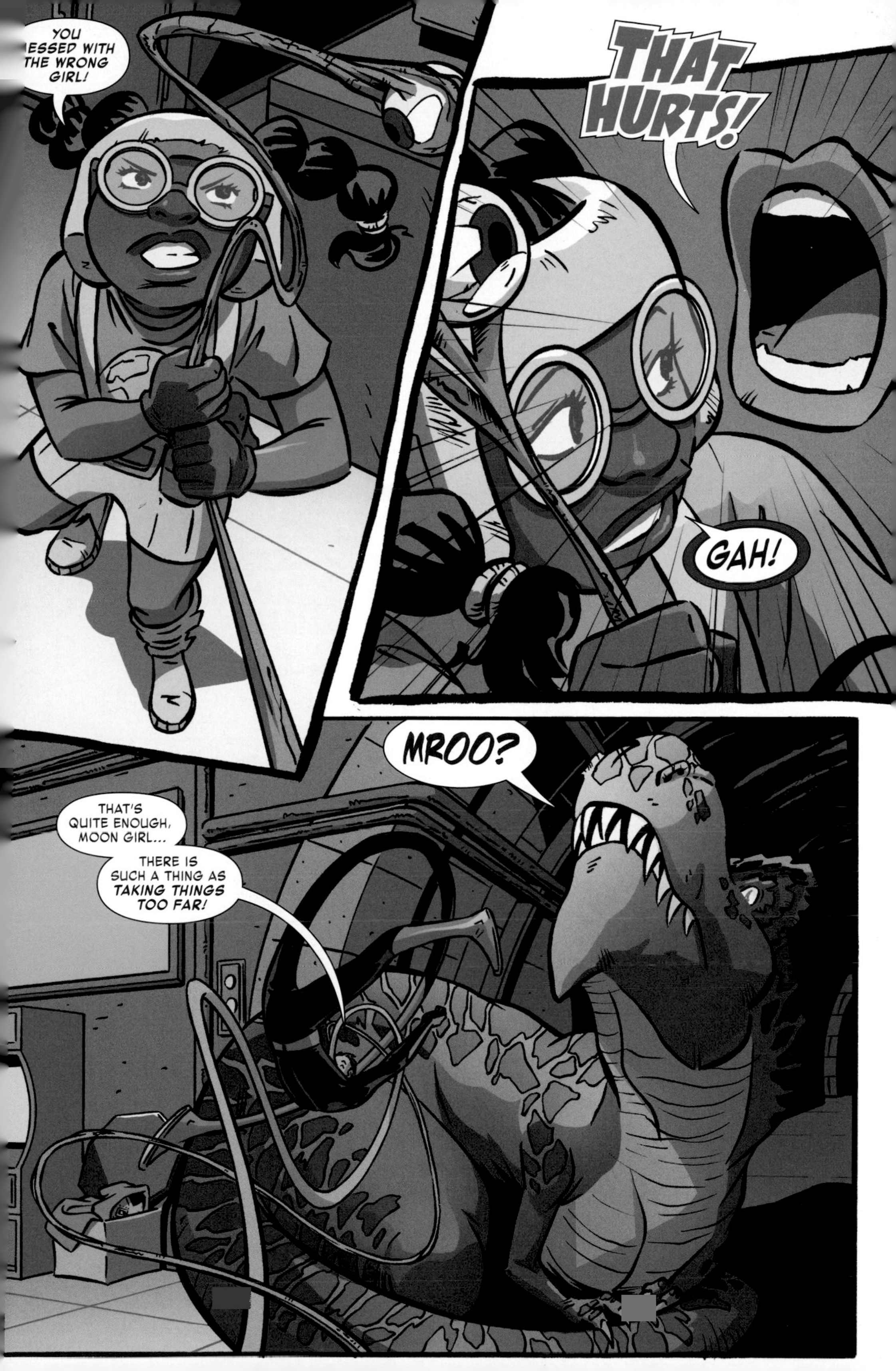
YOU MESSED WITH THE WRONG GIRL!
THAT HURTS!
GAH!
MROO?
THAT'S QUITE ENOUGH, MOON GIRL...
THERE IS SUCH A THING AS TAKING THINGS TOO FAR!

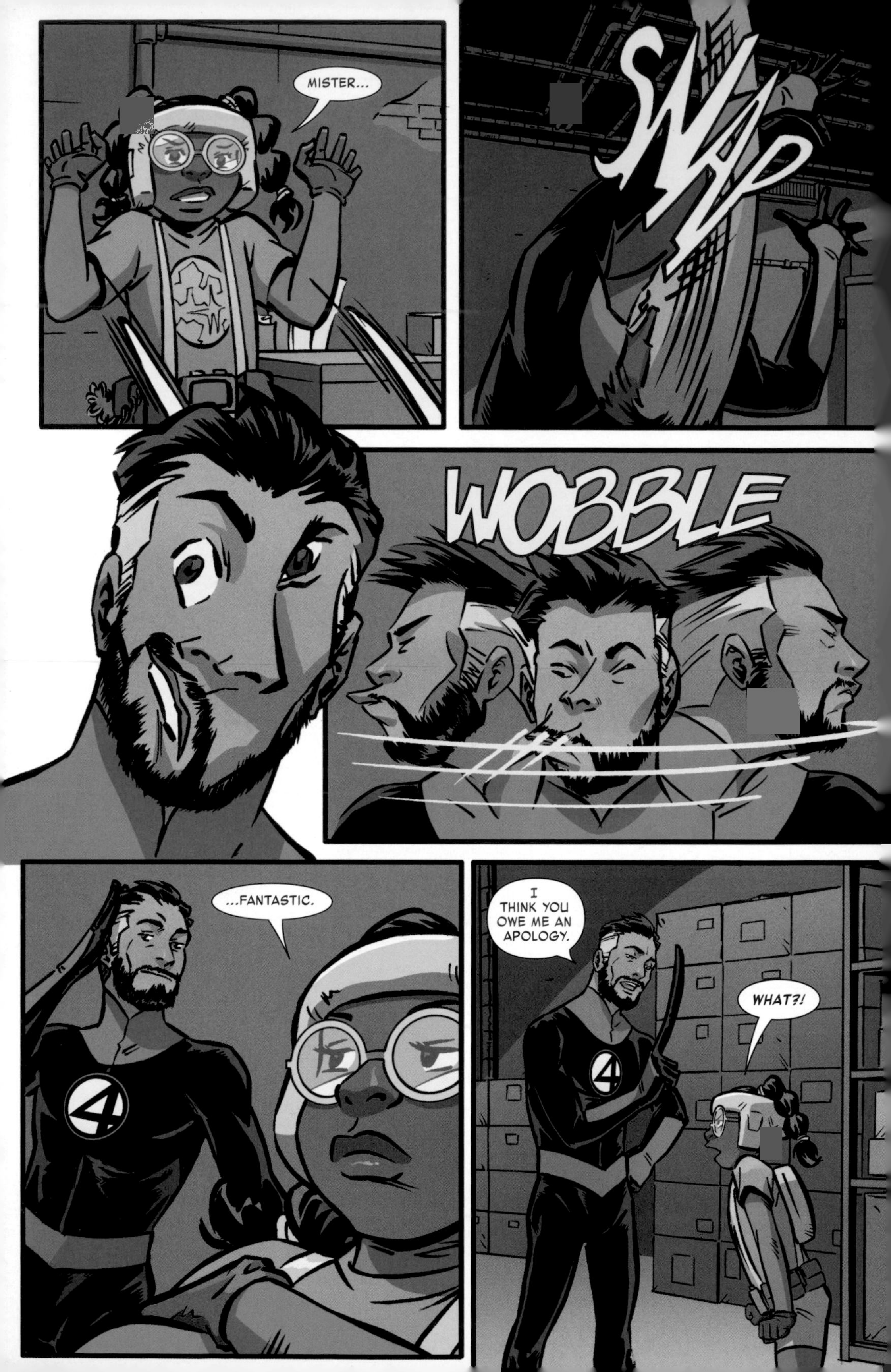
MISTER...
SNAP
WOBBLE
...FANTASTIC.
I THINK YOU OWE ME AN APOLOGY.
WHAT?!

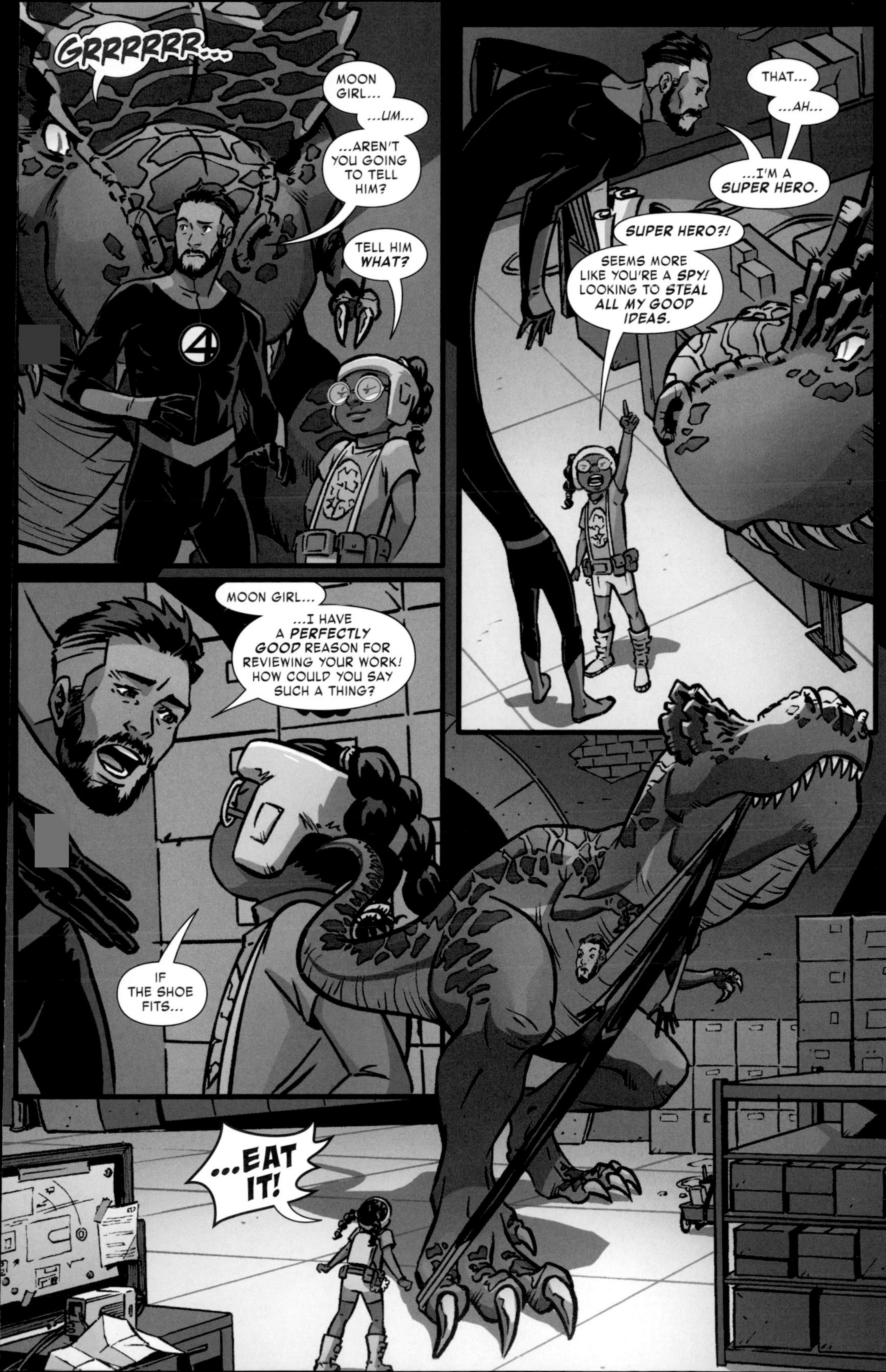
GRRRRRR...
MOON GIRL...
...UM...
...AREN'T YOU GOING TO TELL HIM?
TELL HIM WHAT?
THAT...
...AH...
...I'M A SUPER HERO.
SUPER HERO?!
SEEMS MORE LIKE YOU'RE A SPY! LOOKING TO STEAL ALL MY GOOD IDEAS.
MOON GIRL...
...I HAVE A PERFECTLY GOOD REASON FOR REVIEWING YOUR WORK! HOW COULD YOU SAY SUCH A THING?
IF THE SHOE FITS...
...EAT IT!

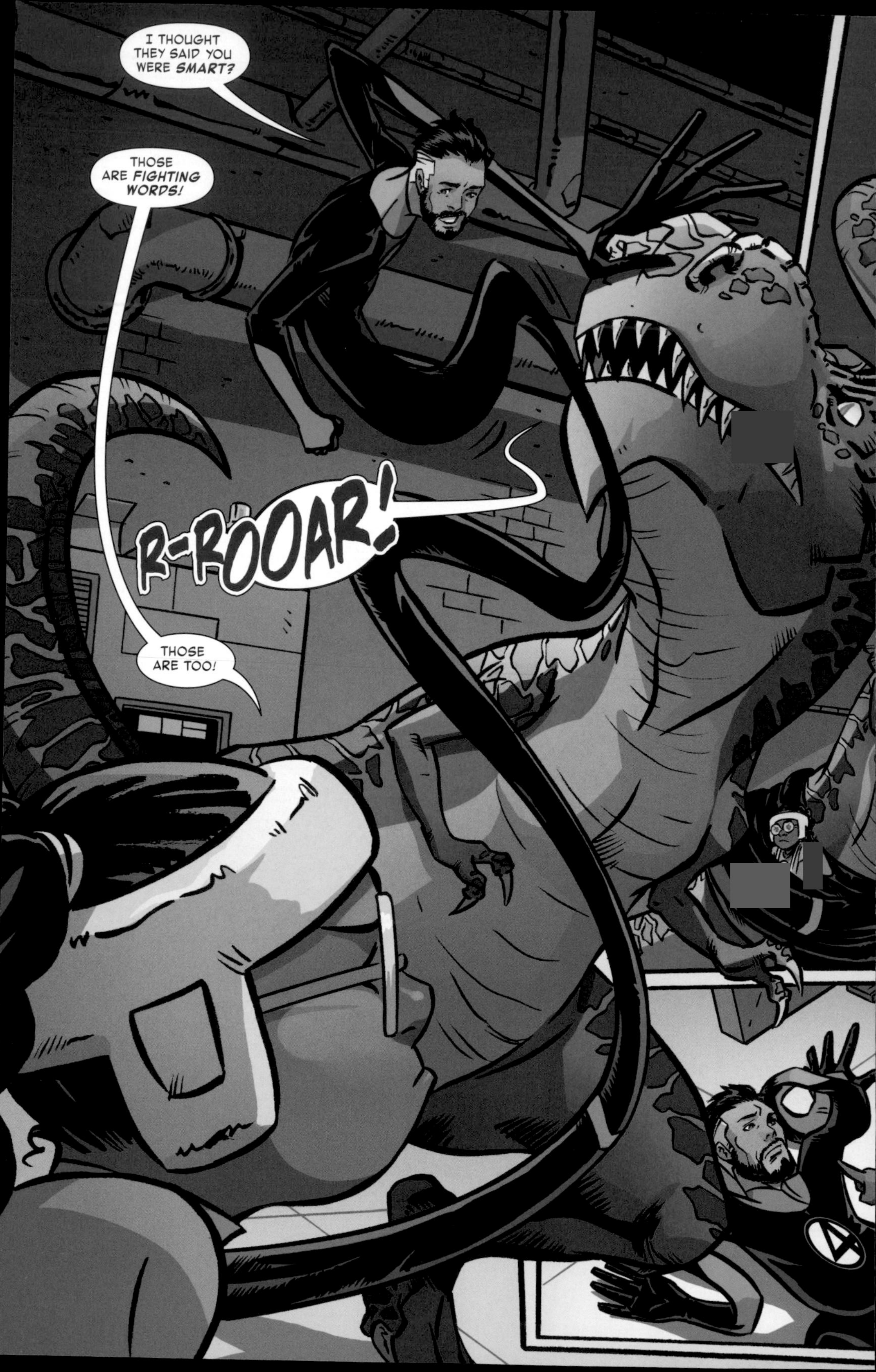
I THOUGHT THEY SAID YOU WERE SMART?
THOSE ARE FIGHTING WORDS!
R-ROOAR!
THOSE ARE TOO!

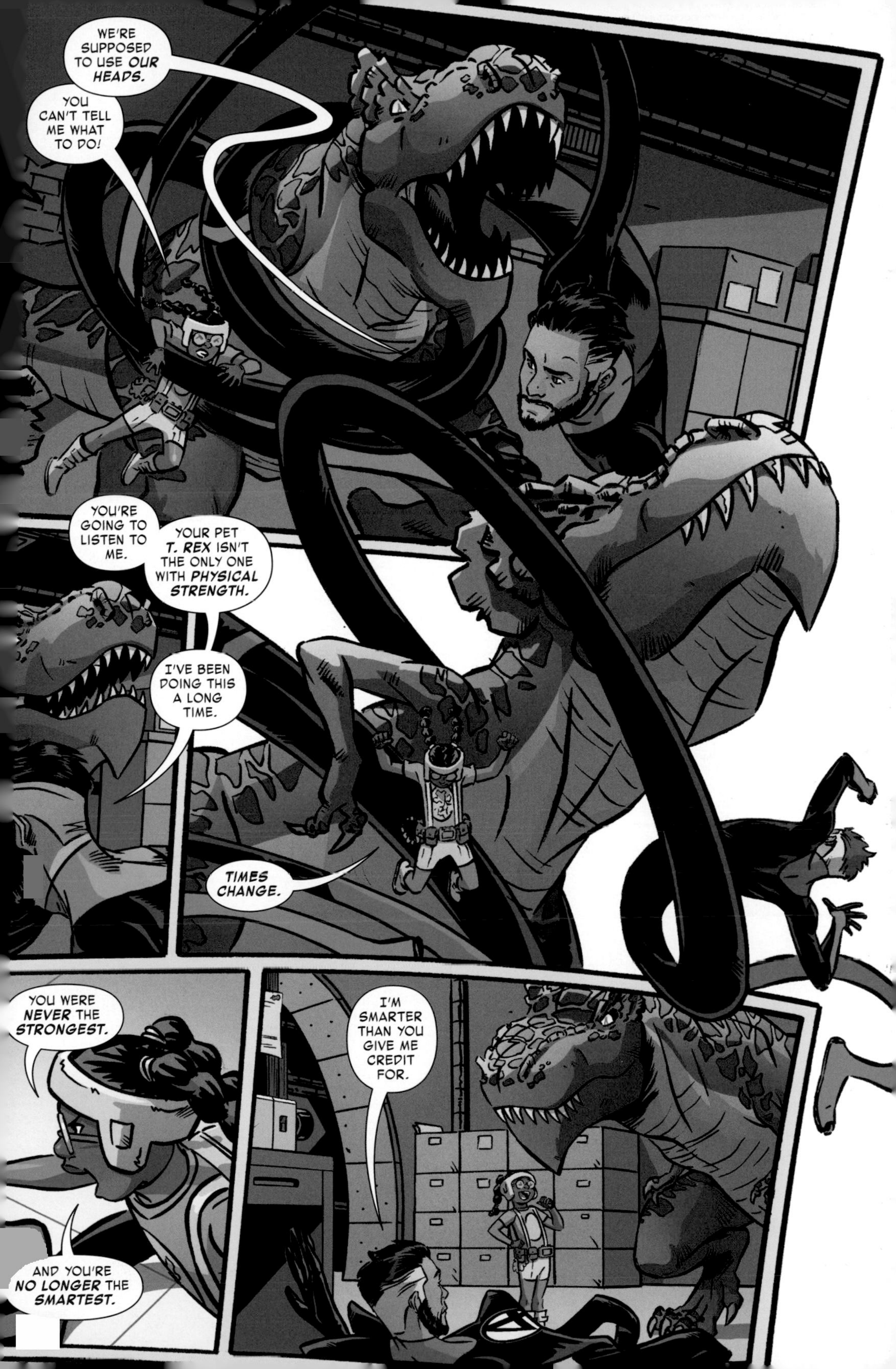
WE'RE SUPPOSED TO USE OUR HEADS.
YOU CAN'T TELL ME WHAT TO DO!
YOU'RE GOING TO LISTEN TO ME.
YOUR PET T. REX ISN'T THE ONLY ONE WITH PHYSICAL STRENGTH.
I'VE BEEN DOING THIS A LONG TIME.
TIMES CHANGE.
YOU WERE NEVER THE STRONGEST.
AND YOU'RE NO LONGER THE SMARTEST.
I'M SMARTER THAN YOU GIVE ME CREDIT FOR.

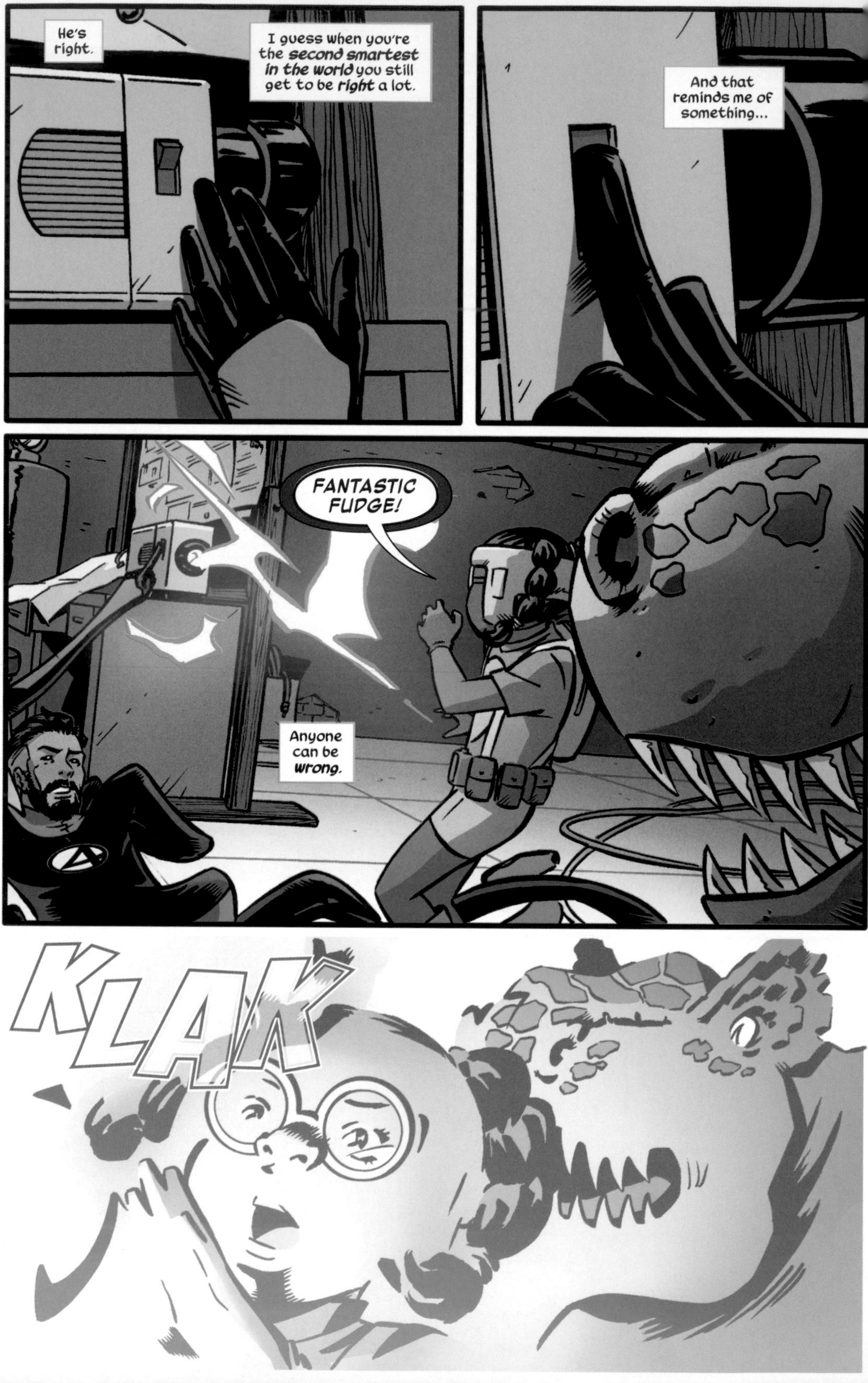
He's right.
I guess when you're the second smartest in the world you still get to be right a lot.
And that reminds me of something...
FANTASTIC FUDGE!
Anyone can be wrong.
KLAK

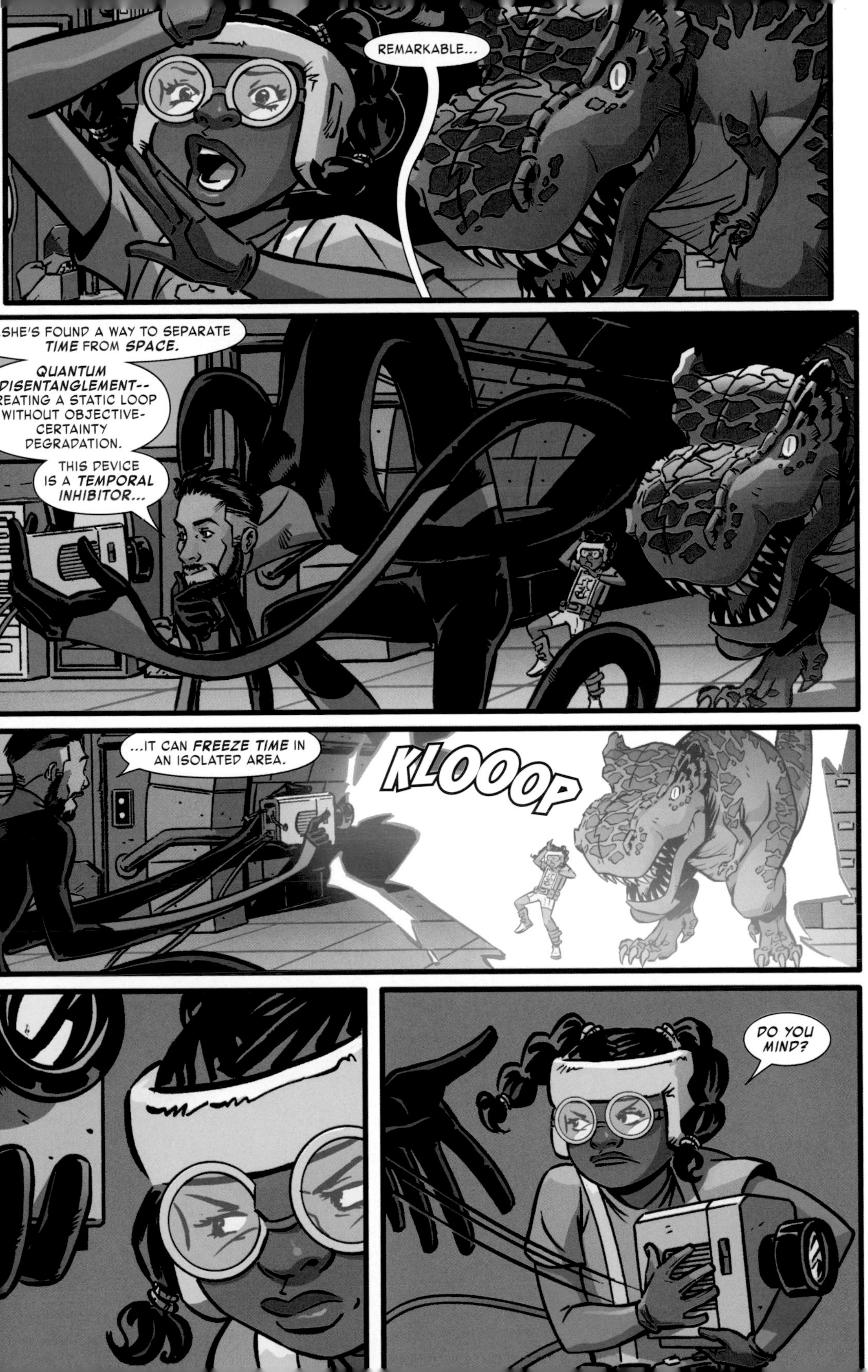
REMARKABLE...
..SHE'S FOUND A WAY TO SEPARATE TIME FROM SPACE.
QUANTUM DISENTANGLEMENT-- REATING A STATIC LOOP WITHOUT OBJECTIVE-CERTAINTY DEGRADATION.
THIS DEVICE IS A TEMPORAL INHIBITOR...
...IT CAN FREEZE TIME IN AN ISOLATED AREA.
KLOOOP
DO YOU MIND?

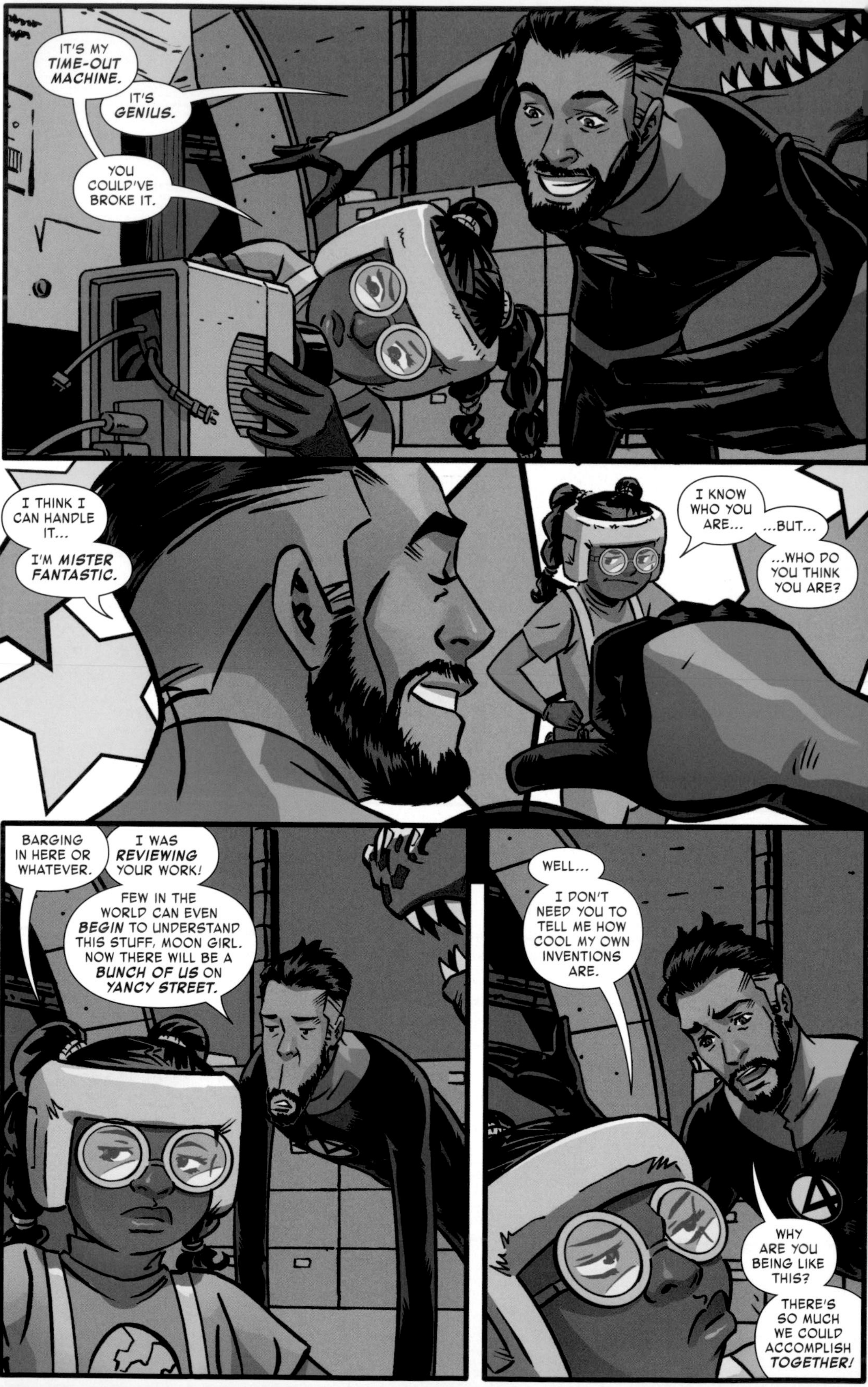

IT'S MY TIME-OUT MACHINE.
IT'S GENIUS.
YOU COULD'VE BROKE IT.
I THINK I CAN HANDLE IT...
I'M MISTER FANTASTIC.
I KNOW WHO YOU ARE...
...BUT...
...WHO DO YOU THINK YOU ARE?
BARGING IN HERE OR WHATEVER.
I WAS REVIEWING YOUR WORK!
FEW IN THE WORLD CAN EVEN BEGIN TO UNDERSTAND THIS STUFF, MOON GIRL. NOW THERE WILL BE A BUNCH OF US ON YANCY STREET.
WELL...
I DON'T NEED YOU TO TELL ME HOW COOL MY OWN INVENTIONS ARE.
WHY ARE YOU BEING LIKE THIS?
THERE'S SO MUCH WE COULD ACCOMPLISH TOGETHER!

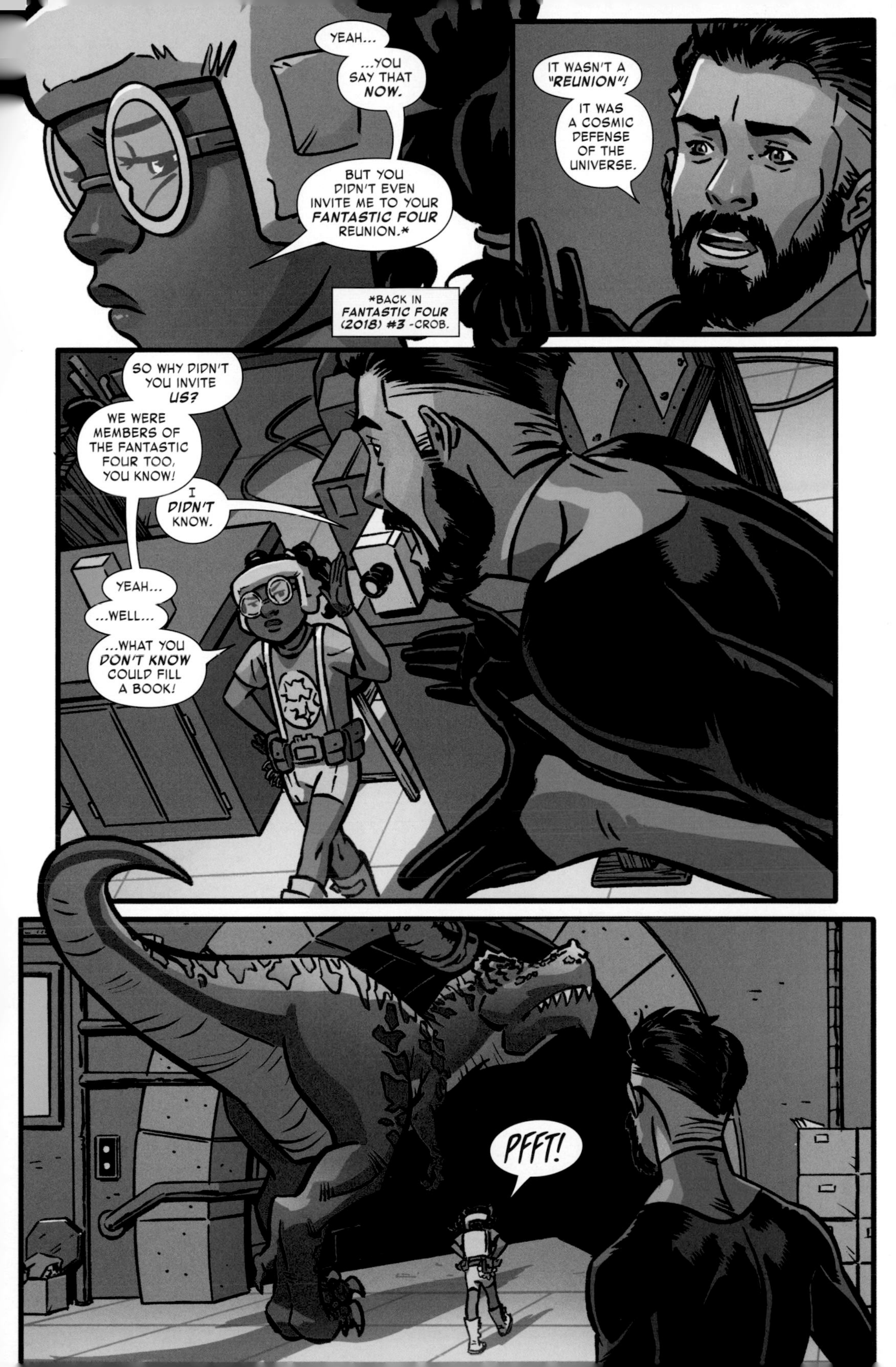
YEAH...
...YOU SAY THAT NOW.
BUT YOU DIDN'T EVEN INVITE ME TO YOUR FANTASTIC FOUR REUNION.*
*BACK IN FANTASTIC FOUR (2018) #3 -CROB.
IT WASN'T A "REUNION"!
IT WAS A COSMIC DEFENSE OF THE UNIVERSE.
SO WHY DIDN'T YOU INVITE US?
WE WERE MEMBERS OF THE FANTASTIC FOUR TOO, YOU KNOW!
I DIDN'T KNOW.
YEAH...
...WELL...
...WHAT YOU DON'T KNOW COULD FILL A BOOK!
PFFT!

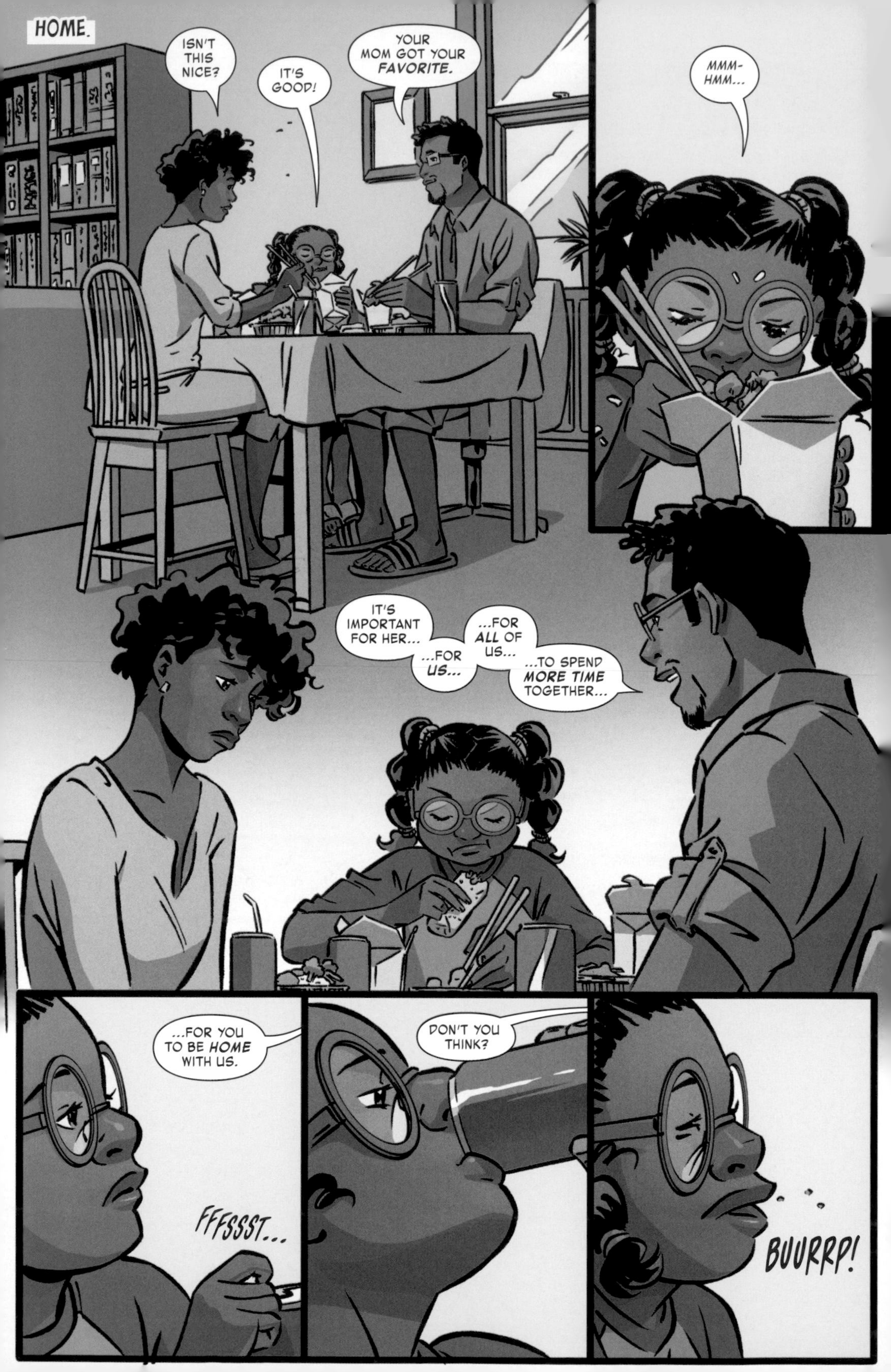
HOME.
ISN'T THIS NICE?
IT'S GOOD!
YOUR MOM GOT YOUR FAVORITE.
MMM-HMM...
IT'S IMPORTANT FOR HER...
...FOR US...
...FOR ALL OF US...
...TO SPEND MORE TIME TOGETHER...
...FOR YOU TO BE HOME WITH US.
FFFSSST...
DON'T YOU THINK?
BUURRP!

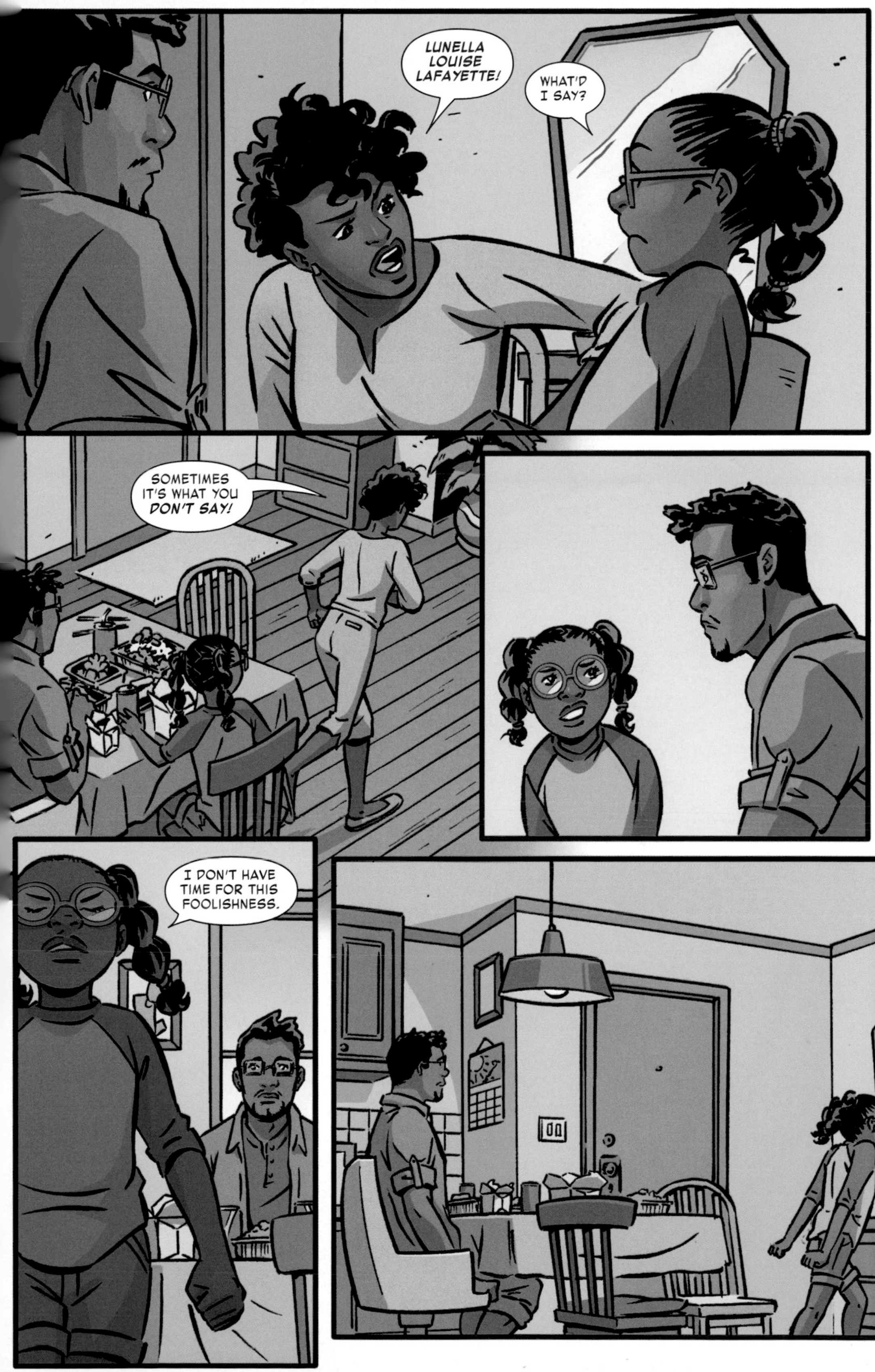
LUNELLA LOUISE LAFAYETTE!
WHAT'D I SAY?
SOMETIMES IT'S WHAT YOU *DON'T SAY!*
I DON'T HAVE TIME FOR THIS FOOLISHNESS.

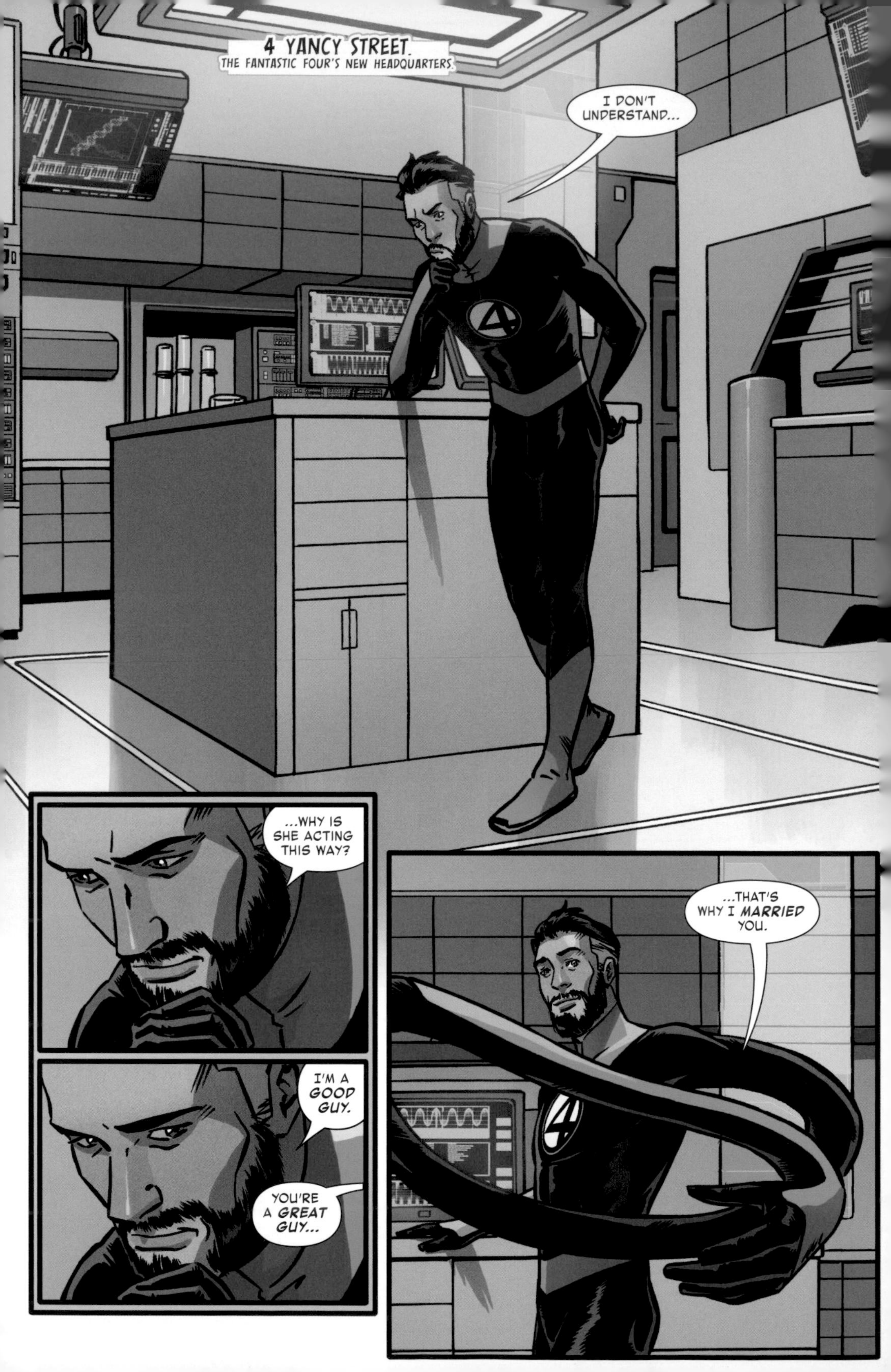
4 YANCY STREET.
THE FANTASTIC FOUR'S NEW HEADQUARTERS.
I DON'T UNDERSTAND...
...WHY IS SHE ACTING THIS WAY?
I'M A GOOD GUY.
YOU'RE A GREAT GUY...
...THAT'S WHY I MARRIED YOU.

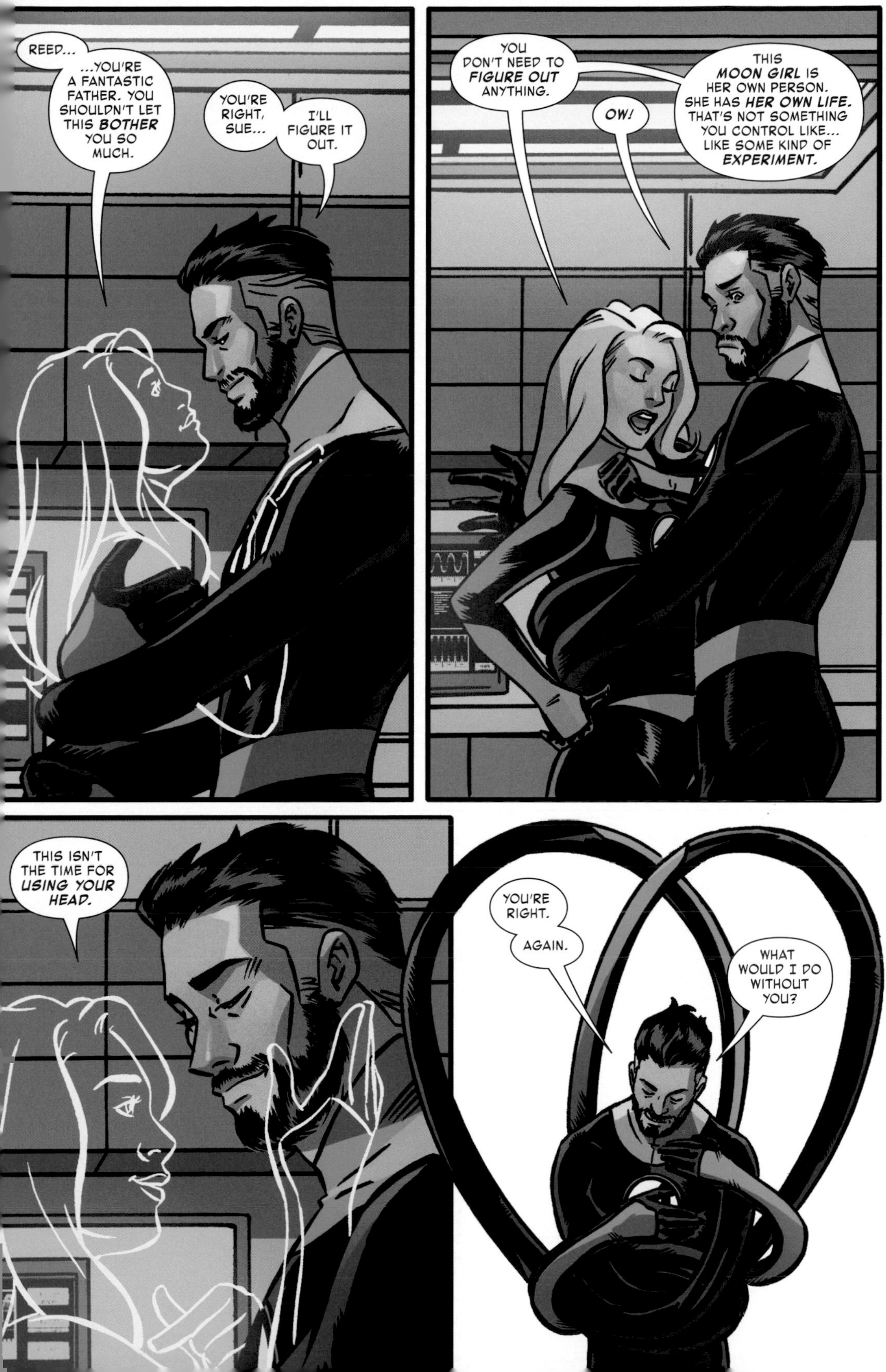
REED...
...YOU'RE A FANTASTIC FATHER. YOU SHOULDN'T LET THIS BOTHER YOU SO MUCH.
YOU'RE RIGHT, SUE...
I'LL FIGURE IT OUT.
YOU DON'T NEED TO FIGURE OUT ANYTHING.
THIS MOON GIRL IS HER OWN PERSON. SHE HAS HER OWN LIFE. THAT'S NOT SOMETHING YOU CONTROL LIKE... LIKE SOME KIND OF EXPERIMENT.
OW!
THIS ISN'T THE TIME FOR USING YOUR HEAD.
YOU'RE RIGHT.
AGAIN.
WHAT WOULD I DO WITHOUT YOU?

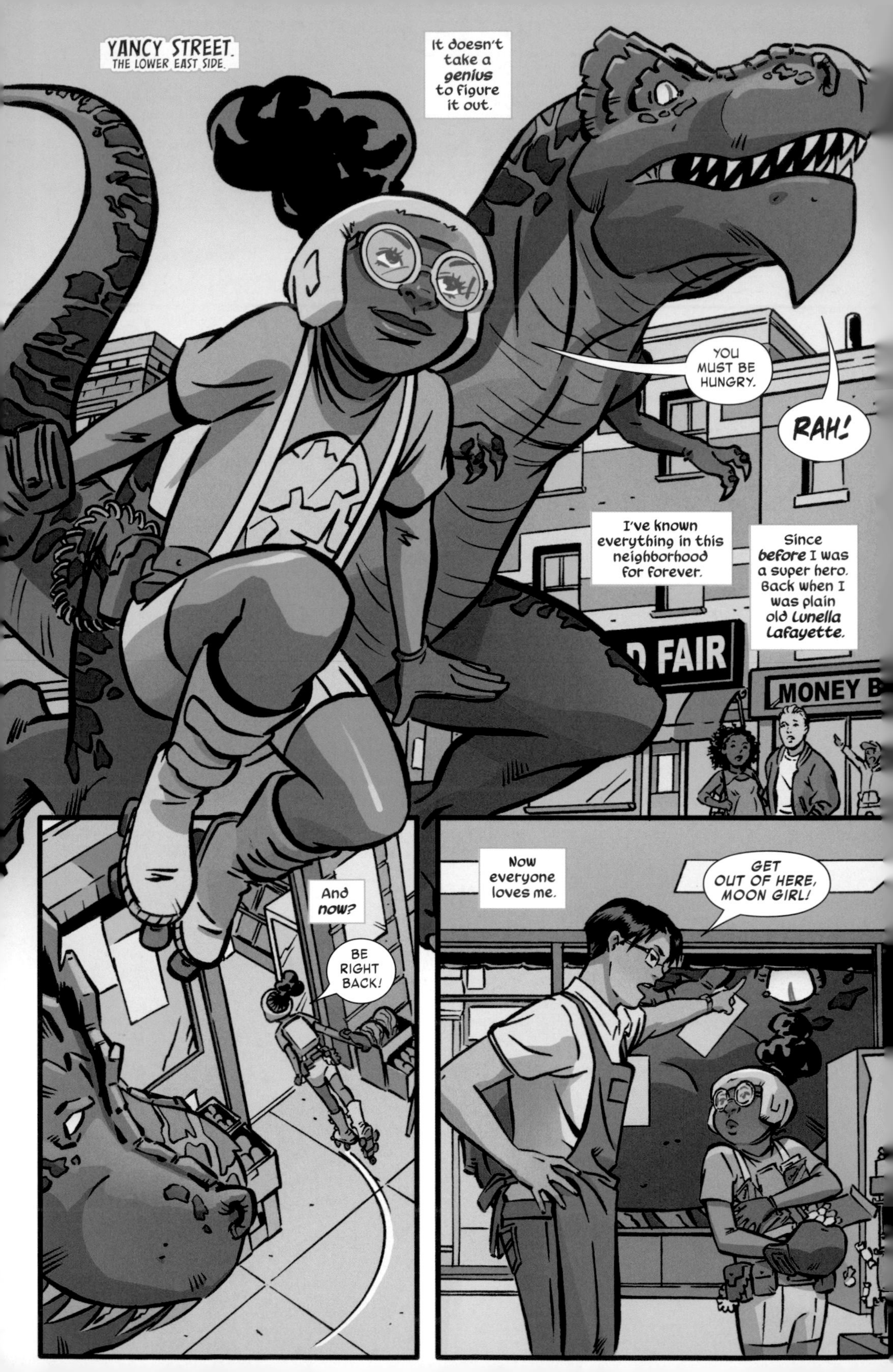

YANCY STREET. THE LOWER EAST SIDE.
It doesn't take a genius to figure it out.
YOU MUST BE HUNGRY.
RAH!
I've known everything in this neighborhood for forever.
Since before I was a super hero. Back when I was plain old Lunella Lafayette.
D FAIR
MONEY B
And now?
BE RIGHT BACK!
Now everyone loves me.
GET OUT OF HERE, MOON GIRL!

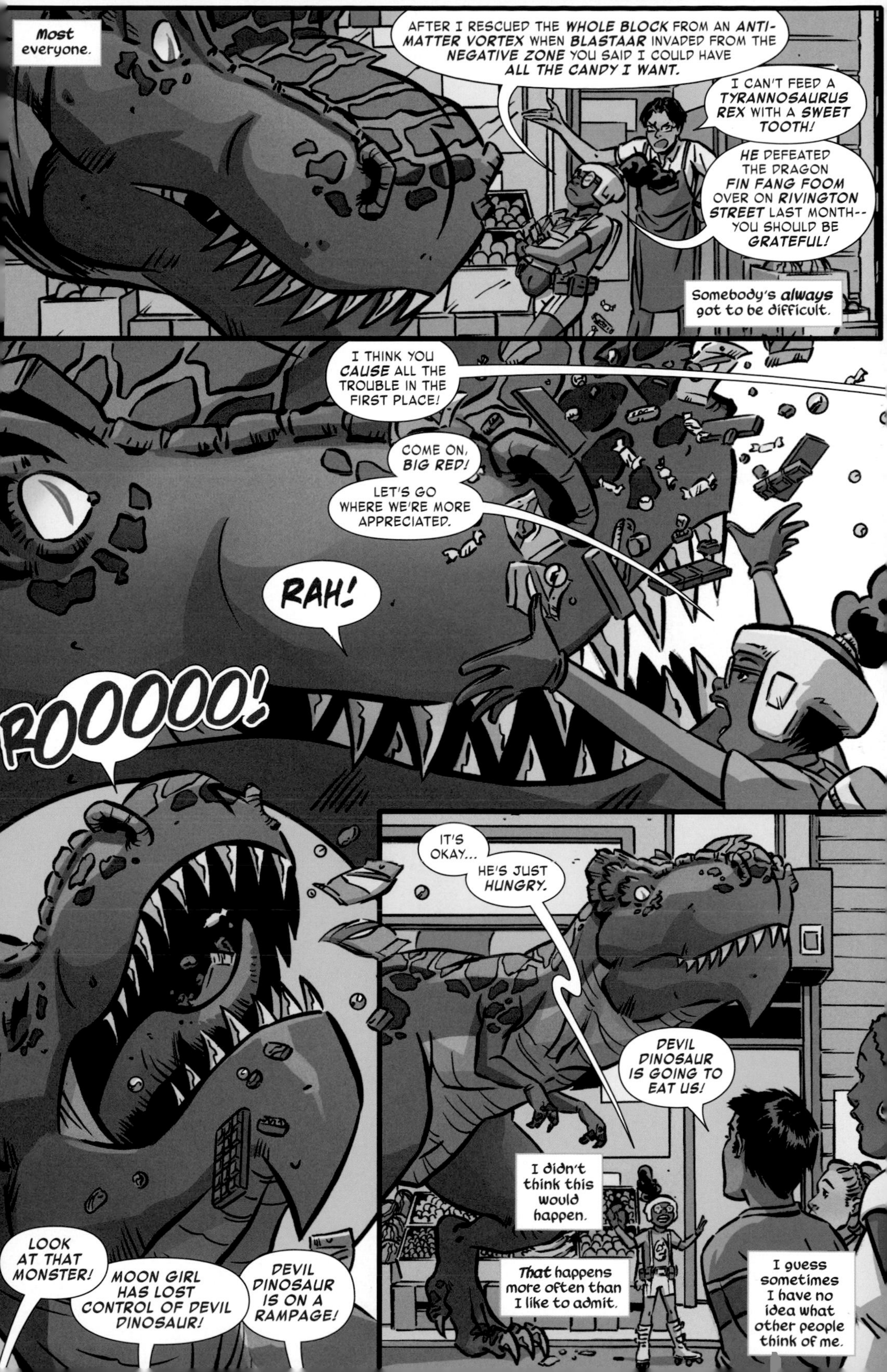

Most everyone.
AFTER I RESCUED THE WHOLE BLOCK FROM AN ANTI-MATTER VORTEX WHEN BLASTAAR INVADED FROM THE NEGATIVE ZONE YOU SAID I COULD HAVE ALL THE CANDY I WANT.
I CAN'T FEED A TYRANNOSAURUS REX WITH A SWEET TOOTH!
HE DEFEATED THE DRAGON FIN FANG FOOM OVER ON RIVINGTON STREET LAST MONTH--YOU SHOULD BE GRATEFUL!
Somebody's always got to be difficult.
I THINK YOU CAUSE ALL THE TROUBLE IN THE FIRST PLACE!
COME ON, BIG RED!
LET'S GO WHERE WE'RE MORE APPRECIATED.
RAH!
ROOOOOO!
LOOK AT THAT MONSTER!
MOON GIRL HAS LOST CONTROL OF DEVIL DINOSAUR!
DEVIL DINOSAUR IS ON A RAMPAGE!
IT'S OKAY...
HE'S JUST HUNGRY.
DEVIL DINOSAUR IS GOING TO EAT US!
I didn't think this would happen.
That happens more often than I like to admit.
I guess sometimes I have no idea what other people think of me.

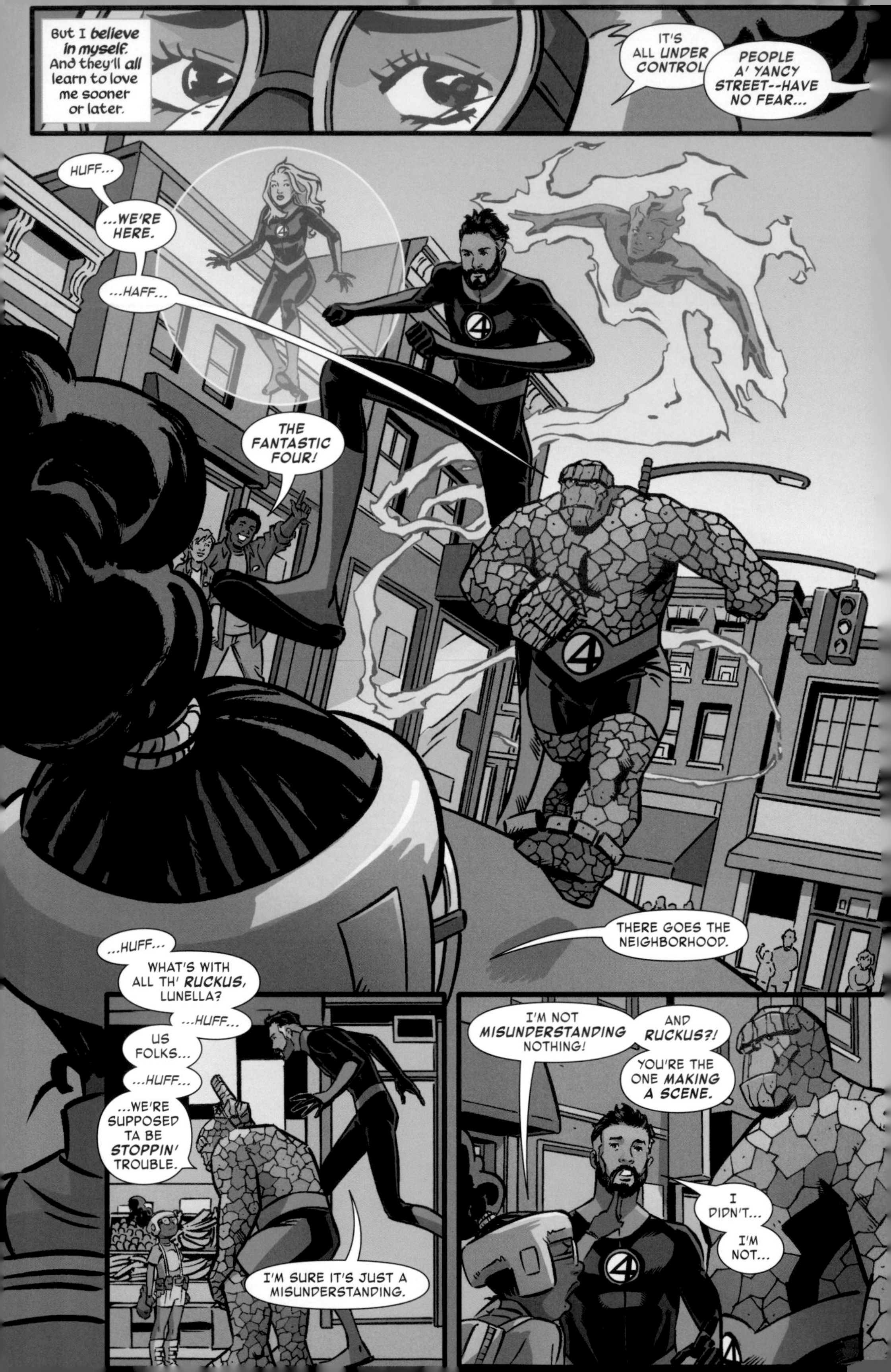
But I *believe in myself*. And they'll *all* learn to love me sooner or later.
IT'S ALL UNDER CONTROL
PEOPLE A' YANCY STREET--HAVE NO FEAR...
HUFF...
...WE'RE HERE.
...HAFF...
THE FANTASTIC FOUR!
THERE GOES THE NEIGHBORHOOD.
...HUFF...
WHAT'S WITH ALL TH' RUCKUS, LUNELLA?
...HUFF...
US FOLKS...
...HUFF...
...WE'RE SUPPOSED TA BE STOPPIN' TROUBLE.
I'M SURE IT'S JUST A MISUNDERSTANDING.
I'M NOT MISUNDERSTANDING NOTHING!
AND RUCKUS?!
YOU'RE THE ONE MAKING A SCENE.
I DIDN'T...
I'M NOT...

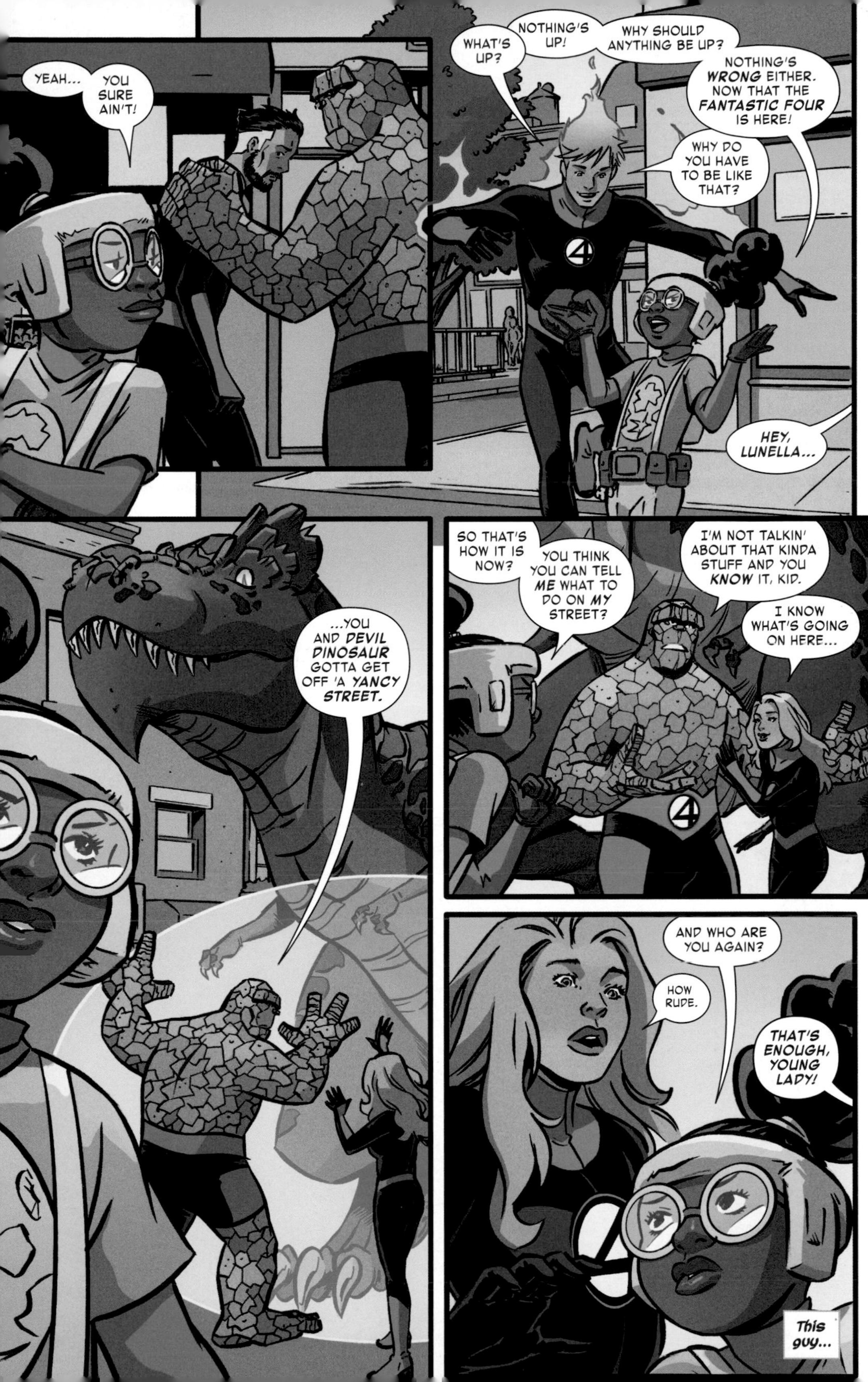
YEAH...
YOU SURE AIN'T!
WHAT'S UP?
NOTHING'S UP!
WHY SHOULD ANYTHING BE UP?
NOTHING'S WRONG EITHER. NOW THAT THE FANTASTIC FOUR IS HERE!
WHY DO YOU HAVE TO BE LIKE THAT?
HEY, LUNELLA...
...YOU AND DEVIL DINOSAUR GOTTA GET OFF 'A YANCY STREET.
SO THAT'S HOW IT IS NOW?
YOU THINK YOU CAN TELL ME WHAT TO DO ON MY STREET?
I'M NOT TALKIN' ABOUT THAT KINDA STUFF AND YOU KNOW IT, KID.
I KNOW WHAT'S GOING ON HERE...
AND WHO ARE YOU AGAIN?
HOW RUDE.
THAT'S ENOUGH, YOUNG LADY!
This guy...

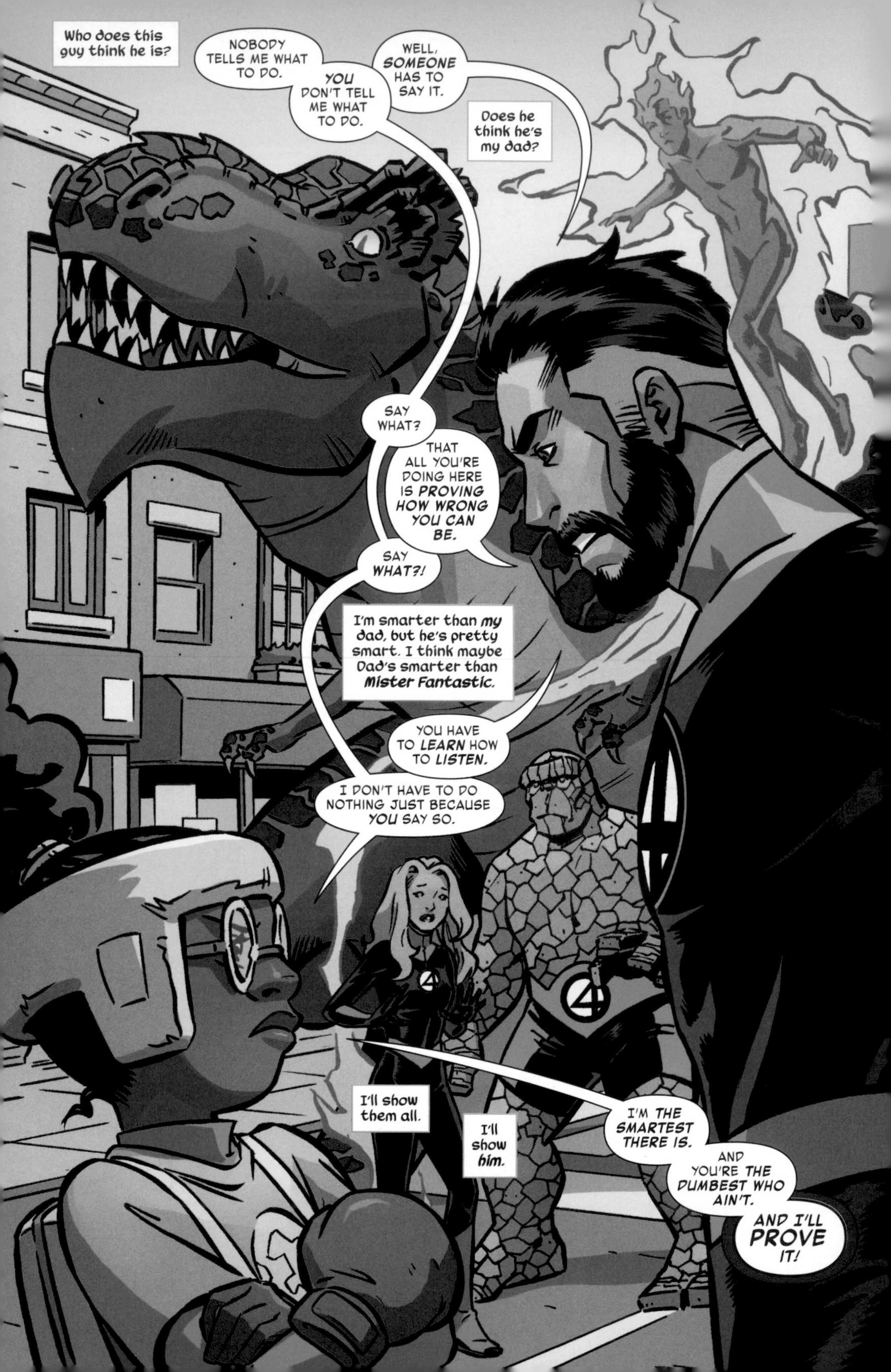
Who does this guy think he is?
NOBODY TELLS ME WHAT TO DO.
YOU DON'T TELL ME WHAT TO DO.
WELL, SOMEONE HAS TO SAY IT.
Does he think he's my dad?
SAY WHAT?
THAT ALL YOU'RE DOING HERE IS PROVING HOW WRONG YOU CAN BE.
SAY WHAT?!
I'm smarter than my dad, but he's pretty smart. I think maybe Dad's smarter than Mister Fantastic.
YOU HAVE TO LEARN HOW TO LISTEN.
I DON'T HAVE TO DO NOTHING JUST BECAUSE YOU SAY SO.
I'll show them all.
I'll show him.
I'M THE SMARTEST THERE IS.
AND YOU'RE THE DUMBEST WHO AIN'T.
AND I'LL PROVE IT!

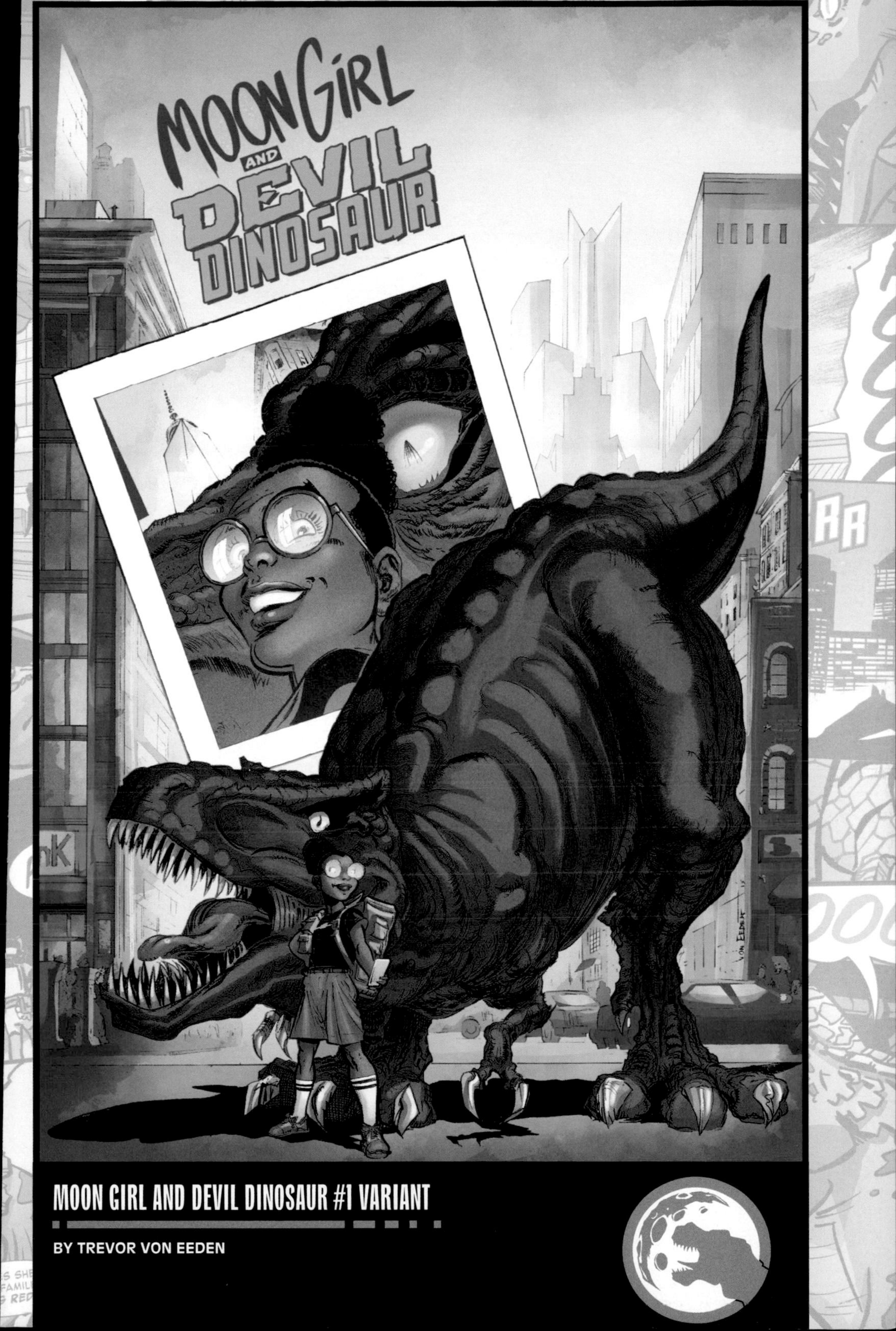
MOON GIRL AND DEVIL DINOSAUR

MOON GIRL AND DEVIL DINOSAUR #1 VARIANT

BY TREVOR VON EEDEN

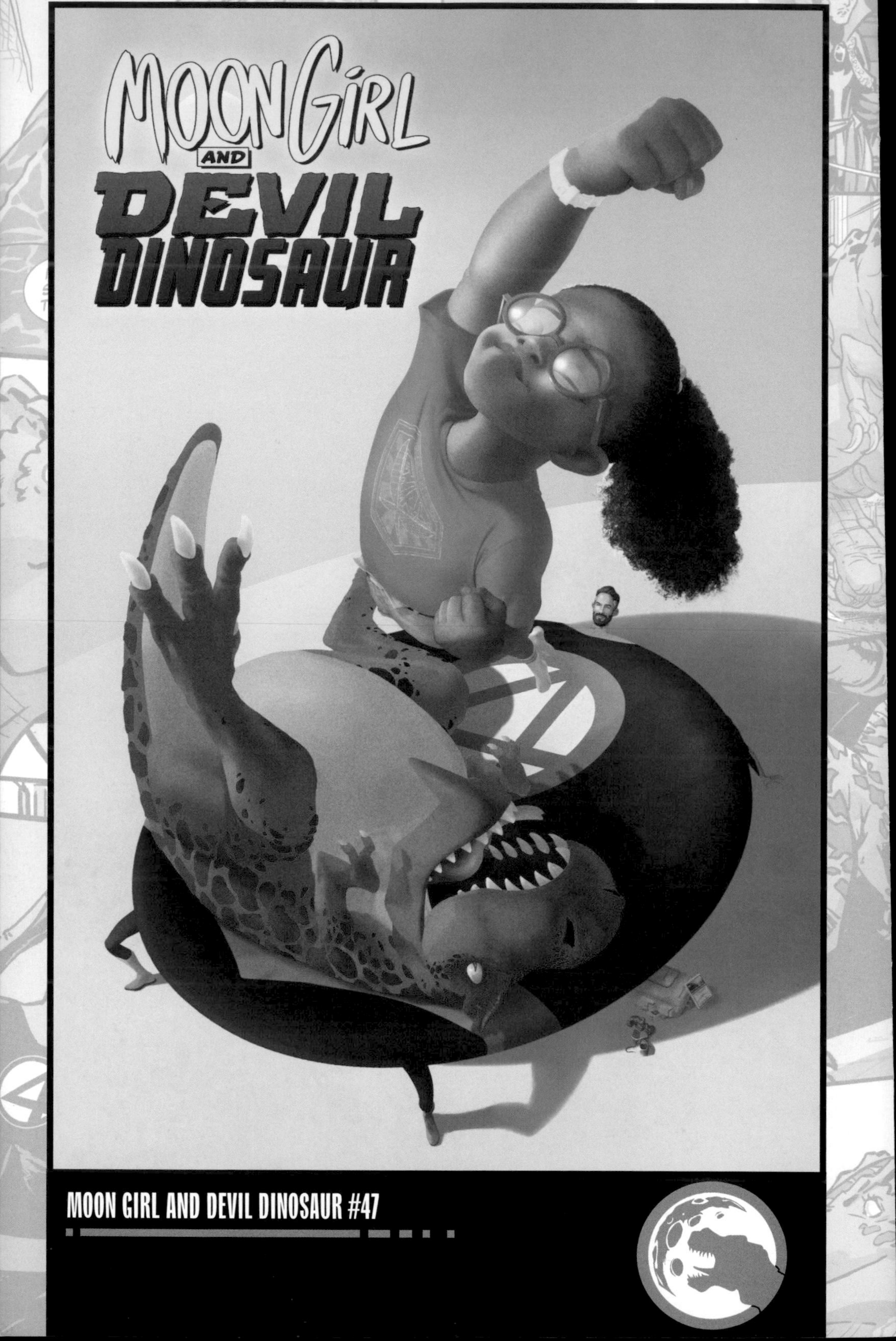
MOON GIRL
AND
DEVIL DINOSAUR

MOON GIRL AND DEVIL DINOSAUR #47

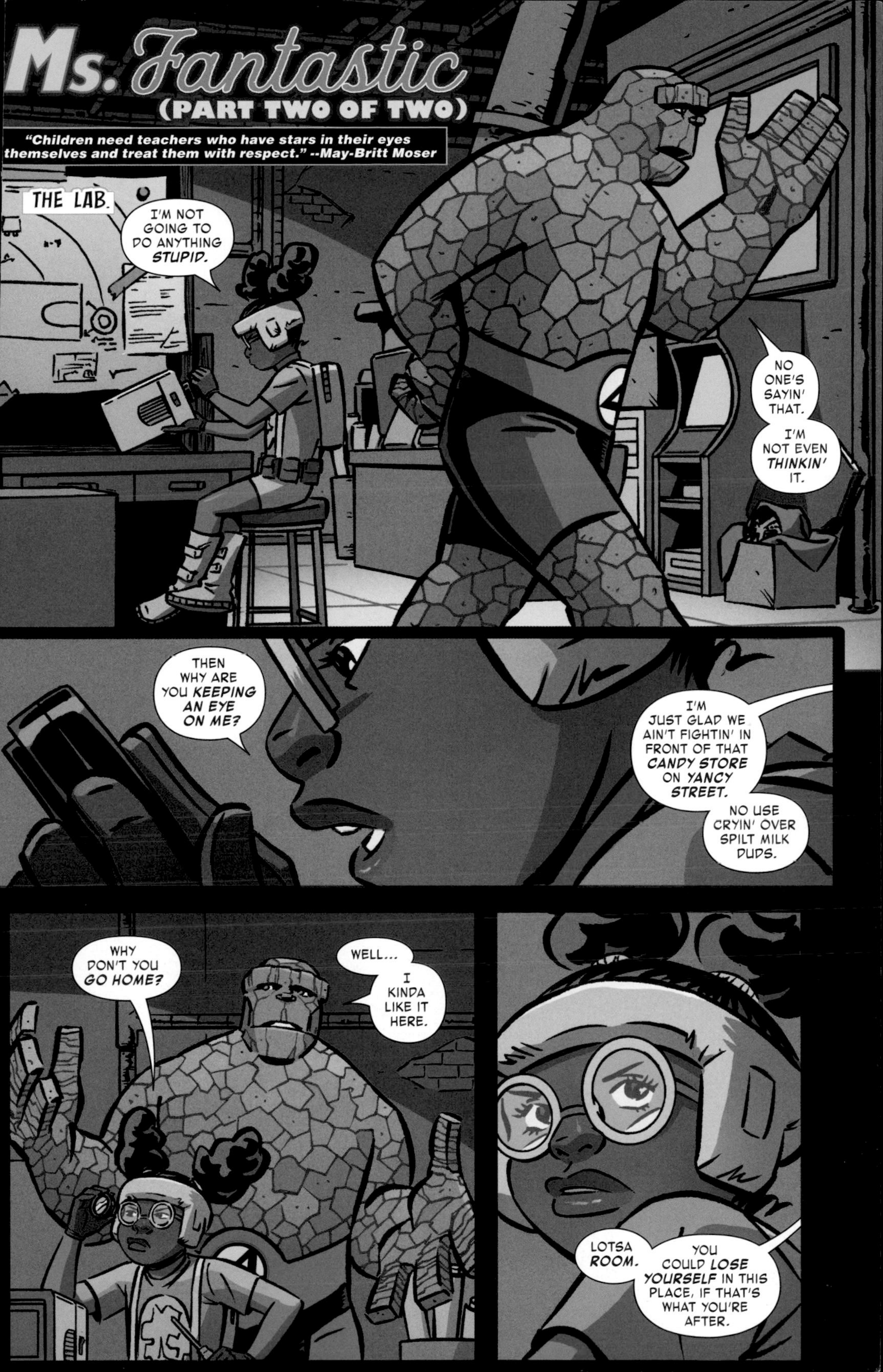
Ms. Fantastic
(PART TWO OF TWO)
"Children need teachers who have stars in their eyes themselves and treat them with respect." --May-Britt Moser
THE LAB.
I'M NOT GOING TO DO ANYTHING STUPID.
NO ONE'S SAYIN' THAT.
I'M NOT EVEN THINKIN' IT.
THEN WHY ARE YOU KEEPING AN EYE ON ME?
I'M JUST GLAD WE AIN'T FIGHTIN' IN FRONT OF THAT CANDY STORE ON YANCY STREET.
NO USE CRYIN' OVER SPILT MILK DUDS.
WHY DON'T YOU GO HOME?
WELL...
I KINDA LIKE IT HERE.
LOTSA ROOM.
YOU COULD LOSE YOURSELF IN THIS PLACE, IF THAT'S WHAT YOU'RE AFTER.

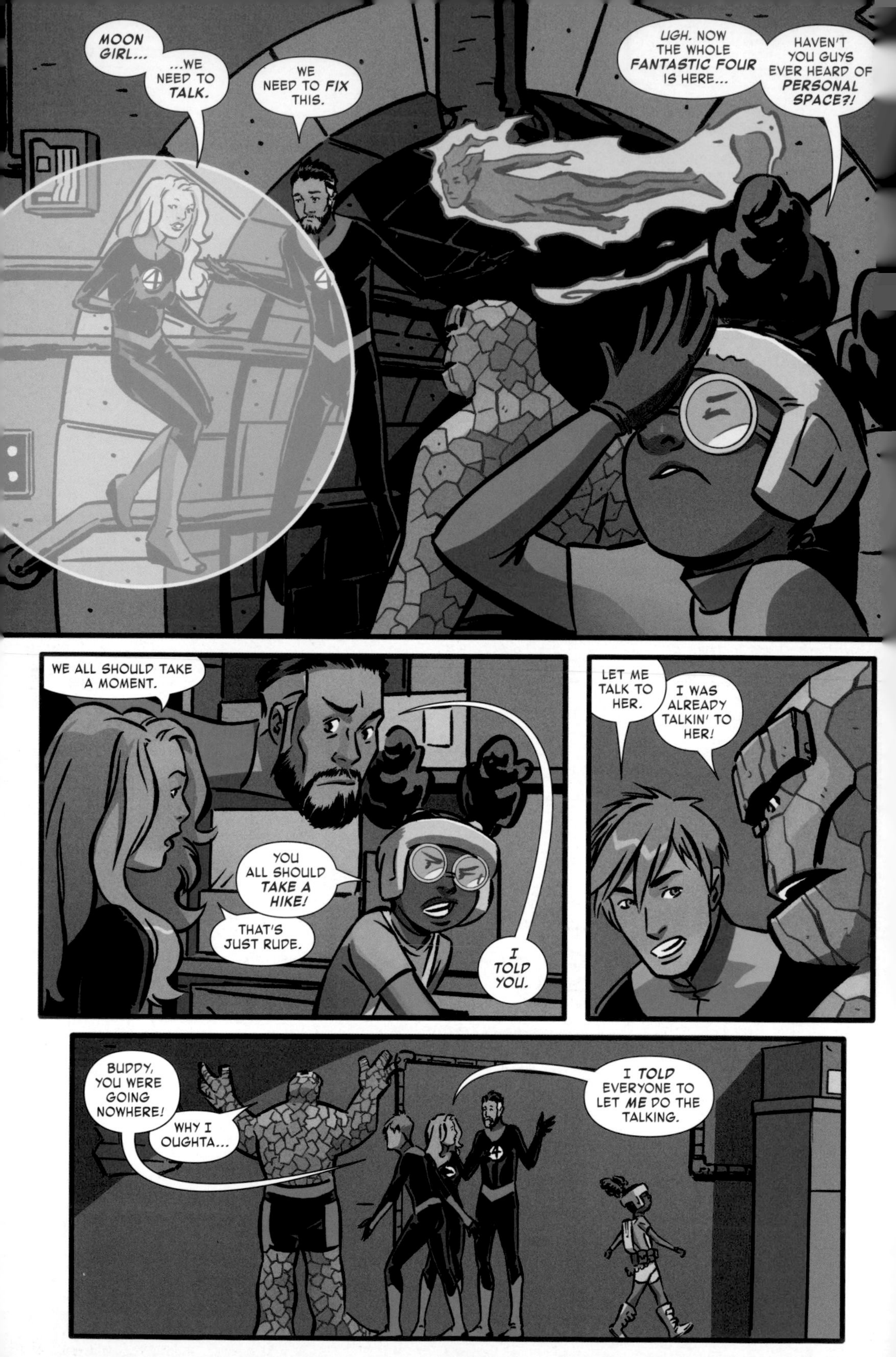
MOON GIRL...
...WE NEED TO TALK.
WE NEED TO FIX THIS.
UGH. NOW THE WHOLE FANTASTIC FOUR IS HERE...
HAVEN'T YOU GUYS EVER HEARD OF PERSONAL SPACE?!
WE ALL SHOULD TAKE A MOMENT.
YOU ALL SHOULD TAKE A HIKE!
THAT'S JUST RUDE.
I TOLD YOU.
LET ME TALK TO HER.
I WAS ALREADY TALKIN' TO HER!
BUDDY, YOU WERE GOING NOWHERE!
WHY I OUGHTA...
I TOLD EVERYONE TO LET ME DO THE TALKING.

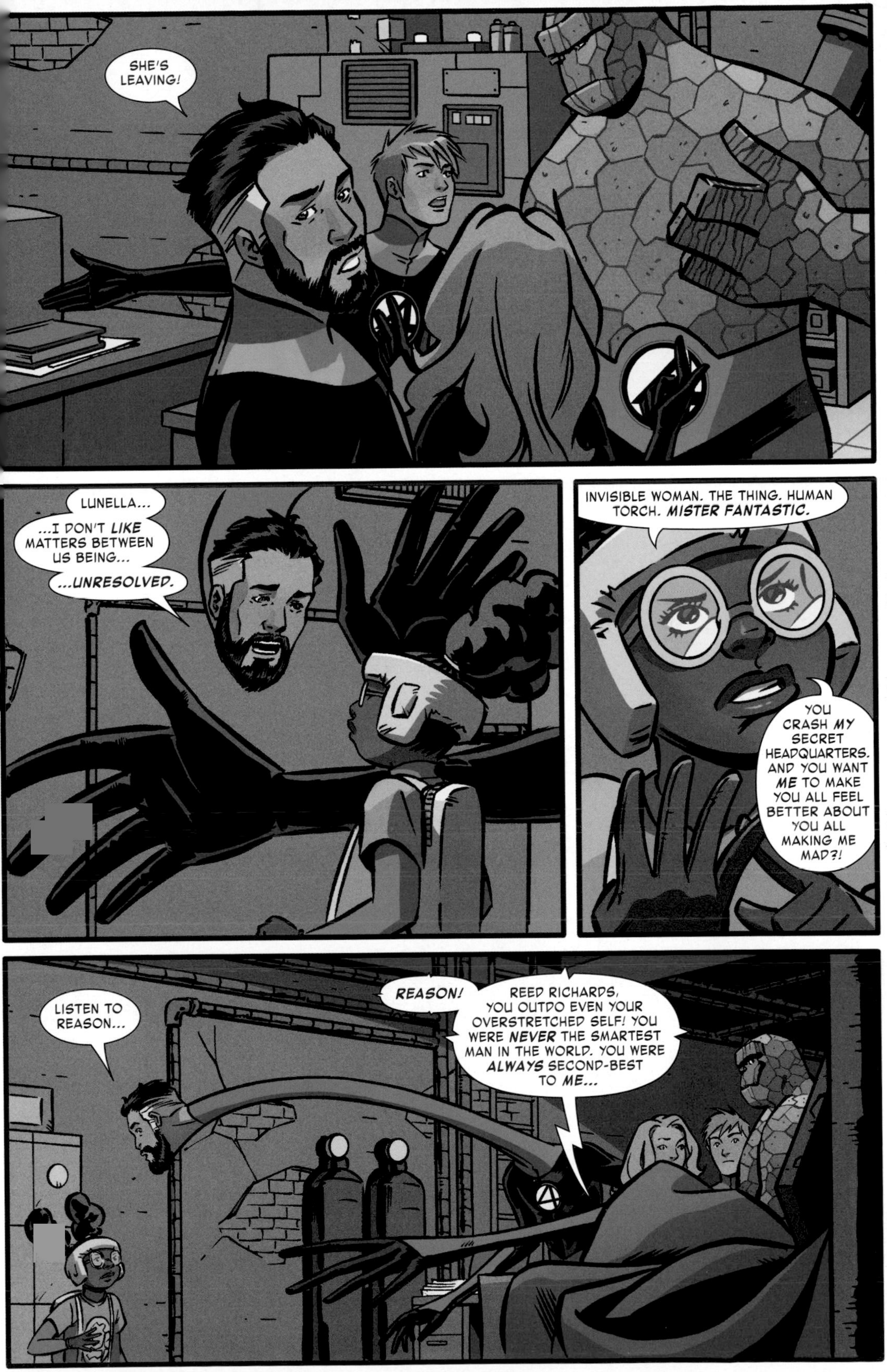
SHE'S LEAVING!
LUNELLA...
...I DON'T LIKE MATTERS BETWEEN US BEING...
...UNRESOLVED.
INVISIBLE WOMAN. THE THING. HUMAN TORCH. MISTER FANTASTIC.
YOU CRASH MY SECRET HEADQUARTERS. AND YOU WANT ME TO MAKE YOU ALL FEEL BETTER ABOUT YOU ALL MAKING ME MAD?!
LISTEN TO REASON...
REASON!
REED RICHARDS, YOU OUTDO EVEN YOUR OVERSTRETCHED SELF! YOU WERE NEVER THE SMARTEST MAN IN THE WORLD. YOU WERE ALWAYS SECOND-BEST TO ME...

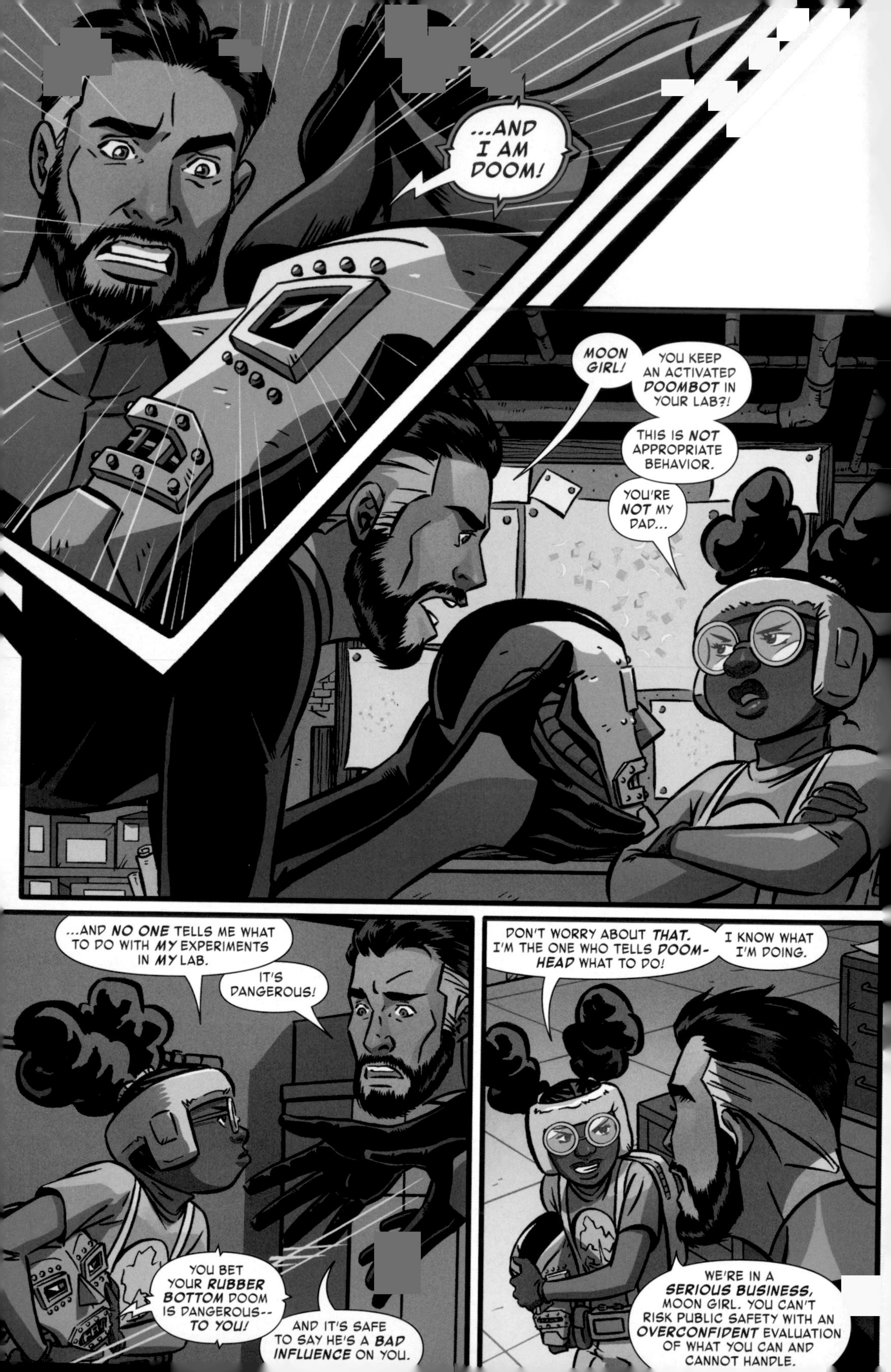

...AND I AM DOOM!
MOON GIRL!
YOU KEEP AN ACTIVATED DOOMBOT IN YOUR LAB?!
THIS IS NOT APPROPRIATE BEHAVIOR.
YOU'RE NOT MY DAD...
...AND NO ONE TELLS ME WHAT TO DO WITH MY EXPERIMENTS IN MY LAB.
IT'S DANGEROUS!
YOU BET YOUR RUBBER BOTTOM DOOM IS DANGEROUS-- TO YOU!
AND IT'S SAFE TO SAY HE'S A BAD INFLUENCE ON YOU.
DON'T WORRY ABOUT THAT. I'M THE ONE WHO TELLS DOOM-HEAD WHAT TO DO!
I KNOW WHAT I'M DOING.
WE'RE IN A SERIOUS BUSINESS, MOON GIRL. YOU CAN'T RISK PUBLIC SAFETY WITH AN OVERCONFIDENT EVALUATION OF WHAT YOU CAN AND CANNOT HANDLE.

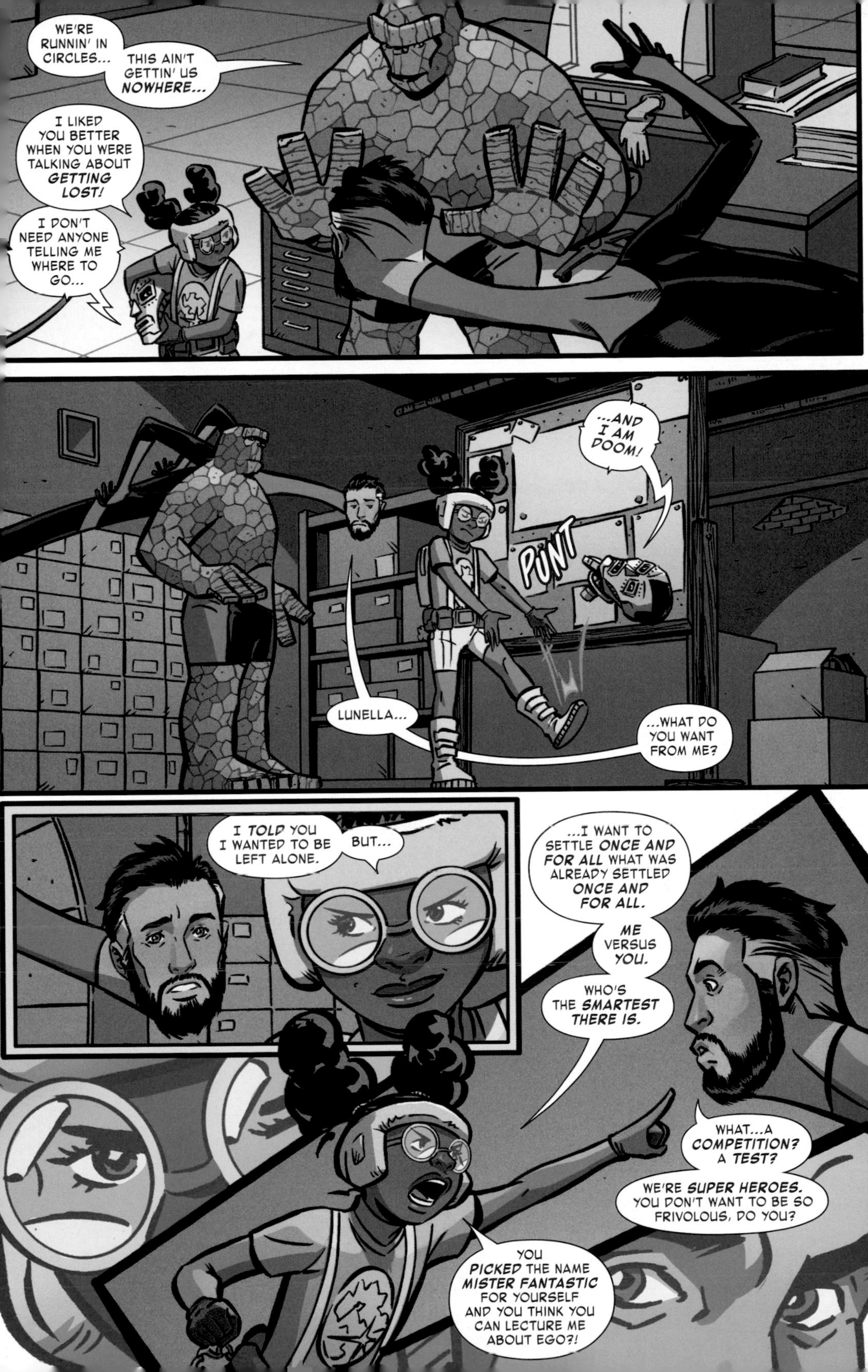
WE'RE RUNNIN' IN CIRCLES...
THIS AIN'T GETTIN' US NOWHERE...
I LIKED YOU BETTER WHEN YOU WERE TALKING ABOUT GETTING LOST!
I DON'T NEED ANYONE TELLING ME WHERE TO GO...
...AND I AM DOOM!
PUNT
LUNELLA...
...WHAT DO YOU WANT FROM ME?
I TOLD YOU I WANTED TO BE LEFT ALONE.
BUT...
...I WANT TO SETTLE ONCE AND FOR ALL WHAT WAS ALREADY SETTLED ONCE AND FOR ALL.
ME VERSUS YOU.
WHO'S THE SMARTEST THERE IS.
WHAT...A COMPETITION? A TEST?
WE'RE SUPER HEROES. YOU DON'T WANT TO BE SO FRIVOLOUS, DO YOU?
YOU PICKED THE NAME MISTER FANTASTIC FOR YOURSELF AND YOU THINK YOU CAN LECTURE ME ABOUT EGO?!

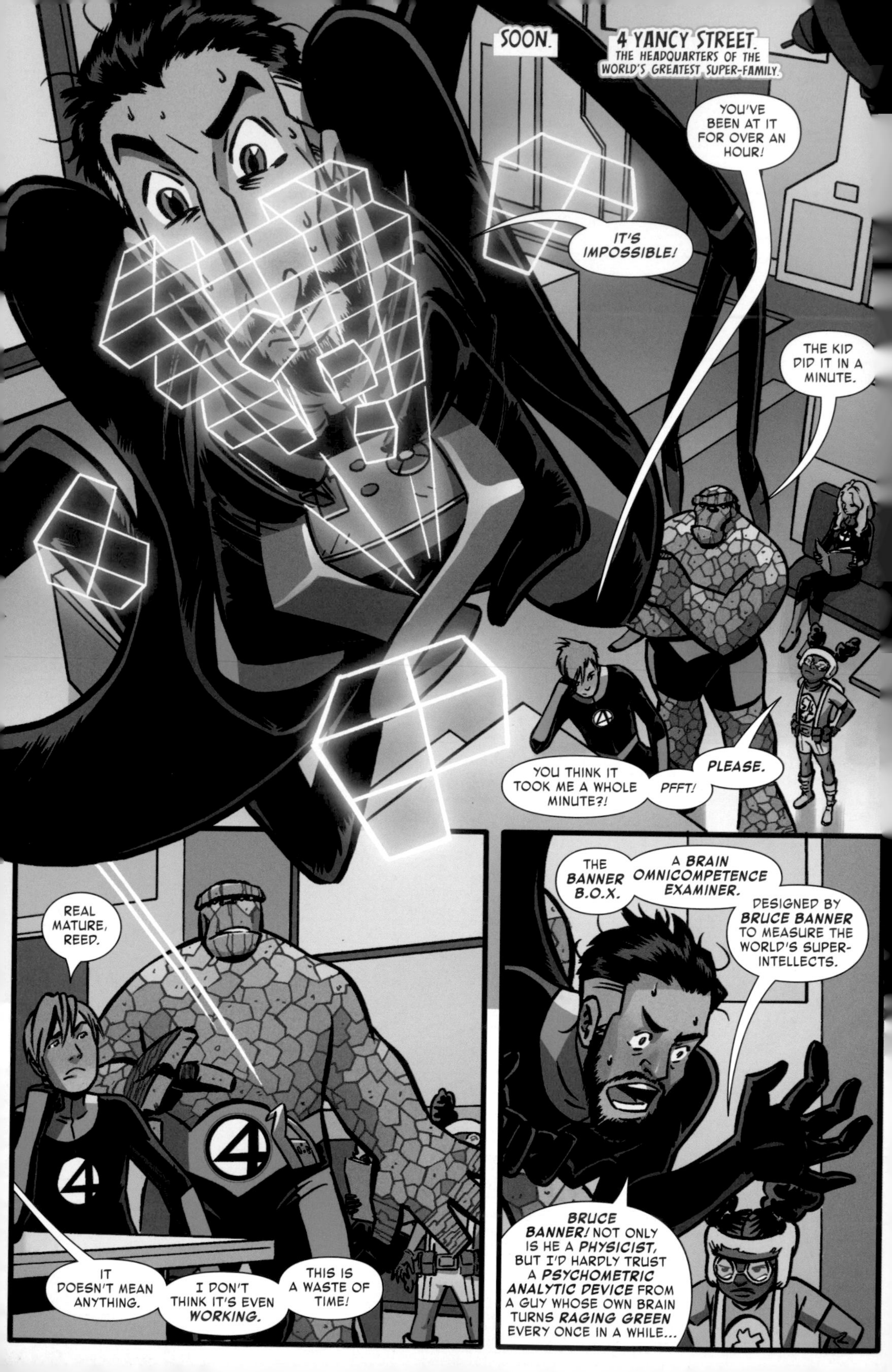
SOON.
4 YANCY STREET.
THE HEADQUARTERS OF THE WORLD'S GREATEST SUPER-FAMILY.
YOU'VE BEEN AT IT FOR OVER AN HOUR!
IT'S IMPOSSIBLE!
THE KID DID IT IN A MINUTE.
YOU THINK IT TOOK ME A WHOLE MINUTE?!
PFFT!
PLEASE.
REAL MATURE, REED.
IT DOESN'T MEAN ANYTHING.
I DON'T THINK IT'S EVEN WORKING.
THIS IS A WASTE OF TIME!
THE BANNER B.O.X.
A BRAIN OMNICOMPETENCE EXAMINER.
DESIGNED BY BRUCE BANNER TO MEASURE THE WORLD'S SUPER-INTELLECTS.
BRUCE BANNER! NOT ONLY IS HE A PHYSICIST, BUT I'D HARDLY TRUST A PSYCHOMETRIC ANALYTIC DEVICE FROM A GUY WHOSE OWN BRAIN TURNS RAGING GREEN EVERY ONCE IN A WHILE...

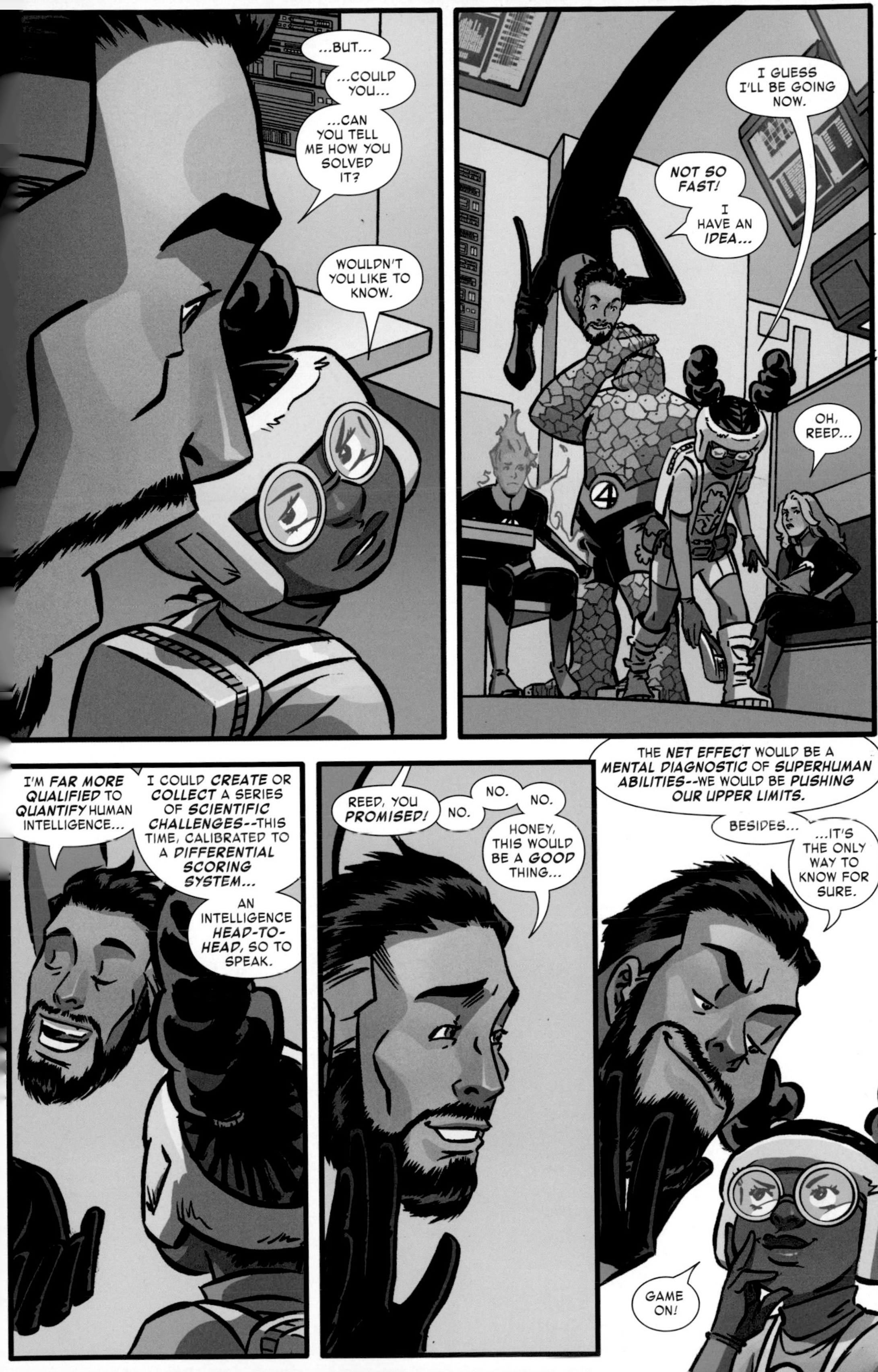
...BUT...
...COULD YOU...
...CAN YOU TELL ME HOW YOU SOLVED IT?
WOULDN'T YOU LIKE TO KNOW.
I GUESS I'LL BE GOING NOW.
NOT SO FAST!
I HAVE AN IDEA...
OH, REED...
I'M FAR MORE QUALIFIED TO QUANTIFY HUMAN INTELLIGENCE...
I COULD CREATE OR COLLECT A SERIES OF SCIENTIFIC CHALLENGES--THIS TIME, CALIBRATED TO A DIFFERENTIAL SCORING SYSTEM...
AN INTELLIGENCE HEAD-TO-HEAD, SO TO SPEAK.
REED, YOU PROMISED!
NO.
NO.
NO.
HONEY, THIS WOULD BE A GOOD THING...
THE NET EFFECT WOULD BE A MENTAL DIAGNOSTIC OF SUPERHUMAN ABILITIES--WE WOULD BE PUSHING OUR UPPER LIMITS.
BESIDES...
...IT'S THE ONLY WAY TO KNOW FOR SURE.
GAME ON!

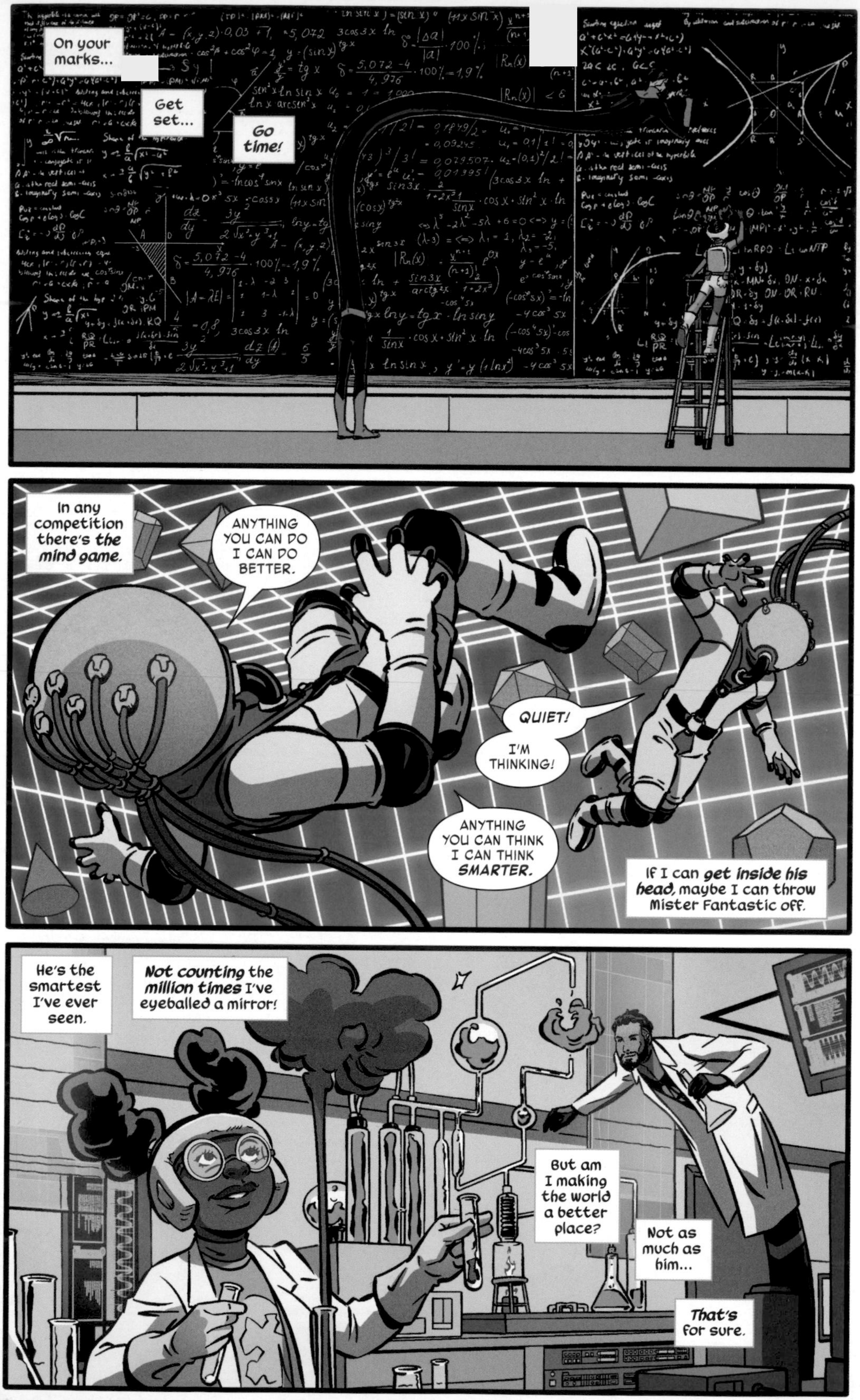
On your marks...
Get set...
Go time!
In any competition there's the mind game.
ANYTHING YOU CAN DO I CAN DO BETTER.
QUIET!
I'M THINKING!
ANYTHING YOU CAN THINK I CAN THINK SMARTER.
If I can get inside his head, maybe I can throw Mister Fantastic off.
He's the smartest I've ever seen.
Not counting the million times I've eyeballed a mirror!
But am I making the world a better place?
Not as much as him...
That's for sure.

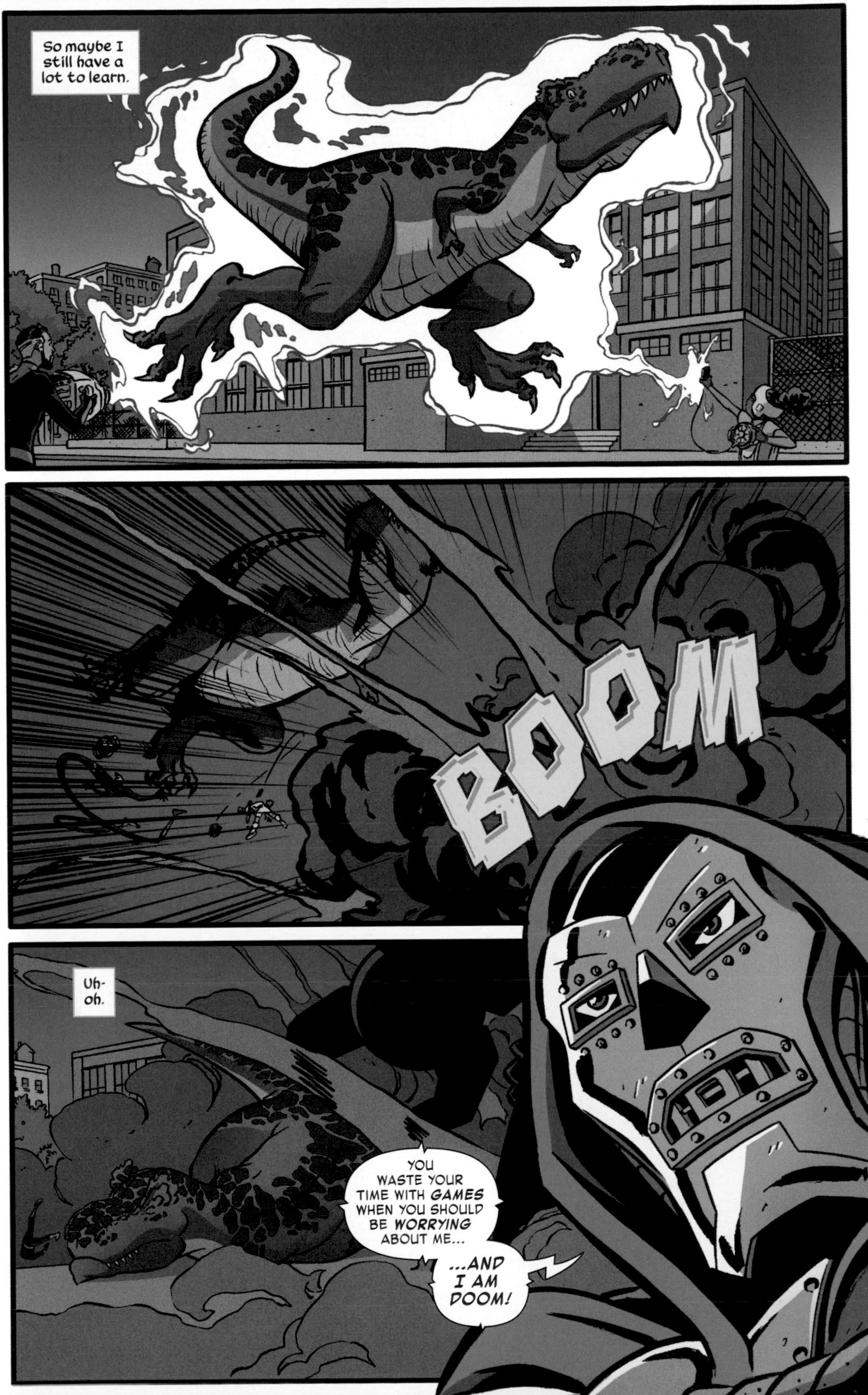
So maybe I still have a lot to learn.
BOOM
Uh-oh.
YOU WASTE YOUR TIME WITH GAMES WHEN YOU SHOULD BE WORRYING ABOUT ME...
...AND I AM DOOM!

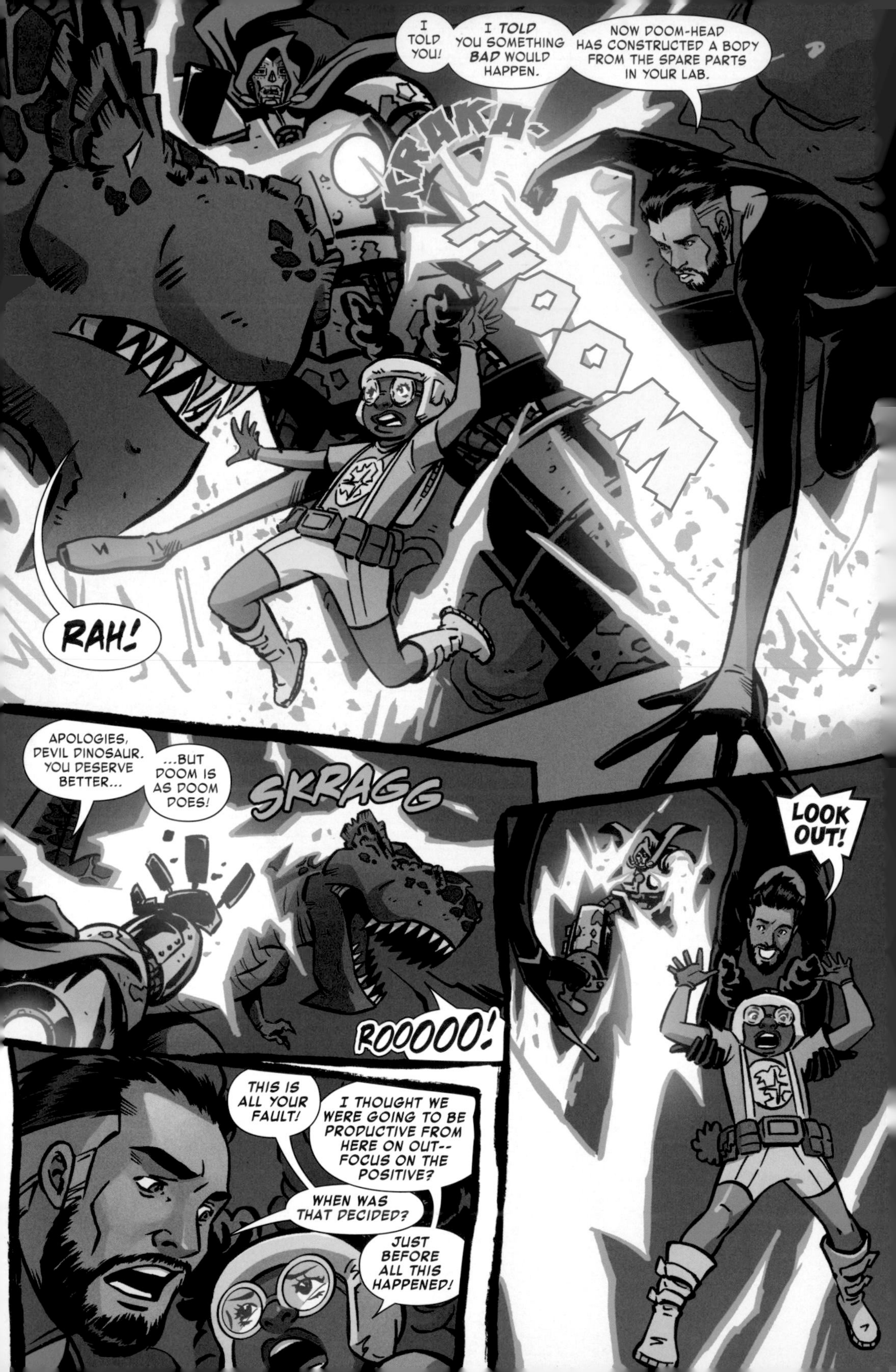
I TOLD YOU!
I *TOLD* YOU SOMETHING *BAD* WOULD HAPPEN.
NOW DOOM-HEAD HAS CONSTRUCTED A BODY FROM THE SPARE PARTS IN YOUR LAB.
KRAKA-THOOOM
RAH!
APOLOGIES, DEVIL DINOSAUR. YOU DESERVE BETTER...
...BUT DOOM IS AS DOOM DOES!
SKRAGG
ROOOOO!
LOOK OUT!
THIS IS ALL YOUR FAULT!
I THOUGHT WE WERE GOING TO BE PRODUCTIVE FROM HERE ON OUT--FOCUS ON THE POSITIVE?
WHEN WAS THAT DECIDED?
JUST BEFORE ALL THIS HAPPENED!

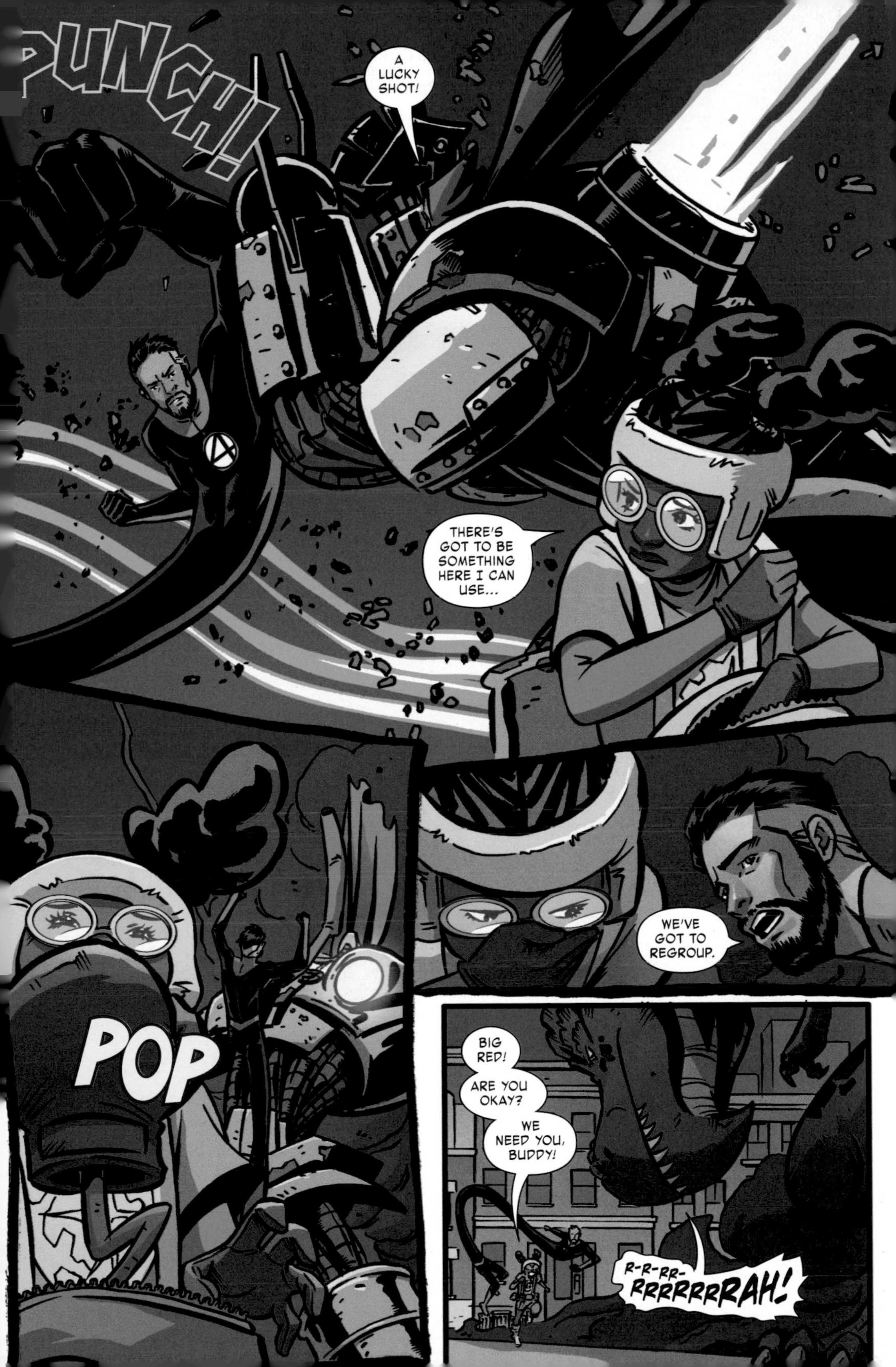
PUNCH!
A LUCKY SHOT!
THERE'S GOT TO BE SOMETHING HERE I CAN USE...
POP
WE'VE GOT TO REGROUP.
BIG RED!
ARE YOU OKAY?
WE NEED YOU, BUDDY!
R-R-RR-RRRRRRRAH!

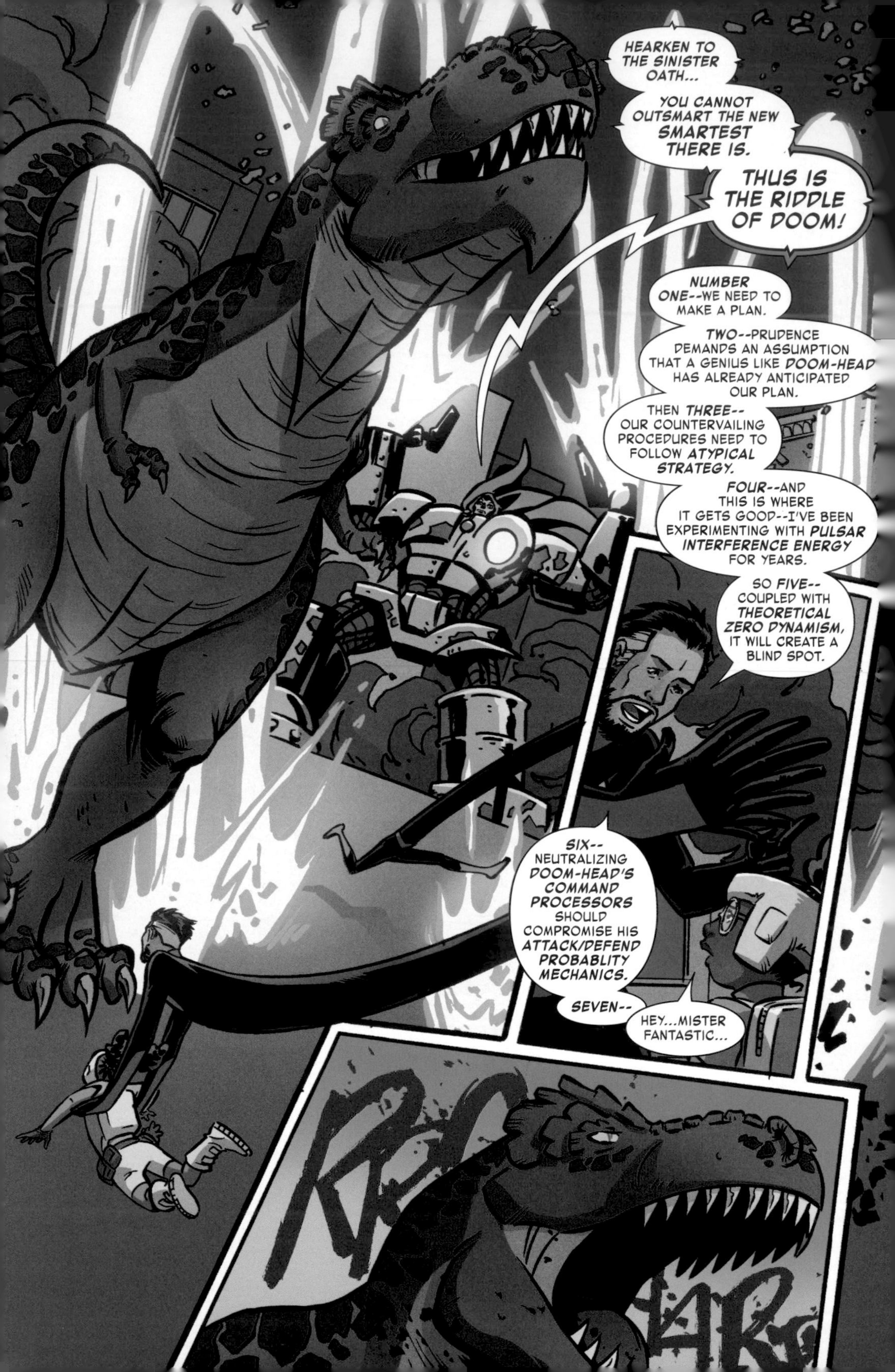
HEARKEN TO THE SINISTER OATH...
YOU CANNOT OUTSMART THE NEW SMARTEST THERE IS.
THUS IS THE RIDDLE OF DOOM!
NUMBER ONE--WE NEED TO MAKE A PLAN.
TWO--PRUDENCE DEMANDS AN ASSUMPTION THAT A GENIUS LIKE DOOM-HEAD HAS ALREADY ANTICIPATED OUR PLAN.
THEN THREE--OUR COUNTERVAILING PROCEDURES NEED TO FOLLOW ATYPICAL STRATEGY.
FOUR--AND THIS IS WHERE IT GETS GOOD--I'VE BEEN EXPERIMENTING WITH PULSAR INTERFERENCE ENERGY FOR YEARS.
SO FIVE--COUPLED WITH THEORETICAL ZERO DYNAMISM, IT WILL CREATE A BLIND SPOT.
SIX--NEUTRALIZING DOOM-HEAD'S COMMAND PROCESSORS SHOULD COMPROMISE HIS ATTACK/DEFEND PROBABLITY MECHANICS.
SEVEN--
HEY...MISTER FANTASTIC...

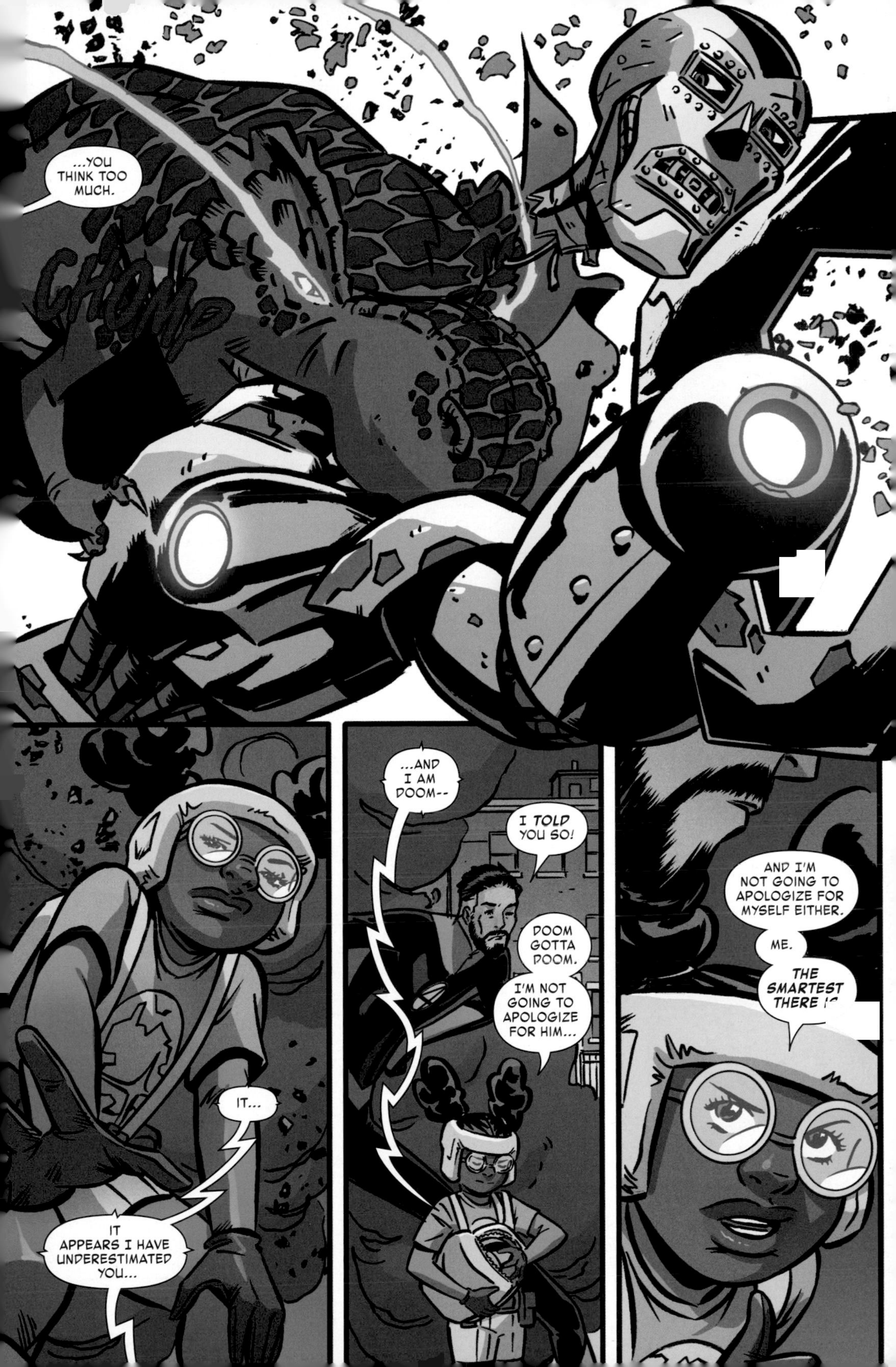

...YOU THINK TOO MUCH.
CHOMP
IT...
IT APPEARS I HAVE UNDERESTIMATED YOU...
...AND I AM DOOM--
I *TOLD* YOU SO!
DOOM GOTTA DOOM.
I'M NOT GOING TO APOLOGIZE FOR HIM...
AND I'M NOT GOING TO APOLOGIZE FOR MYSELF EITHER.
ME.
THE SMARTEST THERE IS

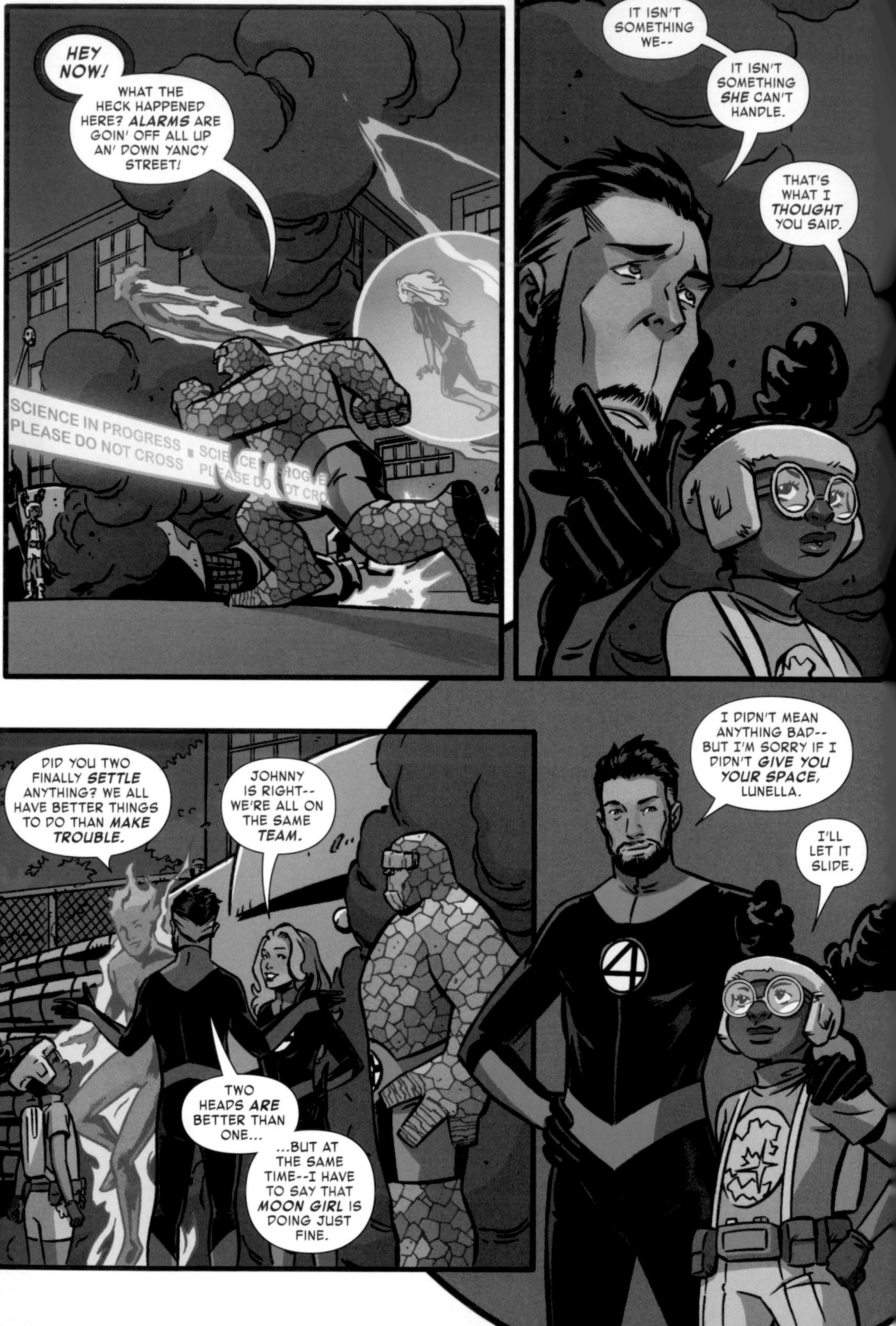
HEY NOW!
WHAT THE HECK HAPPENED HERE? ALARMS ARE GOIN' OFF ALL UP AN' DOWN YANCY STREET!
SCIENCE IN PROGRESS PLEASE DO NOT CROSS
IT ISN'T SOMETHING WE--
IT ISN'T SOMETHING SHE CAN'T HANDLE.
THAT'S WHAT I THOUGHT YOU SAID.
DID YOU TWO FINALLY SETTLE ANYTHING? WE ALL HAVE BETTER THINGS TO DO THAN MAKE TROUBLE.
JOHNNY IS RIGHT--WE'RE ALL ON THE SAME TEAM.
TWO HEADS ARE BETTER THAN ONE...
...BUT AT THE SAME TIME--I HAVE TO SAY THAT MOON GIRL IS DOING JUST FINE.
I DIDN'T MEAN ANYTHING BAD--BUT I'M SORRY IF I DIDN'T GIVE YOU YOUR SPACE, LUNELLA.
I'LL LET IT SLIDE.

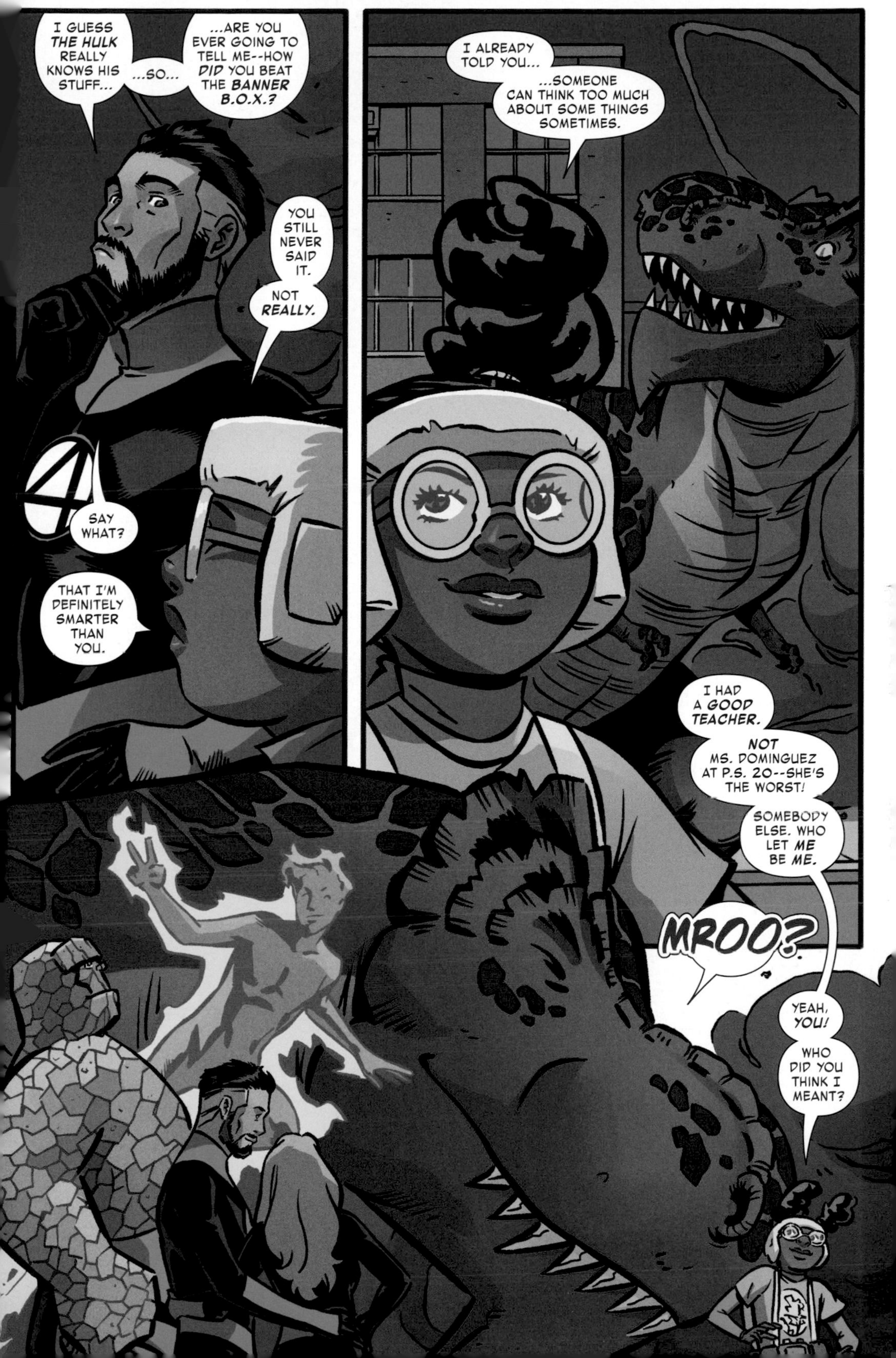
I GUESS THE HULK REALLY KNOWS HIS STUFF...
...SO...
...ARE YOU EVER GOING TO TELL ME--HOW DID YOU BEAT THE BANNER B.O.X.?
YOU STILL NEVER SAID IT.
NOT REALLY.
SAY WHAT?
THAT I'M DEFINITELY SMARTER THAN YOU.
I ALREADY TOLD YOU...
...SOMEONE CAN THINK TOO MUCH ABOUT SOME THINGS SOMETIMES.
I HAD A GOOD TEACHER.
NOT MS. DOMINGUEZ AT P.S. 20--SHE'S THE WORST!
SOMEBODY ELSE. WHO LET ME BE ME.
MROO?
YEAH, YOU!
WHO DID YOU THINK I MEANT?

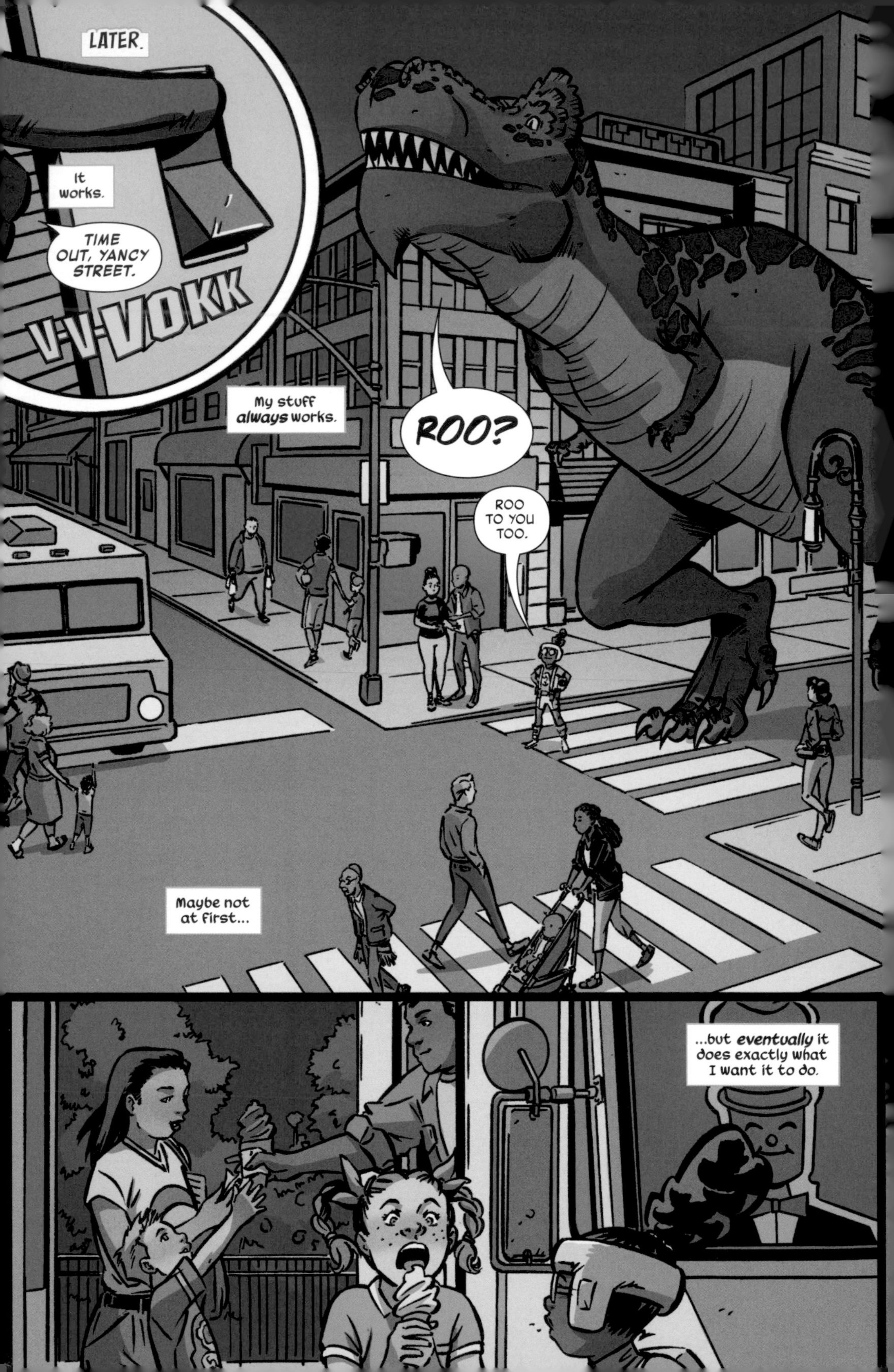
LATER.
It works.
TIME OUT, YANCY STREET.
V-V-VOKK
My stuff *always* works.
ROO?
ROO TO YOU TOO.
Maybe not at first...
...but *eventually* it does exactly what I want it to do.

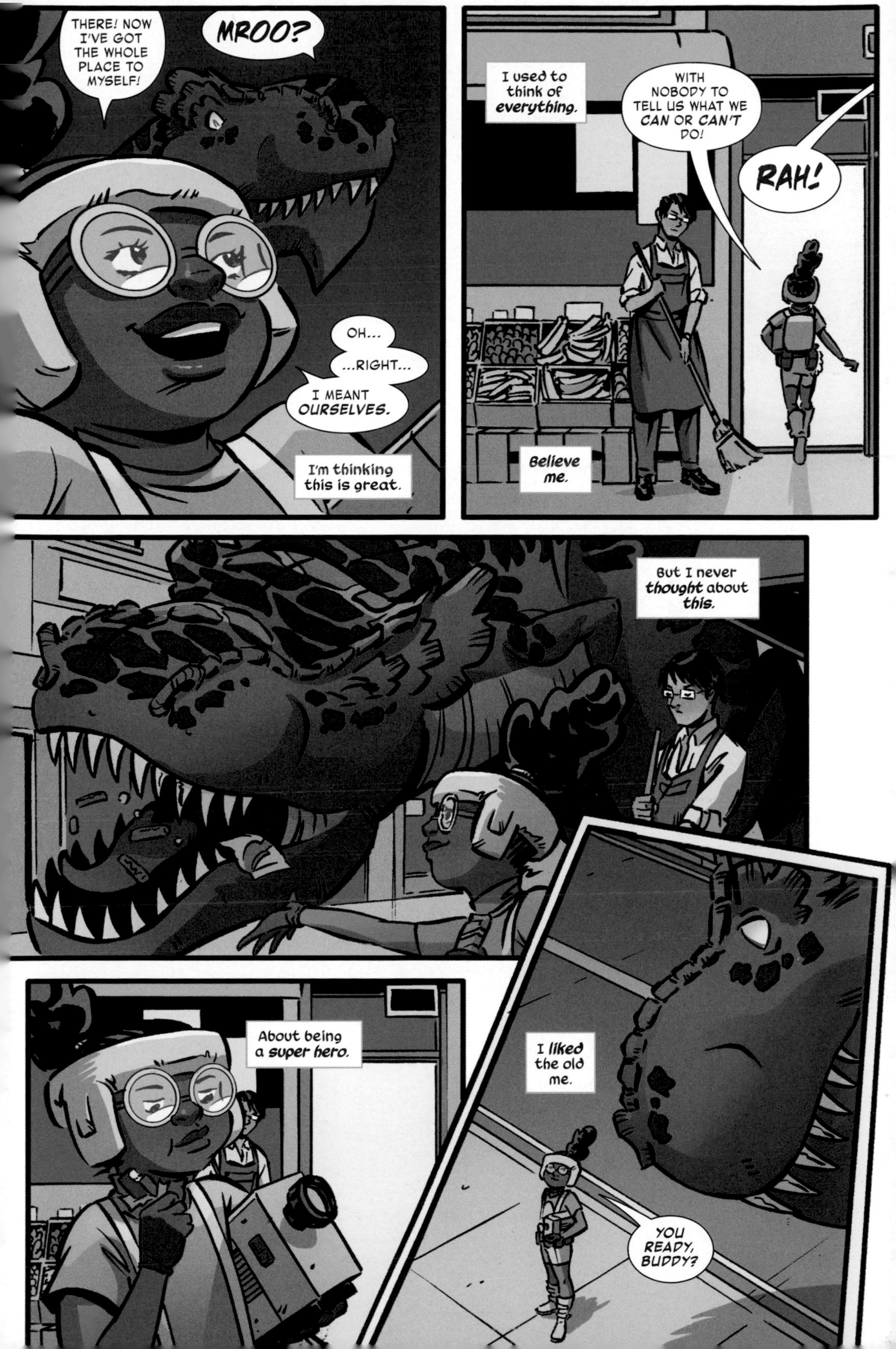

THERE! NOW I'VE GOT THE WHOLE PLACE TO MYSELF!
MROO?
OH...
...RIGHT...
I MEANT OURSELVES.
I'm thinking this is great.
I used to think of everything.
WITH NOBODY TO TELL US WHAT WE CAN OR CAN'T DO!
RAH!
Believe me.
But I never thought about this.
About being a super hero.
I liked the old me.
YOU READY, BUDDY?

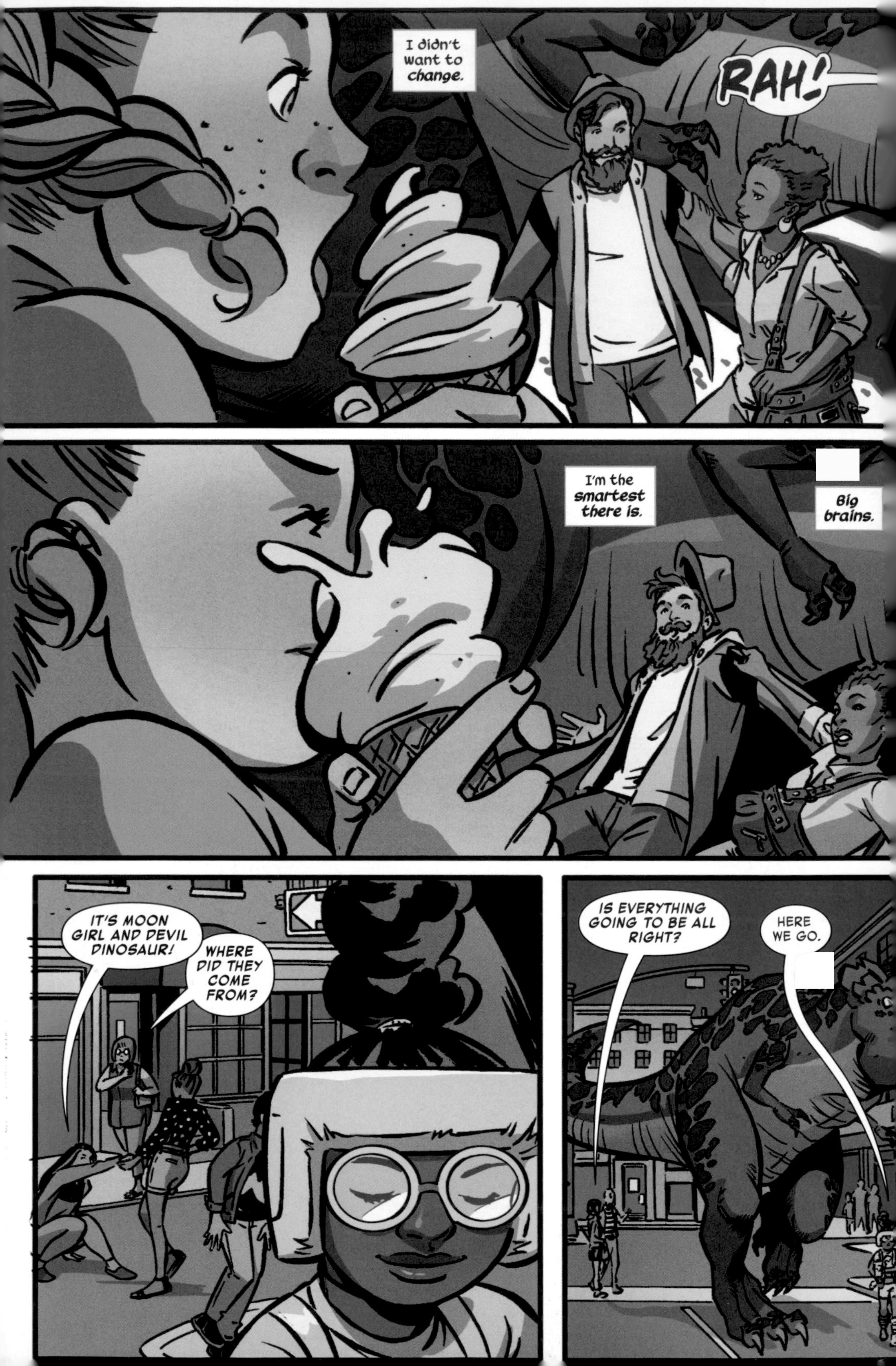
I didn't want to change.
RAH!
I'm the smartest there is.
Big brains.
IT'S MOON GIRL AND DEVIL DINOSAUR!
WHERE DID THEY COME FROM?
IS EVERYTHING GOING TO BE ALL RIGHT?
HERE WE GO.

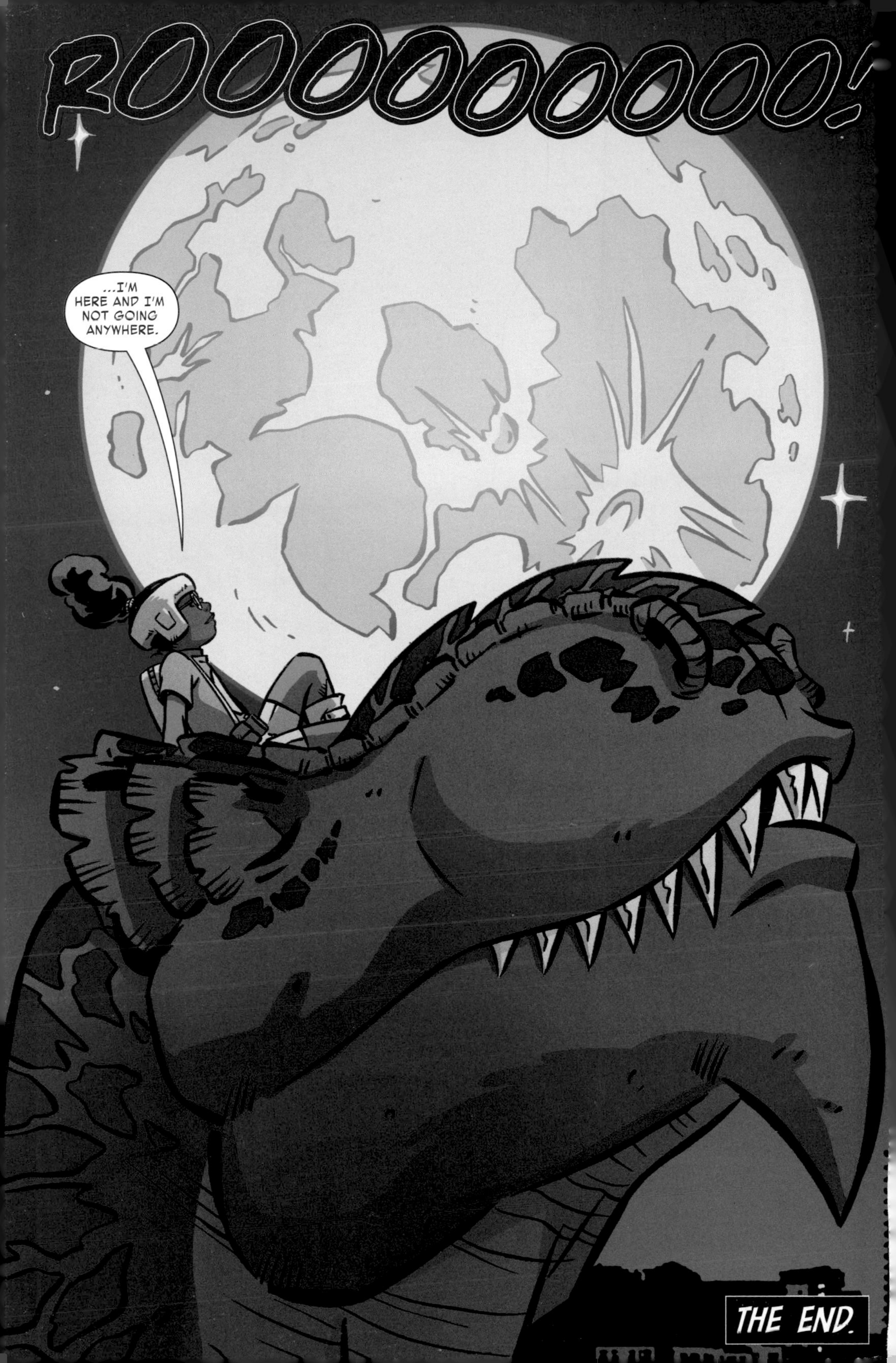
ROOOOOOOOOO!
...I'M HERE AND I'M NOT GOING ANYWHERE.
THE END.

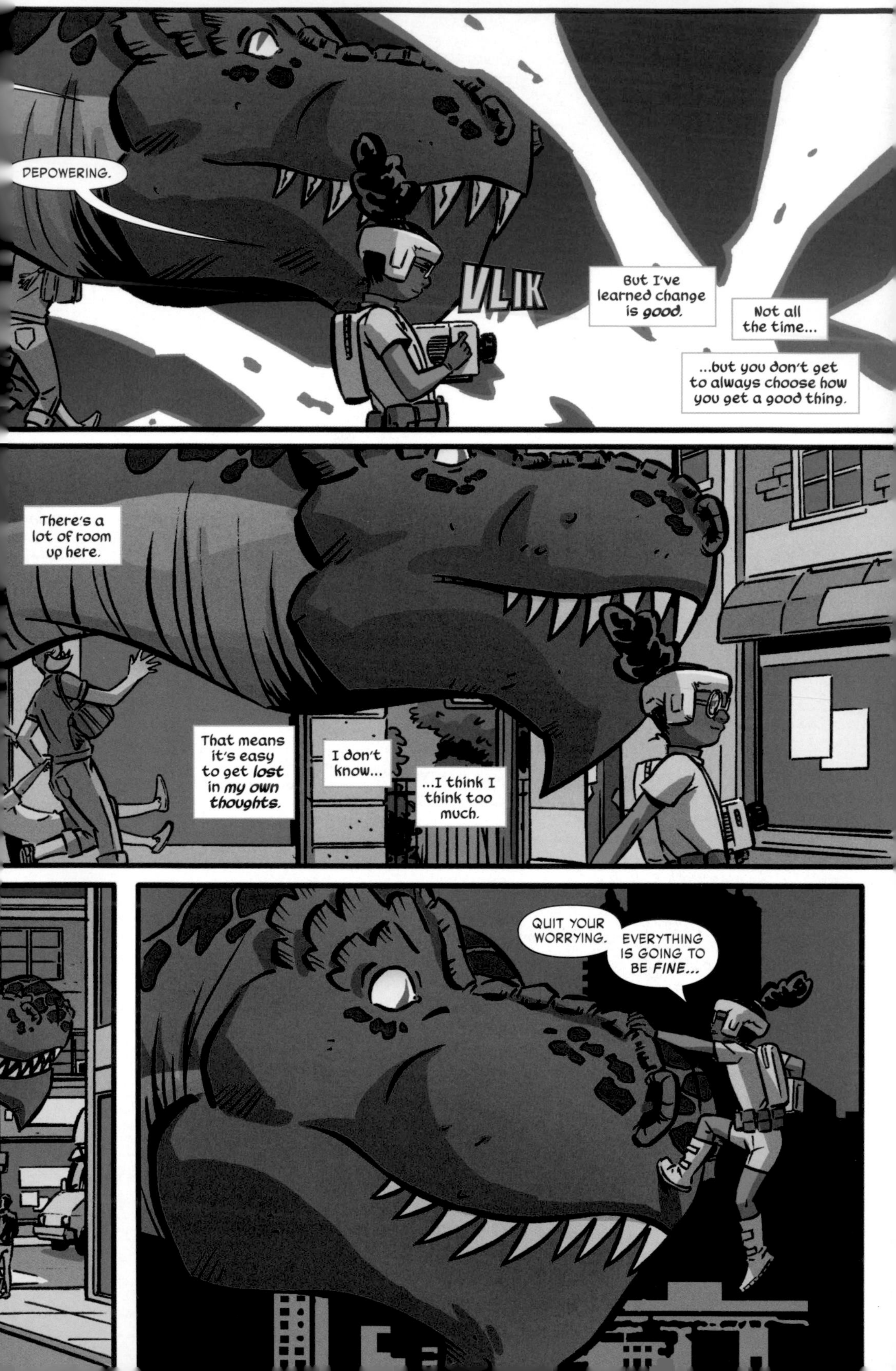
DEPOWERING.
VLIK
But I've learned change is good.
Not all the time...
...but you don't get to always choose how you get a good thing.
There's a lot of room up here.
That means it's easy to get lost in my own thoughts.
I don't know...
...I think I think too much.
QUIT YOUR WORRYING.
EVERYTHING IS GOING TO BE FINE...